THROUGH
HOLLOW
LANDS

THROUGH
HOLLOW
LANDS

WELCOME
TO *Fabulous*
LAS VEGAS
NEVADA

Urbane
PUBLICATIONS
urbanepublications.com

THOMAS PAUL BURGESS

First published in Great Britain in 2018
by Urbane Publications Ltd
Suite 3, Brown Europe House, 33/34 Gleaming Wood Drive,
Chatham, Kent ME5 8RZ
Thomas Paul Burgess, 2018

A CIP catalogue record for this book is available
from the British Library.

ISBN 978-1-911583-58-5
MOBI 978-1-911583-59-2

Design and Typeset by Michelle Morgan

Cover by Ben Thomas Design

Printed and bound by 4edge Ltd, UK

Urbane
PUBLICATIONS
urbanepublications.com

WELCOME

For Ruby & Mary

GAS

A

Acknowledgments

Thanks to Mary for reading countless drafts over numerous years. Recognition is due to the editing skills of Averill Buchanan. I would also like to express my thanks to Matthew Smith and all at Urbane Publishing. I request indulgence from the estate of the late, great Michel Tournier for my attempted homage to his peerless ' Erl-King'. To the many friends on social media who consistently inquired after a follow up to 'White Church, Black Mountain'. This is a somewhat different beast ... but I hope you enjoy it nonetheless.

DISCLAIMER

Contains graphic descriptions of sexual violence.

THROUGH HOLLOW LANDS

An allegory on the death of American innocence

A Novel by
THOMAS PAUL BURGESS

Though I am old with wandering
Through hollow lands and hilly lands,
I will find out where she has gone,
And kiss her lips and take her hands;
And walk among long dappled grass,
And pluck till time and times are done,
The silver apples of the moon,
The golden apples of the sun.

W. B. Yeats,
'The Song of Wandering Aengus'

Midway upon this road of our life,
I found myself within a forest dark.
For the right way had been missed ...

Dante Alighieri, Inferno

WELCOME

Part 1

Chapter 1
NEVADA

George Bailey lobbed the tightly crumpled ball of paper at the wastebasket again. It ran around the rim and bounced back out, rolling across the road maps and flight tickets strewn around the floor and came to rest at his foot.

He stared at it with a mixture of malice and regret, then nudged it a little with his instep, before bringing the full weight of his suede loafer down on it. It disappeared underfoot, only to spring up again when he released it. It looked no different than it had when she'd first balled it and bounced it off his forehead in exasperated rage.

He sighed heavily for the umpteenth time in the two hours since she had left. Sitting on the edge of the bed, head propped in one hand, he reached down and picked up the offending item. He smoothed the wrinkled page out on his knee and read aloud the words – printed in an elaborate serif font – that he now knew off by heart.

> *Because I reached deep down inside you,*
> *and struggled with the lock*
> *on the flimsy picket fence,*
> *that separates your passion from your will,*
> *you ran away from me.*

And running still, you gulp,
the oxygen of common sense and reason.
Reasoning for the best.
That gate's now firmly shut.
Be careful that the hinges do not rust.

It was supposed to be a love poem, something with which to win her back, something that showed off his new sensitive side. Something he hoped Beatrice would embrace, along with the flight itinerary and the hotel reservations. A trip out West and the promise of a new beginning for them. Love lost, love found.

It had completely the opposite effect.

The lesbian chick, Kim, the flat-chested girl with retainers and piercings who worked weekends with him at Lou's Video Emporium, thought George's idea to write a poem was 'like, sooooo romantic'. He was a little weirded out by Kim: she had a tattoo of a naked Madonna on her thigh but puzzlingly always covered up the singer's breasts with a flesh-toned sticking plaster. She was studying literature at college and had loaned him some books – W. B. Yeats, Shelley, and John Donne – but it was Kim who ended up writing most of his poem under his tentative, awkward instruction, drawing on some past heartbreak of her own involving a married woman.

As George read the poem again, he began to understand why it had been so spectacularly counterproductive. He could see more of his own hand in it than he'd intended. Had it all really just slipped in there subliminally? The veiled threat, the implication that he was stronger than her, that he could survive a separation better than her. That she was the lucky one to have him. But wasn't that the truth? Hadn't she always signalled her acquiescence with silence and tears?

The TV in the Comfort Inn Motel room blared on. Pyramids of tanned, leggy teens, toothy and blond, extolling the virtues of The Southern Star Cheerleaders Boot Camp in Alabama. Some podgy, balding instructors with whistles and clipboards leering and clapping from the sidelines. Nice work if you could get it, George thought.

Beatrice was from Alabama, of Sunday go-to-meeting Baptist stock, father an industrial shelving salesman, mother a home- and baby-maker. Bee had five siblings who lived within a loud holler of their mother's voice. George had taken her away from all of that. He had played on her conventional upbringing and strong family values to lead her on a wild goose chase across seven towns and six states in as many years.

She had variously stood by her man in Little Rock, Georgia; Jackson, Tennessee; Gainesville, Florida; and now New York, New York as George meandered from one dark night of the soul to the next, seeking personal redemption by taking half-baked shots at some kind of career – film school, creative writing school, dolphin trainer school, bereavement counselling college. They'd all seemed like great ideas at the time.

It was Beatrice who held down temping jobs in dead-end secretarial positions and managed the bills so his tuition fees could be met, Beatrice who stocked the refrigerator and paid the rent. She'd taken to her bed in their apartment since their break-up the day before. That was why George was holed up in a motel – giving her her 'space' like she asked – but he'd persuaded her to come see him for one last stab at a reconciliation.

The cleaning cart rumbled by the window again. He heard a sigh and the sound of sucking teeth. The maid was clearly becoming annoyed at the 'Do not disturb' sign that still hung on George's door. It was 4:37 p.m. and his blinds remained drawn.

The high-pressure shower was beating off the plastic bathroom curtain. He'd turned it on twenty minutes earlier but couldn't convince his hungover bones to stand beneath the stinging needles of water. The sound made him smile. He associated it with Beatrice crooning Elvis songs in her Southern drawl while she soaped and shampooed for what seemed like an eternity, oblivious to all but her happy ablutions. He would stand by the bathroom door waiting to hear her attempts to affect the King's distinctive riff – 'uh-huh-huh' – it made him laugh out loud every goddam time.

Another jet on approach to Newark Airport rattled the window frame.

George slid onto the floor, his back against the bed, and began to sob. He didn't know why. Deep inhalations of breath, gagging occasionally – a sound that no one would hear. He pulled the tickets closer to him with an outstretched foot: George Bailey, Beatrice Hatcher, United Airlines, Flight 93, Newark to San Francisco, departing 8:40 a.m., September 11th, 2001.

He flipped through the flight boarding cards and the car hire vouchers for the road trip down the Pacific Coast highway to LA, then on into Vegas. It was meant to be a surprise for Beatrice – the trip of a lifetime, finishing up in the city of second chances – all paid for online with her Visa and American Express cards. That would be a surprise to her too. He'd thought he could maybe pay it off by winning at the tables or roulette wheels. Besides, they'd be back home before the credit card bills arrived. And she'd have forgiven him by then for borrowing her cards; she always forgave him.

Except this time, it seemed. This time there was the not inconsiderable matter of Jaffé Losoko, the young African student whom George had befriended, fucked and left with child. This time, it felt very different.

Jaffé Losoko was a strikingly attractive young Ethiopian woman who had moved into their apartment block when they lived in Florida some years back. At the time, George, as always between jobs, spent his days in the cinema at the nearby mall or aimlessly browsing the internet at home.

He had established, through casual conversation with Jaffé, that she was claiming political asylum in the US while studying here. Her only contact with her family back in Africa was via the internet.

George liked Jaffé. Her sunny disposition, flawless ebony skin and perfect bone structure, her killer smile and broken English caused him to feel somewhat protective toward her, an unusual sentiment for him. That feeling deepened when she confided that a return to her country would mean certain imprisonment, rape and possibly death due to the political activities of her two older brothers.

Like most Americans, George engaged with Jaffé's plight, albeit superficially, on an uninformed, wholly personal dimension. The fact that latent or open hostilities affected many African nations was of little or no interest to him. It didn't take long, however, before he was offering the young woman access to the computer in their apartment rather than have her pay for it at the mall.

He began to take an interest in her appearance, suggesting that she abandon her long-sleeved, ankle-length dresses for more suggestive figure-hugging attire. Jaffé explained that her Muslim beliefs forbade the exposure of her perfect skin. But George waxed lyrical for an hour about how American women were graceful, distinctive, enlightened and self-regulating in these matters. Besides, how could she stand the Floridian heat in get-ups that looked like they'd been cut from old curtains?

In bed, Jaffé was tentative but trusting, naive but willing, shy but emboldened.

'Teach me things,' she pleaded, and lifted the duvet with one arm to invite him under.

He still sometimes thought about the shiny ebony of her long firm legs, her full breasts and hard nipples, the whites of her eyes and her white teeth standing out against the black of her skin, the elaborate cascade of her coiled and braided hair as it framed her face and fell around her shoulders. She was shaved smooth.

He had abandoned all previous boudoir conventions with Jaffé. She neither wanted nor required them. She identified early on what she liked and, after three or four afternoon 'fact-finding' sessions, she would roll onto her front, arch her beautifully smooth, rounded ass-cheeks toward him and smile over her shoulder. That smile. Pitched somewhere between innocence and awakening.

'It's sweet,' she would moan, her intonation emerging from the dark continent in breathless discovery. 'It's sweet!' Her full lips would part in pleasure and the tip of her tongue poke out, pink, between her perfect teeth.

When he'd looked at her lying asleep beside him, so young and blameless, he had almost believed they might have a life together, that their diametrically opposed worlds might be joined in an idyll of him teaching her and her soaking it all up. He would provide, nourish and stimulate her; she would care for him. No complicated power relationships, no emasculating; gender equality, man and woman. Simple.

This delusion lasted for as long as it took George to drunkenly boast of his conquest to some casual acquaintances in the local sports bar.

'You ol' dawg! How old did you say she was?'

'You know what they say, Georgie – once ya have black, ya can never go back.'

'Mick Jagger says "Black girls just wanna get fucked all night. I just don't have that much jam." You got that kinda jam, Georgie?'

It wasn't long before he'd stopped using condoms, trying – at first desperately, then carelessly – to pull out in time, the danger making it hotter. And it was so very hot to be inside her: she was hotter than anything he'd ever known, as searing as sub-Saharan Africa.

Four months later, a noticeably crestfallen Jaffé informed him that, although she was some weeks late with her period, she had enrolled in a regime of vigorous physical exercise at the local gym and was confident this would alleviate the problem. George, horrified, told her that he wasn't so sure her proposed course of action would work. So she sought to reassure him by cataloguing a list of barbaric schemes, each more extreme than the next, that might be brought into play to dislodge the ... inconvenience.

He just couldn't allow her to take such drastic measures. Even for him, amoral and without scruples, what she was suggesting seemed an altogether different class of indiscretion, beyond the pale. Abortion. Termination. Even when it was done legally it was still baby-killing. His gut ached with the worry of it, but he had to go along with what Jaffé wanted.

That evening he had borrowed Beatrice's car and drove it to an almost-empty multistorey parking lot. There, buckled in tight, he threw the VW into reverse and slammed the rear end into the nearest concrete pillar. Then, having psyched himself up on the way home to give the performance of his life, George ranted convincingly to Beatrice about the motherfucking asshole who had rammed into her parked car and left the scene of the crime without detection. He went so far as to report the incident, within earshot of Beatrice, to the speaking clock.

By next morning, he had a cheque made out to cash and a grateful Beatrice who, as she ran out to catch the bus for work, thanked him for taking care of the repairs.

Jaffé met him at a bohemian coffee bar near the university. George was at once both dismayed and relieved to find that she was having second thoughts. Perhaps she could have the child after all and George could help raise it by providing funds, she suggested. Or maybe she could go back to Africa clandestinely, where her family might help out.

This presented George with a new dilemma. Quite prepared to pay the bill fiscally, if not morally or emotionally, he was now being asked to decide upon the life and death of his unborn child and its mother. His emotions swung backwards and forwards like a pendulum. It was more responsibility in his adult life than he could ever have imagined and it petrified him.

He had waxed lyrical for an hour on how American women were strong, individualistic, liberated and independent. He spoke of the promising career she had in front of her and how this would be put in jeopardy by the responsibilities of motherhood. He reminded her of the high expectations of her parents back in the Third World. But, he said, he didn't want to sway her – oh no, this must be her call.

When he had finished, Jaffé agreed that this was indeed her decision and her decision alone. George felt better about that, as if it partially exonerated him from what was going to happen next. His alma mater, St Augustine's, cast a long shadow. The Catholic-schooled George believed that if he died with venial sins on his soul, then he would only go to purgatory. But a mortal sin such as abortion? Well, it was straight to eternal damnation, do not pass Go, do not collect $200.

He knew this wasn't the end of it. Not by a long shot. Somehow, somewhere, there would have to be atonement, restitution made, penance endured, in this life or the next. But this did not prevent him from suggesting to Jaffé that they do it bareback, just one last time. After all, with her already being pregnant and all … well, what was there to lose? He would, of course, provide the money for the termination – he pushed a brown manila envelope across the Formica table – but he couldn't be responsible for the outcome. That was important to him.

She decided there and then to attend a local clinic she had found in the Yellow Pages, and within three weeks had left the apartment block and disappeared, much to George's guilty but considerable relief.

A legacy of the whole sorry episode was that George would never again eat shrimp salad, the crustaceans resembling too closely, in his mind, small foetuses.

Beatrice drove her car around for months afterwards, a piece of string holding down the flapping, clunking trunk door.

'Goddamn mechanics … buncha crooks. You shoulda heard what they wanted to charge,' he told her. 'I won't pay that price … I simply won't pay it on principle.'

The question of the return of Beatrice's repair money never came up again.

George threw the tickets onto the table, dried his eyes with a sleeve and lay on top of the bed. How had it come to this?

NEVADA

Chapter 2

'Uhh huh … But Mama … he's not a bad man. You know how sweet he can be …'

Beatrice Hatcher cradled the phone receiver between head and shoulder while blowing her nose and pulling the duvet up around herself.

'… I have stopped crying, Mama. I have the flu … Uhh huh … No, George says the girl had the – you know, procedure – then just upped and left. He don't know where … Uhh huh … Well, you know, Mama, some of those girls from overseas, why they're just trying to git their hooks into any ole American boy so as they can weasel themselves into this country. Probably was fixin' to git with child all along.'

She was careful to withhold any unnecessary details of George's dalliance with Jaffé Losoko – specifically that she was black and African. The menfolk in her family back in Tuscaloosa, Alabama, most assuredly did not need to know those facts.

'Uhh huh … What are you telling me now – that I should have gone with him anyhow? … Well, Mama, I don't know 'bout that … He could be trying to get through to me right now … Uhh huh … Well, is Sissy there? … Well, put her on.'

Beatrice reached for a hand mirror beside the bed and studied her red, chapped nose.

'Hi Sissy! ... Well, not too good, baby. Mama told you everything, I guess.' She dipped two fingers into a jar of Vaseline and smeared her nostrils. 'Well, honey, I *am* thirty-four years of age, for crying out loud – and, well, some of the things he said in that bullshit poem ...' Beatrice began to sob again. 'No, honey, I'm okay – just a little low.'

A black trash bag half full of George's clothes lay by the open wardrobe. She had started to fling in items, hoping it would make her feel better, but it had had the opposite effect. She felt tired – tired to the bone.

She had tried to get some sleep when she got back from George's motel room, but the kid in the apartment below had been practising his scales again. 'Tuba-Boy', George called him. The perpetual farting and parffing was bad enough – every time she closed her eyes, it conjured up the vivid picture of a baby hippopotamus in a tutu – but then he attempted a maniac travesty of 'Blowin' in the Wind'. It was probably the routine chosen for the school gala by some ageing hippy music instructor. Against her better judgement Beatrice had found herself following his laborious efforts, straining with him to complete the chorus. Tuba-Boy failed every goddamn time.

Sissy talked on. She could talk all-state for Alabama. She was now informing Beatrice that in the seven years of matrimony to Jim Walker Jnr, the prosthetics salesman, he had never given her so much as an anniversary card – a card of any description – never mind a poem. The poem was a good thing and showed that George was, at heart, a sensitive soul. Why, hadn't her own two sugar-powered cherubs asked about 'Uncle George' only last week? My, he'd made a big impression on them when he'd visited.

Beatrice smiled a little at the memory. George had pulled out all the stops to impress, playing peewee baseball with her siblings' progeny in the yard and wrestling with Gooch, their old hound dog, on the porch. They'd all loved him. He could do that kind of thing effortlessly when he put his mind to it. On the journey back in the rented car, though, he'd cut loose about 'those sacks of fast-food blubber' and lamented the stink of dog that hung about him. She hadn't minded that; he'd held it together for appearances' sake and that was the important thing.

She tugged at her thermal bed socks and dropped another vitamin C tablet into the glass of water beside her bed.

'Well, I ain't callin' him, that's for goddamn sure!' she said. 'Uhh huh … Uhh huh … Uhh huh … Christ, Sissy, I thought I'd get some support from you, of all people, but you're just soundin' like Mama … Well, if he *is* tryin' to git through, let him goddamn wait a while!'

Beatrice reached across the bedside table for a throat lozenge; in negotiating an almost-empty tub of cookie dough ice cream and half a dozen Reese's Peanut Butter Cups, she sent the glass of water tumbling. Dropping the phone into her lap, she pinched her eyes in an attempt to staunch the flow of tears, but huge racking sobs now took hold of her small frame. Sissy's voice, reduced to a mosquito's drone, prattled on regardless.

Beatrice cut in. 'Sissy, honey, I gotta go right now … No, I'm fine … Love you, baby. Tell Mama I love her and to pray for me that I do the right thing … Well, if I can honey, but driving down to Alabama ain't like going to the corner store, you know … Love y'all … Bye now.'

She dabbed Kleenex around the bedside table, creating sodden paper balls that seemed to sum up her current mood better than anything she'd seen that day. Then she crossed to the bathroom, taking care not to catch her reflection in the mirror, and located her insulin pen pump and glucose meter kit. She was still a novice at this and had to give it her full attention.

She placed her finger on the small plastic device. The machine gave it a prick, she winced, as usual, and the required droplet of blood was extracted. The window lit up green and the meter emitted a self-satisfied bleep. 'Let's hear it for Reese's Pieces,' she said aloud and sighed. She'd have to watch her glucose levels. She pushed down the waistband of her fluffy pink pyjama pants, pinched a roll of fat between thumb and forefinger and stabbed it with the insulin pen.

Returning to bed, she plumped up her pillows and decided to watch a little TV from beneath the duvet, a luxury she didn't often get to enjoy, before deciding whether to phone her temping agency to let them know she wouldn't be in again tomorrow. It was money she could ill-afford to lose. Besides, she had only just taken up the position in the World Trade Center building as cover for someone on maternity leave and there was a whisper that the post could be made permanent.

Please God she'd have the opportunity to announce her own pregnancy some day. She knew the diabetes would have an impact on this, especially at her age. A great wave of longing surged through her, the only barren daughter of four sisters, with time running out. The only Hatcher who failed to lay.

She flicked through the channels with well-practised ease, pausing just long enough to gauge possible interest before settling on *Oprah*.

A phalanx of beautiful, glowing, coffee-coloured cherubs smiled back at her from the screen. 'Today we'll be discussing the children of mixed-race relationships,' announced the voice-over. 'Are they truly God's golden family?'

Beatrice let out a little whimper and collapsed in on herself, sliding further down in the bed.

'Goddamn you to hell, George Bailey!'

In his Tribeca apartment, Lou Plutus was feeling the worse for wear. He stood in his vest and boxers, staring hard at the toaster containing his fruit pop tarts, silently coercing them to return to him browned and crisped. Patches of dark, matted body hair peeped out from under his wife-beater vest, and a couple of boils close to eruption on his bulbous nose and the back of his thick neck throbbed menacingly. Wedges of greasy black hair skirted the periphery of his head and were tied up with an elastic band into a stunted ponytail.

With a huge blue flash, the toaster suddenly ejected the soggy pop tarts, oozing a hot, purple mess. Must get that fucker fixed before I fry myself, he thought, and scratched the sagging belly that protruded over the top of his boxers like the bottom lip of a petulant child.

After pouring himself a cup of coffee, he raised each arm and sniffed under his armpits. The stale smell of three-day-old sweat wafted out. He shuffled across the apartment in his ragged tartan slippers to the water heater switch and flipped it. The red light glowed. Then the sound of utility bills hitting the mat in the hallway made him look round. He sniffed under his pits again. He didn't have much to do that day – just the rounds of his various video stores – his 'emporiums', as he liked to call them.

'Fuck it, I can get by for another day,' he said aloud and flicked the switch off again.

'Sorry, were you talking to me?' asked a high-pitched voice coming from the direction of the living room.

Lou froze and then released an impatient sigh. 'Sonny, what the fuck are you still doing here?'

A young man, about sixteen, stepped into the doorway. He had razor-sharp cheekbones, big brown oval eyes and tousled jet-black hair with a side parting. He wore a three-quarter-length leather coat and tight corduroy pants. At first sight he looked serene and cherubic, but on closer inspection, his eyes and sallow complexion betrayed a recreational narcotics habit and a lucrative career in oral sex.

'Well, that's a fine good morning,' Sonny said sarcastically.

'You know how it works. The envelope with your money is on the hall table. You get up before I do. You take it and you leave.'

'I thought I might stay around and watch the movie. I *am* the star after all.'

'You thought fuckin' wrong.'

'Don't I even get a cup of coffee?'

'Sure you do,' said Lou and flung his mug of steaming brew at the youth, who just managed to get a hand up to his face in time.

'OKAY, OKAY. I'm GONE!' he yelled, picking up the envelope and moving toward the door. He stopped and turned. 'Will you need me later this week?'

'Why should I need you? You're in there now with all the rest.' Lou nodded toward his small digital camera.

Sonny looked crestfallen. 'Why d'ya have to be so—'

Lou bounded across the room surprisingly quickly for a small, squat man in his late fifties. His whole body weight thudded into the boy who whimpered as he was pressed flat against the door.

Lou sniffed his hair and neck and licked his face in one feral motion.

'Look, bitch, if I want ya I'll yank yer chain. But if you're ever here again in the morning … well, remember Tony G?'

Sonny nodded, looking down, terrified.

'You heard right. I put my cigar out in his eye. That's why he wears a patch. Nobody loves you when you're sixteen with an ashtray for an eye, geddit?'

The boy was snivelling now.

'Off you go, Sonny. Some of us gotta work.'

Lou opened the door and pushed him out, slamming it behind him. 'Little cocksucker,' he said, laughing, and crossed to the sideboard.

He picked up the camera and pressed the release mechanism. It whirred and delivered the DVD. He crossed to the large plasma screen TV and slipped the disc into the drive. He poured himself another cup of coffee, set it on the glass table in front of him beside the plate of pop tarts and fetched a long, thin wax candle and a kitchen gas lighter. Next, he unrolled and carefully spread a heavy plastic sheet across the couch. It crackled when he sat down on it. Then he pressed play on the remote control.

He fast-forwarded, speeding through the frames, all young boys, all in a blur of pink flesh and juddering motion, until he came to the previous night's encounter. It showed Sonny entering the bedroom wearing nothing but his leather coat.

'About here, right?' Sonny was saying, smiling as he shuffled on his knees across the bed to face the camera full on.

His demeanour became business-like – an amalgam of concentration and faux ecstasy – and he started to jerk off. The camera shook and there was a cutaway. The next clip showed Lou behind the boy, who was now on all fours. The fat man pumped away, making no sound at all, save for the occasional emotionless instruction.

'Head up. Look at the camera.'

Sonny, grimacing, his eyes shut tight, let go a few little yelps and hisses.

Lou took a sip of coffee, flipped back a few frames and began again. Then he lit the candle and pulled down his boxer shorts to reveal genitalia encrusted with angry red welts. He began to drip hot wax onto his crotch.

'You bad little boys,' he whined. 'Look what you made me do. Look what you made me do …'

Chapter 4

NEVADA

George had told Beatrice that he'd paid for the flights to San Francisco with the money he'd won in a sweepstake at the community college where he supposedly taught 'Communications Skills 101' in the evenings. In fact he had been working in Lou's Video Emporium for the past eight months, saving a little, lifting a little more from the register, and, more recently, cultivating a lucrative sideline in selling quantities of Lou's DVD reserve stock and video games from the newly repaired trunk of Beatrice's car. What Lou Plutus didn't know wouldn't hurt him.

This gave him the pocket money that would strategically pay for one classy meal and one expensive item of clothing for her. He could play the regular guy for a little while and she would buy it, buy right into it. She'd believe him. Believe in him. She always wanted to believe in him.

They would fly to Frisco, do the Golden Gate, China Town, Fisherman's Wharf, then on to Vegas. Maybe visit that motherfucker big-hole-in-the-ground canyon too. From Sin City, pick up the car and drive west, until the Pacific breakers force them south, and down Route One to LA. Why not? First class all the way.

The origins of his predilection for wilful deception, and his seeming indifference to the suffering of others whom he viewed

THROUGH HOLLOW LANDS

merely as collateral damage in the wider scheme of his quest for 'an even break', lay in the perplexing period of George's formative years.

'Might as well be hung for a sheep as a lamb ... eh, Georgie boy?' his stepfather, Arnie Futterman, had unhelpfully pointed out in the company of the arresting officers of the Pittsburgh PD on George's thirteenth birthday. It had been a watershed – a turning point – in his troubled childhood.

George's school, the North Canton Elementary School, had launched a charity drive in collaboration with the Pittsburgh State Hospice Foundation. Each child had been given a small envelope imprinted with the crests of both institutions and the words, 'Open your heart to the terminally ill for comfort and for care.' The photograph of an ailing woman, who bore a striking resemblance to Mother Teresa of Calcutta, looked out at potential benefactors.

Students had been sent home with instructions to request donations from immediate family, lick and seal the envelope, and duly return it to Mrs Abernathy. George, precocious, charmingly manipulative and seeking to teach an indifferent world a lesson or two, spotted the potential immediately.

He began modestly enough, explaining to good-hearted old Mrs A that there were some extended family members staying with them on vacation and please could he have a few more envelopes. Then he staked out his territory.

South Canton was close enough by bicycle but far enough away for anonymity. By knocking on doors, batting his impossibly long eyelashes and proffering the official envelopes, he amassed $322.69 within a three-block radius on the first morning alone. To discourage detection, four envelopes were returned to the school, each containing a single dollar bill.

These riches brought clandestine binges on candy, comic books and ice cream, but George began to think big. By the end of the month he was managing a small team of five junior operatives, each one personally schooled by him in the art of door-to-door deception. They descended, locust-like, into the wider suburbs. When he was apprehended with two boxes of one hundred official envelopes taken surreptitiously from the school secretary's office, the scale of the scam had become clear. The local newspaper calculated that they had amassed $2,657 within a two-week period, most of it now unaccounted for. His associates folded like a house of cards, whingeing that George had made them do it.

A few echoed the observations of many fleeced contributors – that the boy had an uncanny knack for maudlin authenticity, drawing on the details of his own late mother's illness for effect. Most agreed that he was a plausible, sweetheart sociopath with slow-burning eyes. But his eyes implied an awareness, a soulfulness much deeper than George would ever possess. They were to remain a considerable asset.

For a brief, wonderful period, he became the cause célèbre of social workers, agony aunts, child psychiatrists and newspaper columnists, all of whom seemed happy to defer to his unsettled domestic history as justification for such an appallingly selfish act: natural father goes missing, reported dead; hard-drinking mother ups and dies; George left in the care of a sullen, embittered stepfather and reluctant half-siblings. Was George's turn to petty crime not simply a cry for attention, for help?

His stepsisters cried themselves to sleep at night, distraught at the unwanted association with 'Bad-Boy Bailey', as he was now known around town. His stepfather studiously said nothing, remaining deaf to the many inferences to bad parenting on his part. Then, when it had all died down and things had returned to normal, Arnie phoned the school to say that George would not be in for two weeks as they were taking a family trip away.

When the boy arrived home that afternoon, he found Arnie waiting in his bedroom. At no time before had his stepfather, a small, fish-eyed linoleum salesman with a passion for military history and machines of war, evidenced a capacity for physical violence. So George was completely taken unawares when, in one sweeping movement, the man produced from behind his back a clicking sock full of pool balls and thudded it hard into the boy's midriff.

George, doubled over in pain and surprise, was sent whirling sideward by another blow that caused him to split his eyebrow on the corner of the dressing table. Blinded by blood, he closed up into a foetal position as the man spat out each word, punctuated with a kick to the boy's crumpled body.

'You – little – cocksucker.'

The beating went on for some twenty minutes, Arnie panting throughout and telling George that he was tolerated in his household only out of respect for his late lamented mother, who'd drunk herself into an early grave after the tragic death of her youngest son, Harry, and her desertion by that useless husband.

'Only thing that good-for-nothing was worth a shit for was playin' that piece-a-crap harmonica. Man, he could blow that harp and no mistake,' Arnie said, unapologetically smiling at the memory of George's father, breathing hard from his exertions and wiping the sweat from his forehead.

After a while, the words began to hurt George more than the blows. He remembered his pa playing slow, haunting laments to Harry at bedtime, and his signature tune, the old rebel standard, 'The Bonnie Blue Flag'.

Arnie took the opportunity to once again point out how

George's negligence had resulted in his brother's death and the eventual disintegration of the Bailey family.

'Ya might as well have put the rope around his neck yourself,' he taunted. 'Yer about as useless as yer old man was.'

As George slowly healed in the semi-darkness of Arnie's locked fruit cellar, he had cried hard at first, more in frustrated anger than in pain, and then trashed everything breakable he could lay his hands on. But his culpability for Harry's death swarmed around like a suffocating wave of blowflies and wouldn't leave him alone. It still plagued him, twenty-five years later.

George's younger brother Harry had been a strangely serious child, an 'old soul' as his doting mother called him. His middle name, Shankill, came from a Scots-Irish great-grandfather on his maternal side.

His pale complexion and straight, blond, pudding-bowl haircut framed a round, freckled moon-face, while his large eyes, magnified by thick-lensed spectacles, indicated a mostly vacant space, a blank page that had yet to be written on. Externally, little was on show to suggest any predominant characteristics or temperamental tendencies. No one ever commented on his similarity to one or other of his parents, or indeed to his older brother, save for the obvious and wholly accurate observation that he was 'a dreamer like his old man'. The dissimilarity was accentuated by the child's cobalt-blue eyes, a markedly different colour from either of his parents and his older brother.

George, of course, knew the reason for this only too well.

As a baby, Harry had been handed to him to hold so that a photograph might be taken of them together. The older boy promptly dropped his brother on his head, eliciting screeched pandemonium from those around him, and detached retinas and a life of fuzzy vision for poor Harry.

That's what started the feelings of obligation and culpability – a sense of having let the kid down literally and figuratively – that the older boy had to learn to live with. And it was portentous of much, much worse to come.

Harry lived much of his life within the fantastic, limitless spaces of his imagination and, at eight years old, much of that centred on the cowboy code of *The High Chaparral*. The popular television series became something of an obsession for the boy, and he would hold imaginary conversations with Buck, Blue, Manolito and Big John in the way that little girls talked to their dolls. He sported a cowboy hat, bandana and a holstered six-shooter, looking vulnerable and achingly incongruous behind his big glasses.

As George lay on the bed in his motel room, his mind went back over the events of that sunny March afternoon which changed their lives forever.

He had been spending less time with the kid lately. Word had got around school that if you looked at the pictures of brassiere models in your mom's clothing catalogue while gently squeezing in between your legs – well, something quite magical, if a little messy, happened. And for George it had – again and again and again.

Harry had been pestering him to play cowboys, but the older boy was disinterested. He could still smell the new ink from those glossy catalogues in his nostrils. It made things tingle and grow. The kid, however, was excited about a recent episode where someone had shot a taut hangman's rope, snapping it and saving the hero. Wouldn't George come down and shoot invisible bullets to snap Harry's invisible rope? The kid pleaded for ages, shouting up at the partially open window of his brother's room.

The ensuing silence should have alerted George to the danger. Later, the screams of his mother, arriving home from her cleaning job to find her youngest child turning lifelessly at the end of an unforgiving plastic washing line, alerted the entire neighbourhood. His father had gone out one day soon after the funeral service and just never came home, thus guaranteeing for George an existence in which sex, guilt, death and loss melded together into anguished, gut-wrenching confusion.

After the thrashing by his stepfather, George had decided to leave Canton, PA, as soon as it was legally or financially possible, whichever came first. But when he emerged, sore and chastened, from his incarceration, he was immediately confronted by a packed suitcase sitting on the porch with a letter taped to it, outlining details of the coming years he was to spend at St Augustine's Roman Catholic Boarding School for Boys in Minnesota. It seemed that his stepfather had remained true to the promise he made a dying woman and refrained from sending Edna Bailey's firstborn to military school in Kentucky, as was his preference.

Instead, George was being dispatched to the next best – or worst – place, all paid for by his mother's life insurance policy. Maybe those Irish priests could thrash some respect into the little prick. And thus began George Bailey's concise sojourn into the world of Latin verbs, corporal punishment, dormitory conventions and icy-cold showers.

The school had a profound effect on him, and George, the impressionable adolescent with the winning smile and plausible patter, was assimilated completely into the uncomplicated dichotomy of rigid authoritarian routines and the easy, rebellious camaraderie of young men at their flowering.

Built in 1886, St Augustine's was housed in an austere if impressive set of stone buildings and outhouses spread out over ninety-two acres of grey-green scrubland and surrounded by high walls and trees. While the school most closely resembled a correctional facility, in its brochure it professed to provide 'a safe, stimulating and supportive Christian environment for young men'. It boarded its students in seven large detached houses, with about forty to each house, supervised by teams of five priests apiece.

George Bailey could not have known it then, but the synthesis of social skills, self-confidence and passable academic qualifications he got there proved to be the bedrock of all future triumphs and, indeed, disasters for the remainder of his span.

He developed a short-lived but intense interest in literature, particularly poetry. Through a crash course in Catholicism, his time at the school also guaranteed a new, more vividly terrifying collection of nightmarish images to haunt him. Those RCs could deliver on hell, damnation, purgatory and excommunication like no Baptist minister he'd ever come across.

Soon after his arrival, George was quick to befriend Kelly, the obese, nervy and unpopular son of the school caretaker. In a charm offensive that, in later life, was to become second nature to him, George also soon ingratiated himself with Kelly's father, the school secretaries, grounds warden and several senior prefects. Favours, of course, ensued, but the most beneficial advantage in assembling such an entourage was the protective buffer zone it sometimes afforded him from his arch-nemesis, Father Francis 'Gusher' Geryon.

Father Geryon was a pompous, podgy underachiever from some bog county in middle Ireland. He dyed and waved his hair, plucked his eyebrows and affected the air of a country squire, but his palate and taste in literature proved as bogus as the reasons he offered for ministering to what he called 'the new world'. 'Where the Holy Father directs we cannot question,' he was fond of saying over his after-dinner whiskey and untipped cigarette.

But it had been no papal directive that led him to take the passage from Cobh, County Cork, to Ellis Island. Rather, his indifferent academic performance in a family of high-achieving surgeons meant that he was always destined for the dullard's path to the pulpit.

Father Geryon had the misfortune to suffer from a severe case of haemorrhoids, coupled with a digestive complaint that ensured that no meal stayed long enough in his stomach to become fully absorbed and therefore provide the required nutrients. It also meant that he had to defecate several times a day, thus exacerbating the former complaint to truly epic proportions. None of this seemed to hinder the maintenance of his considerable bulk.

His critical mistake was to seek solace among his students by alluding to personal details that would have been better left to the imagination. 'I'm wrapped up like a woman at her time of the month,' he would confide while squirming atop a number of cushions on his wooden seat at the head of the classroom. 'Jaysus, boys, it's like a baboon's arse, I don't mind tellin' ya!' he said to the weekly detention classes he supervised like a Stalag commandant.

Such forthrightness with teenage boys, already obsessed with all things genital, could only end in tears. When he revealed that he 'had to wear a type of diaper', the sobriquet of 'Gusher' emerged quite naturally. Written up on toilet walls and shouted after him down stone corridors, the name was soon in universal use, and George Bailey was fingered as the boy to blame for it – correctly, as it happened.

But the antipathy between George and Father Geryon ran much deeper than name-calling. As one of the few non-Catholics at the school, George was absented from many of the religious services that were compulsory for his peers. This apparently stoked Geryon's anti-reformation, anti-imperial prejudices, and ensured that the boy became the regular target of unwanted attention and rigorous schooling in the many Catholic saints and martyrs who had been persecuted unto death. Thereafter, the re-education of George Bailey became Geryon's main business in life – that and the absolute despotism he wielded over all at St Augustine's. When Father Geryon requested and was granted a transfer to become master at George's house, the boy realised it was personal for sure. 'If ever a boy was in sore need of confession and repentance it's you, Bailey,' Gusher would say.

Father Geryon had his particular brand of physical redemption that he doled out to all the boys. For example, there was 'The Crew', in which a long line of offenders would silently walk in single file around the covered pathway of the playground for a minimum of fifteen minutes or a maximum of an hour – longer if it behove Gusher. 'Sequestration' forbade the boy being punished to communicate with others, except in answer to a direct question by the priest. And 'The Erectum' required a boy to eat standing up, alone in the dining hall.

Geryon's bedtime inspections were particularly loathsome. Each boy had to line up, military-fashion, beside their bed so that the ogre could inspect the cleanliness of their hands and feet. It was primarily the feet that he was interested in. He would have each boy place a foot on their metal bed frame and he would walk down the line of beds, running a fat finger between their toes, collecting the black sweaty skin he found there. Rolling these into balls, he savoured their texture and odour before snorting them up his nostril like a man taking a pinch of snuff.

But it was the command, 'Bailey, *ad inexplorata!*' which held the most dread for George. That meant immediate expulsion from the classroom and the weary climb up three flights of stairs to the outer door of the office of Prefect of Studies.

Geryon's instruction was for the offender to enter and kneel down on a prayer stool placed in the centre of the room, facing the office door he had just come through. On the wall opposite the door hung an austere picture of Christ wearing a crown of thorns; he was being struck in the face by a soldier. It was the inspiration behind Geryon's claim, made frequently in chapel, that any human face, however vile, becomes the face of Christ when struck. From the prayer stool, the boy had to reach over and ring a small ornate brass bell that was on the floor beside the stool. It was a perverse parody of the celebration of the Mass.

Having rung the bell, the boy might wait anything from a few seconds to an hour in dreadful anticipation. It was the awful expectation, of course, that rendered *ad inexplorata* so fiendish.

Eventually, sooner or later, a door behind the boy would be flung open with a violent crash and, cassock rustling furiously, Father Geryon would dash at the prayer stool, administering smacks about the offender's face and head. A chit was then shoved into the boy's hand, signifying that he had received due punishment.

One month, when George had already accrued three trips to the office, Geryon chose to reveal another facet to his preoccupation with the boy. As George assumed the position on the prayer stool yet again and reached for the bell that would begin the rite, he heard the door behind him open, then close quietly.

Surprised at this deviation from the routine, George automatically raised his eyes from the floor and tried to glance round.

'Don't look at me!' bellowed Geryon, his voice suggesting a mix of fury, self-loathing and … something else. Longing perhaps?

For fifteen minutes nothing happened.

A half-hour passed and the only sound in the room was George's shallow breathing – the fat priest must still be in the room with him, watching, waiting. After more than an hour, the boy began to wilt. Then just at the moment when fatigue, discomfort and boredom combined to transport George's imagination elsewhere, Geryon acted.

The creak of wooden floorboards underfoot, the slow pacing toward the stool. But instead of the customary polished brown brogues, it was the man's bare feet that arrived in the periphery of George's vision. They were squat, calloused and bunioned; grey, flaking ingrown nails sat like hard snail shells on hairy, thick toes.

Suddenly George's face was pushed hard into the ground by one of them. The force contorted his features into a fish mouth and he drooled. An eternity passed before the priest spoke again.

'Look up,' he said, swallowing hard and removing his foot.

George sensed that it augured something much worse than the slap in the face he expected.

'Don't want to sir,' he blurted out.

'Look up!' demanded Geryon, trying to stifle a high, whining sound that was now escaping his throat.

When George did as he was bid, he could scarcely believe the sight that awaited him. There was Geryon's full bulk standing above him, his cassock hitched up to chest level. At eye level were three or four rolls of naked fat, each belly reducing in size until they reached the bald V of his crotch, where Geryon's tiny lifeless penis sat, corrugated into flaccid wrinkles. A small corpuscle of greyish opaque semen sat on the tip of the foreskin like a dark pearl.

'Will you … touch it?' said Geryon pleadingly.

George had never heard the priest's voice betray such vulnerability, such humanity before.

'I will not force you.' He sighed. 'It must be of your own volition.'

It was a petition.

George made a face as he got a waft of shit and lavender water.

'Or better still, will you touch it … with your own? That's all. Just touching. Will you?'

For a young man who now associated carnal pleasure with guilt for the premature death of his little brother, the corpulent priest's designs were bewildering to say the least. Dumbstruck, George shifted his weight from one knee to the other.

'I have comic books!' Geryon bargained, desperate now.

All the boys had heard of Gusher's fabled comic book collection, DC classics of *Batman, Superman, Captain America* and *The Silver Surfer*. Add to these the latest popular music magazines he brought back from exeat and all agreed that the ogre possessed the ideal currency for transacting any business with young boys.

It was perhaps the first time that George realised he had something other people wanted, something they'd trade for. He had looked unabashedly into the man's eyes and reached for his own flies.

Despite, or perhaps because of, his legacy of sexually charged remorse, George's subsequent success with women gave him countless opportunities to escape from untenable situations, and continued to do so for many years.

Doris, a thirty-three-year-old bleached blond divorcee and Walmart employee, offered the tall, handsome fifteen-year-old George a tantalising glimpse of things to come. When she accepted a transfer to Anderson, Indiana, George, home on summer vacation, packed an overnight bag, took a steaming dump on his stepfather's meticulously detailed table model of the battlefield at Gettysburg, and tagged along. He became a surrogate big brother to her young son, Stevie, and a willing, perpetual erection for her.

In the way that other men moved from place to place, accepting career opportunities, George soon realised that his particular aptitude lay in attaching himself to working women with professional ambition.

At first, of course, it wasn't by design. Nor was it even because he was a particularly good lover. Quite the opposite. As with many young men, he developed an obsession with bedding any member of the opposite sex who crossed his path. And due to his selfish drive 'to cum first and at all costs', his sexual proclivity was as much a surprise to him as to anyone. Things just always seemed to happen that way.

Two years here, in a trailer park in St Paul, Minneapolis, with a nicotine-fingered, chicken factory worker; two years there, in a Pensacola commune with a bisexual mural painter with genital herpes and a trust fund. His twenties seemed to slip away in a lather of sexual inconsequentiality. That was, until he met Beatrice Hatcher.

She was someone he thought he'd like to stay with for a while, to make a go of it with. Or perhaps he just recognised a good thing when he saw it. She was the first younger woman he'd had a relationship with.

He'd felt drawn to her from day one when she'd stopped to give him a lift on an ochre-dusted panhandle back road. That copper-red hair, the porcelain white skin; that flowery cotton summer dress. She looked so small and delicate. Like a little fairy queen, he thought. But she was tough. And sexy, with a teasing maybe-I-will-maybe-I-won't smile. He liked that.

She was such a go-getter, afraid of nothing, certain she was Southern by the grace of God and righteous because of the love of her dear family. She had such an energy and zest for life, and all within that small frame. She blazed in a way he'd never seen before.

Now here he was in a crappy motel room, exiled from Beatrice's life. It was all ruined. Now he'd never get the opportunity to tell her all the things he'd always wanted to, all those silly, important things.

George peeked out through the blinds of the motel room window.

The trip to Vegas would be like a second honeymoon, he'd told her. She'd pointed out that they'd never had a first. And in case it had escaped his notice, they weren't actually married. *Bitch, bitch, bitch.*

It comes from the religious thing, he thought, sitting down again. Her mama never let up on the sanctity-of-marriage routine. And the need 'to give any children y'all bring into this world their rightful and proper family name'.

The Hatchers lovingly referred to their eldest daughter as 'Bee', an affectation that he studiously rejected. Hardly a birthday or Christmas went by without a little crochet bumblebee, a bumblebee coffee mug or a fridge magnet arriving in the mail from the family. Sissy, her stick-thin, anorexic sister would say, 'George, you're now the official Bee-keeper. Don't let us down, ya hear?'

George winced at the memory of the one and only Thanksgiving he'd spent among the Hatchers of Tuscaloosa, Alabama. The house wasn't near big enough to accommodate all Beatrice's brothers and sisters and their corpulent, puffing, sweaty offspring. Everyone headed off to Thanksgiving service where the Reverend Pyle had preached love and fear, forgiveness and penance with no apparent sense of irony or contradiction – New and Old Testament arm in arm. There was Beatrice, eyes closed, hands held high in the air, evoking the spirit in song and celebration. In that moment George realised, not for the first time, that he knew little or nothing about this woman. None of the important stuff anyhow.

She had something – some depth of character or sense of self – which both attracted and shamed him. It wasn't so difficult to admit that, in the ways that mattered most, she was a better person than he was. He recalled his favourite mantra: 'You gotta love yourself before you can love anyone else.' It had conveniently excused a multitude of sins, but recently it had been wearing a bit thin.

Yeah, well maybe if I'd had the better upbringing, he thought resentfully.

He tried to phone her again. Still a busy tone. She'd taken it off the hook. *She's really pissed, and I know why.* It was because of Jaffé Losoko, of course, and the whole sorry story that he had kept from Beatrice for nigh on six years.

George crossed the room to the mini-refrigerator. Having removed the middle and bottom shelves, he'd been able to fit two six-packs of Miller long necks into the compartment.

He darkest fear was that she was finished with him for good this time. She'd been talking about having kids, getting married, starting a family. Why the fuck did he have to tell her about Jaffé now, right before their trip out West together?

Only five weeks earlier, Beatrice had been diagnosed with late-onset Type 1 diabetes. She goddamn needed this trip more than he did. Why hurt her like that? Why, why, why? Dr Witchel, the psychotherapist she'd set him up with and paid for, had been able to answer that straight out.

'You fear illness and death. The loss of your brother at an early age, then your mother, means that you are visiting that trepidation again and again upon your significant other. Put simply, you resent her for becoming ill.'

George had wanted to believe it. It made sense. In Dr Witchel's world, nobody was personally responsible for anything.

'And why did I choose now, when things were going good, to tell her about Jaffé?' George had leaned forward in the leather chair, sensing another emotional parachute.

Dr Witchel flashed him his best, shit-eating grin. 'Classic anxiety regarding commitment and frustrated emotional expression, leading to feelings of self-hatred. You want the relationship to fail, but you aren't brave enough to end it.' He had lightly slapped his thighs as if delivering the punchline to a joke.

George slipped out a beer and flipped off the top with his belt buckle. It was going to be a long night. A large bag of barbecue-flavoured twist chips lay open on the bed; a brochure with a picture of the Hoover Dam sat on the bedside table.

For maybe the third time since he'd locked and chained the motel door and drawn the blinds he said aloud, 'Fuck it, with or without her I'm goin' anyway. And I'm goin' all the way!'

Chapter 5

NEVADA

Beatrice was showered and out the door by 7 a.m., despite her cold. If she took the scenic walk by Kissena Boulevard and made the subway connection via Forest Hills, she should be able to alight at Church Street, grab a quick coffee from Starbucks and still be at her desk at Barrett, Barrett & Downey on the 95th floor of the North Tower by 8:30.

A thought pulled her up short. *Christ, he was right – I'm doing it again!* The daily ritual, superstition taking over, like avoiding cracks in the pavement or not walking under ladders. 'The lucky way', as she'd come to call it: two cups of coffee and half a grapefruit for breakfast; leave the apartment at exactly the same time each day and take the same route, adjusting her walking speed so as to coincide with the Walk/Don't Walk signs at the intersections. It was important to never, ever have to pause at a kerb, as if doing so would invite her precariously balanced world to come crashing down around her ears. It drove George crazy.

What a truly glorious day, she thought as the early September sunshine picked out some prematurely browning leaves on the old oak trees that skirted Queen's College. Force of habit, learned from clean living in Tuscaloosa, prompted her to breathe in deeply, filling her lungs with what she took to be a morning haze rather than the petrol fumes from a passing security truck. She immediately broke into a racking cough, which shook her so violently that passers-by looked around in concern. Her cold had refused to abate completely, but needs must.

She contented herself with the thought that being outside on such a magnificent morning was surely preferable to being stuck at home with her head over a basin of hot water and eucalyptus salts to ease her sinuses.

Despite its many challenges, Beatrice had surprised herself by how much she had come to enjoy living in the big city. Sure, it was hard work at times, but it was without doubt a full-on, no-holds-barred metropolis and she defied any of those guys at Lancy's Watering Hole back home to say any different.

If she had been forced to reflect on why, exactly, she had taken that path out of town, the one so rarely chosen by her high-school contemporaries, she would probably have pointed to a balmy Sunday evening in January 1995 when Super Bowl XXIX was being played out between the San Francisco 49ers and the San Diego Chargers in a packed Joe Robbie Stadium in Miami, Florida. The Alabama Crimson Tide had seven local players who had graduated to the big leagues that year and all of them were taking the field for one finalist or the other. Such was the furore in Tuscaloosa and across the state that a number of buses had been organised and were Florida-bound.

Beatrice and two girlfriends had squeezed into bikini tops and Daisy Duke denim cut-offs and packed their sunscreen. It was an enjoyable enough game by any conventional standard. Kathie Lee Gifford sang the national anthem; Tony Bennett, Patti LaBelle, and Miami Sound Machine provided the half-time entertainment.

As usual, the big networks, ABC, NBC and CBS, scanned the crowd for brief head-and-shoulder shots of the more garishly attired uberfans. Just before play resumed for the third quarter, the cameras swept over a sea of painted beer bellies, giant foam fingers and ludicrous hats to momentarily settle on a beaming Beatrice.

The giant screen had filled with her milk-white complexion, copper-red hair and dimpled smile, and one hundred and six million people who had tuned in to watch the game subliminally ingested a perfect Southern belle. Maybe ten girls in the crowd were briefly featured in close-up that day; it's hard to say how their fortunes were affected, if at all. But for Bee Hatcher, it profoundly changed the trajectory of her life without her ever realising it. The attention she received on her return home as a result of her appearance at the game gave her the confidence to believe that there was more waiting for her in life beyond the Tuscaloosa city boundary. Back at Lancy's Watering Hole celebrity was short-lived, and forgotten altogether years later when she let it be known that she was moving to New York.

Shoot, those old boys had never been out of the county, much less out of the state, she thought as she approached the subway station. They'd no business jibing her about living among the Yankees, not to mention marrying one of them. *Damn it! Not even at the subway yet and I'm thinkin' 'bout him already,* she scolded herself.

Why the hell hadn't George phoned? Was he really going to go out West without her? And what would it mean if he did?

It all came crowding in again.

She produced a Vicks inhaler from her bag and gave herself a double nostril hit. Popping two pieces of menthol gum into her mouth, she sought solace in her permissible mini-high.

Chapter 6

On the morning of September 11th, George woke five minutes before his alarm went off. He lay in the darkness awaiting the bleep on his mobile phone, happily scratching around his semi-erection. The old George, the survivor, the opportunist, the charmer, had returned in the twilight zone of half-sleep. He felt emboldened.

If Beatrice passed on this opportunity, there would be plenty more pretty travelling companions along the way. The idea cheered him up considerably; all he'd needed was to consider his split with Beatrice from another angle. His member grew harder. He thought of reaching for the box of tissues beside the bed.

But then he remembered that Beatrice was paying for it all. Somehow, that didn't seem right – too much of a liberty. *My God, have I no pride?* His erection vanished.

That early morning pain in the pit of his stomach welled up again. It appeared every morning in these waking moments and always when he couldn't escape the thoughts of his crimes and misdemeanours. Guilt? Gas?

'Helicobacter pylori,' the quack had said.

What the sweet Christ was that?

'Think ulcers,' said the doc.

Think stomach cancer, more like, thought a worried George.

Beep-beep-beep-beep-beep-beep-beep! 6:00 a.m.

He jumped, startled. Why did he always jump when he knew what was coming? At least he wouldn't just lie there this morning, staring into the darkness, listening to the disgruntled newspaper delivery guy working his way along the corridor toward him – thwack! thwack! THWACK! – slapping down copies of *USA Today*, huge and heavily laden with advertising supplements and pizza delivery offers.

George rubbed his eyes.

Flight at 8:45 a.m., check-in 7:45 a.m.? Tight but manageable. Booking into the airport Comfort Inn had been smart. Besides, he had nowhere else to go since Beatrice called time on him.

He peeped around the blinds furtively. A cloudless azure sky seemed to say 'Georgie boy, go West. Life is what you make it!' He snapped the blinds open.

'Ha ha!' he exclaimed aloud and clapped his hands, rubbing them together. 'If you're going to Sannn Frannnn-cis-co,' he sang, jigging around the room, collecting up complimentary toiletries, pens, notepads and anything he hadn't packed into the case the night before.

George Bailey, survivor, opportunist, optimist, was back and irrepressible as ever.

The grey Italian casual suit hung where he'd left it last night in preparation for a smooth exit. He was going with the black, rather than white, open-necked shirt. Black Chelsea boots, mail order from London, England, a birthday gift from Beatrice. When he wore this outfit, along with the Ray-Bans borrowed from his boss, Lou Plutus, George felt gooood. 'Yer not a bad lookin' guy,' Lou would remark. 'Clean up good, ya know? Like George Clooney's second cousin or somethin'. Yeah, Clooney with a beer gut.'

George liked Lou. He was a throwback to another time and something of a legend among the store employees. He wore cheap suits, stained under the arms, and suspenders to keep his socks up; and he chomped on old stogies, hawked up, spat out and didn't give a damn who was there to see it.

George met Lou two or three times a week, when his boss called for the takings at the video store, one of half a dozen that he had around town. The video stores were only a secondary earner for Lou. He had a day job as a cameraman with local TV news; he was old-school, unionised and revered among the station team from top to bottom. Lou's adage was, 'When the talent shows, shoot it,' and that's precisely what he did. His cardinal rule was to make sure the camera was running before, during, and after the interview.

This meant that Lou had all the gaffs, the unintended, overheard conversations. The chokes from politicians, celebrities and sports stars. In conversation with George he would casually and routinely mention Oprah Winfrey's chronic flatulence, Elton John's bald head sans wig, and Jay Leno's colostomy bag. He swore on his mother's grave that he'd filmed Dick Cheney, smiling straight to camera, say, 'White man's burden', then spit on a dollar bill tip before giving it to a black waitress. He boasted that he had recorded Hillary Rodham Clinton, the worse for afternoon cocktails, violently argue with herself in a dressing-room mirror before punching it and cutting her hand.

Now, all of this made Lou very popular at parties, but the best parties of all were the ones that he himself threw. Poker parties, where a lucky few got to see his edited out-takes, having undertaken with solemnity and considerable gravitas never to share the details with anyone.

Lou had tapes going back some forty-five years, but he refused point blank to sell them. Rumour had it that he was in possession of a Kennedy porn tape, and an interview with Michael Jackson in which he claimed, categorically, that he and his sister La Toya were one and the same person. 'That crazy Louie,' Lou's friends would say fondly, 'he's the J. Edgar Hoover of the celebrity circuit!'

In his younger days, Lou had flirted with the porn business, and rumour had it that he was still connected. He'd confided in George that he had always suffered from unremitting premature ejaculation, a distinct disadvantage given the ample opportunities afforded him. But George had to agree with Lou's philosophy on the matter. 'Describe your worst blow job!' Lou used to ask, laughing. 'There's no such thing, right? Even the worst is good.'

George, being George, wondered how he could gain access to some of Lou's exclusive out-take footage for commercial gain. So after several months on a charm offensive, he'd eventually got himself invited to a poker game two nights ago, ostensibly because he made Lou laugh. Both he and his host understood that he wouldn't be able to pack the kind of ante required for this breed of cash-heavy clientele. No, his job for the evening was to make with the jokes and mix the drinks. So when Lou called him to the side and braced him $100, George was surprised.

'Get yerself in the game, Georgie boy. Maybe make a few bucks. These guys are assholes.'

'Shit! Thanks, Lou! I'm not sure when I'll have the green to pay you off, ya know.'

Lou had guffawed. 'It's a gift! Christ, kid, I'm only gonna take it all back from you in two or three games anyhow!'

Lou was right, of course. George knew enough about Texas Hold'em to realise that second place in any poker hand was the worst place to be.

Two-a-clubs, three-a-hearts. Go beat!

Five-a-spades, two-a-diamonds. Go beat!

When he was dealt shit, he knew what to do with it.

But it was the good hands, the great hands, that sucked him in and invariably shafted him. He had to keep raising with two pair. Or he had to go all the way with a flush. What could possibly be beating three queens, for fuck's sake? Bet and raise, bet and raise. Hooked and pulled in every fucking time.

It was getting into the wee hours and George had been instructed to open another bottle of JD and freshen the ice. Cigar smoke hung low. The conversation had earlier turned to what Lou was going to serve up by way of video entertainment. A bald Italian restaurant owner named Tardelli and a young but wizened-looking securities salesman called Owens from the Upper East Side excitedly talked up a rumour that some spic bodyguards had filmed Stevie Wonder at play with his schlong.

'The spade maestro didn't even know they were in the room!'

'Like a goddamn baby's arm with an apple in its fist, I'm tellin' ya!' laughed the restaurateur and illustrated the point by rolling his sleeve up.

George excused himself for a piss with all the nonchalance of a lifetime grifter and headed to the far end of the apartment to have a look around. Two bedrooms lay down the hallway. On cruise control he scoped the first, dismissing it as a guest room, rarely used, of no importance, and proceeded to what he assumed was the master bedroom. Surprisingly it was neat and tidy. George figured Lou must have a maid come in once a week.

Then he saw a circular wall safe at the far corner of the room. Incredibly it was open. He looked over his shoulder. Laughter and insults still carried up the hallway from the living room. Why have a wall safe and just leave it open? Was this a set-up? Were they watching him on closed-circuit TV, waiting for him to filch something so they could bust him on his return?

He looked around the room. No cameras in sight. He swallowed. Second thoughts. Maybe he'd just close the safe door and leave the room. He crossed to the wall with that thought still in his mind and had a look inside.

There was a stack of cardboard folders held together with an elastic band and – his adrenaline surged – about half a dozen cans of film stock, another three or four VCR tapes, maybe twelve smaller Digital8 and MiniDV cassettes, and one bulging brown manila envelope. It looked important.

Before he'd really thought it through, George had reached into the envelope and pulled out the single Digital8 cassette it contained, replacing it with one from the middle of the row and pushing the others together to fill the gap.

The tape's info sticker was blank, so there was no means of discerning its content. He stuffed it down the front of his baggy chinos, inside his elasticised Calvin Klein authentic copies. Time to split.

As he headed back down the corridor, the toilet flushed and the restaurateur Tardelli emerged, shaking water from his hands. The man turned and looked straight at him.

'Great apartment,' said George lamely. 'Great party.'

The man stood staring suspiciously at George, who brass-necked it and, squeezing by him, returned to his seat. Tardelli sat down opposite him again. The whole thing took only about two minutes but it ensured that the rest of the evening was agony for George Bailey.

When Tardelli mentioned that he'd had a car radio jacked from his car parked right outside his apartment, and commented that you couldn't trust anyone these days, George was convinced that he had been busted.

'It was happening all the goddamn time. Freaking crime wave.

Real hassle taking the car to the shop. So I leaves a note on the windshield – "radio already stolen!" I come down next mornin'. Fuckin' door lock's broke again. Side window smashed. Sonofabitch has taken a dump on the seat and there's a note on the dashboard – "Just checkin'!"'

The company exploded into laughter. But Tardelli continued to look right at George, and Lou only smiled grimly and chomped down hard on his Cuban stogie. When he did speak, George was reminded of the company he was keeping.

'That's the difference between you and me, Guido. Me, I used to live up in Flatbush, before I moved on to Bensonhurst for a while. White man had the same kinda problems up there. But I had my own way of dealing with that shit – old-school. Got me a ball of twine, wrapped that sucker up in every kinda fish hook and fly hook I could find. Hid it in there. Pushed right back, behind the fixins of the radio. Well now, when I gets down next morning, nigger's legs is hangin' out the door. Bucking and kickin' just like the catch-o-the-day! Can't detach hisself from the hooks, see. Figures he's gonna pull his whole goddamn hand right off! Well, I takes my old Louisville Slugger and I beats that boy till there's pink suds flyin' out of his nose and mouth – and I mean bubbles!'

The room fell silent. Then someone said, 'Fuckin' A!' and they all banged on the table in agreement.

George felt nauseous. Every time the Italian leaned over to speak to Lou, or when they were out of the room together, George almost pissed his pants. He could feel the sharp plastic edges of the cassette tape dig into his inner thigh.

Just when he was on the verge of calling Lou into the hall and confessing the whole thing, the fat host brought the proceedings to a halt.

'I'm beat. Ya don't gotta go home but ya can't stay here.'

He stood at the door as guests filed out. Owens complained that they hadn't seen the show yet. Lou moved him along with a hand to the small of his back.

'Anyone would think yez came here for something other than my company. Now beat it!'

As George drew level with Lou he extended a hand, preparing to thank him for his generosity when Lou grabbed his face between his hands and squeezed. He looked like he might kiss him.

'Ah, Georgie, Georgie. Ya remind me of me back in the day. But that ain't no good thing, ya understand!' He laughed.

George laughed, one hand in his trouser pocket, clenching the tape tightly.

'Here, I've got something for the flight – take the edge off, help you sleep.' Lou slipped him a handful of small white pills and tapped his nose. 'You might need my shades too. That West Coast sun'll melt your brain if you're not used to it.' He handed George his prize Ray-Bans.

'Wow, thanks, Lou. Much appreciated.'

'You take care now. Have a good trip.' Lou sniggered as he closed the door.

George had driven home and studied the tape for any indication of what it might contain. No markings, no time codes, nothing, save for a sticker. A logo. 'Webcore', it read.

It might be anything. It might be nada. There might be money in it. It might be *Gone-with-the-Fucking-Wind* for all he knew. But why, then, keep it in a wall safe?

Anyway, it would have to wait. He'd had the presence of mind to lob it into his suitcase before he left the apartment for the motel.

George hoped Beatrice would change her mind about coming on the trip. He figured he'd buy one of those handheld portable camcorders out West when they got there and make a record of their trip, something they'd always have. Then he could have a quick peek at his contraband, weigh up the options. If he suspected that Lou's tape was celebrity fodder, he'd maybe let Beatrice have a look – she read enough of those trashy magazines to identify any of those kids who passed for Hollywood royalty these days. One thing was for sure, though. It was too late to return it now. That boat had sailed.

Lou Plutus had some very, very heavy friends heading up Russian-backed enterprises. Kneecappings with Black & Deckers were their established MO. Nobody fucked with those guys. Come to think of it, Lou could be a pretty dangerous guy himself. Maybe George should cool it a little on the stock theft when he got back to work at the store.

Besides, George liked Lou.

Chapter 7
NEVADA

Lou Plutus stood in the doorway of his bedroom looking at the wall safe, perplexed. He'd been too fucked up yesterday to notice. Now, looking at the contents with a clearer head, he had a gut feeling that something was wrong. Something was missing. But what? Why hadn't he got around to indexing that material? Christ, it had been on his to-do list for about five years.

Tardelli, the pasta maker, had got him thinking: you really couldn't trust anyone these days. Had the Italian helped himself to Lou's stash? He was a dangerous individual and higher up the food chain than his humble day-to-day labours might suggest. Like Lou, he was interested in pornography and 'rarities', as he described them, captured surreptitiously on film.

Maybe Lou had been too slipshod with his bonhomie; maybe he was letting it slip. Leaving the safe unlocked was unforgivable, tantamount to senility, especially with so many kids putting stuff out on the internet these days, and the paparazzi paying top dollar.

Get a fucking grip, Plutus!

He returned down the hallway and snapped open the locks on a small brown leather case that he had placed in his lap. Inside was a variety of bottles and bags, pills and potions. He held up a little plastic bag with a quantity of rolled joints inside, another with an ounce of oiled, black hashish. He shook a number of dark-coloured pill bottles to ascertain content, and then held an amber glass bottle with a rubber stopper up close to his eye. His amyl nitrate supply was low. Those young guys could sure hoover that stuff up.

The sun was streaming in through the window and hurt his eyes. He raised a hand to shield them and shifted in the chair to avoid it. It would be another day spent trying to fill up the hours. Work for the news crews was slow lately. It was getting harder to stay on the good side of those infantile, hotshot editors down at the station. Reputation and chutzpah counted for less with them. Maybe he'd throw another of his infamous parties soon, invite a few working girls and see if he couldn't get some of those jerks on camera doing something they shouldn't be. That had always provided good collateral in the past.

He'd probably spend the day dropping into his stores, making the collections. The Russians were getting twitchy these days, wanting to renegotiate their arrangement. Always a bad sign.

Raoul, that new Hispanic kid he had working in his Upper East Side joint, was hot, but a little old at seventeen. Maybe he'd offer to get him into the movies.

The morning sun was still pouring through the open blinds, blinding him. He crossed to where his jacket hung on the back of the door and felt the pockets for his shades. Oh yeah, he'd loaned them to Georgie boy. He must be embarking on his odyssey West by now.

George Bailey.

A wide grin spread over Lou's face. If that lying, two-faced prick thought he could steal merchandise from his stores and get away with it he could think again. He fished around in the case, pulled out a bottle of pills, unscrewed the lid and emptied what was left of the contents into the palm of his hand.

He laughed. 'Wait until he drops these muthas,' he said aloud. 'They'll be takin' him off that goddamn plane in a straitjacket.'

Chapter 8

NEVADA

George threw open the motel room door and stood in the glorious early morning sunshine. Looking down on the parking lot below, he thought about the convertible he'd reserved which would be waiting for him at San Francisco Airport, and amused himself by spotting the out-of-state plates and rental cars. There was already a lot of activity down there.

The brunette with the big seventies sunglasses was looking at a map spread out on the hood of her car, an elderly couple were checking each other's golf slacks for unwanted fluff balls and cotton threads, and two of the four immaculately coiffured Arab guys were loading bags into their car.

He'd thought they were South Americans until they'd politely asked him for change for a worn five-dollar bill they'd been trying to feed unsuccessfully into a food vending machine. 'Eeeebraham Lincoln, face up, face up!' they'd chided each other at every failed attempt.

Maybe there was time for a quick muffin and coffee at the godawful plastic hotel breakfast bar.

He conducted a last sweep of the room for any wayward items, slipped the downers Lou had given him into his coat pocket, and stood for the last time in front of the full-length mirror. His shirt still hung out over his pants. Tucking it in tight, he inhaled deeply and fastened the black Italian leather belt a notch further. That gut would have to go.

He extended his arms to either side and raised them up and down until the shirt rode up and sat snugly on the waistband of his pants, the way his mother had taught him as a boy. One of the Arab guys happened to pass by his open door just then, trailing his luggage behind him, and gave him a bewildered look. George, catching his own reflection in the mirror and seeing a middle-aged man in a suit flapping his arms up and down, smiled self-consciously. The Arab smiled back, wished him good morning and carried on.

From the taxi window, the used car lots and diners gave way to factories, warehouses and container yards the closer they got to the airport. George thought of the opening title sequence of *The Sopranos* and began to whistle the theme tune.

It seldom required much encouragement for George to look on the bright side of any reversal of fortune. The sunny early autumn morning and the road ahead, stretching all the way to pre-booked flights and hotels at someone else's expense, helped him live in the moment and anticipate the immediate future with relish.

'Beautiful day,' George said to the turbaned driver hermetically sealed in his cab.

He got no response.

George leaned forward, lifted his sunglasses to squint at the permit swinging to and fro from the radio control knob on the dashboard and tried again.

'Beautiful day, Ashok.'

The driver started a little at the familiar use of his name, glanced in the rear-view mirror and, following the line of George's sight, solved the conundrum instantly.

'Please sit well back in the cab, sir. It's for your own safety.'

George bristled a little but was determined that no one, least of all a goddamn, twelve-to-a-room Sikh incense burner, was going to rain on his parade. He launched into his tried-and-tested catalogue of sure-fire gambits that he reserved especially for cab drivers.

'Just starting out or finishing?'

There was silence but George knew that, as often as not, any cab driver at the beginning or end of a long, solitary shift would eventually melt to enquires after his well-being.

'I came on at six thirty last evening, sir. This run to the airport should finish me. Then I sleep and begin again at six thirty.'

'Damn, that's a long day!' George said, full of pseudo-concern.

'You had better believe it.'

'Still, if the cab's off the road, you're losing money, right? And I know what that's like. Say, how much they charging for insurance these days? I bet you barely break even.'

'Oh my, don't even go there!'

'Well, I'll tell you what. I couldn't do your job, that's for sure. On the gas, then on the brake. Crawling through traffic, having to deal with road rage. Man, that's some stressful shit.'

By the time they were pulling off at the exit for the airport, Ashok had explained that he preferred working nights, anti-social as that was, because he loathed the manic rush hour and enjoyed his own company. There were inherent dangers in this approach, however, and he showed George the angry weal across his forearm, the legacy of a machete attack by a late-night fare-cum-robber.

George also learned that Ashok was betrothed to a second cousin back in Hyderabad, had six brothers and was the seventh son of a seventh son. His older brother, Kelkar, was supposed to alternate shifts with him, but they had recently discovered that on days like today the speeding cab and rapid flickering of passing shadows cast by the bright sunlight had a stroboscopic effect causing Kelkar to twitch and foam at the mouth. Epileptic episodes, previously undiscovered. It was one more thing for Ashok to worry about and George to empathise with. Empathy was one of the things George did well. 'People love to talk about themselves,' his mother had said. 'You let 'em talk and they'll love you for it.'

Ashok was all smiles now. He was looking for the correct set-down bay.

'Well, sir, which airline are you travelling with please?'

'United Airlines ... UA.'

Suddenly the driver's smile froze and his brow furrowed. George assumed the man was returning to business mode as the serious matter of payment and a tip drew near.

'UA ... AA ... capital letters. They're all the same, I guess,' George joked.

But Ashok was already out of the car and around the back to the trunk. George's case stood on the pavement awaiting collection.

George had creased a few bills while in the cab and had them folded, ready to give the driver.

'I hope your brother's health improves and you get back to India sometime soon,' George said.

He held the notes out toward the driver, but was startled when the man grabbed him by both hands and turned his palms up.

'I have been given a gift, sir. Will you indulge me?' Ashok said.

George looked around. The entrance to the concourse buzzed and the usual hubbub of commuter activity continued all around him. What kind of riff was this?

'Please?' Ashok smiled.

The penny dropped with George. 'Hey, right! Seventh son of a seventh son. Look fella, I don't normally buy into this kinda stuff, so ...'

The driver had drawn George's hands up close to his face and was studying them. An airport cop noticed them and was looking in their direction. Another yellow cab pulled in behind theirs, its hazard lights flashing, a little staccato stab on the horn indicating impatience.

Ashok looked up into George's eyes. He had tears in his own.

'Make your peace with God, forgive your debtors, for they keep the airways open for capital letters.'

A jet engine roared in the distance.

'Keep the airways what?' said George.

Beeeeeeeep, Beeeeeeeep!

George jumped and looked over his shoulder. 'Hey, I'm standing here!'

'You stayin' or goin' buddy?' yelled the cab driver behind, leaning out his window and gesticulating angrily. A smartly dressed young woman sat in the back, making no attempt to disembark until the cab got her as close to the luggage trolleys as was physically possible.

The cop was moving toward them with more purpose now, unholstering his book and pencil.

When George turned around again, his hands in the air in front of him, still clutching the fare and tip, he was alone. He caught the brake lights of Ashok's cab, blinking on and off, as he disappeared into the distance.

Chapter 9

Beatrice stood outside the entrance to the North Tower of the World Trade Center. As was her custom since taking the job, she craned her neck and gazed skyward. The structure virtually disappeared into the blue sky overhead. Beatrice had never yet failed to be impressed.

'Good gosh almighty,' she said, shaking her head in bewilderment. 'What a creature is mankind that he can produce such a glorious creation ... two such creations.'

She felt a little dizzy and, as always, self-conscious as she set off a chain reaction of busy New Yorkers all looking skyward to see what she was staring at. Like the sunrise, it truly hurts to look at that marvel for too long, she thought.

She arrived in the glass and marble lobby and got in the elevator. Her finger hovered over the button. She'd intended stopping off at the third-floor Broadway ticket office. She had been trying to convince George to go with her to see *Les Misérables* as a treat for her forthcoming birthday. It would have been nice if it had been his idea, but she'd given up expecting him to take the initiative. She thought about how those tickets wouldn't be necessary now. It was one of the thousand little things that would have to change in her life. For the first time in a long while, she felt conscious of being on her own and a long way from home.

A large black arm with a string of golden bracelets pushed through the gap in the elevator doors just as they were closing, causing it to 'ching' and reopen.

'Hold up there. Weeze goin' up.'

Beatrice recognised the accent immediately as south of the Mason–Dixon Line.

A small boy of about six years old got in followed by huge black woman. She wore a summer dress of yellow and red, with a matching turban-style headdress – a kind of African ensemble. The boy was in short pants and a school blazer, and wore a stiff white collar and tartan bow tie. His black shoes were shined to perfection. The woman offered Beatrice a big, toothy smile.

'Why, you're quite the little gentleman,' said Beatrice, hunkering down to be in the boy's eyeline. 'And what's your name?'

'Don't be frightened, Daniel. His name's Daniel, mam.' The woman licked her fingers, reached over and flattened his hair where it threatened to spring loose.

The boy sighed and rolled his big eyes adorably.

Beatrice smiled. 'Y'all don't sound like you're from around here.'

'No, mam. Daniel and me is up here in New York City from Mobile, Alabama.'

'Well shoot, I'm a Bama girl myself, born and raised!'

A man in a business suit with a newspaper under his arm arrived at the still-open elevator and was about to join them when he turned away at the last minute and headed for the other elevator. The two women looked at each other and burst out laughing.

'Beatrice Hatcher,' said Beatrice, extending her hand. 'Call me Bee.'

'Gabriella,' said the woman, shaking it.

Beatrice's finger hovered over the floor buttons again. 'I'm on ninety-five. Where're you goin'?'

'Oh, weeze goin' all the ways to the top. Ain't that right, Daniel?'

The boy smiled at Beatrice. 'All the ways,' he said.

The door slid closed with a cushioned hiss and a clunk.

Bee looked at her watch. It was 8:44. She wondered if George had really left without her.

Chapter 10

Weaving through the pushcarts and suitcases, George was making good time. The check-in line inched its way toward the smiling UA girl, and he pushed his bag along with his foot, hands deep in his trouser pockets, while other passengers wrestled with shoulder straps and wriggling infants. He smiled to himself at the notable representation of even Pacific tans, Hawaiian shirts worn out over chinos, sockless loafers, casual business types. The general West Coast dudeness of it all. On reaching the end of the line, he gave the pretty Asian girl behind the desk a killer smile and prepared to field the usual formalities. The girl smiled back, but pointed to her eyes while doing so. George just kept smiling.

'Your sunglasses, sir – can you take them off for me, please?'

'Oh sure! Sorry,' he said, feeling a little the poseur.

'Travelling alone?'

'Ah … yes. Alone.' A pang of something resembling remorse swept over him. He made a mental note to call Beatrice one last time before take-off.

'We have a small number of passengers on today's flight, sir. So we're able to upgrade you to business class at no extra charge, if you like.'

This is a break! Better service, more leg room, proper cutlery, he thought. And didn't they recycle the air more thoroughly in there?

'Sure!' said George. 'What's not to like.'

George Bailey wasn't a great flyer. He wasn't petrified exactly but he was certainly reticent. He and Beatrice had driven long distances many times with their belongings packed into a U-Haul and an interstate map spread out on their knees. Ostensibly, this was because they were always on a tight budget, but it was also due to George's lack of confidence in commercial aviation.

The leisure aspects of flying appealed to him greatly, and the whole experience, up to and including the boarding of the aircraft, was embraced with his characteristic swagger. However, once he sat down and belted up, his body would slowly begin to tense, like a fist clenching until the knuckles went white.

The fear usually began in earnest with the flight details and evacuation procedures, which George viewed as fundamentally flawed. 'A life jacket? A life jacket? I want a goddamn PARACHUTE!' His mantra to Beatrice on these occasions was always the same: 'It's a hollowed-out metal tube, right? Thirty thousand feet off the ground. Okay, you've gotta suspend belief even to consider going through with it, right?' Take-offs and landings presented him with the greatest challenge: 'Yeah, and what about that high-octane aviation fuel? They don't measure that in gallons, ya know. It's in tonnes. TONNES, FOR CHRISSAKES!' He would perspire and grip Beatrice's hand tightly, repeating to himself 'I'm okay, I'm okay, I'm okay' until the plane had levelled out and the seat belt signs were switched off.

After that, it was as if he became another person. He'd walk around the cabin, vodka and tonic in hand, treating his surroundings like one big nightclub in the sky and the cabin crew as his personal bar staff. George always availed of the complimentary drinks from the bar, claiming Beatrice's full allocation as well as his own.

But this time, for the first time, he'd be flying alone.

He reached inside his jacket pocket and reassuringly fingered the sleeping tablets Lou had given him. *A couple of drinks at the bar, drop these babies, and see ya at the finishing line*, he thought. Six hours from now he'd be on Pacific Standard Time. Should he change the hands of his watch now? It would still be morning out there. Hell, he could be watching the seagulls on Pier 39 while having lunch, for Christ's sake.

Okay, plan of action needed. He closed his eyes and thought about it. He didn't want to be seen popping pills at the bar, not first thing in the morning. *Into the john, drop the Diazepam, another vodka tonic and float on up in the big silver bird. If all goes to plan, I'll have the eye shades on and the earphones up loud before anyone can say 'emergency exit' … Oh yeah, and phone the woman I love!*

George moved away from the check-in desk and went straight to the airport bar. He admired his reflection in the shiny panel behind the counter and ordered a dish of green olives and cashew nuts with his drink. The first boarding call caught him by surprise and he asked the barmaid to make it a double.

The group of fellow travellers assembling at the gate was indeed small. He counted thirty-six in all. He knocked back the drink and ordered another.

'United Airlines, Flight 93 to San Francisco. Final boarding call.'

Dispatching the second drink with similar haste, he paid and grabbed a handful of nuts. The barmaid looked at him disapprovingly.

'Gotta run, honey,' he said, smiling at her apologetically and making for the restroom.

It was empty but for one man, who was supporting himself with his hands on the stainless steel countertop, his face low, almost touching a sinkful of water.

A few basins down, George ran the cold tap and took the pills from his pocket. Better take the three, he thought, just to be sure. He put them all in his mouth, scooped up some water in the cup of his hand and swallowed. Furtively he looked toward the man, his face still suspended above the pool of water. Amid the discarded paper towels and pools of liquid soap, it was as if he was looking for something profound or important deep in the stainless steel bowl. Suddenly, he sprang erect and began splashing the water from the basin onto his face while mumbling something imperceptible.

George noticed for the first time that it was one of the Arab guys from the motel. 'Hey, how's that for a coincidence?' he said genially.

The man turned and looked right through him.

'The Comfort Inn … this morning?'

There was a flicker of a smile by way of recognition, then the man picked up an attaché case and left.

'United Airlines, Flight 93 to San Francisco. Last and final boarding call.'

Yeah, ya jerkoff, next time you need change for a Hershey bar you can blow it out your ass, George thought.

He followed the man out the door to the boarding gate. The phone call to Beatrice would have to wait.

Chapter 11

NEVADA

In his mind's eye, he'd been playing their last day together over and over again.

'All I ask is pleeease will you load the dishes into the dishwasher. I mean, is that too much to ask?'

'I'm watchin' the game. Can't you SEE I'm watchin' the game?'

'Did you read that article I told you about on mood swings?'

'I'm watchin' THE FRICKING GAME!'

'Yeah, my mom's blood pressure is sky high. She's just not well. And I'm getting a cold. Do you listen? Do you CARE?'

'Look, I had a shitty day. Maybe I don't want to hear about your mom ... or my mom ... or ANYBODY'S MOM!'

'Yeah, well that's just fine. That's real adult, ya know. Adults don't walk away from their responsibilities.'

'Yeah, and who the fuck are you now – the grown-up police?'

Christ, what had they become?

George had never balked at moving on from struggling relationships in the past. Should the necessity arise, he had a talent for making cohabitation with him so unbearable that the woman had practically no option but to show him the door, thus allowing George to occupy whatever moral high ground remained: 'Hey, you finished with me. Just remember that.'

So was that why he'd spilled his guts, unprompted, to Beatrice?

She'd never have known about Jaffé Losoko otherwise. It brought up all those deep, troubling questions he worked so hard to avoid. He was never going to be one of those guys who suggested they saw other people. It wasn't his style. In the past, if it was over, he simply left. Moved on and put it all down to experience.

For her part, Beatrice had exhibited remarkable maturity at the start of their relationship when she insisted that George should never, ever confess his infidelities to her, reasoning that she didn't possess the wherewithal to forgive and forget. Better not to know.

While he was impressed by her candour, he couldn't help but notice that Beatrice was, in effect, sanctioning a kind of moral duplicity, and that she might apply this code to her own indiscretions, although a more scrupulously faithful woman it would have been difficult to find.

She had of late been staying out into the wee small hours with two unattached girlfriends from the office. And as for gay guys? Well, they just adored her. Lou hadn't helped matters by insisting that all women wanted to 'turn' a faggot, so he should be warned and take nothing for granted.

So what had kept them together, through thick and thin, for seven long years? Love? Habit? And where was all this coming from all of a sudden? He knew what Lou would say: 'Yer growin' a conscience, kid.' Yeah, good old Lou. He took no shit from women.

George had taken his seat on the plane and, luxuriating in the extra leg room of business class, was watching as people filed along the aisles quietly, stowing luggage in overhead lockers, removing coats, making themselves comfortable for the trip. He thought about the poor schmucks in cattle class and looked forward to stretching out across all three seats once they got into the air.

The pills that Lou had given him seemed to be doing their job. He felt the dullish surge and muted roar of adrenaline somewhere deep in his guts, and a tingling sensation where the top of his spine joined the base of his skull. It was not unpleasant. God, he could murder a drink. Maybe first class gets that first-class service.

He leaned into the aisle and touched the arm of a stewardess. She turned to face him. It was the stern, older woman on the flight crew. He'd hoped for the blond babe with the hair pulled back in a ponytail.

'Hi, I was just wondering if I could get a vodka tonic on the rocks, please?' He tried to appear the opposite of desperate.

'I'm sorry, sir, the drinks service will be available only after we're airborne and the captain has switched off the seat belt signs.'

She said all this through a fixed, toothy smile that screamed, 'Jesus Christ, can't you even wait for five minutes, you lush!'

'No harm in asking.'

'None at all, sir.'

She turned on her heel and walked away to the back of the plane. George quickly looked after her to see if she'd kept her figure. It was a reflex.

He spotted two of the four Arab men sitting together three rows back. First class too, huh? It's gotta be oil money, he figured. Maybe one of their old men is a sheik.

A few other passengers were dotted around the cabin. One man, wearing a 49ers cap, was working on a laptop; an elderly woman laid out a number of vitamin bottles, oils and creams on the seat beside her, checked them off on her fingers and returned them to her case.

George clipped on his seat belt and flicked nervously through the in-flight magazine. Working in a DVD rental store meant that the movie programme would inevitably be disappointing. He turned the pages. Seen it ... Seen it ... Crap ... Crap ... *The Wizard of Oz*? Christ! ... TCM Classics ...

The Boeing 757 taxied steadily to take-off position but held there for what seemed an eternity. He fantasised about Beatrice running across the tarmac, waving her ticket, ready to forgive and forget. Just like in the movies.

The captain came on the intercom with the usual calming, reassuring nonsense designed to placate the unmedicated.

George suddenly felt the urge to look down at his left leg. It was bouncing up and down uncontrollably. He willed it to stop, but it was as if the limb had become disengaged from his central nervous system. He pushed it down with both hands and felt it subdue, but quiver, under the restraint. In a panic he looked around again. The row next to him was empty. He looked behind. One of the Arab men was deep in conversation with his friend in the window seat and obscured from view. No one had seen him.

Then George noticed that his black silk shirt was stuck to his body, sodden and limp with sweat. Sweat ran down his forehead into his eyes, stinging them. *Fuck, am I having some kind of seizure here?* he wondered, and clenched his eyes tight.

He tried to conjure up Beatrice's face and imagine what she might say to reassure him in such circumstances. Instead, a kaleidoscope of colours and flashes, like a firework display of giant cartwheels and sparklers assailed him, burning painfully bright behind his closed lids. For a moment he thought he might throw up.

'Cabin crew to take-off positions,' blurted the intercom and the big jet engines revved in preparation to accelerate.

Panic welled up in him, and then, just as quickly, he was enveloped by some giant, unseen chemical comfort blanket. It wrapped the dread up and smothered it reassuringly. George felt disorientated and looked behind him once more. Only the Arab at the window remained in the row of seats. George could see his hand drumming nervously on the arm of the leather chair.

Where have the others gone? he wondered distractedly. They were strapped in and ready for take-off. Can't be in the toilet. Not all of 'em. Not even one of 'em. Not allowed.

He was diverted from his ruminations by the fact that his right leg had now joined the other in manically jiggling around. He had to push down on both to gain some control.

George had smoked a little grass in his time and had once or twice tooted a line or two of Bolivia's finest, but hallucinogenics were a definite no-no. Except that one time when, aged twenty-two, he'd left some frat boys he'd been hanging with and went home by himself to drop a surreptitious tab that an older hippy chick had given him. He had become fixated on a print of Munch's *The Scream* that was taped to a wall by a previous tenant and spent the evening watching the unscheduled show unfold. When it was over, George was cured of any remaining curiosity regarding narcotically assisted astral travel. He hated the lack of control, the unpredictability of the high, the not being able to come down, the not being able to make it stop.

As United Airways Flight 93 rattled down Runway 4, pulled up into the air and banked to the west, he heard some passengers on the right-hand side of the plane remark that on an overcast day, the only things poking above the clouds were the two towers of the World Trade Center.

But today it was perfectly clear. As was George's dawning realisation that he was now fully in the grip of a powerful LSD excursion.

Chapter 12

The floors flew by in the illuminated window on the elevator wall. Little Daniel began to hum a tune. Gabriella smiled and ruffled his hair.

Beatrice smiled too. 'What brings y'all to the big smoke?'

'Daniel here, he's up in New York City on account of him winning the Alabama All-State Singing Champeenship – best soloist in his age group. Daniel, he's a proper singin' sensation. Ain't that right, Daniel?'

The boy just smiled and continued to hum to himself.

Beatrice was enchanted. 'Why, you must be so proud.'

'Yes, mam. See, Daniel's an orphan, brought up in and around the 32nd Tabernacle Gospel Choir. That's my church. We likes to think some of our music and prayers rubbed off on the boy. "Jesus Loves Me" – that's his winning song. Ain't that right, Daniel? You just nailed that sucker.'

'Well, it would be just a privilege and an honour to have Daniel come sing for us at service in Tuscaloosa. Do you think that might be possible?'

'Don't see why not,' Gabriella said, smiling. 'This boy is gonna tour the world someday.'

She bent at the waist with some difficulty and kissed Daniel's cheek. He carried right on smiling and humming.

'Are you going to the top for the views?' Beatrice asked.

'Sure are. It's a truly beautiful day. Why don't you join us?'

Bee looked at her watch again. 'Well, I really should be—'

'My, girl, you'll have plenty of time to sit behind a desk,' scolded Gabriella playfully. 'Besides, Daniel here likes you. Might even be fixin' to give you a rendition of something.'

The boy looked a little embarrassed and Beatrice couldn't stop herself from giggling like a schoolgirl about to play hooky with her new-found friends.

'Well, that's about the best offer I've had in a while.' She smiled. 'Thank you. I believe I will.'

The floors flew on by – 93, 95, 97, 99 …

At 8:46 a.m., American Airlines Flight 11 slammed into the World Trade Center's North Tower, creating an impact hole that extended from the 92nd to 98th floors.

At the massive noise of the explosion coming from below, Beatrice, Gabriella and Daniel instantly hunkered down and covered their heads. The elevator bucked and buffeted, throwing them all to the floor. The white strip light sparked and went out, then immediately an orange glow from the emergency lighting enveloped the small space.

The elevator had stopped.

'God almighty,' wailed Gabriella and pulled the boy close to her.

Beatrice moved toward them too and all three hugged the back wall of the elevator.

'It's okay. We're okay. We'll be okay,' said Beatrice, not really aware that she was speaking at all. It made her think of George. It was what he always said before take-off.

'Shussh,' ordered Gabriella urgently, and she placed her finger to her lips, her eyes big with fear.

There was a deep roar coming from beneath them now. It

sounded like the sea, but Beatrice knew that was impossible. No, it sounded more like her mom's old stove cooker, gushing gas before ignition. But enormous. Then there was a pop and a roar as if a massive pilot light had just been lit.

'HELP! HELP! CAN ANYBODY HEAR US? HELP!' the two women yelled in unison.

'Let's get these doors open,' said Beatrice.

They scratched and pulled at the central split in the door. It gave way only partially, creating an opening of only about a foot or so across.

'Daniel, honey? You okay?'

The boy rubbed at his eyes but nodded. Already there was a distinct smell of burning and the insidious beginnings of noxious fumes were causing his eyes to smart.

The elevator shuddered, dropped and shook again, battering them from side to side like some low-budget sci-fi spaceship under attack. When it came to rest they could see that they were just below a floor.

Beatrice wiggled herself into the gap between the elevator doors and, by pushing her backside against one door, tried to prise them apart. The opening increased enough to see that above was the floor of a lobby, while straight ahead was only brickwork and coiled cables hung like jungle vines, under which yawned the bottomless drop of the elevator shaft.

'Move ya-sel, honey,' said Gabriella.

She levered her big frame into the door gap, roaring with the strain, pushing and bucking her well-appointed buttocks to good effect. The door was almost shoved back fully now and stayed in place. She was panting, and big balloons of sweat ran down her face and arms.

She smiled sadly at Beatrice. 'The bigger the cushion, the better the pushin.'

Beatrice peered down. The darkness below was absolute, save for a dull pulsating orange glow. Then she noted the smoke. It was thick with a red blush behind it, mesmerising, suddenly stirring itself, darting and shimmying like a snake in the eddies of air rising up the shaft, then jumping and swirling again, coming right up the duct. Very soon it would reach them.

'HELP! … HELP US!'

Beatrice looked up at the gap overhead, the pile carpet, the glimpse of sunlight.

'Are you thinkin' what I'm thinkin'?' said Gabriella. 'Sweetie, even if you could lift me up to that, you just know these hips would git jammed up in there.'

'Yes, but maybe—'

Suddenly Gabriella screamed. 'Daniel, you come away from the edge right now, ya hear!'

The boy had been looking down into the abyss. He stumbled backward into the elevator. He looked terrified.

'Maybe it's too tight for us,' said Beatrice, 'but we could lift Daniel up and out.'

'Yes! Yes, maybe we could.'

The boy clenched his fists, jutted out his bottom lip and went stiff. He shook his head furiously.

'No, no, no, no, no. I's like to fall.'

The smoke was filling up the shaft quite noticeably now. The sound of falling debris and of screams – human voices in pain and duress – were clearly audible.

Gabriella crouched down to Daniel's height and looked him in the eye. 'Remember when we went up the Empire State, just like ol' King Kong? Remember what I told you 'bout those Indians?'

The boy nodded.

'Well, you go right ahead and tell this nice lady that story.'

Daniel turned his big eyes, welling up with tears, to Beatrice and said, 'Canadian Indians from near Montreal built the Empire State Building. They got the job cuz they didn't have a word for "heights", so they weren't feared of fallin' or nuthin.'

'And now you're gonna be just like those Indians, little man,' said Gabriella. 'You're gonna be an Indian brave and you're gonna climb right out through that gap and run right out of this building, ya hear?'

Chapter 13

The phone rang in Lou's apartment.

'Lou? It's Eddie. Getta hold of Sammy Chan and get down to the World Trade Center. There's been some kinda accident.'

Lou scratched his head but was already moving to pack his camera. 'I ain't seen nuthin' on the news.' He looked around for shoes but had to settle for open-toed sandals.

'Wise guy! We are the news ... at least until somebody gets there ahead of us.'

'Are you breakin' my balls?'

'Louie, Louie, whatever it is, it's big. Less talkin' more filmin'.'

'I'm out the door already.'

When he arrived at Sammy Chan's place, the soundman was virtually jumping up and down on the spot. They threw his boom stand, mic, headphones and assorted paraphernalia into the back of Lou's station wagon and floored it.

Sammy told him that early reports were sketchy but, incredible as it sounded, it seemed that a plane had barrelled into one of the towers. Real horror show stuff.

'What ... like a single prop plane or something?' asked Lou.

'Hell no. A goddamn commercial airliner!' screamed Sammy.

'Christ, I love this town,' said Lou, making a mental note to switch to a wide-angle lens. 'Switch over. You're drivin'.'

Lou and Sammy were negotiating the West Side Elevated Highway when the tower came into view.

'Mother o' God, it's smoking like a goddamn chimney stack!' Lou focused in to get a good motion shot.

'Do you think there are still people in there?' asked Sammy who, like everyone else on the highway, was transfixed by the juxtaposition of disintegrating iconography and human peril while endeavouring not to crash into the car in front of him.

By the time they reached Cedar Street, radio pundits were churning out commentary to accompany the images. No one seemed to know what was happening. Fire trucks, ambulances and cop cars were swarming around the place.

Lou reached inside his canvas bag and pulled out a masking-tape gun. Ripping off strips of tape, he used it to write the huge letters 'TV' in reverse on the inside of the windscreen, forcing Sammy to duck, squint and swerve.

They had driven as far as they could. The only progress likely now would be on foot. Sammy pulled the car sharply into a loading zone and both men jumped out to make their final adjustments to equipment.

Just then there was a roaring noise overhead.

Lou looked across the street. A crowd of people had covered their mouths in horror. Many pointed skyward. People yelled and screamed in disbelief. A large shadow passed over them. Lou felt it before he heard it.

At 9:03 a.m., a second jet airliner smashed into the South Tower, creating an impact hole that extended from the 78th to 84th floors. Large fireballs emerged from the south-west, south-east and north-east faces, and the east corner. The impact rocked the tower, causing it to sway several feet. Much of the fuselage of the jet emerged from the eastern corner of the tower.

'Sweet Christ in the morning,' whispered Lou. He dropped the camera on the big toe of his left foot, instantly fracturing it. For the first time in thirty years of covering the news, Lou Plutus missed the shot.

Chapter 14

The conditions all around them were seriously deteriorating by the minute, yet neither Beatrice nor Gabriella contemplated death. It had all happened so quickly and was so ludicrously fantastical that denial of the undeniable gravity of the situation seemed the least complicated standpoint to adopt.

For the moment, they had a clear priority: Daniel, and his escape. Only when that had been secured would they allow their attention to turn to their own predicament.

Through the gap above, Beatrice could see feet running the length of the lobby: Adidas trainers, black stilettos, brown brogues, heavy work boots.

'Help ... HELP! Somebody help us! There's a child in here ... PLEASE!'

A bald man with glasses got down on all fours and peered through the opening into the elevator. A few people bumped into him. A woman fell over him, got up, stumbled and ran on.

'How many of you are in there?' he asked.

Gabriella held up Daniel. 'Mister, if I can reach the boy to you ... you can take him.'

The man hesitated, then lay flat and extended his arm as far as he could. 'It's too far. You're too far down ... I can't reach.'

'Murray, move your goddamn ass,' a voice commanded from behind the man.

'There are people trapped here … a kid … and women.'

'We got to make it to the stairwells, Murray, or we're all fucked. We'll send someone back for them.'

'Lady, there's no time,' Murray said down into the elevator. 'We'll send the rescue service straight to ya.'

'No! No! You've gotta help us out.' Gabriella couldn't keep the panic out of her voice.

'What the hell happened?' shouted Beatrice.

'A plane flew into us – full speed right into us.'

'Which floor is this?'

'One-oh-one … we're on one-oh-one.'

Some masonry and a lighting panel crashed to the floor in the lobby, throwing out sparks. Dust rose in a cloud.

'That's it. I'm outa here,' said the man behind Murray and a pair of suede desert boots ran by.

'The boy!' Gabriella screamed and held Daniel high again.

Murray looked like his heart might break. 'Lady, I'm sorry. I've got kids of my own.' He pushed himself up on his hands and was gone.

The fire below them was raging up the shaft and smoke billowed all around them. It was now or never.

'If Daniel holds on around my neck and you give me a lift up, I'm sure he could reach the floor and pull himself out. I'm sure he could!' reasoned Beatrice.

'I ain't too clever with lifting.'

'I'm small. You could do it. Look, this is the way we learned in the Girl Scouts: cup your hands together, I step into them like a stirrup, and you boost me up.'

Beatrice was removing her shoes as she spoke.

Chapter 15

L ou had a decision to make, and fast. Tower one or tower two?

Strips of paper came fluttering to the ground like some insane ticker tape parade. Above, the smoke was becoming thicker and blacker. He decided on the North Tower, as the impact site seemed further up and so he figured he could get higher in the building himself.

Sammy wasn't so sure. 'Man, you're not actually going up there?'

'Whadaya think you're gettin' paid for, asshole?'

'Let's shoot it from down here. Besides, we don't have a reporter to talk to camera.' Sammy was grasping at straws.

'If I know Sally Dandridge she's in there ahead of us already. If not, we'll grab a talkin' head from somewhere.'

Lou was already making his way into the building. Streams of people were coming in the opposite direction, pushing past them out of the building in various states of confusion and injury.

'Fire Department comin' through,' came a cry, and a group of firefighters in masks and breathing apparatus forced Lou flat against the wall. Pandemonium reigned. His toe hurt like hell.

'The elevators are out. We'll take the stairs,' Lou said.

'Where exactly are we going?' asked Sammy.

'You'll know when we get there,' Lou replied.

He had to admit it. He was enjoying this. They climbed against the current of fleeing New Yorkers, hell-bent on escape in the opposite direction. Many tried to convince them to retreat.

'Man, are you crazy? You don't know what it's like up there!'

'Buddy, what's wrong with this picture? You're going the wrong way. This whole place could come down.'

Lou said he found that hard to believe, but Sammy had heard enough and, by the 58th floor, announced he was turning back.

'You Chink motherfucker. You yellow lily-livered piece-a-shit. You'll never work with me again!' spluttered Lou.

Plastic was melting and running down the walls of the stairwell. Sammy covered up as some ceiling material collapsed around him.

'You got that right, you fat fuck!' he said and began his descent.

Lou continued the climb alone and then ducked into the foyer of the 66th floor.

It was deserted. Plants were scattered around, the earth spilled from their pots. Bits of ceiling, papers, briefcases and discarded shoes all littered the area. A water cooler lay on its side, still glugging, soaking the beige carpet.

Lou looked at the plaque on the wall outside the frosted glass double doors. 'William Morris Agency' it read. Hey, he thought, Celebrity Central. Who knows what a rummage around in here might throw up? Besides, he needed a break; his toe was blue-black and swollen to twice its size and his crotch was itching like crazy. He went in, his camera hanging down by his side.

'Hello?' he called out. 'Anyone here? Press.'

There was silence, save for the low roar of intense combustion above his head. It didn't register with Lou. He immediately made a beeline for the CEO's office and switched on the desk computer. While it booted up he pulled out drawers from filing cabinets, looking for a familiar celebrity name to refine his search. He noted an abandoned pot of coffee percolating in the corner. Don't mind if I do, he thought, sliding into the luxury executive leather. His toe ached bad. Maybe they had a medical kit somewhere.

Suddenly there was an almighty crash out in the foyer. Lou limped his way back through the agency and saw almost immediately that huge chunks of masonry had ploughed downward and were now piled high at angles across the entrance to the office.

'You have got to be fucking kidding me,' he said aloud and grabbed the corner of a desk for support.

A solid wall of concrete debris rose high above his head. There was no longer any exit from the office, let alone the floor. For a moment he considered falling upon the rubble, clawing at it like a madman until his fingers bled. Instead, he went back into the CEO's office and freshened his coffee cup.

He crossed to the window and looked down on the only town he'd ever felt at home in – perhaps the only thing he'd ever truly loved. Maybe it was fitting to check out this way.

He was just taking some solace in the ironic romanticism of the moment when a dark shape fell by the window, causing him to jerk backward from the pane and spill the hot coffee. A moment later another fell past, this time discernible – a young woman cartwheeling out of control, all the way down to the pavement. Her hair plumed smoke as she fell. It was a serious wake-up call.

'Shit! I'm not ready! Oh fuck ... no,' he said aloud, starting at the sound of his own voice.

He imagined the NYPD obtaining the master key from that Jew landlord. Thick, potato-head Micks, crawling all over his apartment, finding the movies, photos and sex toys. The other guys at the TV station laughing at Lou, the fudge-packer. Who would have thought it? they'd say. Good old Lou.

He considered the business, the video stores, passed to those prick Russians without so much as a dollar changing hands. Then there were the documents on hard drives and in paper files linking Lou with the traffic and pimping of Eastern European girls to whorehouses in Atlantic City and downtown Las Vegas and their subsequent appearance in his 'Webcore Adult Video' enterprise.

The Russians would certainly be concerned about that. Not that any of that mattered now. He could already smell the burning, feel the heat from above.

He returned to the office entrance. This time he *did* fall on the debris, wailing, trying uselessly to clear a path. His fingernails cracked and splintered to the quick. He felt pathetic. Then he had the idea that somebody might keep a pistol in a desk drawer. It would be a better way to go than being burnt alive. He ransacked the place but found nothing. Stupid! Why would anyone keep a gun in the William Morris Agency, unless it was to shoot some Heb lawyer.

The ceiling overhead was beginning to smoke.

I'm gonna burn. He raised both hands to his head. It wasn't like the pain from the candle-wax ... no. It was heat so bad it'd melt the skin right off your bones, turn you into soap right there and then. He crossed again to the window but tried not to look down. He couldn't settle and paced around the office. Soon he was balling his hands into fists and slamming them into the debris, then into the reinforced glass of the windows.

Rivulets of liquid fire started to snake down the walls.

He began to rant, to complain – to himself and God and Sammy Chan and Sonny and George Bailey and anyone else he could think of. 'I'm not ready yet. I'm not ready,' he repeated aloud and returned to the CEO's office.

There, Lou desperately sought to compose himself. As he prepared to meet his maker, he could do little else but sit down again behind the big desk and flick distractedly through a projected twelve-month promotional plan for Britney Spears.

Chapter 16

NEVADA

Thirty floors or so above, Gabriella was grunting and groaning as she supported the weight of Beatrice, with Daniel on her shoulders.

The heat in the elevator was becoming unbearable and Gabriella was hopping from foot to foot as if she were standing on a hot griddle. Daniel had made it up to the gap at floor level but hesitated, unsure of the final climb into the unknown and the prospect of falling back into the fiery abyss below.

'Daniel Stockton … boy, if I have to come up there after you with a switch …' said Gabriella. 'Pinch him. Reach up and pinch him,' she told Beatrice. 'He hates that.'

Beatrice did it and the boy began to cry, but he squirmed up and out of the elevator and emerged like a shelled pea into the lobby of floor 101.

'Good boy! Brave boy!' called Beatrice.

'You a winner, Daniel Stockton. You a wonderment, boy. Now git goin',' added Gabriella.

Daniel stood up and looked around him. The floor was in chaos. Smoke hung low, just above his head.

'To the stairs, Daniel, to the stairs!' shouted Beatrice, pointing and gesturing desperately.

The boy could clearly see the exit sign still illuminated by the emergency lighting. He moved toward it. A metallic wrenching noise screeched into the lobby as a stanchion from the roof supports sheared through. The elevator bumped and shook again. Beatrice and Gabriella hugged each other tightly.

'He'll be all right. You'll see. Lil' Daniel will make it.'

Then they heard it, high and pure above the noise of falling masonry and exploding, sizzling electrics:

'Jes-us loves me, this I know … for the Bi-ble tells me so … Little ones to him be-long … They are weak but he is strong.'

The voice seemed ethereal, soaring above and around them. The clarity, pronunciation and tone was as beautiful as any castrato performing for a Renaissance Florentine court.

Through the gap, the women could see only his small, highly polished shoes standing to attention and his clenched hands held straight down by his sides, as he'd been trained to do when sharing his gift.

'Yes, Je-sus loves me … Yes, Je-sus loves me … Yes, Je-sus loves me … The Bi-ble tells me so.'

'Didn't I tell you that boy could sing,' Gabriella said proudly through her tears. 'Ain't he a wonderment?'

At 10:28 precisely, Beatrice offered up a final prayer for the salvation of her soul and for divine guidance to be granted to her one true love, the errant George Bailey, wherever he might be.

Just then, the entire overhanging section of the tower began its telescoping plunge into oblivion. Fifteen seconds later, the huge permanent steel structure disintegrated into a colossal, billowing cloud of dust.

George was rocking back and forth and from side to side, twisting and jerking like some spluttering felon strapped into an electric chair, oblivious to all but his altered state of reality.

It was relentless: twisting paisley-patterned tunnels and canyons of psychedelic light; African dancers leaping up and down as their bangles jangled and trinkets rattled on unfeasibly long necks; impossibly coloured flowers rapidly opening and closing; headlights hurtling toward him at speed; him running on all fours through a high wheat field; endless lines of Nazis at the Nuremberg rallies; him plunging down a ski slope; metal butterflies opening and closing their wings, making some awful grinding noise; an electro-luminescent desert prairie; multiplying, mushrooming, organisms devouring themselves; the overhead yellow glare of a dentist's unforgiving lamp. The accumulated disposable images of twenty-four hours holed up with cable TV. Sensory detritus. So easily dismissed and forgotten, now returning, warped and malign, to torment him.

George grabbed at the airline-issue eye mask behind which he'd sought some kind of sanctuary. It had made things worse, somehow augmenting this kaleidoscope of psycho-chemical mayhem. The elastic snapped and stung his ear. It felt like he'd been punched hard.

He was now deep in the throes of a narcotic-induced seizure.

All around him people seemed to be running up and down the aisles of the airplane, pulsing forward and then retreating back, as if engaged in a gargantuan struggle. Some were crying into cell phones.

Figures appeared to him as heat sources, dark red at the centre, then changing colour outward in concentric bands of orange, yellow, green and blue. They wrestled back and forth in a sort of vaudevillian choreography, pushing and pulling, falling over one another. He saw all of this through a forest of hanging cables and oxygen masks that swayed back and forth like jungle creepers. Everything sounded dulled, as if he were underwater.

A face, appearing to him as a prism of colours, pushed itself close to his and yelled something that sounded a little like, 'Let's roll!' George tried hard to explain his predicament, tried to ask for help, tried to form words. Lou had spiked him good. His speech centre was shot and his cerebral cortex felt fried.

Then the entire cabin seemed to turn upside down.

He remained pinned to his seat as his anal sphincter let go, bathing him in a warm, reassuring excretion. He managed to force one cogent thought to the fore and in doing so, an idiot smile spread over his pallid, perspiring face, fixing itself into a death-mask grin.

'None of this is real,' he blurted out.

And in that very moment he was surrounded by light and air and space.

He gripped the arms of his seat and found himself enjoying the sensation of falling that now overtook him. A vortex of paper cups and plates, serviettes and plastic knives and forks flew up all around him. Through tightly closed eyes, George imagined he saw pools of liquid fire falling with him.

The sensation of tumbling, head-over-heels got faster and faster. Whole sections of seating, fully intact, fell around him. Fellow passengers, still strapped in by their seat belts, smiled and waved as they passed by. George felt strangely compelled to wave back. Then abruptly

SWISSSSZZZZZZUUUUUPPPPP!!!

It was as if all the air had imploded, been sucked back in.

He awoke with a start to the salvation of the dimly lit, air-conditioned cabin, the low ambient drone of purring engines all around him. He allowed a little yelp to escape his lips. His ear still stung from the elastic slap of the eye mask. Although bathed in sweat, he was greatly relieved to see that he had not evacuated his bowels after all.

A man walked by leading a child to the bathroom. A hushed, ordered calm prevailed, and a few passengers lay stretched out, sleeping.

George felt like he wanted to hug someone. He yelped again like a puppy dog.

A woman who looked like Judge Judy glowered at him from the row to his right. He did his best to smile at her, but it felt wholly inadequate. *What the fuck just happened?* He grabbed for the in-flight magazine and opened it close to his face, desperate for some time to compose himself.

There was a double-spread feature on the art of Roy Lichtenstein staring back at him. The artist's cartoon drawing of a jet fighter and exploding plane, all billowing reds and yellows, assailed George's senses, mirroring the inner-space ride he'd just hurtled through. 'I pressed the fire control … and ahead of me rockets blazed through the sky …' read the speech bubble. Whaam! It was just too much. He slapped the magazine closed, rolled it into a tight baton and pushed it deep into the net pocket of the seat in front.

Calm, Georgie boy, calm, he thought, clenching his buttocks and smiling at anyone who cared to look his way. He reached for the in-flight entertainment controls. He was shaking badly and couldn't compute the on-screen instructions that appeared in the tiny square monitor on the back of the seat.

Get to the restroom, he thought. *Privacy. Clean up. Calm down. Pull yourself together.*

He pushed himself up from the seat and felt his legs buckle beneath him. Looking down the aisle, he saw a queue of maybe four or five passengers standing patiently outside the locked toilet door.

Okay, okay, stay in your seat. Deep breaths. Calm. He sniggered aloud, he wasn't quite sure why. *Focus. FOCUS! Watch a goddamn movie, for Chrissakes!* He tried again to master the controls, with more success this time.

'Channel 3: *The Wizard of Oz*' read the menu. Perfect. An old friend in a time of trouble. Good old Dorothy, good old Toto. There's no place like home.

He lay back in the gun-metal grey seat. The titles rolled. Then he felt something leaden deep in his guts. Something was wrong. *The Blizzard of Odd* read the title, although everything else about the movie seemed as it should be. Except for the soundtrack: 'Strawberry Fields Forever' by the Beatles.

Uh-oh, this ain't over yet. Here we go again.

And so it began. The early black-and-white sequences, the house in Kansas, the twister, the segue to rich Technicolor. There was the yellow brick road, spiralling out from its centre, unrolling further than the eye could see, but it seemed to have a frosty, greyish skin as if it was … yes, ice. A yellow brick ice road.

A small, fragile figure far off in the distance was slowly and artistically skating in arcs and little jumps and pirouettes, all the while coming closer to the camera. The strains of an orchestrated 'Somewhere Over the Rainbow' swelled.

George ground his teeth and pushed his head back into the seat. A low groan broke from him. On the screen a reed-thin black girl in purple latex and a tutu spun in a tight circle to a stop. Ice particles and vapour thrown up by her blades caught the light and glistened like magic, surrounding her in a bright vaporous haze. The skates were ruby red, sequinned, dazzling. She gave him a broad, toothy grin in close-up. Ice particles glistened on the downy moustache on her upper lip.

'Hi, I'm Condi, and I'd like to—'

A large group of Munchkins skated toward her and formed a circle, holding hands and chanting in little squeaky voices, 'Won't you lower your head and join us in a moment's prayer?' This they all did, until interrupted by the thrashing and whirling of the Scarecrow.

George smiled. Yeah, right. This has to be one of those spoof take-offs of a classic. A pastiche. That's it. He guffawed a little too loudly. *I'll be damned if that guy isn't the spittin' image of old George W. himself.* The simian resemblance was striking.

The Scarecrow bemoaned the fact that he could think for himself and set the world to rights 'if he only had a brain'. They were presently joined by the Tin Man, who introduced himself as 'Rummy'. He mumbled almost to the point of incoherence but seemed to be suggesting that if he'd been in possession of a heart, then thousands need not have died. He raised an oil can marked 'Enron' to his tin mouth, swallowed and said in a gargle, 'Death has a tendency to encourage a depressing view of war.'

This isn't what I had in mind, thought George and pushed the button to change the channel. Nothing happened. He pushed again. The screen flickered and returned. Munchkins and friends were still playing out their drama right there on the yellow brick road ice rink.

Condi flashed another smile at the camera, clicked her heels three times, said, 'I wish I was back on Capitol Hill', and skated off stage left where an upright grand piano was waiting. She lifted a large albino python from under the lid, kissed it and said, 'There, there, Toto,' before placing it around her shoulders.

She settled herself on the piano stool and began to play 'God Bless America', while reciting her biography: 'I was born November 14, 1954 in Birmingham, Alabama …'

A shriek from her audience drew everyone's attention. The Lion had arrived.

He was a big black man with round, studious glasses. His lion costume seemed to be amalgamated with some kind of military uniform, and on his chest were pinned a number of medals. Distraught and seeking validation from the Munchkins, he flapped at his outsized whiskers and insisted that he would have run for the highest office if only he'd had 'the nerve'. He had just begun a rather maudlin song about MLK and political assassination when George decided enough was enough.

Unable to change channels or turn the bizarre spectacle off completely, he decided the best course of action was to relocate to one of the empty rows across the aisle. As he moved over, he noticed his reflection in the window. Goddamn it, he looked rough – waxen, embalmed, like some prematurely aged version of himself. A little thinner, a little greyer, a lot more harassed.

He noticed that it was dark outside and that the cabin was lit predominately by overhead reading lights. But how could that be? They were due to arrive in San Francisco in daylight – at lunchtime, in fact.

He took a deep breath, dug his fingernails into his palms and looked closely at his reflection in the window. He asked himself as soberly as he had ever done before, 'Am I now, right now, right this minute, hallucinating?'

Once he decided that the answer was most definitely in the negative, he made a silent vow to take a baseball bat to the plate glass shopfronts of all Lou Plutus's stores when he got back to New York, then he pressed the call button for a stewardess.

A brunette with her hair pinned up stopped speaking to her friend in the galley, looked down toward him, tightened her cravat and made her way down the aisle. She spoke before he had a chance.

'We were all getting a little worried about you.'

'Oh? Why's that?'

'Well, for a minute we thought, me and the girls, that you were having some kinda seizure.'

'Nah, I just don't like flying is all.'

'Is there anything I can do for you?'

'Have we been delayed or something?'

'No sir, not at all. In fact we're ahead of schedule. Should be landing in Vegas in about one hour.'

George sat bolt upright as if he'd been tazered. 'Vegas! Did you say Vegas?'

'That's right.'

'But I'm going to San Francisco!'

'Sir, now you know that's just not possible.'

George was trying not to lose it again. 'I mean, we ... I was going to Vegas, sure, but only after Frisco. I mean I was flying into Frisco. That was the plan.'

'Sir, there's just no way you would have been allowed to board the plane without the proper ticket. Do you have your ticket?'

He plunged his hand into the inside pocket of his jacket and fished it out, damp and crumpled, and thrust it at her.

The woman read it and smiled. 'Just like I said – Vegas.'

He grabbed it from her. Incredibly, it was there in black-and-white: Newark to McCarran, Las Vegas. George reached deep into the fast-dwindling reservoir of cool that he kept for dealing with authority figures and smiled.

'My mistake ...' He squinted at her name tag in the half-light. '... Ruth. Say, could you get me a vodka tonic when you get a chance?'

'Sir, do you mind if I enquire if you're taking some kind of medication, because if you are—'

'Look, I'm fine.' He looked her straight in the eye and smiled. 'Really.'

As he watched her return to the galley to make his drink, George wrestled with himself behind an untroubled façade. Could he really have made such a mistake? No, he was utterly convinced he had booked tickets to fly first to the West Coast. He looked desperately in his document wallet for the car reservation papers confirming the vehicle he was to collect at San Francisco Airport. No deal.

Is that really something that someone could get wrong? To board an aircraft thinking you were going to one destination only to learn that you were headed to another? Maybe it happened all the time. Despite his addled state, he still couldn't believe it was true. Yet here he was, sipping on his drink and looking down at the jewelled blanket beneath him of the suburbs of Las Vegas.

The captain announced ten minutes to landing.

He peered more keenly out of the window, shielding the interior glare with his hand. He could make out the vast neon signs for the MGM Grand, the Bellagio and the Mandalay, splendid and exciting and sexy in their red and green and blue electro-luminescence. Most prominent of all was the stark white bar of light that shot straight up into the night sky like a laser beam from the pinnacle of the huge glass pyramid that was the Luxor Hotel.

George looked again at the reservations brochure that had tumbled from his documents wallet and now lay open in his lap. According to it, a room, pre-paid by Beatrice, awaited him there.

No checkout date was given.

WELCOME

Part 2

The first thing George noticed as he climbed from his cab was the huge pseudo-Sphinx that towered above him, guarding the entrance to the pyramid hotel. It seemed perfect in every derivative facet.

The taxi driver nudged him and said proudly, 'She's a big'un.' He placed George's bag on the sidewalk.

'Sure is.'

'Twice as big as the one they got in Cairo, Egypt.'

George noted he didn't say the 'real' one in Egypt. After all, this was the town where artifice and reality got turned around and no one seemed to care.

'I'll have to take your word for it,' George replied dryly and, lifting his bag, walked down the main hotel thoroughfare lit by flaming oil lamps.

Above him, the massive glass triangle loomed, a baleful, matt black edifice. At night, no reflection seemed apparent and no light escaped its seamless joins. It reminded George of the dull, secret materials they used on the Stealth Bombers to keep them invisible to radar. Yet he guessed that behind each of the huge glass blocks was a luxury room where guests could see out but could not be seen, where ecstasy and decadence and sexual abandon were being savoured.

And he wanted some. But for now, mostly he wanted a shower and a drink and the ability to close a door and to be alone.

He pushed through a small group of Pro-Life protesters in the hotel concourse. They seemed to be targeting a conference being held there. The electronic welcome board trailed an explanation: 'The Luxor Hotel Welcomes Clinical Termination Professionals'. The protesters, mostly women, carried placards with graphic depictions of aborted foetuses. Two men in smart suits were trying to confiscate them. Given his history with Jaffé Losoko, it all made George feel rather queasy and uncomfortable.

Through the whispering double doors the Egyptian theme continued, where an inner passageway was bedecked with fake palms, cascading fountains and imperious pharaohs. A colossal obelisk with archaic carvings loomed above. Fake pillars, made to look sand-bitten and ancient, lay here and there. Piped music with a Middle Eastern theme, designed to convey romance, intrigue and Arabian nights, floated out over the tinkling water splashes. Beatrice would have loved this, George thought, and for a moment he felt a pang of regret that she had chosen not to be here. He reflected again on the instantaneous thrill he'd got when he saw the booking in her name. Like the old times.

Now his cheeks coloured. Could it be that she'd arranged all of this on her own and was going to surprise him by joining him later? Could she be up in the room waiting for him right now?

He thought of Jaffé, then of Beatrice's face when he'd told her the news of his infidelity, how she'd collapsed in on herself and crumpled in that moment. And he knew right away that he was kidding himself. She wasn't planning to join him. Still, she was capable of something like that. Like the surprise birthday parties she'd thrown or the court-side basketball seats she'd won in a radio phone-in show. She'd convinced the station to go the whole hog and get George a pass into the changing rooms with the Knicks. Off-the-cuff impetuosity. He'd always loved her for it. But those kinds of things seemed to belong to their long-distant courtship. Lately, they'd been too tired or too bored or too resentful of each other for such ruses. Besides, he remembered, he'd booked everything on her credit cards, so it wasn't surprising that her name should turn up on all the documentation.

Yet as he passed through the mock-ancient archway into the main lobby of the Luxor Hotel, none of it made sense. He'd never seen the booking documents before. In fact, for this leg of the trip he had reserved five nights in the Double Down Motel, a far less salubrious establishment off the Strip on the seedier side of town. And their reservation was for later in the trip, after they had driven to Vegas from San Francisco.

He closed his eyes for a moment to focus. So, Georgie boy, you arrived on a flight you don't remember booking, to check into a hotel you can't recall reserving. Time for a little nightcap, don't you think?

First he had to check in.

The cavernous front desk and lobby was the picture of efficiency. The swirled marble floor had been buffed to a high sheen, and the uplighters threw shadows onto the statues and rippling water. The four sides of the pyramid soared up to the apex in perfect symmetry. Elevators slid effortlessly up and down at unfeasible angles, seemingly defying gravity and not wholly incongruous with the pre-modern Egyptian premise. It was like being inside a giant, ancient spacecraft, he thought. The feat of architectural engineering was undeniable.

A young man in a bright red blazer sporting a fez cracked a perfect smile. George looked along the length of the front desk, bedecked in green baize and brass. A team of the man's colleagues, identically attired, looked back in unison and beamed at him rather disconcertingly.

'And how may I help you this evening, sir?' asked the young man.

'Checking in. Hatcher's the name.'

The young man flicked at a few keys on his computer and studied the screen.

'Yeeessssss. Double. How many nights are you with us, Mr Hatcher?'

'It's … I'm not Hatcher. Ms Hatcher was taken ill and couldn't travel.'

'I see,' the man said, in a tone of voice that suggested he'd seen something untoward on his screen.

George felt awkward. He'd been pulling one scam or another for so long that he as often as not felt guilty even when there was nothing to feel guilty about. Exhausted as he was, he braced himself to go for it one more time.

'Well, let me explain. You see, the paperwork doesn't—'

The phone buzzed beside the clerk. 'Excuse me for a moment please.'

The receptionist put the receiver to his ear and nodded. Then a slow smile tugged at the corners of his mouth. He hung up.

'That will be fine, Mr Bailey. The reservation is paid in full. You're in room five-ten – fifth floor, elevator on your right.' He gestured toward the elevator. 'You have full privileges to the RA Pavilion, the Giza Galleria, the Oasis Spa and the Pharaoh's Nightclub. We hope you enjoy your stay with us.'

George was turning to walk away when the young man spoke again.

'George Bailey? Why I'm sure that's the name of Jimmy Stewart's character in that movie. What's it called? … *It's a Wonderful Death*.'

'*It's a Wonderful Life*,' George corrected him.

'Quite. I guess people must tell you that all the time.'

'No.'

George looked at his watch, the one Beatrice had bought him and had inscribed with 'Love always, B'. It had either stopped or was wrong. But he didn't have the required faculties to work out the time differential with New York. The prospect of crisp white sheets and fluffy pillows propelled him on. Just go with the flow. It's like pushin' at an open door, he thought.

As he ascended in the ultra-quiet elevator, with melancholy Egyptian music tastefully piping through the speakers, only one mosquito buzz of disquiet fought against the clouds of weariness now enveloping him.

I don't remember telling them my name was Bailey.

Chapter 19

NEVADA

George awoke next morning to the sound of a telephone ringing. He opened one eye warily and saw the evidence of just how tired he had been the night before. A glass, can of tonic water and ice bucket stood on the bedside table. Beside them, several miniature bottles of vodka were neatly lined up in a row where he had placed them before falling asleep, fully clothed. Not one had a broken seal.

He was lying face down on top of the bed, his head at an angle that made it difficult to breathe. The phone continued to ring. *Christ, that's loud,* he thought, and raised his face slowly from the pocket of saliva that had collected underneath it. He picked up the receiver.

'Hello?'

The telephone answered him with a steady dialling tone. Then he noticed that the ringing was continuing, incessant, unrelenting. He lifted the phone from the table, looked underneath and shook it. Immediately he felt ridiculous. It wasn't his phone that was ringing at all. Rather, it seemed like every telephone on his floor – maybe in the entire hotel – was sounding off in perfect unison. For a moment he wondered if it was a fire drill ... but no, it was definitely the sound of many, many telephones all ringing at once.

He heard the dull thud of footsteps hurrying by outside in the corridor. He hit the zero digit on the phone for reception.

'What in the hell is going on?' he demanded.

There was a pause, then, 'Oh Mr Bailey. Do you have your television set on, sir?'

'What? No … why?'

'I suggest you switch it on, sir.'

'What!' He looked around for the remote control. 'What channel?'

'Any channel, sir.' The receptionist hung up.

George zapped the TV. It was set in a heavy, polished wooden unit in the corner of the room. Egyptian motifs and symbols were engraved on the doors. The red light blinked to green and the large screen hummed slowly to life. Out of the darkness emerged what George took to be a huge chimney funnel belching out thick black smoke from its maw. Another stood beside it, leaking smoke and flicking tongues of flame from its middle.

The phones were still ringing.

He was confused and changed the channel, but all he got was the same picture from a slightly different angle. Wary of his in-flight Yellow Brick Road episode, George rubbed his eyes hard.

The phones continued to ring.

It was only when he turned on the volume, heard the voices of commentators, that he realised what he was looking at.

'Oh. My. Gawd. Oh. My. Gawd. Those poor people!'

The voice of the anchorman brought him up to speed like a kick in the balls.

'Just to recap, ladies and gentlemen, what you are watching is the aftermath of what would appear to be an attack on the World Trade Center. The North Tower was hit by a jet airliner at eight forty-six this morning at around the 95th floor. The South Tower was hit by a jet airliner at nine oh three this morning at around the

80th floor. The emergency services are at the scene. We have no news of injuries or fatalities as yet but we'll bring that to you just as soon as we have anything.'

George hit the mute button and let the control slide from his grip. He slipped off the end of the bed and onto the floor, and sat with his back against the bed, never allowing his gaze to waver for a second from the unbelievable spectacle unfolding in front of him.

Was … could Beatrice be in there? No, no way. She was sick, right? She was off work sick. Besides, she only worked there part-time. And didn't he hear her say she'd finished her contract with fucking Barrett, Barlett and whoever? Christ, he wished he'd listened to her now, prattling on about sore feet and rude bus drivers, cholesterol levels and Wenge furniture. He wished he'd listened to what she'd said about goddamn work. Anyhow, Beatrice went south to her family after big rows, the break-ups. Hadn't she said she would do that? Goddamn it, he wished he'd listened.

George watched as the South Tower began its precipitous collapse. At first, the part of the tower above the crash zone began to tilt to the south-east, while the first explosions of dust began at the collision section. People screamed. Then the top was completely swallowed up by the huge growing dust cloud. George watched in silence, his mouth open in disbelief.

The cacophony of ringing telephones continued. Footsteps pounded up and down the corridor outside. Someone dropped a tray of cutlery and cursed. The blazing Nevadan sun outside was trying to slink in and around the edges of the drawn black-out blinds.

The North Tower collapse seemed an inevitability now. No one was leaving for beers and chips. Orange balls of fire bellowed out from the crumbling edifice and within a couple of seconds, the exploding clouds of dust erupted like some concrete and steel abscess and swallowed up the tower's top completely.

In that moment, all the telephones in the hotel stopped ringing. The silence was the loudest thing George Bailey had ever heard.

He struggled to believe what he had just witnessed. Perhaps he should go back to bed and pull the blankets over his head. When he woke up, some new order of reality would likely have established itself and he could start his odyssey over at some new point.

He moved to the blinds and paused, reluctant to let in the light of the new day to authenticate what he had just seen. He tugged twice and the desert morning light decanted into the room, filling it completely, leaving no corner unlit.

Instinctively he raised a hand to shield his eyes, but then noticed that the windows had been treated in some material designed to save the valued guest from just such an inconvenience. It had the disconcerting effect of making the world outside appear as if it had been shrink-wrapped in orange cellophane.

Below him, but at a distance, Las Vegas Airport stretched out like a huge concrete spider. Jet aircraft of different types sat on the runway at a variety of angles but there was no activity. Nothing landing, nothing taking off. No flight crews or baggage carts or catering trucks. Nothing. No one.

George thought again of the anti-abortionists protesting outside: 'The unnecessary termination of a healthy living being'. At least developments in NYC must have distracted them for a while. It was all much too close to home. Jaffé's actions, bankrolled by him with money stolen from Beatrice. He was determined not to give in to it, but he couldn't shake the undeniable certainty of culpability. The whole sorry mess reminded him of the unfortunate tale of Harvey.

Harvey was a Golden Cocker that George had insisted on buying when he and Bee had been enjoying one of their all too rare 'happy families' episodes. A surrogate child perhaps, although Beatrice would never have admitted to such an outlandish thing. Nevertheless, all were agreed that Harvey was a beautiful creature indeed. Full pedigree, registered papers with lineage – the works.

But questionable breeding practices had rendered the pup temperamentally unstable. He began to snarl at George and snap at Beatrice if she ventured too near at feeding times. It was only a matter of time before Harvey attracted a lawsuit. So when he jumped up on a child playing with a ball in the local park, nipping him in the process, the writing was on the wall.

After several futile attempts to pass Harvey on to friends and acquaintances, George, with heavy heart, brought Harvey into the veterinarian surgery for termination. As the dog stood trustingly looking into his eyes, his pink tongue lolling to one side, his long cartoon-like ears, his burnished autumnal red coat pristine in the full expression of youthful vigour and health, George had watched the needle go in. What a waste, he'd thought. He'd wondered ever since what role he'd played in making the dog so anti-social.

The young black bellhop who came to collect George's soiled suit and shirt for cleaning brought him up to speed with events.

'Unbelievable man. Un-beee-leeevable. I ain't never seen anything like this shit. Whole goddamn country is grounded. Only thing flyin' is birds, man. Birds … by order of GW!'

George was simply relieved and delighted to have someone else confirm this latest assault on his sensibilities.

'You know, I was there. I was just there, man,' he told the bellhop. 'Newark – flew in from there just last night.'

'Dawg – I mean sir – you're one lucky son-of-a-gun, I tell ya. Those A-rabs were lifting any flight with a shit-load of fuel onboard. West Coast mostly. LA, San Francisco …'

George froze. He remembered the phrase – prophetic, as it turned out – his mother used to use when she felt a shiver: 'Like someone walking over my grave'. Arabs … San Francisco. He saw the young man look at him quizzically.

'You feeling okay, sir?'

'There were Arabs on my plane.'

'Shit, there are ragheads all over this town,' the young man said, laughing and gesturing around the room. He tickled one of the Sphinx-shaped bedside lamps under the chin. 'Or had you forgot where you're staying at?'

'But I thought I was flying to—'

'It's those poor people got trapped in them towers I feel sorry for.'

'My girlfriend worked in there.'

'No shit! She okay?'

'She didn't go in yesterday.'

The young man rubbed his head and blew out his cheeks. 'Now, that is some lucky shit. The two of you have some powerful medicine happening right there, maaan.' He pointed a bony finger at George. It had a large silver skull-and-crossbones ring on it. 'Man, you'll probably never come as close again.'

'I'm gonna call her.'

'Yeah, you do that.' The bellhop had been backing toward the door and was now shifting from foot to foot. 'First time in Vegas?' he asked, rubbing thumb and forefinger together.

'Yes,' said George, belatedly realising that the man was awaiting his tip. 'Let me get my wallet.'

'Yeah, well, I'm a little sorry for you, ya know. The Strip's like a ghost town out there. Ain't never seen it this way before. Bad timing I guess.'

'I guess,' George said and pressed a dollar bill into his hand.

The man was not impressed. He opened the door to leave, saying over his shoulder, 'Talk's cheap but it ain't free.'

'Guess this shit's going to be bad for business all round,' George said and closed the door after him.

He looked again for his mobile phone but couldn't find it. Maybe he'd left it on the plane, or at the lounge bar, or maybe in the airport bathroom. He remembered again the Arab dousing himself with water. The four men on the plane, three of whom seemed to disappear on take-off. He never saw them again. Could they really have been part of some wider conspiracy? Just how close had he come?

Regular news bulletins brought him up to speed. When the full picture became apparent, the fate of Flight UA 93 – his flight – shook him to the core. It was then that George began to ruminate on the potentialities of his unique circumstance. It never took him long to judge an opportunity for what it was worth.

He supposed that Beatrice, Lou and anyone else he had spoken to over the last few days believed he was heading for Frisco. *If people think I was on that San Francisco flight, the one apparently en route to crash into the White House ... that went down into the dirt of western Pennsylvania ... then to all intents and purposes I'm a dead man.*

He crossed to the mirror and studied his reflection. Better still, if there was a fuck-up on the passenger manifest, if he really did get the wrong flight ... He was smiling now. Irrepressible.

A new start, a clean slate. Pitch up somewhere claiming amnesia, with a few carefully selected memories. Christ, the possibilities! He remembered when Lou introduced him to his pal Anton Grimovski – 'Grimmo' – from Donetsk in the Ukraine.

Grimmo drank coffee mugs of vodka in a gulp and talked primarily about two things: how Sergei Bubka, a Donetsk native and medal-winning athlete, was a second cousin of his, and how he knew a place in the Bronx where it was possible to get fake social security numbers, passports, driver's licences, even college diplomas and references. Any documentation you wanted for the right price and no questions asked. The dilapidated brownstone usually had a queue of Poles, Turks, Irish and Mexicans whose permits had expired stretching down the hall and out onto the steps.

Why the hell couldn't he do that? Maybe a rebirth as André Dupree, a paralegal from Baton Rouge, or Roger Stembridge, a college professor from Boston with a major in Criminology. Yeah, that would be sweet. The possibilities seemed endless. All debts cleared, all obligations void, all past digressions wiped away. It would mean he could never go back, of course. Never phone. But other than Beatrice there was really nothing to go back for.

He imagined sitting across the street from her apartment, dark glasses, baseball cap pulled down, watching her at the window wrestle with the tragic grief of her loss and her guilt at not reconciling with him before it was too late. Or loitering behind an old oak at Collingwood cemetery back in Canton while she placed a single red rose on his empty grave. He liked that.

He threw himself on the bed, unintentionally landing on the TV remote. The channel changed to the in-room menu. The voice-over purred on about the opulent facilities on offer in the Luxor Hotel, and showed images of slot machines and gaming tables which seemed to stretch for miles. The voice was replaced by Sinatra and a big-band rendition of 'Luck be a Lady Tonight'.

He grinned. Lucky for sure. Lucky to be alive. For now anyway, he was George Bailey. Good ole Georgie boy, in a fully paid luxury pad. In Las Vegas. With money to spend and all week to do it in.

Lou Plutus stirred slowly. He was completely naked. As he pulled himself into a foetal ball, his muscles ached and the entire left side of his body, from his scalp to the sole of his left foot, was racked with pain. His teeth, eyes and fists were clenched shut against the hurt. His nostrils were filled with the smell of sulphur and smoke.

'You're a very lucky man,' said a voice. The timbre suggested a younger man. The enunciation betrayed an Eastern European inflexion. The acoustics suggested a high-ceilinged room.

Lou was frightened to open his eyes. 'Where am I?'

'Where do you want to be?'

'Anywhere but ...' Lou half-opened one eye, the one that didn't feel tight and burnt.

He saw his own saliva sticking to the cement dust and the debris of metal shavings on the floor close to his face. Turning his head to the side, he noticed the nondescript legs of some industrial furniture. Further across the floor, beyond the irregularly shaped pieces of scrap metal and balled newspaper, he saw black basketball boots and the zipped bottoms of a pair of black combat pants. He closed his eyes tightly again and forced himself to speak.

'Who are you?'

There was a long silence. Then, 'My name is Virgil.'

The stench of smoke was slowly clearing from his nostrils. He thought he recognised the smell of salt air and diesel. Maybe turpentine. Certainly piss. Something resembling a ship's foghorn seemed to sound off in the distance.

'Why am I here?'

'Ahhh, now that *is* a good question, and one I don't feel fully qualified to answer,' said the young man. 'Suffice to say that the people who wanted you here … well, they always get what they want.'

Lou was gradually uncurling his body now and trying to push himself up on his left hand. He looked at his forearm and the back of his hand and winced in pain. They were nothing but raw flesh, the skin blistered and peeling. He let out a wail of anguish.

'No one is listening. No one cares,' said the young man dispassionately.

'But how did I get here? I mean, it was over for me.'

'They had you brought here. For a reason, I expect.'

'Who are they?'

'The Triptych. The Three.'

Lou tried to turn around to face the direction the voice was coming from. He let out a howl of pain as the skin around his midriff tightened and cracked.

'What is it you Americans say? "Ouch! That's gotta hurt!"'

Lou edged his legs and buttocks around to face the direction the voice was coming from. Through one eye he saw a stick-thin young man well over six feet tall. His head and most of his pale face was covered by the hood of his black Adidas sweatshirt. White wires crept up from the pockets where his hands were thrust and into small earphones that disappeared under the hood. He sat languidly on the edge of a dilapidated desk, his long legs stretched out in front of him.

Lou pushed himself up with difficulty onto his knees. The room was an old disused shipping office of some kind. A rusted cast-iron plaque read 'New York Port Authority'. Maritime charts and schedules still hung on the walls. Metal cabinets lay tipped on their sides, spewing files and papers onto the floor. The windowpanes were dirty and broken. Through them Lou could see a steel fire escape, a few large commercial shipping containers and the lit windows of small offices in the building opposite.

'I need help. I've been burnt,' he said.

'I can see that.'

Virgil stood up and reached across the desk, grabbing something with his bony fingers. It was a large piece of broken mirror, jagged and discoloured. He held it up to Lou. 'Now you can see too.'

The image reflected back caused Lou to gag. A whimper escaped his dry, tight lips. The whole left side of the man in the mirror was lobster red with blistering burns. It was as if a straight line ran down his exact middle, from head to toe, red on one side, white on the other, scorched versus saved. Even his penis was half and half. Under other circumstances, it might be comical.

'I expect it'll eventually die down – become less noticeable,' said Virgil indifferently as he lit a cigarette. 'There are some clothes over there. Why don't you put them on?'

He gestured to a swivel chair on wheels, over the back of which was draped a navy-blue one-piece jumpsuit. Plimsolls were on the ground.

Lou limped over and tried to ease the material over his roasted flesh. He looked back at Virgil. 'You're Russian, right?'

'Latvia, Lithuania, Moldova, Belarus, Ukraine. From the Urals to the Crimea – why do you always assume we are Russians?'

'Whadaya gonna do? You lost. Gedd-over-it!'

Virgil laughed. He split his sides. 'You know, we say that for every one, genuinely interesting and intelligent Yank you have to wade through one hundred thousand assholes.'

'Yeah, well I know Russians. I work with them.'

'You mean you steal from them.'

Lou started. 'Is that what this is about? Is it?'

'All shall be revealed,' said Virgil and he smiled, gesturing toward the open door.

'Cuz if it is, I can explain. Let me speak with Gregor … or Andre.'

'I think first we see the Anvil, no?'

He ushered Lou out of the room and into a filthy corridor.

'The Anvil?'

'One of the Triptych.'

'Are they bosses?'

Virgil laughed. 'Much further up the food chain.'

As Lou shuffled along behind Virgil, crunching over rubble and broken glass, he glanced this way and that through the muted glare of dirty fluorescent tubes. Occasionally, small dark shapes darted across their path. Virgil sucked his teeth and cursed an oath against rats. It was turning colder. Lou could see traces of his breath in the dank and musty air.

Rooms lay to either side of the corridor. Dimly lit, their windows blacked out, each one had a metal chair in the centre with leather restraining straps and a head restraint. The single bulb of an overhead light shone down on each chair. Lou swallowed hard.

On one seat sat a simple nylon rucksack with a Canadian maple leaf embossed on it. A blue bikini top lay on the floor. Two rooms down on the left, another chair exhibited an immaculately pressed tuxedo with a yellow carnation in the lapel. A bowl of rotting fruit sat on the ground. In yet another, a bloodied baseball bat lay across the armrests. In this room Lou thought he caught a glimpse of a man's wig lying at the foot of the chair. It was only when they had moved on that his terror caught up with his conscious thought. The wig was bloodied. It was … it could be … a scalp! Despite his lesions, Lou's whole body chilled, the short scorched hairs on his neck standing up. Virgil seemed more interested in his MP3 player.

As they came to the end of the corridor, Virgil took a sharp right into a better-lit, cleaner passageway. At the end stood a telescopic gate, similar to the ones on old elevator shafts, behind which was a lacquered teak door. Virgil stopped and turned around to face Lou. Much to the small man's surprise, he began to arrange and smooth Lou's jumpsuit, as a mother might prepare her son before entering the headmaster's office.

Virgil, noting Lou's surprise, mumbled, 'You have been given to me. You belong to me now. How well we both carry out our instructions will reflect very seriously' – he searched for the correct phrase, looking grave beyond his years – 'will have serious ramifications for us both. You understand this?'

Lou could see for the first time that Virgil's eyes were a pinkish-red, that the young man was in fact an albino. His eyes seemed to glow with an unnatural inner light. Lou nodded his assent.

Virgil slid back the gate and knocked. A bolt was shot on the inside and the large wooden door opened a crack. Lou could hear the muted sound of electric guitar music. Heavy footsteps on the other side walked off into the distance. Virgil pushed at the door warily and shepherded Lou ahead of him into the bright light.

The room itself smelled of stale sweat, fast food and baby oil. The music, a wall of electronic metal and power chords, thumped out from a huge, ancient, seventies-style ghetto blaster sitting on a card table to their left.

'I am the master of this universe,' sang the synthesised, nasal vocal.

Lou could see the cassette sleeve. It read *'Space Ritual Hawkwind.'*

The brightness in the room was cruel. Two large, mounted stage-lighting units stood on tripods on either side of the space, their aluminium casing multiplying and maximising the white light bursting from chubby, mega high-wattage bulbs.

Virgil had slipped on a pair of dark glasses; Lou tried to shield his eyes with a hand. The heat emanating from the light sources was aggravating the burns all down his left side. He edged away from the one closest to him.

'I give you … the two-tone man,' shouted Virgil above the music.

Lou was scouring the room through slit eyes, the unrelenting pain just about keeping his awful dread in check. The first discernible image he identified almost made him laugh with relief and recognition.

It was a large poster of Michael Jackson, from his 'Billie Jean' period, tacked to a door. The singer, poised forever on the toes of his arched, patent leather feet, was wearing a fedora, a sequinned suit and a glove. Iconic. It had adorned the bedrooms of countless teens and the walls of innumerable greasy fast-food outlets and taxi cab offices. Lou noticed that the face of the superstar had been altered. The eyes and mouth had been carelessly removed and replaced with what looked like the eyes and indecipherable smirk of the Mona Lisa.

Beside the poster hung a large and well-worn star-spangled banner. It was heavily wrinkled, pock-marked and, in places, ripped and holed.

Virgil had poured himself a cup of coffee from a percolator in the corner and was sipping it.

The music from the player suddenly ended, leaving only a loud, sub-Dolby hiss filling the room. The wheels of the cassette tape squealed a little as they reached the end of their spool, then the mechanism thumped off with a thunderous clunk. There was silence, save for the dull hum of what sounded like a small generator powering the electricity.

Lou felt like he badly needed to pee. He was about to say so, when a figure emerged from the shadow behind the incandescent glare.

The Anvil was a muscular six-footer wearing the black, fishnet sleeveless vest and leather pants uniform of the S&M set. His shaven head was covered with tattoos, as were his arms, like some Maori warrior. He wore round, wire-rimmed dark glasses and had a walrus-like handlebar moustache. He moved with slow steps across the room and lowered himself behind an old desk on which sat an open laptop.

Lou squirmed, uncomfortable and in pain, caught like a moth in the crosshairs of the coruscating beams.

'You fear the light?' said the Anvil in an accent that sounded like pure, hammed-up Bela Lugosi.

Before Lou could answer, a metallic click brought the generator to a rattling stop and the lights went out. The room was changed utterly, now lit only by the greenish glow from the laptop on the desk. Lou felt instantly relieved as the heat died down.

The Anvil leaned his face into the light from the computer. It glinted with studs and piercings. He removed his dark glasses and looked up at Lou. His eyes were heavily lined and he wore long, false eyelashes. Pure Nadset 'Droog'.

'Better?' he asked.

'Sure.'

'You are a very lucky guy, no?'

Beaten as he was, Lou was getting tired of hearing this and, despite himself, answered acerbically, gesturing at his clothes and his physical state with a theatrical flourish.

'Lucky? Yeah, sure.'

The Anvil seemed a little displeased. 'You'd rather be back there?'

Lou was growing bolder. 'Look, Anvil – whatever your name is – I'm in fucking pain here. I mean, when can I go home to a doctor. What gives?'

The Anvil said nothing and sat staring at Lou for what seemed a long time. He nodded over Lou's shoulder to Virgil. At this, Virgil lifted the bubbling Pyrex coffee pot from its stand, crossed to Lou and began to pour the boiling contents up and down his left arm.

'Arrrrghhh!' Lou grabbed his limb in pain and fell on the floor, writhing in agony. 'You mutha-fucking faggot!'

The Anvil spoke in Russian to Virgil who translated: 'Do you now understand …' He finished his question himself in English '… the dynamic of our relationship?'

'Arrrrghhh! Yes! Fucking YES!' said Lou and passed out.

When he woke up he was slouched in a candy-striped deck chair. A plastic bottle of 'Australian Gold After-Sun Lotion' sat on the Anvil's desk beside a bottle of Vicodin. Lou looked up at Virgil pleadingly.

'Yes. Take,' said Virgil indulgently.

Lou picked up the lotion. It felt cold, as if it had been in the refrigerator. He squeezed some onto his hand and forearm, gently spreading it in tiny circles. The relief was immediate, if short-lived. Then he emptied out a fistful of Vicodin and slammed them into his mouth hungrily, crunching and swallowing without water. Some minutes passed as they sat in the semi-darkness. Eventually, Lou, more contrite now, took the initiative.

'You guys know me, right? I mean I work with Gregor, Andre and Sergei out of Brighton Beach. They'll speak for me. We run the skin-flick business. Atlantic City. Las Vegas. You know me, right?'

'I know of you,' said the Anvil, rolling a cigarette.

'Whatever it is we can work it out, okay?'

The Anvil said nothing.

'It's the money, right?' said Lou, unable to leave the silence alone for fear of what it might lead to. 'The video stores … Look, I have dirtbags scamming offa me all the time so it's only natural I look to my own credits column, right?'

Silence.

'Whatever it is, I can get it for you. We can do this thing, whatever it takes. You'll be happy. Really! Let me fix it. What'll it take, for Chrissakes?'

'I am only one of three,' said the Anvil and he leaned back into the darkness, creaking in the chair.

'Get your friends. We can make a deal. Really.'

The Anvil laughed mirthlessly. 'My friends … quite.' He laughed again.

'What are you into, my man? What do you need?' Lou was becoming desperate. 'Your guys will tell you. Ol' Lou Plutus, he can get your itch scratched.'

That seemed to amuse the Anvil. After a while he said, 'You pathetic little man. You know … of what you remind me? Like a …' He spoke in Russian again to Virgil. '… like a turtle that has flopped onto its back in the baking sun and cannot turn itself over. And the ants … yes, the ants are coming.' He made a scurrying noise on the desk with his fingers and laughed again.

Lou began to sob quietly. 'Anything,' he pleaded. 'Anything.'

'I want you to see something,' said the Anvil, turning the laptop around to face Lou.

The Vicodin seemed to be kicking in now and Lou leaned forward, despite the tight stretching of burnt skin across half his belly. On the screen, looking bemused and moving in a jerky webcam fashion, appeared the head and shoulders of a moon-faced man in his late thirties or early forties. He pushed a floppy fringe out of his eyes and pulled his chair closer to his computer screen.

'It's me. I'm here now ... I'm back,' he said, in a nervous, expectant way, made more disturbing by the tinny quality of his voice through the small laptop speaker.

Lou looked at the Anvil questioningly, who smiled back at him.

'You dare ask me what I want, insect, what I need.' The Anvil spat out the last word angrily.

Lou bit his bottom lip.

'Then watch.'

Virgil slipped silently back into the shadows, putting his dark glasses back on, as if he preferred not to see.

'Are they there?' asked the Anvil.

The man in the laptop swallowed hard. 'Yes.'

'What ages?'

'Four and seven'

'Two boys?'

'A boy and a girl.'

'Better. They are asleep?'

'Yes.'

'You are alone?'

'Yes. As agreed. My wife has gone out to work her shift.'

'You have been to their room?'

'Yes ... but ...' The man bit on his knuckles. 'I was waiting for you.'

'As it should be.'

Lou didn't like the way this was shaping up. He squirmed a little in his chair. The Anvil ignored him.

'I want you to go now and bring the boy. Try not to wake him.'

The younger man got up. Lou could see that he was wearing a pair of beat-up jeans and a check-pattern work shirt. Just some nobody from the swaying wheat fields of Montana or the Black Hills of Dakota. Just somebody's dad.

'And Steven,' said the Anvil, 'remember I showed you how to lift them … where to put your hand … your fingers.'

The man turned back to the webcam and smiled a vacant affirmation.

In its bland, matter-of-fact ordinariness it was the most quintessentially evil thing Lou had ever seen in his life. The Anvil sniffed his own fingers, closed his eyes and laughed. He said something in Russian. Virgil, in a voice tired with resignation, translated.

'He says he has lost his moral centre.'

'*Niet! Niet!*' protested the Anvil.

Virgil sighed. 'I stand corrected. He has relocated his moral centre.'

'*Da! Da!*' said the Anvil, laughing, and he began to unbutton his pants.

Lou saw movement on the laptop screen. A door opened and the man returned clutching a small, sleeping dark bundle in a blue woollen romper suit.

Lou's eyes involuntarily sank to the floor.

'Come, come, Mr Plutus,' protested Virgil, goading from the darkness. 'Still some sacred cows to slay? Surely not? Not if you are to serve the Triptych.'

Lou cried softly to himself as he thought of all the dreadful things he had seen and done, all the things that had brought him here, now, to this terrible place.

All across the Las Vegas and Canyon County to the shores of Lake Meade, throughout the length and breadth of Nevada and Arizona states, along the Strip, in every temple of avarice and den of iniquity, from the silver champagne ice buckets and corporate junkets of the Bellagio, MGM Grand and Caesar's Palace to the frayed toothpicks and peptic ulcers of downtown Las Vegas – Glitter Gulch, Fremont Street and the Stratosphere Tower – punters were struggling to come to terms with the savage bite someone had just taken out of the Big Apple, half a continent away.

In keeping with the entire nation, Sin City simply did not know how to react or behave. The city's clumsy emotional response was crystallised in the sorry spectacle of the New York, New York Hotel and Casino Complex on the south end of the Strip.

The elaborate steel and plywood construction that fronted the street was fussily designed to mimic the Manhattan skyline as faithfully as possible and dramatically lit. It was easy to spot all the main landmarks – the Statue of Liberty, the Empire State Building, the World Trade Center. It was now eerily deserted, framed in twinkling neon and spotlights while empty roller coaster cars climbed and dived in and out of the counterfeit structures. Those gamblers and holidaymakers who might otherwise have been screaming and laughing in mock alarm as they hurtled to and fro, now congregated quietly in small groups, some crying, most taking pictures of a pretend city tableau that no longer existed in real life.

Around dusk, George, suited and booted, descended to the lobby of the hotel. He was still agonising about that phone call to Beatrice, unsure whether to reveal that he was still alive or let things stand as they were – release her from a love and a life that even he had to admit fell far below any reasonable expectation of what she truly deserved. He still couldn't shake the uneasy notion that she had been caught up in the catastrophe. Perhaps one phone call, just to hear her voice, then hang up immediately.

But could he really do that? Could he listen to that distraught Dixie drawl struggling with bereavement for him and say nothing to release her from it, this woman who had never denied him anything? It seemed a too, too spiteful act.

The lobby of the Luxor was still sparsely populated. It was as if people felt self-conscious about having a good time in the wake of what they'd just seen on TV. Images of the World Trade Center, smoking, then collapsing, seemed to be on every screen in every bar and restaurant. Security guards were peering at their small black-and-white sets intoning disbelief into their lapel mics. Small groups of onlookers, mostly weekenders or tourists from overseas now stranded in this Tinseltown, stood in small groups agog, trance-like, watching it over and over again.

The out-of-work actors up from LA, who made a buck by dressing up in the theme costumes of each hotel, looked awkward and incongruous. Here and there, clusters of semi-clad Cleopatras and pharaohs in sequins, feathers and fake gold shivered in the chilly air-conditioned evening. Temple guards with plastic swords and spears and handmaidens brandishing baskets of fake fabric flower petals, looked at each other self-consciously. They were employed to work the crowds, to steer them into the casinos and drinking dens. But the tables remained largely empty while croupiers pulled straight their waistcoats, rubbed their chins and did card tricks for each other to pass the time.

A pit boss touched his earpiece and laughed. The boys in the control room were wisecracking; no scams or cons to concern them this evening. The blaring sirens and clanging bells of the ranked masses of slot machines seemed like gangs of drunken college kids loudly crashing a funeral. Just fucking great, thought George. Undeterred, he set out to look in on the hotel's attractions.

The RA Pavilion and Giza Galleria were impressive in their soulless, opulent emptiness. The Oasis Spa glowed in a warm luxuriant orange light, its hot tubs and plunge pools steaming and bubbling away irrepressibly. At the Pharaoh's Nightclub, George paused to pick up a flyer. Performing this week, it said, were 'The Redskins, on their third successful Vegas residency'. Turning the flyer over, he started.

Peering back at him in a rather unnerving way was a close-up of three red-faced, bald men. The blurb explained that this was a theatrical trio of mute performers in red latex bald caps and black clothing. 'See their hilarious take on information overload and popular culture pollution,' read the ad. *Yeah, right. Hilarious! Good luck getting some laughs in this town tonight, guys.*

George crumpled the flyer and dropped it in the bin. Turning as he did so, he noticed a door ajar. Looking directly at him through the gap was one of the Redskin trio he had just been reading about.

'Hey, Redskins!' George called out, punching the air with mock gusto, slightly embarrassed at having been caught dumping their promo material.

The man widened his eyes so that the whites appeared huge against his red face. His lips parted and his mouth broke open, revealing a slash of uneven white teeth. George immediately felt uneasy. Then the man smiled, raised a finger and drew it slowly across his throat. George couldn't suppress a shudder. A moment later the red man took a step backward into the shadow and the door swung closed. *All part of the act I guess,* George told himself and moved off faster than he had arrived.

The prestige casinos on the Strip were largely linked by air-conditioned tunnels and walkways, ensuring that guests never needed to venture out into any environment that wasn't carefully controlled. Thus George found himself meandering through the medieval court of King Arthur and his knights via the Excalibur Hotel and Casino. *Oh to be in merry England*, he thought … in Las Vegas, in the scorching Nevada desert. 'Everything you want, we got it right here in the USA,' sang Chuck Berry through the concealed ceiling speakers and behind the plastic trees.

The surreal vision of medieval ladies-in-waiting, with their conical hats, golden tresses and trailing trains, chewing gum and pulling hard on Marlboro Lights stretched all credulity.

Further on into the Vegas night, the motorised gondolas of the Venetian Hotel and Casino stood tied to moorings, still and quiet. The Paris Hotel and Casino had closed its scale replica of the Eiffel Tower for fear of attack by aircraft. The 'Fabulous Illuminated Dancing Fountains' of the Bellagio Hotel and Casino lay maudlin and motionless, save for a pathetic half-spurt here and there.

Only in America.

Numbers in the bars and casinos were still sparse, so George thought he would venture out onto the Strip itself, breathe in some of that good-to-be-alive desert evening air.

An enormous moon hung low in the early twilight sky, which was streaked with fingers of pinky-red clouds. Light-sensitive lamps and spotlights on timers were kicking in. Hundreds of car tail lights twinkled and flashed. Millions of light bulbs were now generating a night-time heat to rival that of the baking day.

The massive Sony Jumbotron screens that, as a rule, carried video footage of casino entertainments stretching off into the distance – Roy and Siegfried, David Copperfield, Billy Joel. But tonight, every massive monitor along the Strip featured the same image: the star-spangled banner, Old Glory herself, flapping and waving at half-mast; a hundred or more giant electronic flags, forlornly fluttering in the breathless evening air. Las Vegas was paying its respects in its own inimitable fashion.

George thought about grabbing a burger and fries, although he noted to his surprise that he had no appetite whatsoever. Besides, a cursory burrow through his pockets produced only loose change. He tapped the seat of his pants where his wallet should be, a habit he'd developed from mimicking his old man, and slipped out the leather. Four crisp, unused pristine fifty dollar bills. Can't be right, he thought. I had one fifty that I broke at the airport bar. The rest should be in tens and twenties. Figuring that it would be best to run up a tab at the Luxor (and worry about paying for it later), he decided to stroll back to the hotel.

The night air felt good. As he drew level with the New York, New York Casino, he stopped dead in his tracks. Unbelievably the Twin Towers – the World Trade Center – had disappeared from the make-believe Manhattan skyline.

'How's that possible?' he said aloud, his mouth open in amazement. 'I was here like fifteen minutes ago. I saw it!'

George looked around for some sign of construction work with no real expectation of finding any. It simply wasn't possible that the replica model could have been changed so rapidly. The only person around was an old-timer bum. He had with him a shaggy-looking dog. On the dog's back sat a small cat, and on the cat's back sat a white mouse. On a cardboard sign the man had written, 'No point lyin'. Need money for beer!'

George considered approaching him to ask about the missing building, but he couldn't help but be impressed by the old man's street show and his chutzpah.

'Two dollars a photograph,' the bum said and smiled, scratching the matted hair underneath his sweat-stained 'I ♥ LV' baseball cap.

'Don't suppose you'll tell me how you get yer critters to do that?'

'I could tell ya … but then I'd have to kill ya!'

'They're drugged, right?'

'Maybe you're drugged!' said the bum, smiling.

'You don't … glue 'em on or nuthin' like that?' George screwed up his face.

'Mister, I care more about 'em than I do 'bout you, so you'd best be on your way now, lessen yer makin' a donation here?' He nudged a tin pot with his foot.

George looked again at the New York skyline and then at the old man. 'I don't suppose you …'

The bum began to jiggle with laughter. He could barely contain himself. He placed a dirty, fingerless-gloved hand over his mouth in the manner of a coy Japanese schoolgirl.

'Nah, forget it,' said George, flapping his hand dismissively.

As he walked off he could hear the man sing, 'Start spreading the news, I'm leaving today, I want to be a part of it, New York, New York.' The dog began to howl along.

George wondered again about lasting damage to his grey matter following Lou's spike, and why the fat fuck had juiced him in the first place. Had he audited the stores and noted the missing stock and cash? Or was it that tape? George made a mental note to purchase that camcorder tomorrow and see just what might be on it.

In the meantime, it was cocktail hour.

The Luxor bar and restaurant areas were buzzing a little more than they had been earlier. He'd sink a quick one or three and maybe go down to the gaming floor for a look. Passing two large black men in Egyptian costume, he left the marble-floored area and moved into a deep-pile burgundy carpeted corridor that led to elevators and bedrooms. Beyond this he could see a tiered lounge quarter that seemed to ease up on the whole full-on Ancient Egyptian vibe.

Deano's looked good to him. Piano music piped. George decided instantly that this would be his adopted watering hole for the duration of his stay. Only a few barflies buzzed around while a grumpy-looking barkeep worked a towel on wet glasses. Perfect. He could already taste the first of the day.

Suddenly, from around a blind turn in the corridor off to the right, a throng of children emerged, pushing him back against the wall. George did a double take. Not children. They were small, wizened adults. They stopped in the centre of the passageway, held hands and formed into three circles.

A tiny woman with a creased, pinched face and wearing a headscarf noticed the ill-at-ease George trying imperceptibly to skirt the ensemble. He had been preoccupied with the barman, who he could still see from where he stood; would he fix his drink with a lemon or lime twist? Now he found himself wondering what the difference was between dwarfs and midgets. The small woman put herself between George and escape.

'Won't you lower your head and join us in a moment's prayer?' she said.

George got goosebumps. He'd heard the voice – the question – some place before. But where?

About to make his apologies, George suddenly and for no apparent reason became overwhelmed by an undeniable sense of Beatrice – her smell, her feel, her irrefutable presence. It was a feeling so strong that he looked around to see whether she had actually walked into the corridor and joined them. He instantly ached with anxiety for her. He missed her like she was a physical part of him – the way he used to miss her, only much, much worse.

Beatrice would want him to pray with them, so he closed his eyes. But nothing would come. He opened them again and looked down at the group of little people. They broke hands, opened their circle and surrounded him, placing him at the middle of their new circle.

The tiny woman with the pinched face beamed up at George. Her whole visage seemed entirely transfigured, as if smiling had released something trapped inside her – something loving and giving. Her eyes teared up; she took both his hands in hers.

'The quality of mercy is not strained. It droppeth as the gentle rain from heaven upon the place beneath,' she said.

Chapter 22

NEVADA

The cotton jumpsuit they had given Lou itched like hell. Dark damp stains covered it from the lotion, which plastered the material to his skin. They had offered him a docker's three-quarter length coat that he had draped around his shoulders. It felt heavy and awkward but it countered the early morning chill coming in off the river. His burns stung at every pothole the yellow cab bounced across, like a tin box on rubber balls.

He felt perfectly wretched. As they sped across the Brooklyn Bridge, Manhattan-bound to see this Baba Yaga chick, his discomfort and debasement carried him beyond any trepidation at the encounter. His curiosity at precisely what their beef with him was and how they proposed to extract recompense was being swallowed whole by his total fatigue and gnawing discomfort. It gave him some balls back.

'Hey, Virg, when am I gonna get some shut-eye?'

Virgil was all silence and disdain.

'Young guy like you, you don't wanna be hangin' with lowlifes like that Anvil fella,' Lou continued. 'That's one sick sonofabitch. Ya know what I'm sayin?'

'Youth is wasted on the young, and life on the living.'

'What? There you go with that gobbledygook, pseudo-intellectual baloney again. How come I can't get a straight answer to anything around here?'

Virgil stared into the middle distance and was silent.

'What about you, buddy?' said Lou, addressing the back of the cab driver's head. 'Who do you like for the Super Bowl?'

The cab driver made no acknowledgement of him whatsoever.

'Yeah, okay then. Step on it, bozo!' said Lou, frustration masquerading as bravado. 'What time ya got, Virg? I make it about eight thirty in the a.m.'

'Believe me, there's no hurry,' said Virgil sardonically.

'Maybe not for you, but I need time. I want to give you people what you want – square things away, get back to normal.'

'People try to pass time. People fill it up. People leave it behind. But you, my friend, you have more time than you can possibly imagine.'

Lou rubbed a circle on the window where it had become fogged up. The traffic should have been brutal by now as midtown office workers made their way into the city. Lou blinked and rubbed again. Empty streets, empty roads. No cars, no people.

'Kinda quiet out there,' he said, a little unease creeping into his voice.

Virgil said nothing.

'Ain't no public holiday that I know of,' Lou went on. 'Place closed down cuza what went on at the towers yesterday?'

Virgil said nothing.

Lou was reaching now. The fear was back. He knew that a city like New York does not – cannot – simply misplace all its people and transport. It was as if a neutron bomb had hit the place. Theatres and billboards sailed by, manholes steamed, traffic lights blinked and changed. Nothing human moved.

On the giant telescreen, footage of the World Trade Center disaster played out over and over again, the towers first crumbling into dust, then flying back up again, emerging from a cloud of dirt, pristine, straight and erect. It looked like a bad joke, a 1920s silent movie.

Lou craned his neck to watch the image as the cab pulled level. He was dumbstruck when the footage of his last home video, the one he had recorded with Sonny the day before, flashed up on the massive monitor: Sonny, on all fours, taking it up the ass from him. *In Times Square for Chrissakes!* He felt woozy all over and fell back into the seat.

'Still in such a hurry?' said Virgil, smiling as he readjusted his earphones.

They travelled on in silence, cross-town, East to Upper West Side.

How can any of this be possible? Lou thought, but the words wouldn't come out in any direct question. Little point asking. It defied explanation. Roll with it. Ride it out.

They drew up at 72nd Street and Central Park West – The Dakota Building – and got out. The doors slammed, echoing down the empty thoroughfares. No distant traffic hubbub. Not even the birds were singing. The cab left them behind and rattled off into the distance, all squeaks and groans.

Virgil pulled the cords of his hood down, tightening it further around his face. Lou considered making a run for it. But to where? Manhattan was a ghost town. Besides, Virgil would catch him easily and God knows what hell there would be to pay. He'd have to bite the bullet and hang around.

High over the 72nd Street entrance, the stern figure of a wooden Dakota Indian looked down on them from above. The building's high gables and deep roofs with their profusion of dormers, terracotta panels, balconies and balustrades resembled a shadowy German schloss. It induced no little dread in Lou, but as a native New Yorker and possessing an indomitable wise-assed backsass he couldn't resist whistling the theme from *The Addams Family* and clicking his fingers.

They passed by the concierge's glass booth. A small TV was on with the sound down – some kind of game show. The morning paper was spread out on the desk beside a steaming coffee cup and a half-eaten muffin. But there was no sign of human occupancy.

They climbed into the elevator and Virgil pushed the button marked 'Penthouse'.

'I guess you'd better fill me in on this Baba dame,' Lou said.

'What would you like to know?'

'Man, you can't begin to imagine.' Lou pulled his sleeves away from his sticky flesh. 'Is she mobbed up?'

Virgil laughed. 'Maybe we start with her ... reputation. In Russian folklore there are many stories of Baba Yaga. "Yaga Kostianaya Noga", the fearsome witch with iron teeth. She is also known as "Bony Legs" because, in spite of a ferocious appetite, she is as thin as a skeleton.'

'Nursery rhymes to frighten children?'

'In some stories she has two older brothers. Perhaps you have met one of them already?'

'The Anvil?'

Virgil smiled. 'She appears to have no power over the pure of heart and those of us gifted with the power of love, virtue or a mother's blessing. Do you have a mother's blessing, Mr Plutus?'

Lou rounded on him. 'My mother was a drunk and a whore who burned me with a lighter when I pissed the bed.'

The elevator wheezed to a stop.

Virgil placed his hand on the sliding gate and paused. A steely tone entered his voice. 'This is not a woman to be trifled with. You understand?'

'Yeah, whatever it takes,' Lou said dismissively.

Virgil swung around in an instant and with one hand grabbed Lou by his windpipe. He raised him effortlessly off the ground. Lou spluttered and struggled to breathe.

'We hang in the balance between hell and hallowed ground, you and I, Louis. Do you understand?'

'Yezzz. Yezzz,' rasped Lou.

The young man let him drop and slid back the gate.

The elevator accessed directly onto a large open-plan apartment with pinewood walls and floors. Some green baize panelling acted as a relief. All the windows were blacked out with electrical tape. An orange glow from several large table lamps set around the floor illuminated the main living area. The corners and recesses were cast in dark shadows. Japanese music – a shamisen string sound box and tsuzumi drums – lilted discreetly, plaintively.

Virgil took his shoes off and motioned for Lou to do the same.

Green metal filing cabinets lined the walls of the room, ceiling to floor. Hundreds of exquisitely ornate lacquered boxes were stacked in front of them. Some were opened. Neat ordered piles of photographs spilled out of them and covered the floor.

In the centre of it all stood Baba Yaga, a tiny figure, small enough to be a child. Facing away from the men as they exited the elevator, she swayed almost imperceptibly to the music, the red and gold layered silk of her highly wrought oriental gowns rustling, whispering, sighing. She seemed to be holding something in her arms.

'He is here, Old Mother. I have delivered him to you,' said Virgil, looking somewhat in awe of the tiny woman.

She raised a heavily powdered, pure white hand, demanding silence. She had unfeasibly long fingers, and nails meticulously painted crimson red, with solid silver, intricately tooled, pointed nail extensions on each little finger. She stayed that way until the music stopped, and for some time afterward.

Then: 'And how has my little snowflake been treating you, Mr Plutus?' The voice was Eastern European; well-educated, matriarchal, imperious.

Before Lou could answer, she turned around slowly, theatrically.

He jolted. Baba Yaga was wearing the full make-up of the kumadori kabuki performer. Her face was a radiant, dazzling white, illuminated by the rice powder base of the oshiroi. The bold lines of colour highlighting her eyes, cheekbones and jawline magnified every expression extravagantly. Her magnificent brocade robe flooded the ground around her. An enormous jet-black wig was skirted by a jade-encrusted headband. And in her arms she carried a small, black porcelain Russian doll that she rocked and caressed.

'Green tea, Mr Plutus?' she asked.

'Certainly. Why not.'

'Virgil, dahlink, would you?'

She gestured toward a ceramic pot suspended above a burner. Beside it sat an old stone-and-wood opium pipe. She folded in on herself, dropping down to sit cross-legged on the floor, the doll cradled in her lap.

'Make yourself at home, Lou. May I call you Lou?'

'That's my name,' he said, arranging himself carefully on the floor opposite her.

'We have so much to talk about, you and I.' She stroked the doll's head and bent low to kiss it on the cheek.

Virgil returned with the tea and poured. As he filled Lou's cup, he leaned in and whispered in his ear, 'Don't mention the doll.'

'That's a pretty doll,' said Lou perversely.

Virgil rolled his eyes.

'Doll ... DOLL! Do you speak of little Mikhailavich?' She grasped the black doll to her bosom.

'I only meant—'

'Look around you. I have one million Polaroids of Mikhail. Look! See?'

Frantic, she leapt up and went around the room yanking out the drawers of the steel filing cabinets until they clanged to a stop on their runners. She threw hundreds of snaps into the air.

'Look! See?'

She handed a pile to Lou.

They all showed a young black child of around five or six years of age. Each photograph was virtually identical – perhaps slight differences in the placement of the child's arm or head. She gathered a wad of them together and put her face close to Lou's. Her breath smelled of mould and rotting compost.

'Look! See Mikhail laugh! See Mikhail play!' She flicked the photographs rapidly between thumb and finger as if they were a flipbook animation, causing the boy's image to indeed appear to be in motion.

'Old Mother, we deliver a higher purpose. We serve a greater master.' Virgil's appeal was subservient but to the point.

Baba Yaga recovered herself, smiling. 'Do you like what I've done with the place, Lou?' She gestured around the room with her elongated fingers.

'Not my taste, but it sure makes an impression.'

'Ah yes, your taste. That would run to the putrid Tribeca hovel where you root and fornicate in your own filth!'

Lou did not fail to note the change in her tone – mocking, angry. His mouth went dry.

'You know my place?'

'Dahlink, that's why you're here. The scene of the crime and all that.'

'What? I don't follow.'

'First things first, my dear. You've been less than reasonable with certain assets that my colleagues and I maintain an interest in.' She took a sip of tea.

'I don't know what—'

'Oh dear, I hope you're not going to make this difficult, Lou.' She frowned dramatically. 'After all the trouble we've gone to for you.'

'Maybe if you—'

'Webcore, Lou … WEBCORE!' She screamed the word.

Lou's heart jumped in his chest.

'Now see what you've done,' she said, calm once again. 'You've woken baby.' She stroked the head of the doll and reached into the folds of her gown, her hand emerging with a pacifier which she placed first in her own mouth, then in the doll's.

'I'm gonna make good on anything I skimmed. I swear. From the takings and the stock. I swear it.'

Baba Yaga sighed. 'Lou, Lou … if only it were that easy.' She pulled an open box of photographs toward her and began to lay them out like tarot cards. 'We don't care about that, really we don't. But you know, by placing yourself here with us you have put in jeopardy a very lucrative commercial enterprise.'

'The skin flicks?'

'And the girls, Lou, and the girls. So many little Natalies and Natashas backed up in hotel rooms from Minsk to Miami awaiting their debut on the silver screen. So many whorehouses from Vilnius to Vegas who are now short of new blood.'

'You can't land that on me!'

'Oh really? Not your fault? I see. Then tell me, Lou, who left a wall safe unattended, a wall safe full of just about every Webcore employee and account, every pornographic movie and every brothel address, for the police to read AT THEIR FUCKING LEISURE?'

She dug her nails into the palms of her hands in fury until they bled. Lou's stomach flipped and clenched.

'They won't go to my place,' Lou said unconvincingly.

'They're there right now,' cut in Virgil, closing the flip-top on his mobile phone and pocketing it.

'Why would they go there?' Lou asked, feeling sick.

'Really, Lou, don't you know? Come on now,' said Virgil.

Baba Yaga was giggling, a high-pitched girly snigger. She repeated Virgil's question like a mantra, 'Don't you know? Don't you know? Don't you know?'

'No!'

'Because you're a dead man, dahlink,' she said.

The room was spinning. The music started up again. Something Russian this time – 'Kalinka' maybe. When he could focus once more he saw Baba Yaga dancing around the room, holding the doll up in the air, singing to it. Virgil clapped in time and stomped his foot.

'Please,' said Lou. 'Anything. I'll do anything to go back … to go somewhere … anywhere else.'

Baba Yaga threw back her head and yakked like a crow.

Lou wiped snot and tears from his face.

'But we haven't even got to the best part yet, dahlink.'

She crossed the room and, opening a filing cabinet drawer, removed a bottle of vodka, some glasses and a photograph. She handed the Polaroid to Lou.

'You know this man?'

Lou looked at the snap. 'That's George Bailey. What the fuck has he—'

'He is your friend, no?'

'No, he's just a nobody … a loser I cut a break. He's a funny guy, is all.'

'Oh, a funny guy?' She poured herself and Virgil a glass of vodka, holding the doll all the while. 'This funny guy, he stole something from you, no?'

'No … yes. I dunno, maybe.' Lou began to see where her questions were leading. He struggled not to piss his pants for the second time that day.

'Maybe you have by now worked out what it was he took from the safe?'

Lou whimpered. 'The snuff movie?'

'Correct! The snuff movie. *Na zdorovie!*' The pair clinked glasses, then knocked back the contents. 'You watched it of course,' she said, refilling them.

His eyes sank to the floor. 'I watched it. It scared me.' Lou was shaking.

'The man in the movie – the man with the knife – he is a very dear friend of ours. A very, very influential man. We have high hopes for him in the future. I know you recognised him, Lou. I know you know him. Many, many people know him. You can see the problem.'

'I swear to God, I didn't realise Bailey took that tape. He swiped it blind. He can't know what he's got hold of.'

'We cannot take that chance. Which is why you are here right now and not just teeth and fillings among the rubble of the Twin Towers.'

'What do you know of Russian toasts?' asked Virgil.

Lou was confused. 'Is that the game where a group of guys jerk off, cum onto a slice of bread, and the last guy to cum has to eat the bread?'

Virgil slapped him hard across the face. 'Cretin! Toasting is a highly divisive issue.'

Baba Yaga looked on approvingly as the young man explained.

'Two schools prevail: minimalist – proper Russian – and Caucasian, which includes the Georgians, Armenians, Chechens, whatever. Russian toasting prose may lean toward Nabokov in its brevity or Chekhov in its melancholic uncertainty. It also helps to be a student of Stanislavsky to deliver it properly. In the Caucasus, to deliver a Russian-style toast is an insult and has led to bodily harm and even a vendetta lasting half a dozen generations.'

'I'm sorry,' sobbed Lou pathetically.

'Bailey is in Las Vegas, staying at the Luxor Hotel,' said Baba Yaga. 'You will travel with Virgil, meet with our people there and recover the tape for us. It will not be easy. He may have strong allies interceding for him.' She handed Lou a glass of vodka. 'Before this you will meet with the Monk, the last of the three, who will give you some proper clothes – and your final instructions.'

She looked at Virgil and smiled wickedly. He looked away.

'Yes. Anything, anything,' snivelled Lou, taking the glass with a shaking hand. 'I'll gut the fucker.'

'Good! Good! But for now you will propose a proper Russian toast. You will drink to your hosts' generosity and to the Anvil's wisdom, my great beauty, my snowflake's virtue, Mikhail's good health and the financial prosperity of Webcore.' She licked her lips and smeared her sharp white teeth with red. 'But most importantly of all, you will describe for us what you will do to George Bailey – body and soul – when you take your revenge.'

Chapter 23

The encounter with the little people threw George Bailey badly. First there was that undeniable feeling of déjà vu that he couldn't shake but couldn't pin down either. And then there was that sense of Beatrice.

He floundered in the guilt of it. What a bastard he'd been. What a scumbag. Why not phone her right now, put her out of her misery. She'd be sure to forgive him everything, especially if he rose again, Lazarus-like, from the dead.

Two blond and tanned air stewardesses wearing black armbands gave George the once over as they passed by. Both flashed dazzling smiles. *Guess those babes got stuck here as well,* he thought, instantly compartmentalising Beatrice and vindicating it: *Couldn't fly back to her even if I wanted to,* he rationalised. *Couldn't drive either, if those queues at the car rental desk were anything to go by. Maybe best for all concerned that ol' George stays dead a little while longer.*

He slid onto the leather bar stool. Action on the floor looked slow and Deano's was close to empty.

'What'll it be?' asked the bartender.

'Vodka tonic, double, rocks.'

George noted the touchscreen poker slot machines inlaid into the flat surface of the bar.

'Guess there's no escape,' he said aloud.

'Hey, it's Vegas!' The barkeep, smiling, flopped down a place mat and set George's drink on it.

George threw a fifty on the bar. 'Have one yourself,' he said.

'Thanks, I've been off it for five years now, but here's to y'all.' He raised a glass of ginger ale.

Three screens around the bar were still running the Twin Towers apocalypse, as were some more in the adjoining casino room.

'Hard to believe, huh?' said George, taking a decent pull of his drink.

'Yeah, I was just saying to Margie down there.' He gestured further down the bar.

George heard a racking cough and stretched to look around the pillar that obscured his view. There sat a late middle-aged woman with a hatchet nose, too much make-up and straight platinum-blond hair, which could only have been a wig. She languidly raised her glass to both men.

'Gotham City's gonna bounce right back, ain't that right, Margie?'

The woman raised her drink again and dragged on a plastic nicotine substitute tube. 'Goddamn Nevada smoking prohibition. Yet, as only New Yorkers know, if you can get through the twilight, you'll live through the night.'

George moved his bar stool around so as to see the woman better. 'That's pretty poetic,' he said.

The woman slid a box of matches down the bar toward him – Big Apple Strikes. They had a drawing of the Statue of Liberty on the sleeve.

'It was Dorothy Parker who said it. Says so on the back.'

'Margie's a New Yorker herself. Ain't that right, Margie?' The barman's craggy face cracked into a grin. He seemed glad of the company.

Margie coughed again, shoulders shaking, and wiped her mouth with a napkin. 'Christ, Jeff, I've been here an hour and already you're my biographer.'

'Margie thinks we had it comin' to us. Ain't that right, Margie?'

'I never said that.'

'Says we've been goin' around the world crappin' in other people's backyards long enough.'

'Now me, I gotta sister had a boy killed on the USS *Cole*.' Jeff seemed to be working up to a sermon. He appeared agitated. 'It was the target of a terrorist attack carried out by Al-Qaeda in the Yemeni port of Aden. Twenty-two years old. Proud as hell to be out there. I say we find out who's behind this malarkey and nuke their asses back to buggery.'

Margie smiled. 'Yeah, just don't nuke the oil wells, though. That would defeat the whole purpose of the thing, right?'

'Say what?'

George began to squirm uneasily on his seat. The drink hadn't met his expectations, and now it looked like he might be the unwilling adjudicator in a foreign policy debate.

The woman pulled a strand of hair away from her face and tucked it behind her ear. Her skin was tanned but dry and heavily lined. Her eyes flashed kindness and intelligence.

'Shussh,' she said, raising a finger to her lips. 'Shussssssssh. Can you hear it?'

'Awww ... nope,' said Jeff, looking at George conspiratorially, safe, he presumed, in their shared gender superiority when women were talking politics.

'What am I listening for?' asked George, willing to play along for the moment.

'Why, the sound of all those air conditioning units, those ice-making machines, those central heating boilers up north in winter.

Millions upon millions upon millions of them, all just cranking away out there. Now I'm here to tell you, we can't just go into any country in the world that takes our fancy and seize their natural resources just because we're the biggest kid in the playground with the most toys.'

'We're bringin' freedom to those countries. We're bringin' democracy!' Jeff was getting angry.

'Anyone ask those people if they wanted the goddamn *Simpsons* in the first place? Look, bottom line – Americans don't want their lifestyle choices messed with. This time it's oil. Next time, water. Same deal. We're not going to want to know how that pack of cowboy sleazeballs got it for us, just that they did.'

Jeff looked apoplectic. 'I'm from Houston, mam, and I'll thank you—'

'Yeah? Well, get me my motherfucking check, Tex ... before I call the manager!'

Jeff's face went plum. He wrapped the towel he'd been using around his knuckles and slammed his fist onto the bar. 'Yeah? Why don't you go back to "Jew York"!' he said between clenched teeth.

Margie wasn't fazed. She threw back her drink and slowly returned her sunglasses, book and smokes to her handbag.

Jeff stormed off, muttering to himself, 'Goddamn country's going to hell in a handcart. We need somebody to make this country great again.' By the time he'd got to the opposite end of the bar where a young couple had sat down his demeanour had miraculously changed.

'How y'all doin' this evening?' he said, beaming like the true service industry professional he was.

'Sorry about that,' Margie said to George, rising to go. 'He's been wanting to have a pop at me all evening. Some people ... they see this' – she nodded at the news footage on TV – 'they just think

Alamo or Iwo Jima or something. People get crazy. Well, this ain't no foolin' around, hon. Know what I mean? Ain't nothin' ever gonna be the same again.'

'I just came in from New York myself.' George flashed his best ladies' man smile.

'Yeah, I thought you had the look of a civilised man about you.' She was moving off and speaking over her shoulder, making it clear that social intercourse was all she was open to and that even that was coming to a close.

'George Bailey.' He put his hand out.

'Margie Kaufman.' She came back a few steps to shake his outstretched hand.

'Can I buy you a—'

'No thanks, George. It's been a long day, but nice of you to ask.'

George's face dropped a little.

She noticed and laughed. 'You should be ashamed, George – an old bird like me. I'm almost flattered.'

He felt himself flush.

'You a married man, George? Kids?'

'Nah, I had my chances.'

'You will again.'

'Nah, I blew it. Lightning doesn't strike twice in the same place.'

'Not true! Lightning struck the Empire State Building fifteen times in fifteen minutes.'

George laughed. 'Who would know a thing like that?'

Margie smiled and pointed to the box of matches on the bar. 'Big Apple Strikes. Check it out.'

She sashayed off into the distance.

George finished his drink and picked up his dollar bills from the bar. He was feeling beat and keen to avoid Texas Jeff, who would be looking for exoneration of his outburst. It had been one hell of a day. But one look at the casino floor in action before bed was a must.

It had filled up a little and seemed more like the real thing by this time. Punters were getting their second wind: 'Terrible thing back East, but hell – I'm on vacation!' The PR spiel promised 'an opulent casino gaming area that's as wide as the Nile, with everything your treasure-seeking heart desires', and it certainly was an impressive operation. They had it all – slots, video poker, blackjack, craps, roulette, baccarat, pai gow. A sumptuous poker room and a race and sports book with seventeen giant-screen TVs and one hundred and twenty-eight individual monitors 'for your viewing pleasure'.

He hovered by the craps table for a while and watched them shoot dice. One young guy in a baseball cap and blue jeans seemed to be on fire. A small crowd had gathered around.

'Let's roll!' he kept shouting at the top of his voice. 'Let's roll!'

George found something about this disconcertingly familiar, but for the life of him he couldn't grasp what. It was that feeling of déjà vu once more, of being close to some revelation that stays stubbornly, tantalisingly out of reach.

A giant display stood as the centrepiece of the gaming floor. It was a massive illuminated horseshoe intertwined with a mammoth dollar sign. Flanking it were the corporate sponsor logos of Mobil Oil and Enron. Under the arch sat a sleek red sports car. The leggy models handing out leaflets assured all interested parties that the lucky winner on the premier slots would be guaranteed the car, plus an unlimited lifetime supply of fuel to run it, because 'it's your God-given right as an American to burn gasoline'. Maybe Margie Kaufman had a point, George thought.

He was, in the end, drawn to the poker rooms. Old ladies, fat housewives, Asians and Kentucky drifters seemed to predominate at the low-stakes tables. But it was the high-rollers behind the area cordoned off with velvet ropes that caught his attention. There was a minimum five hundred dollar entry fee, with a lower limit placed on one hundred dollar chips for the pros, rich dudes who got their money quick and easy. Gang members and rap stars. This was the Movie Vegas, the Big Fight Vegas, and George loved it.

Outside looking in; it was as far as he was going to get. Security guards in sharp suits, bald, scary, muscled freaks with walkie-talkies up the ass milled around. An old-timer, ramrod straight, wearing a Stetson, bootlace tie and carrying a silver-topped cane, slipped in and was welcomed deferentially. A fat guy in a Hawaiian shirt and beads. A foxy Asian woman in a sharp business suit. A black bling Emperor. It was all free entertainment, just standing right there.

George remembered his poker night with Lou and made a mental note to score the right video equipment to watch that tape. If he could nail that scumbag in some way following the drug spike, he would.

The lobby was busier now. People milling around, unsure. Guests negotiating special rates and enquiring about availability and insurance reimbursement for their enforced, prolonged stay. The queue at the car hire desks snaked all the way back to the casino entrance.

George had had enough. Anxiety over Beatrice's well-being couldn't be adequately dismissed in a glib one-liner or quenched in a cocktail hour or assuaged by the smile of a trolley dolly. What if she had gone into work, yesterday of all days? He couldn't bear to think about it.

Uncomfortable as it was to admit, he had not been outside a relationship of one kind or another with a woman for as long as he could remember. Now he was floundering without any 'significant other' to define him – no one to fight with, worry about, sulk over or cheat on.

His eyes were heavy. Sleep could be eschewed no longer. He made for the elevator, glancing back toward the hotel entrance. Emerging from a small group of theatrically dressed pharaohs, temple guards and handmaidens who had been giving out promotional literature, a striking young black woman pulled a beige raincoat on over her costume.

It looked like … yes, it was … Jaffé Losoko! George blinked his tired eyes hard and looked again. She was moving fast toward the door now. It was definitely her.

'Jaffé!' he shouted, pushing past a couple with a baby buggy and loaded down with bags.

'Well, excuse me,' said the mother sarcastically.

'Sorry! … Jaffé! Jaffé!'

The black woman slipped through the sliding doors and was gone. George emerged from the hotel only to see the lights of her cab twinkle and disappear among the enormous Humvees and stretch limos on the Strip. He slipped the doorman a five-dollar bill for more information.

'Sorry, man. All I can tell you is she works here maybe three nights a week.'

'Might some of the others know how I can contact her?' George asked this more in hope than in expectation. He moved toward the knot of pharaohs, temple guards and handmaidens giving out leaflets.

The doorman shrugged. 'I doubt it. They're under strict instruction not to give out those kinda details to the public. Young guy – gondolier over at the Venetian – got fucked up real bad by some prick who followed him home last month and ass-raped him. This ain't no dating agency, bud.'

'I'm … an old friend.'

'Sure you are.'

George was walking away when the man called after him.

'Look, I can tell ya this. She left in a Lucky 7 cab. You don't see so many of them around here. They work outa Darktown, if you get my drift. Most of the shines around here settle in West Vegas. Maybe you should take a look around there. I guess it depends on just how good a friend she is.' The doorman gave him a knowing grin.

✳

George collapsed exhausted onto his bed. His mind wrestled with the emotions that seeing Jaffé Losoko had thrown up again. He'd assumed she'd gone East, finished her studies and got a respectable job. What in hell's name was she doing on the fringes of Las Vegas nightlife?

He experienced again the overwhelming guilt he thought he'd put behind him. In truth he felt responsible for her. Had it been his dalliance in the first place that had led her down this path? Had she become so distraught at the termination of the pregnancy that she'd drifted into bad company? Was it really her? So many inexplicable things had happened over the last couple of days. Maybe his mind was playing tricks on him.

Waves of fatigue welled up and pulled him down into a deep and troubled sleep.

He found himself again in the chapel at St Augustine's. It was night-time. The chapel scared him even during the day – all those sacred bleeding hearts and crowns of thorns. The massive organ pipes, like a forest of dead trees, threw shapes and shadows around the walls and ceiling. The confessional boxes, where a curtain might twitch in the moonlight, stood like sentinels.

But the place had been allowed go to seed. The walls were flaky, distempered; streams of water ran down them. Paintings of august historical and mythological figures hung on the walls, with brass plaques under each to identify them – Electra, Aeneas, Saladin, Aristotle, Plato, Orpheus, Cicero, Avicenna, Averroes ... Nine or ten people were ambling around the chapel in a confused and distressed state. They tripped up among the pews and knocked over the chalice that held the ceremonial wine. It spilt and puddled dark red across the tiled floor. For some reason he knew he had to keep the people together, in one place. Something foul was abroad, something evil. They must not meander off down those long aisles and into the dark chapel alone.

A painting sat propped up on the altar – a watercolour of ... Beatrice. She wore that brown calfskin jacket he liked and had her hair tied up as if she was attending a formal occasion. She was smiling. When he looked back again the painting was covered, wrapped up with brown paper and tied with string.

Suddenly there was a loud crash, glass smashing. Someone had thrown something heavy through the great stained-glass window at the end of the chapel. At first it looked like a wheelchair. Then he could see it was an airplane seat. The men and women ran, shielding their heads from the falling debris.

Out of the corner of his eye George saw the St Augustine's school nurse, in full uniform, push a gurney past them, through a pair of swinging double doors. In that moment, in that instant, in the scraggy frame of the elderly nurse, silver hair scraped back, ulcerating sores on her stick legs, he knew he was in the presence of pure unadulterated malevolence, the physical embodiment of evil turned flesh. He caught a glimpse of the maniacal grin on her face as the doors swung closed behind her. It chilled him to the core.

By now he had lost control of his charges. They had wandered off this way and that despite his best efforts. Only one figure walked toward him – his mother. George didn't feel surprised to see her. She smiled at him.

'You always were an impressionable boy, Georgie – a day-dreamer. You and your brother both. You're more alike than you think or know.'

'Tell me how to fix it, Ma. I want to fix it. I want to put it right.'

'You know how to fix it, Georgie. You always have.'

She pointed off into the distance. He saw a low glow of light in the sky. It was coming from somewhere else on the school grounds. He knew deep down in his marrow that he absolutely, positively, did not want to go. The scariest house duty you could pull was the final security check of the buildings at the far end of the school grounds.

His mother smiled again. 'It's your job. It's your responsibility. Someone left the lights on. You gotta turn them off.'

He knew then what he had to do. It was an unshakeable conviction stronger than anything he had ever felt in his life before.

When he awoke, however, he couldn't salvage from the twilight zone of his fast-fading memories just precisely what that might be. He stretched, and the smell from his armpits made him wince.

For a moment there was a scuffling noise outside in the corridor and what sounded like child's laughter, or maybe crying. George saw movement under the door, then heard what sounded like small feet running off into the distance.

He rubbed his eyes and sat up. A sheet of paper had been pushed under the gap of the door. He threw back the sheets and crossed the room. A flyer, maybe, for some evening's entertainment or an in-house show.

What he saw made him sit down slowly on the edge of the bed in bemused disbelief, his eyes clouding with irrational tears.

It was a childlike drawing of an orange dog with floppy ears and lolling tongue. It was Harvey. On the other side, in angry letters cut and pasted from newspaper print, it said, 'Woof … fucking woof!'

Chapter 24

'In many ways, Brighton Beach is no longer part of the USA,' said Virgil, smiling, delighted that the meeting with Baba Yaga had gone so well. The vodka was making him loquacious. 'The people here, they think they must have a passport to travel beyond Coney Island!' He said it boastfully.

They were bumping around New York again in the same taxi cab, heading now to see the Monk for the last of Lou's three 'consultations', as Virgil called them. Maybe then some element of normality might return to this chaotic and infernal expedition. So far, it had been an initiation Lou would never forget.

He steeled himself for yet another encounter with the deeply objectionable, the disturbing, the soul-shrinking, the unknown, for they were entering the heartland of Russian-American communities in south-east Brooklyn, better known as 'Little Odessa'.

Lou had been here before. The Russkies had talked about opening a few video stores in their own backyard. They'd brought him down and shown him around. He hadn't found the experience a particularly enjoyable one. One hundred and fifty thousand Soviet emigrants had settled in Brighton Beach in the last twenty-five years. The former 'poor-man's playground', where hard-working Italian families used to saunter the boardwalk and take the sea air, was no more. Now there were countless Russian restaurants, serving borscht, caviar, vodka, and Russian book-shops, bath-houses, barbers and funeral homes. They bragged about how they had the Africans and Puerto Ricans on the run.

Lou looked out of the window. The street was full of Hasidic Jews, suited businessmen and young thugs concluding commercial deals, quarrelling or talking on their mobile phones. They drove past Coney Island Avenue, Brighton Beach's own 'Broadway'.

Virgil turned up his personal audio, closed his eyes and sang in a passable drawl, 'Oh God said to Abraham, "Kill me a son" … You know Bob Dylan, Mr Plutus?'

'Don't know him exactly. Covered an outside broadcast gig of his once—'

Before Lou could continue he was nudged excitedly on his wounded arm.

'Almost all signs are in Russian,' said Virgil proudly. He was as enthusiastic as a small boy returning home. 'Look!'

Shop windows boasted 'Quality Italian Footwear', 'Bargain Basement Essentials', 'Cheap Goods from Russia' (this shop was owned by Koreans), 'We Accept Food Stamps', and there was a hairdresser's proclaiming that 'Carla' still worked there. All in Russian. Virgil proudly translated every one for him.

The cab came to a stop.

Nestling in the shadow of the elevated New York subway, and squeezed between a block of dilapidated storefronts and a former red-brick blast foundry, was the Monk's aluminium trailer home, rusting and forlorn. The wheels had been removed and replaced with bricks, window boxes and hanging baskets that trailed weeds and mouldy decay. Towering over all was the massive metal skeleton of a previous gasworks.

A line of bedraggled and world-weary people had gathered outside the trailer. They were mostly elderly women with shopping trolleys, absent-mindedly fingering beads and miniature icons. Some of them carried cut flowers. Rough-looking men clutching duty-free packets of Marlboro occasionally cut up the line. No one protested. The talk was of a local jeweller who had been killed, shot in the throat in broad daylight. A train rumbled and screeched overhead.

'Well, Mr Plutus,' said Virgil with a smile. 'Welcome to the underworld.'

He raised his arms high above his head and stretched, as if he had just got out of bed. For the first time, Lou noticed the handle grip of a Glock 17 protruding from his elasticised waistband.

A raised voice could be heard coming from inside the trailer: 'The Mafia? Which Mafia?' The Monk's latest customer emerged from the doorway.

He wore a leather jacket and held a presentation box of Remy Martin Champagne Cognac under his arm. His unfeasibly bushy eyebrows were arched in mock incredulity. He spoke back over his shoulder as he exited: 'All this Russian mafia bullshit is made up. It was invented by those tight-ass New York WASPs who hate us for being so entrepreneurial and successful.'

The punter closed the door, descended the few steps and walked off. The crowd parted to let him through.

Virgil placed a steering hand in the small of Lou's back and pushed him to the head of the queue and up the steps. Cries of rancour and resentment split the air. Curses were hurled, and some of the younger men in the assembly moved forward menacingly.

Virgil slowly put his hood down. His white hair blazed. He took out his earphones, letting them hang around his neck, and turned unhurriedly to face the mob. Instantaneously they cowered as one. The old women crossed themselves repeatedly and bowed low, laying their flowers reverentially on the bottom step. The young men averted their eyes and placed their contraband on the ground before sidling off into the shadowy margins.

Lou was impressed and frightened and dismayed all at once. He caught the sound coming from Virgil's earphones. It was the hiss of static. White noise. Dead air. Had his fellow traveller been listening to this since back at the docks with the Anvil?

Virgil studiously replaced his hood and earphones and pushed Lou through the door into the darkened interior of the trailer.

The room was dim and smelled of damp mould and heavy incense. Identical racks of black suits lined the walls. Identical boxes of white shirts and black patent leather shoes were piled in corners. The room was lit mostly by lava lamps and Christmas fairy lights.

In the centre of the space was some kind of altar. It was a strange hybrid of Russian Orthodox icons, candles and highly wrought gold leaf and leather bibles. The bibles were opened at various places, their pages marked by silk ribbons. Byzantine crucifixes and ornate icons – the Theotokas, the Akathist, the Archangel Michael – were interspersed with Haitian voodoo art. Coloured mirrors glittered and beads hung from around the stunted necks of mummified monkey heads. In the corner, a large plasma screen TV showed *South Park* with the sound on low.

Virgil indicated that Lou should sit on the couch; he remained standing by the door. Lou felt more weary than surprised by it all. It had been that kind of day. On a small coffee table in front of him a tatty school exercise book lay open. It was filled with intricate, indecipherable scribblings. Codes, ciphers, words, diagrams – they were packed tightly together, covering the pages completely. Beside this was another open book, its pages textured by what seemed like Braille.

The sound of a toilet flushing announced the arrival of the Monk. He was tall and thin, and wore a dark kaftan and sandals.

His long hair and beard were matted. He looked pretty much as Lou imagined he would. He had expected some demented preacher type and this guy was sure fitting the bill.

The Monk crossed to the centre of the room and paused. He nipped the bridge of his nose with thumb and forefinger, as if divining who was in the room with him. It was then Lou saw that his eyelids had been sewn shut with what looked like steel wire. It threw him.

'What the fuck's with the eyes?' whispered Lou.

'They made him see so much ... so many terrible things. It was his own choice,' Virgil whispered back.

The Monk walked toward Virgil, who had silently indicated that Lou should stand up, and felt the contours of his face with his bony hands. Virgil put his hood down to facilitate the process. Suddenly, and with deceptive strength, he pushed Virgil hard back against the wall and held him there with one hand. With the other, he pulled the Glock from his waistband and thrust it, handle first, toward Lou.

'Kill me!' he demanded.

'What?' said Lou, taken aback.

'Kill me. Do it now!' He sounded educated, English, a thespian-type – and utterly insistent.

Before Lou could do anything, Virgil had relieved the blind man of the gun. 'Now, now, Old Father, you know that isn't possible.'

The Monk seemed crestfallen and didn't protest. He moved closer to Lou and ran his hand over his face. He felt the burns and blisters.

'The dragon has breathed on you already,' he said, surprised.

Lou winced and drew back. 'I'm here to receive instructions ... for a job. Let's get on with it.'

'Better you should have killed me, then, than to hear from these lips the task I must set you.'

'Fuck that, Rasputin! I wanna be done with all of this. This fuckin' pantomime. I wanna make things right and leave it at that.' Lou was spitting the words at the blind man but he was looking at Virgil.

The Monk threw his head back and laughed.

'Ahhhh, I see! You are an altogether different proposition than I expected.' The tone of his voice had changed. 'An altogether different piece of work.'

'I am what I am.'

'That you are, Mr Plutus, that you are.' He was stroking his beard thoughtfully. 'Tell me, do you believe in your immortal soul?'

Lou was impatient. His face was smarting and weeping where the blind man had broken the crust.

'What is all this bullshit? I lost a video tape. I'll get it back.'

The Monk ignored him. 'Our mutual friend here believes, don't you, Virgil?' His mood seemed to have changed. Virgil cast a look to the floor. 'Will you tell us once again about your adventures in Chechnya, Virgil? Will you show us … your pain?'

Virgil plunged his hands deep in his pockets and squirmed uncomfortably.

'Did your victim cry out to Allah the merciful, Allah the just?'

'Enough!'

'Do you still dream of your boot, pressing down on his head, your knife sawing at his throat?' The Monk turned to Lou. 'Does he still listen to the Soviet crop reports, Mr Plutus? Such a lonely boy, so far away from home, listening to the taped accounts of record Soviet crop yields. How … sad.' His laugh was cruel. 'Show us your pain Virgil. Lift your shirt.'

The young man did as he asked with a slow reluctance that suggested he had no other choice. Lou could see a pink-purple weal, a perfectly straight scar that ran from his upper chest bone to the dip of his navel. Virgil seemed ashamed.

'Do you remember, Virgil? Do you? I do. CPR in progress, bag-mask ventilation, airway established per anaesthesia, no appreciable breath sounds to right chest, chest tube placed, obvious hemothorax. No pulse, no pressure, pupils fixed and dilated. Wounds, one entry site at two to three centimetres below the nipple in the midclavicular line. No obvious exit site, carotid pulse palpated, sinus rhythm. Entering the operating room, massive bleeding relatively controlled but … internal massage, intracardiac epinephrine and cardioversion, some pulse and pressure return. But … Doctor, I think we're losing him.' He smiled maliciously in Virgil's direction. 'Should I go on?'

'That's enough. That's not why we're here,' Virgil said quietly.

'Quite. So let us turn our attention to the matter at hand.'

They both faced Lou, who had no spit left to swallow.

The Monk spoke. 'You took something that did not belong to you. You, in turn, had that thing taken from you. Our patron wants it back.'

'That much I know.'

'That's not all. As a gesture of … what shall we call it?' He looked at Virgil, who shrugged. 'Good faith? Yes, I like that … as a gesture of good faith you will employ your not inconsiderable talent by organising a similar production in which you, Mr Plutus, will be the chief protagonist … the star, if you will.'

Lou protested. 'Look, that ain't necessary, okay? Anyone who knows Lou Plutus knows that I can stay schtum about anything, no exceptions. You don't need this kinda collateral on me. I can keep my mouth shut.'

The Monk reached over and gently touched Lou's eyes, ears and mouth with the tips of his fingers. Lou blanched.

'Dear Lou, we have no fears on that score, none at all. We simply want to see you … get your hands dirty.'

'I don't do snuff. I'm strictly porn.'

'Really, Lou? After all you've seen today, do you really believe you're in a position to negotiate?'

Lou cupped his hand over his mouth and stayed uncharacteristically silent. He was sweating hard. After a while he spoke.

'So you want me to whack some skank on camera. You get the tape and we're quits?'

'No,' the Monk said as if speaking to a dim-witted child. 'You travel to Las Vegas, and locate and return what belongs to us. You deal with the problem of Mr George Bailey and you produce something titillating on camera for the powers that be. Then we will see what we'll see.'

Lou had already gone well beyond any personal line in the sand he may have had. Survival was paramount. He was now operating on the merely logistical.

'Bailey I'll do for free. You'll need to arrange the place for the, uh, movie shoot – hotel room somewhere quiet, maybe the desert. And the girl, the hooker. You can do that.'

'Ahhh,' the Monk said playfully, 'who said anything about a girl?'

'Then a fag. Maybe I can give you some names.'

'Our patron ... he was very precise about this.' The blind man rubbed at the steel thread holding his eyes shut. He rubbed hard. The wounds began to weep tears of blood. 'What was it he said? Oh yes, "a gaining of wisdom necessitates a loss of innocence". That was it.'

Virgil had moved away from the wall and over to the shrine. The Monk took Lou's face between his hands, forcing him to stare at his suppurating eyes.

'It will be a boy. A male child. No older than seven years. A non-Caucasian. A black African. He was very specific about this.'

Virgil fell to his knees in front of the altar. His whole frame shook with remorse. Tears and snot streamed from eyes and nose. He began praying gibberish and crossing himself feverishly at high speed, over and over again.

'Lost souls,' he wailed like a banshee. 'Lost souls!'

NEVADA

'Well, Lucian, if you ask me it's much easier to deal with a criminal who breaks the law than with a person who doesn't know or doesn't care that the law exists in the first place. And that, my friend, is what you're dealing with when you take on these Russki sonsabitches. Over.'

Chief Deputy Sheriff Fox McKinley released the button on the radio handset and pushed his hat back. The sweatband was wet. It was a hot day. Nevada hot.

He'd parked the cruiser in the shade and had the AC up full blast, but he still felt sticky as a thirty-dollar hooker's crotch. His trademark voice growled low and even, a slow reverberating bass timbre that his men swore made inanimate objects resonate in accord with his contemplative pronouncements.

'Hell, Lucian, I figured you'd say that, but we gotta get together on this one. Yeah, I know it … Well, you say hello to the missus for me. Yeah right, ex-missus … Be seein' ya. Out.'

Like his voice, his craggy weathered face had been formed by a lifetime of hard experience, whiskey and tobacco. He smoothed down his thick grey moustache, pulling on the ends repeatedly, a habit he had when lost in thought or frustration.

It was important that he convinced the Las Vegas Metropolitan Police Department boys that these Russian pornography and vice ring shenanigans were worth their attention. He was loath to admit it but without LVMPD, the Clark County Sheriff's Department were going at this with one hand tied behind their backs.

The downtown Fremont Street/Glitter Gulch area beyond the Strip fell within the jurisdiction of the LVMPD. Frequented mostly by the down-at-heel gamblers and locals, it was here that he needed guaranteed easy access. No questions asked. All the intel passed on by the Feds suggested that this so-called Webcore operation had its base smack in the middle of old Sin City herself.

Both agencies worked within each other's jurisdiction by mutual consent. The LVMPD was funded by the City of Las Vegas and Clark County. Funding was based on a complex calculation based on the size of population, calls for their service and felony crimes committed in the prior year. Both jurisdictions approved the annual budget, including their percentage of same. Additionally the department self-generated approximately thirty-three per cent of its funds through property tax and by charging for certain services such as special events, work cards and privileged licence investigations. Put simply, a lot of people's wages each month were dependent on the goodwill and reciprocation of a lot of other people. Rocking the boat was a downright unpopular thing to do.

Both agencies enforced organised crime policies with the implicit support of the Clark County political hierarchy and the Nevada State Legislature. And it was widely acknowledged that both agencies had been comprehensively compromised and corrupted by organised crime.

Officers often doubled up on off-duty security jobs for casinos and acted as plain-clothes enforcers as needs be. McKinley felt pretty sure about who was taking what from whom in his own department, but the Met was another matter. He had to be sure that those Russian sex dollars hadn't already turned the heads of Captain Lucian de los Santos and his boys. Otherwise, he was pissing in the wind.

He needed to get out of the car to stretch his long legs. Those old bones of his weren't what they used to be, certainly not since he'd come off the road doing one hundred miles an hour plus during the high-speed pursuit of a black SUV with New York licence plates and blacked-out windows. That was just over two decades ago. The steel pins they'd put in his leg to hold together the shattered bone could have comfortably earned him early retirement and a consultancy in any number of security firms. But Chief Deputy Sheriff Fox McKinley was an ornery old-school cuss.

Born and bred third-generation Nevadan, he'd met his wife Rita in the late fifties, when she was a flame-haired young singer at the Majestik. They'd been together ever since, despite his claims that not a day passed when she'd failed to bust his balls concerning his predilection for Red Rooster chewing tobacco. He was a throwback to cowboy days, and the men in the department loved him for it.

He had taken a direct hand in recruitment policy and built up from scratch a force of bright young men committed to high standards in public service. Hell, the sheriff himself, Jed Conroy, had asked him to run on his vacant ticket when he stepped down. Fox had declined.

Rita said she understood when he requested and was granted permission to re-engage on active service, said he'd probably get his fool self killed next time. But she knew her husband, knew that he meant what he said when he swore he was 'gonna git those Russki sonsabitches who left me a half gimp'.

He leaned on the hot hood of the car at full stretch, like he was about to be searched, supporting himself with the palms of his hands and fully extending his long legs, trying to iron out those kinks. The joints clicked loudly.

A big rig swept by, bumping and rattling and hissing air brakes. Pigs grunted and squealed through the metal stanchion of its high-sided trailers. It threw a cloud of dust up around him. He narrowed his eyes and spat.

'Don't move a muscle, old-timer. Resume the position,' said a man approaching through the dust.

McKinley squinted harder. He could just about see the flashing blues and reds.

'Now gimmie fifty push-ups or gimmie fifty dollars,' said the man.

McKinley tried not to laugh; he recognised the voice. 'I'll give ya the toe of my boot up yer ass!' he said, straightening up and holding the base of his aching back with both hands.

The sharp outline of a young officer emerged through the cloud of dust. Deputy Harry Shankill Bailey wore his uniform well, like he was born to it. He was tall and thin, reed-like. Straight up and down. In contravention of rules and regulations, he wore his Taurus large frame revolver slung low on his leg, Wild West-style.

'Reckon I'll tell Rita you said that and leave it up to her to soften yer cough some,' Deputy Bailey said.

'Reckon you do that then, and while yer at it, tell her to quit asking young greenhorn, wet-ass punk kids like you to follow me around like I was an old houn' dog 'bout ready for the bone yard.'

'Shoooot, I's just tryin' to learn from the master.'

'Yeah, well you shoulda learned by now that I take it black, no sweetener and that I'm partial to Big Sal's pecan pie around now.'

The young man pushed his hat back on his head and with a smile headed toward the double doors of the diner. McKinley brushed himself down and followed.

Deputy Bailey was already arranging the cutlery on either side of the plates when McKinley joined him. He nodded at Big Sal and placed his hat on the red leatherette seat before sliding in to face the young officer.

Harry Bailey took off his hat and pulled on a pair of wire-rimmed spectacles with thick round lenses, looping the legs around his ears. His straight blond hair and large indigo eyes made him look boyish.

'Contacts still troubling you, boy?'

'A little, sir, but no point in making life any more difficult than it is.'

Young Bailey was referring to the stringent eyesight and hearing tests that the county had put in place for all its officers since the accidental shooting of the Kavanagh boy by Police Officer Ramon Chavez. McKinley had called in a few favours from the station physician in order to smooth Bailey's way. Retina trouble would ordinarily have barred him from a career in the Sheriff's Office. But Fox and Rita McKinley had developed a fondness for this earnest young man who they first encountered as a twelve-year-old, when he had gone calling from door-to-door in their neighbourhood, introducing himself and asking for casual work.

Harry Shankill Bailey claimed no blood kin and had been raised from the age of eight in the state orphanage where he'd been deposited, gasping for air and purple in the face from near asphyxiation, or so it appeared. As time passed he'd taken to idolising the local deputies, becoming something of a mascot for the Sheriff's Office, having bombarded them with homework projects and requests for high-school magazine interviews. As the McKinleys had no children of their own, it wasn't surprising that young Harry found himself invited for Thanksgivings and Halloween trick-or-treating. His fascination for the old West had endeared him to Fox, who shared this interest and found such a thing rare in one so young. When Harry aced his entrance exams for deputy, the boys in the division were determined that a pair of dodgy eyes would not impede his entry. He remained something of a mascot for them all.

The older man was pushing his pie around his plate distractedly and stroking his moustache absent-mindedly. To McKinley's vexation, Harry had become something of a 'minder' since the veteran's return from sick leave, on the express request of the formidable Rita. The deputy adjusted his glasses nervously, cleared his throat and made a tentative enquiry.

'Ya ain't eatin' the pie, so … is somethin' eatin' you?' He bit at a rag nail at the corner of his thumb, preparing to be withered by a dismissive response.

It never came. Instead, following a long pause, McKinley sighed and maintaining his gaze on the table said simply, 'There's been another one.'

Harry knew instantly what the sheriff was talking about and let slip his cup, spilling coffee across the Formica tabletop. He mopped it up with paper napkins.

'Shit, are you sure? That makes five.'

McKinley looked him straight in the eyes, his voice steady. 'What's not to be sure about? You'll read about it tomorrow like everyone else.'

'Same MO?'

'In as much as there is one. Black kid, male, six years old, lifted outa West Vegas. Found him this morning behind some dumpsters. Brought there from someplace else. Propped up nice. Face and hands cleaned, clothes brushed, hair combed. Throat slit – damn near decapitated.'

'And the fried chicken?'

McKinley made a clicking noise behind his teeth. 'Damnedest thing. Same empty box … bones picked clean. From Yardbird

Dixie Wings. The Met boys are all over it for DNA. Nuthin. The sonofabitch fed it to the kids before he—'

Sal arrived to top up the coffee and mop up the mess.

Fox McKinley looked ancient and grey, like he had turned to stone. He stretched one long leg out of the booth and rubbed at the knee.

Sal left to flip burgers.

'No motive, no witnesses, no hard clues, no murder scene, no suspects,' McKinley continued. 'We ain't got one lead.' He popped a toothpick into his mouth.

'We got any theories?'

'Yeah, kids go with strangers.'

McKinley unfolded a colourful glossy flyer and pushed it across the table. Harry looked at it. It showed a drawing of the smiling cartoon *Simpsons* family holding open a scroll. He read the words aloud:

A Message from The Simpsons:
Piano keys, they can't turn locks,
And footstools don't have toes,
And we all know that cabbage heads
Don't have a mouth or nose,
And children know the dangers,
So don't ever go with strangers.

McKinley scratched his head.

'Circulated clear across the county. Car bumper stickers too, radio shows, milk cartons. There's real fear out there, but they still go with strangers – near on one a month now.'

Harry felt chastised. He sipped some coffee and tried again. 'What about the racial thing?'

'Well, we're all prayin' it ain't so, but it can only be a matter of time before this blows the fuck right up in our piggy-pink faces.'

'What does de los Santos say?'

'The Met have specialists from Atlanta flyin' in at the weekend. Those boys up there had somethin' similar a few years back. Never collared anyone for it, so you can see how's they might be interested. If they turn up jack shit, then the whole shootin' match is goin' over to the Feds.'

'Same guys who've been working the Webcore thing with you?'

'Maybe ... maybe not.' The old man cleared his throat.

'Somethin' else on your mind, Fox?'

'Boy, you've been hangin' around me waaay too long.'

'Spit it out.'

McKinley stood up and threw a few dollars on the table. He hitched up his belt, the keys and cuffs jangling. 'Walk with me.'

The two men pushed out through the doors and were swallowed up again by the dry heat and merciless glare. McKinley climbed into his car and placed an arm on the open window.

The young man leaned in and squinted as the sun reflected off the Deputy Sheriff's badge and into his eyes.

'I've told de los Santos and I'm telling you, but no one else for now. Understand?'

Harry nodded.

'Now, I know everyone thinks I'm about fit to be retired and that I have a hard-on for those Russians since they fucked me up.' He focused on the steering column, then looked up at Harry earnestly. 'But I'm here to tell ya, son, I feel it in my water. Those Webcore motherfuckers are up to their necks in this somehow. And if Lucian de los Santos and our brother officers of the Met are being greased by those cocksuckers, then I guess we'll have to do this one all by ourselves.'

The young man winced. 'That's fucked up in so many ways, Fox. I don't know where to begin.'

McKinley laughed out loud. 'We'll see, son, we'll see. You just be ready to back me up when I holler.'

The young man stepped away from the car and dropped into a gunfighter pose. He whipped his revolver from its holster in a blur and was pointing it at McKinley.

'Rita says to pick up a quart-a-milk and some cheese whip, old man.'

'Take off yer spectacles, boy,' said the sheriff. 'You look like an asshole.'

He pulled away in a cloud of dust.

Chapter 26

NEVADA

George had tried to get back to sleep, despite the amateur sexual athletics of the couple next door. They yelled in time, they panted in unison, they grunted and moaned independently of one another, then soared together in pitch and decibel. They rattled the bed springs and the headboard clouted the adjoining wall. They rolled onto the floor with a thump and began the whole choreography anew. It was impossible to sleep.

The Vegas rays were already slinking in around the edges of the blackouts. George, finding it hard to breath from beneath the pillow he had wrapped around his head, simply gave up. He lay looking at the ceiling, then around the room.

A framed picture. Oils, pencil and charcoal. An abstract portrait of what appeared to be a couple in shadow, or perhaps a black child being carried on the shoulders of a white man. Broad strokes, thick oil paint, no discernible features. All outlines and silhouettes. He hadn't noticed it before.

How long had he been in town, in this room? It seemed like a week. But all the indications – his watch, which, he conceded, may only have been working intermittently, the TV news, the in-room hotel welcome page showing his current bill ($0), even the copy of the *Las Vegas Sun* that he'd filched from the bar the previous evening – all said the same thing. It was September 12th, 2001.

How could that be?

George could hear low, intimate post-coital babbling from next door. It made him feel suddenly, desperately alone. And sorry for himself. Misunderstood. It made him think of Beatrice. And of Jaffé. He thought about the pronounced contrast between the two women and their lovemaking.

He and Beatrice had fallen into the occasional perfunctory throwing of sexual shapes, as much out of duty as expectation. All the women's magazines that George browsed through in newsagents without actually buying said the same thing: that this was to be expected in a long-term, monogamous relationship, and that couples had to work at putting the 'jizz' back into their sex lives. The impromptu entry from behind across the ironing board, the surprise leather basque and riding crop before bedtime- -that kind of thing.

But with him and Beatrice things were a little more complicated than that. It all came down to who would make the first move – effectively, who was in control; who wanted it more. The French said, *Il y a d'un qui embrasse et un qui est embrassé*, or so claimed Kim, the lesbian literature student who worked nights with George at Lou's Video Emporium.

He thought that summed things up pretty well. The fear of being subsumed completely by another, the effort it took them to maintain who they were as individuals in the life they shared, had pretty much emasculated him and turned her into a drudge. It was tragic in its way.

Perhaps that was why Jaffé had so intoxicated him and why he had to tell Beatrice about it. She had to know. After all, it was her fault, wasn't it? Scores settled. *Look what you made me do. I hope you're happy now.* But of course his elaborate self-deceptions only worked as long as he was indulged enough to get away with them.

Now Beatrice had drawn the line, pulled the plug. *And that, my friend, is why you're lying here, alone, staring at the ceiling like a schmuck.*

He wondered again if he had really seen Jaffé last night. Jaffé Losoko – in Vegas! Surely not. If mistaken, she had a double waitressing this casino.

He felt the blood rush a little as he recalled their first coupling. So different from Beatrice, even back in the day when Bee had been as insatiable as any flame-haired young Dixie chick on heat.

The waiter from the coffee bar they'd first met in told him he'd only seen Jaffé once after they split up. She had cut off all her hair – her shiny coiled and braided ringlets – to a close plantation-slave crop. George knew why. His sins of omission rendered him just as responsible as that young woman far from her home. He would never be able to shake his complicity in the abortion. Old Gusher Geryon and the other priests had seen to that.

Christ, thought George, swinging his legs over the side of the bed and shaking himself from his reverie, what does a guy have to do to get laid in this town?

Having showered, he thought again about phoning Beatrice – maybe just hear her voice and hang up. He could do it quick, wrong number-style. Put his mind at rest. But he instantly changed his mind.

A plan of action – that's what was required. Take his mind off Beatrice. A trip to the spa and sauna for starters: 'Be sure to enjoy our full facilities,' the flyers said. Maybe later, brace that doorman for some more leads on the Jaffé lookalike. George decided it couldn't really be her. After all, what were the odds? Still, it might be fun making the acquaintance of Jaffé's doppelgänger – 'I know you probably get this all the time, but you really remind me of an old girlfriend.'

He'd left a food order hanging on the outside of the door, and room service arrived with pancakes. From his window he could see that there was still nothing landing at or leaving from McCarran International Airport.

He settled down to breakfast and a read of the local paper that came with it. He flicked through, ostensibly looking for bargain offers on electrical goods, especially handheld video recorder/players, but checking out the events, acts and shows where he might kick back a little.

'LV Still on High Alert. President Bush Seals Skies' read the front page headline. He duly read his horoscope, dripping syrup and coffee on the paper.

Scorpio: You might look for ways to escape reality this week or not be able to focus on your day-to-day responsibilities and duties. It's as if you are living in another world. That's only natural, due to the Sun, Mercury and Venus all in a challenging aspect to Neptune. It could be very hard for you to see and think clearly.

Next up was the Lonely Souls page. George smiled at what he took to be a joke or a typo. 'Should be Lonely Hearts, you assholes,' he muttered under his breath.

Retired Lady, 64. Recently jumped off cliff. Looking for someone to tell my husband I'm much happier now he can no longer hurt me.

His eyes flicked across the page.

Stunning Model, 30-something. Wife of sports star, stabbed to death. It was him and I know how to prove it. Get in touch.

George set down his coffee cup and rubbed his eyes. They couldn't all be misprints. His stomach got flutters.

Black Male, 19 years old. Looking for someone to help stop my younger brother from avenging my death.

This has got to be a prank, George thought. But it ain't April Fool's – or Halloween.

Romantic Female, 27 years old. Died in car crash. Wants to let long-term boyfriend know the answer was 'yes'.

It was like the obituaries had become confused with the dating page. George got serious goosebumps. He felt cold all over.

'To hell with that,' he said out loud and binned the paper. 'I've gotta get out of this room. I'm gettin' cabin fever!'

He threw some cold water on his face and finished dressing quickly. One boot remained stubbornly undetected. Once he found that he'd be off.

He flicked on the television and scrolled down to the pay-per-view sex movies. If those assholes next door could keep him awake all morning, he was sure as hell going to fuck with their afternoon delight. He flipped a finger at the separating wall.

'*Dirty Café*. Maybe. *Persian Pampered Pussies* … better. *Hardcore Secrets of the Sex Slaves*. Perfect!'

George ran the movie. He cranked the volume up to ear-splitting levels. The amateurish titles ran along with an electropop sound track. He hoped for something harder than the soft-focus stroke jobs most of these movies showed. He felt spiteful. He wanted some real heavy action to send a 'fuck you' right back at those bunnies next door. George clumped bootless around the room, gathering together his wallet and coins. The movie continued unwatched in the background, the soundtrack filling the room.

Footsteps. A door being knocked. A door opening.

Woman's voice: 'Master, your mistress has purchased me as a gift for you. I am here to do your bidding.'

George moved to the party wall. He cupped his ear and thought he could hear the first sign of disgruntled voices next door. He smiled, satisfied. He opened his wallet.

'I'll be …'

Four crisp, unused pristine fifty-dollar bills looked back at him.

Man's voice: 'The senate decrees that if you perform well, to the master's satisfaction, you may be freed from slavery.'

Woman's reply: 'I will do whatever is asked of me.'

George was down on the floor now, looking under the bed for his missing boot. It lay on its side, just beyond reach.

Man's voice: 'Do you possess any special talents?'

The sound of clothes being unfastened and falling to the floor. A man's short, sharp intake of breath. The smacking noise of flesh slamming against flesh. Groaning. Moaning. Every sound at full volume.

A fist thumped on the party wall. 'Buddy, turn the goddamn noise down!' yelled his neighbour.

George grinned, content. He crawled around to the other side of the bed on all fours to retrieve his boot and took a quick look at the on-screen antics in passing.

His heart stopped.

There, in full close-up action was the thirty-inch plasma, high-definition screen visage ... of Jaffé Losoko.

She wore stilettos and a frilled animal-skin loincloth. It was pushed up around her waist. A thickset man in a Roman centurion's uniform plunged himself in and out of her, eyes closed, holding her around the middle. Her lips parted in pleasure and the tip of her tongue poked out between her teeth.

'It's sweet,' she murmured in pretend ecstasy. 'It's sweet.'

The man next door beat on the wall and eventually George's door. The phone rang again and again. George sat on the floor until the whole movie had run its course. It had the flimsiest of plot lines, each scene clumsily leading on to the next set piece. Jaffé and her fellow performers assumed the full gamut of sexual positions, with a few popular deviances thrown in for good measure.

Then the end titles ran where he learned that she had taken the stage name 'Jaffé Rossetti'.

George felt his mouth go dry just before the screen went blank. A familiar logo scrolled from bottom to top.

'A Webcore (Las Vegas) Production.'

Chapter 27

The journey to Vegas was no picnic for Lou Plutus. He tried to push to the back of his mind the thoughts of what was required from him when he reached his destination. The murder of an innocent child, for salacious and wanton purpose. All he could do was try to rationalise it, compartmentalise it, keep it contained. But he had fallen a very long way, and he knew it.

He had no recollection of how he and Virgil arrived at the Greyhound bus station, him in shades, a black suit and white shirt he'd taken from the Monk that made him look like a renegade from a bad R&B act. He had assumed they would fly down to Vegas, but with all planes grounded, Virgil announced with some amusement that they were to be fellow Greyhound passengers all the way.

'Only losers take the bus,' moaned Lou as darkness fell and they queued beside the aluminium and wood fifties-style jalopy. On the panel it said 'Silver Stripe Americruiser' in wavy writing. 'I thought they de-commissioned these old birds?'

'You should be happy to be travelling with the salt of the earth,' Virgil said. Something about his tone was mischievous. 'Now this is how to see America – from the underbelly up.'

'It's a fuck of a long trip,' complained Lou. 'I'm dog-tired.'

The pain from his burns had settled to a tolerable level, but it exhausted him. He picked nervously at the scabs that had formed on his face. Virgil maternally slapped his hand away for the hundredth time.

'Then sleep until we get there, if you can.'

Those ahead of them in the queue filed on in silence. They were few in number and all seemed bent at the waist, as if cowering or weighted down with the cares and woes of a life lived in suffering, pain or fear. The interior smelled of old leather, diesel fumes and nicotine. The driver, an elderly black man with deep lines on his face and Brillo-Pad grey hair and moustache, read his newspaper and looked at no one in particular.

Individuals shuffled along the aisle, sitting here and there in ones and twos. A dishevelled Hasidic Jew pulled at his long beard and removed his glasses to clean them on a tasselled scarf. A pair of ancient nuns stared into their laps, their liver-spotted hands clasped together and wrapped in rosaries. A Mexican man with tattoos and bad teeth scratched the crack of his ass and sniffed his fingers. A young man in uniform, carrying a canvas gunny sack with a navy crest and the words 'US Fleet Air Arm, San Diego' on it, slugged from a half pint bottle of Jack Daniels and drunkenly manhandled a skinny Thai girl of seventeen made up to look thirty. A man with Slavic features walked the length of the bus and back, scowling at everyone, and settled eventually behind the driver, looking around him angrily and furtively in turns.

Lou and Virgil went straight to the back seat and spread out. Virgil pulled his hood low over his face, adjusted his earphones and settled into a swift repose.

The driver folded away his paper and started up the bus. It coughed and shuddered into life with a mechanical, guttural rattle. Twilight America began to roll by. Neon urban sprawl gave way to leafy commuter belt, then characterless interstate concrete.

Lou fought hard for a while to keep his eyes open, but eventually they flickered and closed. When the bus jolted or clattered he would waken.

On one of those occasions, the bus had come to a stop at a deserted railroad crossing. Lights flashed, bells clanged, a locomotive percussively roared by: rat-a-tat-tat, rat-a-tat-tat, rat-a-tat-tat. He glanced out beyond the sepia tint of his dark glasses, beyond his own reflection in the window, down a well-lit alleyway running by the train track. Some children were gathered in a small group, laughing and pointing.

At first he couldn't see the object of their attention. Then, as the barriers lifted he saw it. In a nearby junkyard, an adult horse, a grey, was straining and thrashing in distress. A telephone cable had become detached and wrapped around the stallion's neck. The harder it struggled, the more it strangled. The horse sweated and sprayed foam from his mouth. His eyes bulged crazily with panic and effort. His partner, a smaller brown filly, galloped wildly and futilely back and forth, whinnying and smashing her head into the chain link fence that skirted the yard. A junkyard dog yapped and snapped at her hind legs. The children continued to laugh and point. The bus moved off.

Featureless towns and commercial strips flew by, monotonously illuminated and washed in an insipid orange glow: truck stops and convenience stores, signs for liquor and gas, Foot Lockers and Taco Bells. All the same. Never ending.

Lou slept. And woke. And slept again. The netherworld in between was a porous blur that allowed reality and dreams to mix together and seep through. He saw the angry-looking Slavic man stand up, walk down the aisle and call for attention. No one paid any heed. He continued anyway.

'My name is Damir Igric. I am twenty-nine years old and

Croatian. I have fought proudly for the one hundred and eighth brigade of the Muslim-Croat army in our homeland war of independence from Yugoslavia.'

He looked agitated and wiped sweat from his brow.

'Some people say our soldiers … some people have accused us of murdering civilians and destroying churches and desecrating Serbian cemeteries.' He reached into a satchel hanging from his shoulder. 'I am a locksmith. I came to America on a thirty-day visa to work.' His voice sounded strained and barely holding together. 'But I cannot work. I have seen terrible, terrible things.'

He began to cry quietly. No one on the bus seemed to be paying any attention to him whatsoever. He looked around desperately. Imploringly. Then his face hardened with resolve.

'You ignore me now. You laugh at me …'

He removed a short-bladed box cutter from his satchel and held it above his head. He looked at the bus driver's back, his plump neck, the folds of fat spilling over the collar of his shirt.

'… but soon you will know my name, as you know and fear the names of Khalid Almihdhar, Nawaf Alhazmi, Abdulaziz Alomari, Mohamed Atta, blessings and peace be upon them.'

He turned and moved with purpose up the aisle toward the oblivious driver. The bus jumped and rattled onwards. Lou's eyes flicked open. The bus passed through shadow and out the other side, by which time the Slav was seated in his original place, staring steadfastly in front of him, just as if he'd never moved.

Lou slept.

After a while he felt a faint pressure in his bladder and, stirring, wondered when they might make their first scheduled stop. The bus bounced over some rough asphalt, then slowed and bounced again over what felt like speed bumps. Finally, with a hiss and squeal of worn brake pads it shuddered to a halt.

Lou half-opened his eyes. They were in the dimly lit, deserted parking lot of a massive shopping mall.

'Ten minutes!' yelled the driver and the folding doors sprang open.

The driver made no attempt to move; neither did anyone else. Virgil hadn't stirred. Lou gathered himself and stood up. The fat man slowly pulled on his coat and tiptoed down the aisle as if it were a minefield. When he half-turned to look over his shoulder, Virgil was sitting fully upright, arms folded, smiling at his charge's puerile, clumsy stealth.

Lou froze. 'I need to take a piss.'

'Ten minutes.'

'Get you anything?'

'World peace and an end to poverty,' said Virgil sardonically.

'Yeah, right. Well, you can't have everything.'

'Precisely! Where would you put it all?'

'Go fuck yourself!' Lou turned to go.

'Ten minutes. Don't make me come looking for you.'

'Yeah, yeah, yeah, big man,' said Lou and he climbed off the bus.

Lou felt deflated and insulted at Virgil's indifference to the idea that he might try to escape or flee. But the young man's apathy was well-founded, for it was a course of action that Lou had long since given up on.

The concrete and steel temple to consumerism sat cold and unwelcoming. Fluorescent light poured from its interior yet failed to illuminate any area beyond its immediate boundaries. Coloured neon signs proclaimed this to be the home of 24-Hour Shopping, of Miller Time and Nike, Applebee's and Ben and Jerry's.

He looked around the deserted parking lot and back at the Greyhound. It sat surrounded by a light blue-grey mist that was coming from its tail pipe. Its windows were clouded and opaque.

He saw his own breath form as a cloud in front of his face and shuddered. Was it really that cold?

The double doors of the mall glided open with a whisper. Piped music played cocktail cover instrumentals of Steely Dan. On every side stretched long featureless corridors, lit by harsh strips. He was standing at a crossroads of adjoining passageways. Most stores had their metal shutters pulled down. Those few that didn't drew him onward. At the far end of a long row of shuttered shops, Lou saw some movement – a young man in overalls with a bucket and mop.

'Hey, where can I find the john?' he shouted.

The man looked up briefly from his task. He had a patch over one eye.

'Hey, buddy, a toilet?' Lou asked again.

He was suddenly distracted by the sound of bells and whistles. Far down another corridor he saw an empty kiddie train choo-choo across the gap and out of sight.

He looked back toward the cleaner. He was gone. A door slammed.

Down another passageway some elderly people on Zimmer frames shuffled trance-like in the opposite direction. He was about to call after them but couldn't think what to say. A mechanical whirring sound coming from behind caught his attention.

Lou spun around.

Whatever it was remained out of sight but was coming closer. His bladder screamed a reminder about why he had come here in the first place. Then emerging from an adjoining corridor he saw a half dozen battery-powered golf type caddies slowly whirring toward him. It took a moment to register what he was looking at. In each caddy sat a horrendously obese child. A few pushed ice cream sandwiches into their mouths; some scoffed sacks of potato chips and popcorn; others drank from bucket-sized cartons of Coke and Sprite and ate colossal burgers. Their puffed-up arms and legs, swathed in designer T-shirts and cut-offs, jiggled like giant white, pasty worms. Their swollen heads beneath baseball caps trailed portable music player leads from the ears and rolled around on tree-trunk necks. They made no sound, save the slurping of soda and the crushing of food wrappers. Their glacially slow buggies crept closer.

Lou turned and ran as best he could. From the corner of his eye he saw the kiddie train choo-choo by, this time a little closer. It was still empty, except for the final carriage where a single black boy was sitting. Beside him, incongruously squeezed into the kid's seat, was a large black woman. The child appeared to be singing, the woman crying. The golf caddies got closer. Lou tried to make his legs work but they wouldn't respond.

Suddenly he opened his eyes with a start. He was back on the bus and bathed in sweat. The young man in navy uniform had extricated himself from his position entwined around the sleeping girl and come back several seats to stare at Lou.

Lou sat up. The sailor grinned from ear to ear and thrust the sloshing bourbon toward him.

'It'll git ya where yer goin."

Lou, endeavouring to regain his composure, waved the bottle away.

The young man was undeterred. He extended his hand. 'Bradley Streep.'

'Lou.'

'Hi, Lou. Hell of a long night shift to put in, isn't it?'

Lou looked around at Virgil to see if he was still asleep.

'Whoaaaaaaaa! You need to change your aftershave, my man!' said Bradley staring at Lou's burnt face.

Lou touched his cheek self-consciously. 'Are you some fuckin' lounge act or what?'

The sarcasm flew way over the young man's head, who swivelled round to face Lou front on.

'No, man, I'm in the fleet air arm,' he said earnestly. 'I'm a navy pilot but can't get me a flight back to base on account of ...' He frowned. 'Are you guys in a band or somethin'?'

'Yeah, I'm Ray Charles. How did you guess?'

'No seriously, it's usually musicians and ... uh, celebrities who wear shades all the time.'

'If I was a celebrity would I be ridin' this heap of shit?'

'Well, man, I usually ride F16s and I'm on here.'

Lou sighed. 'Look, sport, what can I do for you?'

The young man appeared hurt. 'Just tryin' to be friendly and pass the time is all. San Diego's a long ways off.'

'This bus goes to Vegas, sonny.'

'Sure, I know that. That's where I change.'

Lou realised he couldn't get back to sleep anyhow and relented. 'San Diego. Is that where you're from?'

Bradley, who had half-turned away, brightened up instantly. 'No, sir. I'm from San Luis Obispo, on up the coast, but I'm stationed in SD.'

'Must be nice out there this time of year.'

'Man, surf is just about up by now. Time to oil the board and take her out.'

'And what about sleeping beauty there?' Lou nodded at the girl who was now stretched out on the seat, using Bradley's bag as a pillow and his coat as a blanket.

'Oh shit, that's Pak Bahn or something. Christ, I don't know. I met her in a lap dancin' dive in New Jersey. Fucked her six ways to Sunday!' He lowered his voice and whispered. 'She thinks I'm takin' her home to SD, but I'm gonna ditch her in Vegas. She's such a fuckin' skank, man!' He laughed and took another pull on his bottle.

Lou smiled. 'Maybe I will …' he said and reached for the bourbon.

Bradley held out the bottle then suddenly snatched it back to his chest, violently possessive. His face darkened and his expression changed, making him almost unrecognisable from a moment ago. His voice dropped too.

'That was then, sport, this is now,' he rasped.

'Fuckin' wise guy!' grunted Lou. 'Shove it up yer ass.'

The bus bumped, the cabin lights blinked. Bradley cackled darkly and looked older than he had at first. It unsettled Lou.

'Ha ha, I'm only fuckin' with ya. Tell ya what, Louie. No offence. Have a slug for sure, but answer me a question that's been bothering me.'

'If it's about the face …'

'No, no. That's your own business, man. This has to do with my business.'

Lou studied him warily. 'Shoot.'

'Well, in my line of work it's all about orders – following orders, obeying orders without question. That's how we're trained to do what we sometimes gotta do. Geddit?'

'Sure, I geddit.'

'Okay, let's say for the sake of argument that you were asked to do something that you knew was a bad … a very bad thing?'

Lou began to get suspicious. He jabbed a thumb at the comatose Virgil. 'Did that prick put you up to this?'

'Shit, I never seen that guy before in my life.'

'Well, just what are you gettin' at then?'

'Well, Louie, I don't know your line of work, see, but you know mine, right?'

'So you say.'

Bradley seemed wounded again. 'Squadron's honour! Two tours in the Mediterranean, one in the Gulf.' He crossed his heart. 'Here, have a look.'

He reached into his pocket and handed Lou some photos showing young men in uniform on the deck of a large carrier.

'Those guys beside me are my buddies. We're fixed wing … fighter jets. The guys behind are rotary wing … choppers. Seahawks. They're weak pussy asses.'

Lou glanced at them. 'So what's the big bad thing they wanted you to do?'

Bradley leaned in toward Lou and whispered conspiratorially. 'No fuckin' joke, my man. This is some serous shit.'

'Ya gonna tell me or what?'

Bradley placed his hand on Lou's knee and looked him straight in the eye.

'What if you were me, Lou – scrambled, action stations, up there in the wide blue yonder – and some guy comes on your intercom and orders you to blow some fuckin' commercial airliner out of the sky, eh? Just like that, eh? What would you do then Louie, eh?'

Lou rubbed his head. 'Some Syrians or Koreans or shit? Sure, why not. What's a few less towel heads or Chinks. You're doin' your duty, right?'

Bradley was white and sweating all over. He leaned in closer. His voice fought hysteria. 'Not overseas, Lou. Not the mid-east or Gookville. Right here, right in the good ol' US of A. Would ya do it, Lou … for the greater good and all? Would ya do it?'

Lou looked at him sceptically. 'You yankin' my chain?'

'Man, they can fake a moon landing and shoot a president. Doncha think they can do anything they goddamn want?'

'Get the fuck outa here.'

Bradley looked for a moment like he might cry. Then he sat bolt upright and laughed. He threw his head back and roared with laughter. There was no mirth in it whatsoever.

'That's it! That's it! That's right. What if, Lou, eh? What if?'

He handed Lou the bottle. 'Sorry, buddy, I've been on a bender for days now. Had a bad last few months. Unlucky in love is what's at the back of it all.'

'I heard they love a man in a uniform.'

'Yeah, they do say that, don't they. Look, I've taken up enough of your time.' He got up.

'She ain't worth it, kid.'

'Oh I know that. I know that now. That bitch from La Jolla … she left me for a Jew piece-a-shit precious stones merchant. Can you believe that?'

'Ouch.'

'Yeah, all because of one crazy night with her friend, man.'

'You got busted?'

'Well, as my buddy TC says, when you're caught with yer cock in her mouth and yer finger up her ass, its goodnight Irene!'

They both laughed.

Bradley stood up. 'Ya know La Jolla, Lou?' he asked, towering above Lou. 'La Jolla, California. Some of the most expensive seafront real estate in the country. Seal colonies, fag antiques shops, Botox clinics – my God, you can just smell the money in that town.'

The bus caused him to sway from side to side. He closed his eyes like an evangelical preacher. When he opened them again, they seemed black and dead, like marble.

'She's from La Jolla, Lou. Her dad had the BMW franchise for most of the coast. We were gonna settle there, but that's all gone now, ya know?' He hunkered down awkwardly until he was at eye level with Lou. 'I'm gonna let you into a little secret now. Only you, you and nobody else'.

He whispered into the fat man's ear: 'They let us fly test flights up and down that stretch of coast from time to time.'

He placed his hands behind his neck and rolled his head from side to side. He leaned in again and smiled.

'Me, I'm gonna let things settle down. Let things take their course, ya know what I'm sayin'. And then, when I feel the time is right, I'm gonna load up with some live ordnance, my man, some of that electric soup. Four canisters of napalm oughta do it.' Bradley had little balls of foam forming at the corners of his mouth. 'Think about it, Lou – all those Mercedes chicks with their coiffured poodle dogs and their personal trainers. VOOOOOOOOOOOOM!'

He extended his long arms to their full span and wiggled his fingers. 'Impact with high-order detonation. Have a nice day!'

Lou could see that he was absolutely serious.

Bradley straightened up, rubbed the small of his back and returned to his seat. He prodded Pak Bahn disgustedly with the toe of his boot.

'Shit, bitch, move your skanky ass!'

He looked back at Lou one last time, his eyes wide and huge, and gave him two raised thumbs. 'Light it up, maaaan. Light it all up.'

Captain of Detectives, Lucian de los Santos, considered himself to be a pragmatic man above all else. Growing up in a Salvadorian shanty town had taught him early in life that if you can't join them, then you surely must beat them.

The youngest of five boys, he had had to fight hard just to reach the trough ahead of the rest of the litter by the time his parents brought him stateside. Then, on a hot Miami night while accompanying his father on an errand to the corner store, he saw him get stabbed seventeen times in the throat, head and chest by a Haitian junkie who was looking to intimidate his dealer with an act of wanton, senseless violence.

From that point on, young Lucian knew he couldn't survive without the support of his brothers. And then, following a single-minded application to study and duty, he came to depend on the support of his brother officers in the Miami force. When he took the job in the Las Vegas Police Department he became, at forty-one, the youngest Captain of Detectives ever to hold the position. A meteoric rise through the Miami and Dade County PD had paved the way.

He'd first made his name in narcotics, then vice, becoming the high-profile hammer of the Hispanic crime community. His penchant for sharp suits and loud ties had not transferred easily to

THROUGH HOLLOW LANDS **203**

Nevada law enforcement, the blue-collar beat officers calling him 'spic' and 'spiv' behind his back. His deeply pitted, acne-scarred cheeks, pencil-thin goatee and small, deep-set eyes gave him a haunted, feral look. But Lucian was secretly proud of the cracks they made about him 'never having left the barrio', citing this, to anyone who cared to ask, as the key reason why he succeeded in keeping a lid on the off-Strip activities of Vegas's neon underbelly.

He boasted that he knew the Latino criminals inside out. Body and soul. He thought like them and would have no compunction in meting out summary street justice if that was what was required. But a life spent swimming against the tide had left him with a tendency for moral ambiguity, and he believed it was about time that he got his dues. Put simply, Captain Lucian de los Santos had felt for some time now that he was owed, and owed big time.

Vegas seemed just the town to deliver on that. He knew everyone worth knowing – on both sides of the law. If he was smart and patient, there was no telling where he might end up. But for now, the echoing assembly hall of the Martin Luther King Elementary School, located in the centre of West Las Vegas's African American community, was where it was at.

From his vantage point, seated centre stage on the raised platform area, flanked by some suit from the District Attorney's office, a dried-up bleeding-heart social worker, and a Queen Latifah lookalike from the PTA, he gazed around the room. The shit had truly hit the fan.

The TV and radio reporters had agreed to wait outside, interviewing any black parent, civic representative or school teacher they could lay their hands on. But the print media hacks and concerned parents packed the bleachers at the back. Some workmen were dismantling the basketball poles and hoops, carrying them out through the double doors to make more room.

De los Santos noticed the tall figure of Sheriff Fox McKinley standing conspicuously just inside the hall, hugging the back wall. He was resting his hands on his keys and gun belt, his long arms sticking out incongruously at angles. McKinley always made him uneasy, the same way he had felt as a youth in Miami when a black-and-white cruised by. Some inherent guilt in the DNA. Always something to keep secret, even when he had nothing to hide. Always the fear of being caught, even when he had done nothing wrong.

He leaned forward, bumping the microphone with his chin, causing high-pitched feedback to bounce around the bare walls.

'I'm happy to take that question, Susan.'

The crowd settled down and all eyes turned on him.

'Sure, we've pursued a number of lines of enquiry, but the men you ask about are more to be pitied than feared. They're compulsive confessors who regularly turn themselves in at station houses across the county. They'd tell you they helped OJ if they thought they'd get on TV.'

A ripple of laughter from the hardened hacks went around the room. But the Reverend Jonas McCord standing in the centre of the crowd wasn't laughing. He dabbed his forehead with a neatly folded handkerchief and raised a hand.

'I hardly think, Captain, that levity is an appropriate response, when innocents are being lifted off the streets, when evil stalks my community – my parishioners – like a ravenous wolf.'

There was a flutter of 'hallelujahs'. The suit from the DA's office visibly winced and peered out at the crowd, shielding his eyes with his hand.

'And furthermore, I'm not seeing too many black faces up on that podium this evening,' McCord added.

The sullen sucking of teeth. More 'hallelujahs', louder this time.

Lucian smiled. He enjoyed playing politician. 'Now Reverend McCord, let's try to keep this process focused on the problem at hand. We all need to work together on—'

'That's all fine, Captain, but these ain't no white children ending up down some back alley. Now why do you suppose that is?'

'Amen!'

'Right on!'

'Fuckin' A, man!'

'It's true that we've ruled out the possibility that the victims knew their assailant, and we doubt whether the murderer comes from this community, but that's not the same thing as saying these crimes are race-hate related.'

'Captain …' The Reverend looked around him, secure in the knowledge that he was on home turf. A smile twitched at the corners of his mouth. '… I don't believe that you or your department, or the Sheriff's Department for that matter …' He turned and nodded toward Fox McKinley at the rear of the hall. The crowd looked over their shoulders in unison. Fox lightly tugged the brim of his hat. '… have sensed the real scope of this disaster, the serial catastrophe that is taking over our streets.'

He was hitting stride now, his voice and words taking on the cadences of the pulpit. He began to bounce up and down on the balls of his feet.

'Early on, well, I got me a sick feeling about it, right here in the pit of my stomachaaaah, right after poor little Charles Jonesaaaah, en route to a grocery storeaaaah. I just knew it and I saidaaaah, someone is stealing our kids off the streets. Then came poor little Avery Langaaaah … and Morton Fenderaaaah, bringing books from the library for his sick grandmuthaaaah. Well, brothers and sisters, the fear just grew all through last year.'

The oration was working, the affirmations coming from the

crowd rising in volume. Black people pushed to the front of the hall. Still more came in off the street, swelling the crowd.

'And now little Curtis Owensaaaah, a grade A student, top of his classaaaah, the very seeds of a new generation, the heart and soul of a communitaaaah, whose loving parents I was with last night ...' The Reverend shook his head in disbelief, and lowered his gaze and voice for effect. '... inconsolable ... just inconsolable.'

The crowd went quiet as if on cue. He was in control.

'Now, I am a mild-mannered man, and I don't hold with what some of the younger brothers around here have been shouting for ... don't hold with that vigilante justiceaaaah, but I'm here to tell you today, right now, Captain de los Santos, that this sure smells like the work of the Klan!'

There was uproar. Lucian caught the eye of Fox McKinley across the heads of the crowd. The sheriff imitated a telephone receiver with his thumb and forefinger and mouthed the words 'call me' before slipping out unnoticed through the double doors.

Lucian was keen that the Clark County Sheriff's Department took its fair share of the workload and responsibility for what was fast becoming a national news story. But he also knew that this meant entertaining McKinley's notions of Russian mafia involvement in the murders. If he gave this credence, it would open up a vice angle on the case and indirectly unbolt the door to the FBI. It would also allow McKinley's boys access to files, clubs and casinos that he preferred to retain an exclusive hold over. Like so many of the Vegas enforcement community, de los Santos was happy to dismiss the older man's preoccupations in this regard, not least because of the clandestine relationship he enjoyed with a number of wealthy Eastern Europeans in Florida, some of whom were indirectly investing in the Webcore Corporation, under its auspices as a chain of video stores.

The random nature of the killings had initially supported the race theory. It was inevitable. Nowhere else could they find any emerging motive or link. One kid had multiple stab wounds, one had been garrotted, one shot and yet another bludgeoned to death. None of them had any money or valuables. There seemed no obvious sexual activity; save that the anuses of each victim had been smeared with Vaseline, no trauma seemed evident. All the children were dumped, having been killed somewhere else, all laid out in open view and arranged in natural, relaxed postures. Most were tied upright to a tree or fence, and had been partially eaten by crows and ants by the time they were found. The remains of takeaway fried chicken meals were at every scene. In both the initial and final analyses, the victims had only three things in common: they were poor, they were children, and they were black.

De los Santos would have liked to pursue the race motive, hang it on some loony redneck cult. But he knew it wouldn't fly. Maybe in Mississippi or Tennessee, but not here. Not in Vegas. McKinley wasn't buying it either and had already told him as much. The Reverend Jonas McCord ploughed on, however.

'Looking to bring prosperity out of povertaaaah …'

Lucian pushed his sleeve up by way of scratching his wrist and glanced surreptitiously at his wristwatch. If he wanted to get tickets for the big fight at the MGM, things would have to be brought to a swift conclusion. 'The Beast from the East', Minos Baboov, was in town defending his title. Lucian loved the vibe of boxing matches, liked to hang around with boxers and promoters. This Vegas gig was perfect for that. And he wanted to make this fight tonight. Baboov? More like baboon, he thought. That animal is gonna punch holes through that poor nigger challenger!

There were two kinds of fighters, and all you had to do was look in their eyes to tell which was which. The first was the big guy, the muscle man, the school bully in the playground. Those guys traded off their physique and their potential to cause hurt. But when all was said and done, they didn't like to get hurt themselves. Knowing that, and being able to take advantage of it, could help an underdog in the ring.

The second type of fighter wasn't the biggest or the toughest or the loudest, but when you looked in his eyes you saw something that said, you can hurt me and you can humiliate me, but know this: if I get you down, if I get on top of you, no matter what, nothing and no one will stop me beating on you until you are dead and bloody and still.

That's the kind of fighter Minos Baboov was. He was a bad man and a stone-cold killer. Lucian knew the look.

Some Russian high-rollers were due in town for the match. That meant that Lucian and his boys were expected to iron out any unforeseen predicaments and sanction any irregularities that might impede their guests' unadulterated pursuit of every vice or pleasure that took their fancy. His now annual summer vacation as a guest on a yacht in the Caribbean depended on it.

De los Santos looked again at the rapt audience, all focused on the Reverend McCord, swaying in the middle of the hall, sweating bullets, eyes closed.

The fight aficionados always said 'Bet on the black guy'. Not this time, he thought. No fucking way.

Chapter 29

The fight was a short and brutal affair. George Bailey watched it from his stool at the bar of Deano's, dapper in a cashmere V-neck sweater and casual slacks. The contest, if it could be called that, lasted only two rounds and was shown on the only TV in the hotel not running the Twin Towers catastrophe footage, now accompanied by captioned portraits of moustachioed men in uniform: 'Officer Patrick Maloney, age 31 years. Fire Chief Dan McAvoy, age 53 years …'

Baboov had started the fight as he meant to go on and floored his opponent almost instantly. From the glimpse that viewers caught of the poor sap on his backside, looking to his corner in fear and apprehension, it quickly became clear that he was going to stay down for as long as possible and take any count available to him to avoid being further mashed.

The Russian was indeed an awesome specimen. There had been physically bigger fighters, but something in Minos Baboov's demeanour, in the way he carried himself while felling anyone put in front of him, marked him as a dangerous man in and out of the ring. That, and the fact that he never smiled. Ever. The press ate that up with a spoon. It was his trademark, his USP. Eddie Murphy, who was doing a winter season at Vegas, had even made wager: either he would get Baboov to laugh or he'd go five rounds with him. Everyone wanted a piece of 'The Beast from the East'.

Viewers might have been forgiven for thinking that the Vegas crowd were booing a non-contest, but in fact it was the signature mantra of the thousands of Russian émigrés who followed The Beast fanatically.

'Babooooooooooov!' they chanted in unison.

The barkeep at Deano's this evening was a much more affable character than Texas Jeff. Timmy was happy to talk boxing, baseball and weather – whatever. He also knew when to take himself down to the other end of the bar to polish glasses. And he made a damn fine margarita into the bargain.

The casino floor was beginning to fill. Guests, mostly out-of-towners, mingled with the costumed Egyptian waitresses who worked the floor. George was keeping his eyes peeled for Jaffé.

'Gin and tonic, rocks,' said a voice further up the bar. It was unmistakably Margie Kaufman's.

George leaned back to see her settle herself at the bar. 'Timmy' – he gestured to Margie and saluted her with a raised glass – 'on my tab.'

'My God, a gentleman admirer,' she said, smiling. 'I've always depended on the kindness of strangers.'

She lifted her drink and moved down the bar to join him.

'Here's to you, George. Back for another shift?'

'Dirty job, but someone's got to do it.'

'True, true.' She looked up at the TV and the melee taking place in the ring following Baboov's victory. 'Ah, pugilism. The noble art of self-defence.'

'That black guy's face looks like a busted couch.'

Margie looked again and winced. 'Ouch!'

'Not much of a contest,' said Timmy, who joined them. 'Guy goes into the ring to be beaten senseless, then picks up a tidy purse for carrying advertising on the ass of his pants, which he spends most of his time sitting on!'

'It might be a lot of things but it sure ain't a sport any more,' said George.

Minos Baboov's face filled the screen. He leered manically for the cameras.

'How'd you like to meet that guy down a dark alley?' Margie said and began to laugh. It rapidly turned into a wracking cough.

George was unsettled by the severity of her cough. He could hear the clinging, wheezing phlegm crackle through her lungs and up into her throat, then settle down again.

Timmy brought over a glass of water. Margie drank it down in one.

'What I really need is a Marlboro Light,' she said, wiping tears from her eyes with a tissue.

'You really want to get some sound advice about that cough,' said George.

For a moment she seemed angry and looked like she might scold him. Recovering, she slipped on her oversized seventies sunglasses, smiled and cupped her hands over his.

'Georgie, if you and I are gonna be friends then you're gonna have to lay off with the sage advice. Get me?'

'Gotcha. Whada I know, for Christ's sake?'

'Maybe more than you think,' she said a little wistfully.

She grabbed her handbag and started to rummage through it. 'Anyhow, here's the deal – I simply cannot have a drink without a cigarette, darling. I know you understand.'

'Sure thing.'

'So I have a proposition for you. Normally around this time I have a cocktail and a smoke in the hot tub.'

'They let you do that in the spa?'

'No, silly, by the pool outside.'

'But isn't it getting dark about now?'

'Best time. Representatives from America's finest corporations have vacated the pool area and are dropping Viagra in their hotel rooms for their hooker encounters later on. Besides, dusk ... you can see the desert stars and moon just around now. Whadaya say? Wanna join me?'

George thought about it. 'Well, I'll need to go get my swimming costume and a towel.'

'Me too.'

'Can you get a drink out there?'

'Is the Pope a Catholic? Poolside bar, heated water jets massaging the old bones, madam nicotine. Bliss!'

'What the hell. See you out there in fifteen minutes.'

'It's a date,' she said and began to pack up her things.

George called Timmy, settled his tab and headed for the elevator. He liked Margie. Something about her suggested solidity and dependability, a grounding he had come to take for granted from Beatrice and one that he'd sorely been missing. Margie knew her own shit stank and so did everyone else's. He was also drawn by the hope that he could develop platonic feelings for another human being without the prospect of fucking them. Or of fucking them over.

When he exited the elevator, some movement caught his eye at the far end of the corridor. The maid's cart sat laden with toilet rolls, towels and soaps halfway around the corner. He cursed, remembering that he'd left the 'Do Not Disturb' sign on his door. The room would not be made up. In the gathering shadows the maid worked, crouching behind the trolley. The top of her head showed thin, steely-grey hair. An arm, spindly and liver-spotted, reached around the cart for something.

He quickly swiped his key card and left the door ajar in his haste. The room was just how he'd left it – like a bomb had hit it. The bedside phone was partially obscured by one black sock, but he could still see that a red light was flashing. There was a message.

The late evening sun was low and found its way beneath the treated shrink-wrap coating on the windows, causing George to squint. He found his swimwear and set about changing, pulling the cashmere sweater up from the bottom. It was tight and he struggled to get his arms out, then to get it over his head.

The housekeeping cart rattled to a stop outside his door.

He turned to see if the maid had arrived, struggling to focus through the light wool of the sweater pulled over his head and the sunlight in his eyes. The room suddenly filled with a fetid stench. Moving slowly but steadily toward him was a figure, bent over and trailing one leg. George knew instinctively, incredulously, that it was the decrepit nurse of his nightmares, coming at him now with a bony arm outstretched, holding something indeterminate, long, something that caught a glint of sunlight and flashed. In a panic, he wrestled with the asphyxiating garment, only to become even more entangled.

Then there was another figure in the room. A struggle seemed to be taking place between it and the nurse. George pulled the sweater off and threw it on the floor, just in time to catch a glimpse of a maid's outfit disappear out the door. A loud crash sent cleaning materials, shower gels and pillow mints all over the hallway; toilet rolls cascaded in long white ribbons down the corridor. Urgent footfall on deep-pile carpet faded into the distance.

Margie Kaufman stood in the centre of the room arranging her platinum wig in the mirror. She spoke over her shoulder.

'I came up to make sure you weren't getting cold feet.'

'What the fuck just happened here?' George, out of breath and dripping in sweat, placed a hand on the cupboard housing the minibar for balance.

'Whadaya mean?'

'Someone was just here. I saw them!'

'Oh her! Listen, handsome, some of the maids in these hotels can't be trusted. Rob ya blind, honey. It might be an idea to close the door behind you after you come into the room. Geddit?'

'That's what that was about?'

'That's what what was about? Look, George, I'm serious. Close the goddamn door and keep it locked. It's just common sense, sweetie.'

'Yeah, right. Common sense.'

'Now get a move on, you hunk. Let's get down there.'

'Let me just check the message on the machine.'

Margie folded her arms tight across her chest, tucking her hands under her armpits. 'While you do that can I just use your bathroom, Georgie?'

'Sure! Help yourself.'

He went over to the phone and punched the hash key. It was a cold-call pre-recorded message: 'Can you give a new life to children who desperately need a parent? We are located at 222 Frank Sinatra Drive ...'

'I'm not parental material,' George mumbled aloud and was about to hang up.

'... we are particularly interested in placing children from the African American community with parents who ...'

He slammed the phone down hard on the cradle.

Meanwhile, in the bathroom, Margie Kaufman ran the cold water tap over the deep cuts that striped her palms and fingers where she had clutched the blade. The flow of blood eased up, then stopped completely, and the deep incisions faded imperceptibly into the heavy lines already etched on her hands.

The hot tub was steaming invitingly. Margie had a waiter bring two margaritas, rocks with salt, out to them. She shed her robe to reveal a pink and brown one-piece suit, and carefully negotiated the three steps down into the water while tightly holding onto the rail. The heavy wrinkles, the sacks of semi-atrophied muscles that hung from her arms and legs and her deep-tanned parchment-like skin, convinced George that she'd been telling the truth about her advanced years. He put her now at maybe seventy, where before she would have passed as being in her late fifties. The wonders of paint and powder. She saw him look at her and laughed.

'Why do women wear make-up and perfume, Georgie?' she asked as if she'd read his mind.

'Dunno.'

'Cuz we're ugly and we smell bad!' She threw her head back and guffawed.

He smiled. You had to love her.

'Well, that's it, George – nowhere to hide. Get it all out there, that's what I say!'

'Margie, you're even more beautiful than I—'

'Quit the bullshit and turn that little knob, there's a good boy.'

He did as he was bid and the pool gurgled and bubbled up into life.

He slid in. The hot streams immediately felt good against his tired muscles and he manoeuvred this way and that to direct the flow onto his aching joints. Margie sighed and looked to the skies. Needle points of starlight were beginning to prick the gathering black above. Margaritas came and went. And came and went. George watched the steam from the pool rise into the air. The twinkling lights stayed fixed in the firmament above.

'This has been one hell of a trip … and I feel like I've only just arrived,' George said.

'Relax.'

George dipped down until the frothing water was just above his chin. He frowned.

'Ya know, Margie, lately I've been frightened that I might be – well, losing it a little.'

'Show me a sane man and I'll cure him for you.'

George smiled. 'Don't tell me – Big Apple Strikes?'

'Carl Gustav Jung actually.'

He raised his eyebrows.

'I've had a little therapy over the years, dearie,' she explained.

He looked skyward. 'When do you figure the airports will open again?'

'Beats me. When everyone calms the hell down I expect.'

'How long you give it until it's safe again?'

'Safe? SAFE? It's never been safe! Don't you think these guys can blow a plane out of the sky any place or time they choose?'

'Well, then, what stops them? Security?'

'Hell no! Think about it for a moment. Even if you could stop them getting through on the international flights, what about all the internal ones between US cities – Dallas to Palm Springs, Atlanta to Birmingham – who's gonna check on all of them. If these guys are willing to go down with the ship – well, it's just not possible.'

'If that's true, then why would anyone fly at all?'

'Well, George, now you're getting to the meat of it. See, we all buy into the lie. We all tell ourselves the FBI or the CIA or whoever is gonna bust these guys before it can happen to us. Truth is, it's a zero-sum game.'

'You've lost me.'

Margie pulled herself up to the next step to make her point. Her skin now resembled a prune's.

'The Arabs know we could nuke the goddamn Muslim world back to buggery if we got riled enough. We, on the other hand, know that they can fuck with us big time, fuck with our way of life right here at home.'

'Like what?'

'Like what? Planes falling from the goddamn skies onto our cities, shopping malls in Boise, Idaho, disintegrating in suicide bombs.' She became thoughtful. 'Bottom line, it's not that different from the old Mutually Assured Destruction deal we had going with the commies.'

George was a little intimidated by her passion. 'I hadn't thought of it like that.'

'Listen, my friend, I was one of the forty-nine per cent who didn't vote for that half-wit cowboy retard. We was robbed, buddy!'

Margie got out of the hot tub, moved to a nearby sun lounger and swathed herself in towels. She rooted around in a small canvas bag she had brought with her and pulled out a large pack of Lay's potato chips. On the bag it said: 'Kosher for Passover. 2 packs for $1.99 from Ralphs.'

She smiled. 'I mean, don't get me wrong. This is a great fucking country!'

George climbed out and joined her, drying off before he sat down. The mood seemed to have changed. He was feeling a little melancholy.

'Yeah, a great country, but not one to be alone in,' he said.

She looked at him. 'Oh, come on, George, you're not alone.'

'I used to think I'd have more people in my life – as time went on, I mean.'

'Doesn't work that way,' she said. 'In fact, the opposite is true.

No one really "gets us" in the end. We're the sum total of our lived experience. Not so bad for me though, since I gave my life to Jesus Christ.'

George laughed aloud. 'Yeah right!'

Margie responded merely with a smile.

He looked at her. He could see she wasn't kidding. 'For real?'

'Surprised?'

'I had you down for ... well, Jewish.'

'Jesus was a Jew.' She had a twinkle in her eye.

'Tell me you're not one of those fire-and-brimstone, God-created-the-dinosaurs ball-breakers?'

'Nah, I'm more of a New Testament kinda girl – do unto others and all that jazz.'

'No offence,' he said, 'but you drink like a goddamn fish and smoke like a chimney!'

'None taken.'

'Don't they have rules for that?'

'Rules cramp my style.' She seemed to be enjoying this.

For a moment, George wrestled with the idea of telling her about his great crime, then just blurted it out.

'If you're a Christian I feel I should tell you something. I had an abortion ... I mean, I paid for one ... I mean Beatrice, my partner, she actually paid for it but she doesn't know that ... it wasn't hers ...' He suddenly felt acutely embarrassed.

There was a long silence. Margie's jaw dropped open, then she exploded with laughter.

George wriggled with humiliation. 'Christ, I can't believe I just told you that!'

'What kinda soap opera world have you been living in, my man!' She was rocking backward and forward with laughter.

'Oh gawd.' He was mortified.

'What, you thought I was going to judge you or something?'

'I dunno.' His survival mechanisms were kicking in. He needed to save face. Flattery ought to do it.

'I just thought I could trust you. I know I barely know you, but even in the short time we've known each other …'

'Oh, give it a rest, George!' She nodded at his crotch. 'Got a little shrinkage going on down there, a little corduroy sac?'

He gulped. She was more than a match for him.

'Self-pity and pretty words ain't gonna do it this time, hon. You're in more trouble than you know.'

She was packing up to leave.

'Yeah? Ever since I've been here, I've had a feeling—'

'Listen to your feelings … and lock your goddamn door!'

'Have I said something to …'

Margie set her bag down, crossed to where he sat and cupped his chin in one hand. She looked almost maternal.

'Look, sweetie, you're a good kid. I'm sure you had your reasons. I want you to promise me one thing. If you ever, you know, find yourself in a position to make amends … well, you spoil that child every chance you get.'

George looked at his feet. He felt ashamed.

'One last thing, a little bird tells me that you're getting ready to head into East Vegas.'

George bristled. 'What little bird?'

'Well, Timmy at the bar for a start. You've been asking citizens all over this place if they've seen some black chick you used to know.' Her expression became more serious. 'Be very, very careful, Georgie. I'm older than you. I'm even older than I look.'

He was about to say something flattering but she placed a finger over his lips.

'A fella like you needs to watch his back in this town. You be careful, you hear me?'

She reached inside her bag and pulled out a small velvet pouch. She opened the neck and shook a small silver medal on a chain out onto the metal table. Embossed on the surface of the medal was a figure holding a lance and at his feet was a coiled serpent.

'Know who that is, George?'

'Should I?'

'That's your patron saint.'

'Oh yeah?'

'Saint George is one of the most venerated saints in the Catholic, Anglican, Eastern and Oriental orthodox churches. He's immortalised in the tale of Saint George and the Dragon.'

'I knew that.'

'Yeah right!'

He found this all rather unsettling. 'Margie, as interesting as all this is …'

'The dragon makes its nest at a spring that provides water for the village. The citizens have to dislodge this guy from time to time to collect water. Each time they offer the dragon something – a human sacrifice, an innocent. The victim is chosen by drawing lots. Now, one day this happens to be the infant prince. Very democratic, doncha think? Of course, the king prays for his son's life to be spared and whadaya know, along comes Saint George on his travels. He faces down the dragon, protects himself with the sign of the cross, and – bada bing, bada boom!'

As she was speaking Margie made the sign of the cross over George's head. George squirmed a little and looked around to see if anyone was watching.

'Ooookaaaay!'

Margie continued unabated. 'He slays the dragon and rescues

the prince. The grateful citizens abandon their ancestral paganism and convert to Christianity.'

'And?'

'You don't have to believe any of that, George. Just wear the pendant for me.'

Suddenly there was a hissing sound all around them. The irrigation sprinklers had kicked in, spraying the plant and flower displays around the pool area. They were both instantly showered in a fine mist.

Margie had walked off some distance.

'George, I'm out of here tomorrow in the A.M.' she shouted back. 'I've got a ride with a Canadian family as far as the Coachella Valley.'

He looked at her through the mist. The artificial light created a prism effect, surrounding her in rainbows.

She turned toward him again. 'Although it might not seem like it at times, honey, I want you to understand one thing: you are not alone.'

He glanced down at the religious medal in his hand. When he looked up again she was gone.

Someone opened the door to the bar, and music and laughter tumbled out into the night air. He thought he heard a man's voice say, 'Do the right thing. Make her proud.'

Returning to his room, he collapsed onto his bed. The space still hadn't been cleaned but he felt disinclined to do anything about that. He double locked his door and seriously considered wedging a chair against the handle. He was spooked; there was no denying it. Just another day in Sin City.

It was late now and his eyelids felt heavy. He absent-mindedly fingered the St George medallion that now hung around his neck while flicking through the various TV stations. The highlights of the Baboov fight had just ended on ESPN. The scene he'd witnessed earlier played out again in the ring but this time from a different angle. A perma-tanned, tuxedoed sports presenter with a Botox smile and plastic hair thrust a microphone in the face of the champion. Behind Baboov was a tall wiry Hispanic with pitted cheeks, and wary eyes that darted around the ring. He wore an LVMPD shield on a chain around his neck. To his left stood a young man in a hooded sweatshirt, hands thrust deep into its pockets. He seemed incongruous, but then he looked quickly away from the camera and down at the ground. He manoeuvred himself backward through the crowd, away from the melee while grabbing at the shoulder of another crowd member and pulling him along.

George shot upright on the bed. Wearing Ray-Ban Wayfarers and grinning from ear to ear as he was pulled away from the mob was the unmistakable visage of Lou Plutus. George bounded across the room and threw open the closet door. He reached inside the jacket hanging there, where he knew he'd left Lou's borrowed Ray-Bans. They were gone.

Nothing surprised him any more. Not the wallet that seemed to replenish his cash on a daily basis, nor the clocks, calendars, his watch and the newspapers that all insisted the date remained September 12th, 2001, despite what seemed like an eternity passing. Jet lag, time zones, hallucinogenic flashbacks. Any attempts at rationality didn't cut it any more.

The cameras now turned their full attention on Minos Baboov. He struck a pose with a bodybuilder side view, tensing his massive, sweating bicep. Tattooed on his upper arm were the three heads in profile of Marx, Lenin and Stalin set against a red flag and a hammer and sickle. Below that, on his lower arm, George saw the now familiar logo of the Webcore Corporation.

Chapter 30

Sheriff Fox McKinley went to his office window and anxiously peeked between the wooden slats of the blind – darkness, save for a blue neon sign flashing the word 'Nails' at the front of the Korean beauty parlour across the street.

He snapped the slats closed and smoothed down his thick silver-grey moustache in an agitated fashion. He had been a fool to send Deputy Harry Shankill Bailey on such a potentially dangerous errand but he had had little choice.

He was loath to admit it, but the Sheriff's Office leaked like a sieve these days. To test his theory he'd casually mentioned 'in confidence' to a couple of deputies that he'd received a memo from the Governor's Office in Carson City intimating that the state legislature was about to slash overtime pay rates, beginning with the LVMPD, who were known to have a prodigious annual bill in this regard. Approximately one hour and fifty minutes later, a fraternal Captain of Detectives, Lucian de los Santos, was calling him, asking after his health and that of his good lady wife before enquiring – obliquely, of course – about rumours of pay cuts. The memo had been fictitious and McKinley claimed no knowledge of it, but the ruse had served its purpose.

So when the sheriff decided to put a tail on de los Santos, he knew it had to be done sensitively. It wasn't a task that could be entrusted to just anyone. Additionally, McKinley wanted to make sure that his claim that the spic was up to his ass in shady dealings with the Russian crime families couldn't be dismissed as an old man's preoccupation with the one that got away. He needed hard evidence. De los Santos had never met Harry – never seen him in uniform and definitely never seen him with Fox. In many respects the boy was the obvious choice.

Harry had sat some five rows back from de los Santos and his party at the Baboov match – plaid shirt, casual jacket, glasses, sipping beer from a styrofoam cup like some overgrown frat boy who had got Big-Fight-ticket lucky through a radio show phone-in. Fox figured that his lack of experience with undercover work might even be advantageous.

'Just be yourself,' he'd told the young man, 'and keep your eyes and ears open. Don't make eye contact with the targets, and do not under any circumstances follow any of those under surveillance into a place that is private or away from the public gaze.'

Harry's enthusiasm for the project was predictably unbridled. Fox felt confident in his charge's ability to undertake the task successfully, but there was something about Harry Shankill Bailey that remained an imponderable.

Sometimes he just saw things differently from those around him and, more worryingly, acted on the conclusions he came to with a single-mindedness that didn't take into account any perspectives other than his own.

When he was younger, Rita had taken time to try and curb his tendency for impulsiveness. But both surrogate parents agreed that the origins of Harry's personal vagaries were probably rooted in the time prior to meeting the McKinleys, or, indeed, before being placed in the adoption home. Crucially, Harry could shed no light on this period himself.

One thing was for sure, if Rita got wind that Fox had sent the boy out on such a potentially dangerous errand, she would make the sheriff's life a living hell for the foreseeable future. Shit, never mind Russians or corrupt cops; fear of reprisal from Rita was primarily why they had to meet here in his office, lights out, after hours.

McKinley settled down in his seat and rubbed at the vulnerable joint behind the knee brace he had taken to wearing when off duty. Car headlights swept across the window, briefly illuminating the slats in high beam. He crossed to the door and opened it.

Harry gave him a carefree wave. He had a six-pack of Miller under his arm. The sheriff stood aside and brusquely waved him in.

'What's eatin' you?' Harry asked.

'You think you've come to a party, boy?'

'Just thought you'd appreciate a cool one is all, waitin' here alone.'

'I sent you out to do a job, son.'

Harry could see McKinley was genuinely riled. He felt chastened.

'Now hold up a minute, I'm all ready to make my report. Let me get in through the door first though.'

McKinley took the beers from him, pulled one from the pack and prowled the room looking for an opener in the desk drawers. He cursed, pulled off his belt and opened the bottle with the buckle. Harry slipped out a long-neck, crossed to where McKinley had sat down and made a whole show of twisting off the cap with a fizz.

'Screw-tops,' he said.

They both found it hard to hold back a smile.

'You ever heard of a telephone, boy?'

'Got one right here.' Harry tapped his pocket.

'Ever consider checking in with base?'

'Thought you wanted this low key.'

'Christ, Harry, it was your first time at this kinda thing.'

'You worried about me?'

'I was worried for Rita – worried she'd be worried.'

'But she didn't know 'bout any of this.'

'Exactly! I had to worry for her!'

'Nothing to worry about.'

'So what you got?'

'Party were four in number. De los Santos, a small fat man, a skinny young man, and a spade pimp.'

Fox straightened out his leg with some difficulty and put both feet up on the desk.

'No shit, Sherlock, is that it?'

'Ask me!'

'What?'

'This will go better if you ask me questions.'

He held the young man's gaze, gauging whether he was taking the piss.

Harry pushed back in the chair, rubbed his eyes and yawned.

'Seriously. Ask me somethin.'

'Well, maybe you could put a little more meat on the bones of those … descriptions.'

'Now you're getting it!' Harry said enthusiastically. 'Well, the good captain you know already. The little fat guy looked weird up close. I followed him to the john. It looked like he was wearing a lot of make-up, like he had a bad skin problem or he'd been burned or something.'

'Russian? Eastern European?'

'No, but outa town. New York I'd say.'

'The kid … the skinny guy?'

'Yeah, Russian for sure. Kept his hood up and his cell clamped to the side of his head most of the time. Didn't even watch the fight. Was talkin' to somebody throughout.'

'The black guy?'

'One hundred per cent sleazeball. Kangol cap, velvet suit, blinged up big time.'

'No women?'

'Not that I saw. Not with them, not at the fight.'

Fox took a deep pull on his bottle and burped loudly. 'Pardon me … Did de los Santos seem to you to be making a big deal of anyone in particular?'

'The young guy didn't say much to him directly, but when he did he listened. Besides, he was so keen to kiss Baboov's ass and to look good for the cameras … well, he just couldn't stay outa the ring before or after the fight. You can watch it all on the sports channel.'

'Sounds like Lucian okay. How did you figure the spade for a pimp?'

'A couple of uniforms fingered him for me.'

'What!' McKinley leapt up from behind his desk, knocking over his beer. 'You were made?'

'Calm down, calm down.' Harry patted the air in front of him. 'Billy Bale, I go bowling with him sometimes. He's on crowd duty. I'm chattin' with him outside when this sleaze comes out, so I make a joke of it – what line of work do you imagine that gentleman is engaged in kinda thing?' He looked pleased with himself. 'Billy gave it up right away. Lamont Riddle, "The Riddler" they call him, cuz when they've nabbed him in the past he always gives more questions than answers – what do you take me for? what do you think my lawyer will do with your shitty-ass case? do you know how much this Rolex is worth? – that kinda thing.'

McKinley was still agitated. 'And what if Officer Bale just happens to mention to his boss that he was chatting with you out front of the big fight?'

'So what. I can't go to a fight like any regular citizen? This is a small enough jurisdiction, Fox, and an even smaller law enforcement community.'

The older man ran his hands through his grey hair thoughtfully. He could see his deputy was right.

'Any unexpected calls to you from the LVMPD – any apparently innocent questions coming from that quarter – you tell me immediately, okay?'

'Sheeeiiiit, okay!'

There was an awkward pause.

Fox tried to lighten up. 'Look, kid, ya did good. It's just I need you to realise that if we keep at this there's every likelihood that I'll be puttin' you in harm's way, and that makes me sick to my stomach.'

'I know it.'

'This is an adult dose, son. If I'm right about this, we're fixin' to go up against a group of individuals who are trafficking whores, dope and guns … and who may be covering for someone who murders little black kids. Throw in a senior detective on the take, well, you can see how all this can go belly up in a major way.'

'I hear ya. I'll be careful … Mom.'

McKinley shot him a sideward glance, then abruptly made to go for him but pulled back, smiling. Harry played at closing up in a defensive posture and uncoiled, looking pleased to be back on familiar ground with Fox. The sheriff couldn't suppress a welling up of affection.

'My God, boy, the good citizens of this here Silver State can sleep easy. Deputy Bailey's on the job.'

Harry rose from the chair smiling. He flipped his revolver out of its low-slung holster, spun it around a finger, then cupped the handle in his palm, feeling its weight. He made to toss it from one hand to the other but miscalculated. It fell on the wooden boards with a heavy clunk.

Fox McKinley's grin stiffened into a grimace.

Chapter 31

Lou Plutus emerged from the toilet of his hotel room, fanning his hand in front of his face.

'Pheeewww! You could build a pier with what just fell out of my ass.'

Virgil sat in front of a low glass table arranging Ritz crackers in small piles as if they were casino chips. A contemporary country station played in the background – some gal yowling, 'No more chicken 'n' gravy, til you take me down to that little white church.'

'Did ya hear me, sonny? The world just dropped out of my bottom!'

Lou laughed at his own joke as the cistern gurgled and hissed in the background. He looked askance at Virgil.

'Hey, lighten up why doncha? Why so serious?'

Virgil flipped a cracker into his mouth and leaned back, putting his hands behind his head.

'Because I appreciate the gravity of the situation.'

'And I don't?'

'Given the tasks awaiting you, you seem of a rather cheery disposition.'

'Just tryin' to lighten the load, my man.' Lou was momentarily reflective. 'That Anvil guy was right on. When you cross over – cross that line, I mean – anything's possible.' He smiled.

Virgil feigned surprise. 'What, you mean you are just now coming to that conclusion? Did you not murder your own president?'

Lou shrugged and exuded mock indignation. 'What, me personally?'

'And your people know that, but they deny it to this day.'

'JFK was a pussy hound, and he fucked with the wrong people.'

'In former Soviet, as children we are taught in school that this was a military coup. Your bullshit land of the fucking free!' Virgil spat it out.

Lou looked up at him and smiled. 'I ain't no goddamn patriot. If you're tryin' to get a rise outa me you're wasting your breath.'

Virgil wasn't finished. 'And you cunts never landed on the fucking moon either!'

Lou chuckled and settled back, linking his fingers contently across his gut. 'When do we move on Bailey, get the tape back to you know who.'

'When they say so.'

'And when will that be?'

'When all the pieces are in place. The content of the tape – the Kompromat – is obsolete to us if exposed too soon. The big man, he is not there yet, but he will be.'

Lou appeared suddenly excited. But dread was never far behind his faux bravado. 'What do I call him when I meet him ... you know, the big man?'

Virgil seemed wary. 'You call him "Sir".'

Lou smirked. 'Well, the big guy ... let's face it, he's got cotton candy hair and a face that looks like it's been dipped in Cheetos dust.'

'So?'

'Well, I mean ... he's hard to take seriously.'

Virgil stared at him in disbelief. 'Idiot! Shallow, yes. Vain, of course. But don't be fooled by the act. My advice – you've seen the tape, yes? – just look at the ground and call him sir.'

Virgil crossed to the bathroom and, lifting a can of deodorant, began to spray the air liberally.

Lou chuckled. 'Essence of Plutus.'

'Yes, that would be about right. I imagine your essence is rank,' said the young man, screwing up his face. He returned to the glass table.

Lou mocked his revulsion. 'I'm very, very hurt. I take my anal hygiene very seriously.'

When he saw that he couldn't goad him any further, Lou relented. 'Say, that Baboov – he's some piece of work isn't he? What's the story with all those tatts?'

Virgil looked bored, like he was babysitting a precocious child. He cut the tower of crackers and stacked them into three piles and sighed.

'Russian criminal tattoos have a complex system of symbols.'

'You think Baboov's got one on his cock?'

Virgil ignored him. 'The ink is often made from burning the heel of a shoe, mixing the soot with urine and injecting it into the skin with a sharpened guitar string attached to an electric shaver.'

'Like maybe a worm … that turns into a snake, know what I mean?' Lou laughed.

Virgil closed his eyes and rubbed his temples with his fingertips in little circular motions. He rose slowly, crossed to the window and looked out.

Vegas was coming to life. Trails of cars sat at junctions and stretched in four directions, all blinking lights shimmering slow motion.

'This moronic inferno,' Virgil mumbled under his breath. 'Perhaps the most lamentable sinners of all. They live lives neither meritorious nor reprehensible. They know their past and are even able to see their future, but they know nothing of the present.'

He turned and looked at the fat man quizzically. 'I've never understood why you kept the tape in the first place.'

Lou shrugged. 'It came into my possession. I dunno ... insurance, some leverage for the future, unforeseen circumstances.'

Virgil was astounded. 'Leverage? With him? He's made an art out of hustling.'

'Look, I had no idea what was on it until I watched it. I mean, Christ knows I wish I never had.'

'But you did, Lou, you did, and you sought to profit from it, and then you lost it.' Virgil frowned. 'What did you expect?'

'Well, none of this, that's for fucking sure!'

'How did you obtain it?'

'From that sand jockey, the prick who caught himself on camera at the end of, you know, the action. Guess he had the same idea. Protection, insurance ... whatever.'

There was a bleep from inside Virgil's hooded sweatshirt. He reached in for his phone and looked at the screen.

'It seems that one of his "acolytes" has already located and engaged Mr George Bailey, but there was an intercession. We expected as much. Forces rally to his aid even now.' He placed the phone on the table and looked at Lou gravely. 'We need to ask Minos Baboov for help in this, but it must be you who buries the blade.' A shadow passed across his face. 'And I who must record the deed. That is what he wants.' He seemed crestfallen.

Lou examined his fingernails. 'If I said I'll do it, I'll do it!'

'And the child?'

'One less nigger.'

Virgil's face registered dread and disgust simultaneously. He had previously been instructed by his masters to encourage Plutus to further debase himself. 'He must come to know self-loathing. He must make it his friend,' they had said. Virgil could see now that he needed little encouragement.

The fat man noticed his disdain and snapped, 'You judgin' me, freak?'

Virgil leisurely uncrossed his legs and, crossing the room, smashed his fist full into Lou's leering features.

'What the fuck?' Lou screamed.

'No one told you to enjoy this.'

Blood seeped from Lou's nose and mouth and got caught in his teeth.

Virgil pulled his hood tighter around his face. 'Too bad you don't believe in anything. Then at least you could pray for forgiveness.'

He pocketed his phone and left the room.

Chapter 32

A week ago he never would have never believed it, but George Bailey was tiring of the Las Vegas Strip. He had tarried by the pool for most of the morning without getting wet himself.

The dark surface of the pyramid hotel seemed to soak up the midday desert sun, then reflect it back in waves of almost unbearable heat that seemed capable of knocking you off your feet.

A fine mist of cooling water spray puffed clouds from some of the poolside canopies. Businessmen and vacationers stood in flabby, pink-skinned huddles using floating beach and pool inflatables as tabletops for their drinks. They chatted on mobile phones and hailed each other from across the pool and mezzanine. As the day went on, their laughter grew louder.

George sensed that the trauma from back East was dissipating. Despite the relentless TV images irrevocably burning their way into the collective consciousness, it had all seemed so much like a Hollywood disaster movie that people had begun to treat it that way. Perhaps the alternative was too awful – well, while on vacation anyway.

He had earlier felt a fool when, on spotting the athletic curves of a young black woman squeezed into a white bikini, he had rushed up to her with inappropriate haste and put a hand on her shoulder.

'Jaffé?'

'Oh no, you just didn't! Well, excuuuuse me!' The woman had turned around, indignant, perfectly executing a ghetto head-and-shoulder roll while wagging an accusatory finger.

'Sorry, my mistake,' George had whimpered.

'Ummm, hummm. You bet ya ass!' She had prodded a fat friend picking at her toes. 'Can you believe that?'

The location of the Luxor Hotel at the western end of that pulsating thoroughfare of Strip meant that he could effectively walk from one radiant extremity to the other, passing by or through all the casino hotels of note and their signature attractions.

There was the Excalibur, with its cheesy, plastic 'ye olde' decor and 'Lords' and 'Ladies' washrooms, and the Tropicana and MGM, with their Mob history practically etched on the collapsed faces of the broken and crushed croupiers.

Since his brush with the busker outside New York, New York he'd tried not to look up at the make-believe Manhattan skyline. But he always did. The towers were still missing. Could they ever have been there? He didn't trust his own memory now. It made the hair prickle on the back of his neck.

On down the Strip, the pomp and self-importance of the pretend illuminated Eiffel Tower in the Paris vied with the much-touted 'Dancing Fountains' of the iconic Bellagio for 'big dog' status on this premier central stretch of gambling real estate. George watched the endless lines of Asian tourists wait patiently behind their Nikons and Olympus on tripods for the classical music to start and the free lightshow to begin.

An old lady in a tutu, bent and misshapen, moved in a parody of interpretive dance while hustling for dollars. A tall, shaggy, blue Cookie Monster posed for pictures with children and drunks, as did an army of Elvis impersonators. He wondered how they all survived the relentless searing temperatures in those costumes.

After a while it was a cinch to tell the out-of-town suckers on a weekend bender from the jaded casino workers changing shift. There were the senior couples, retirees who had motivated themselves throughout years of mediocre payslips and mounting medical bills to finally make this 'trip of a lifetime'. There were the tawdry losers who lived out of a shabby backpack, and grabbed soap and hot water privileges from the men's room and furtive sleep from the deep leather chairs of casino sports lounges in front of huge plasmas, their baseball caps pulled down low, always wary of being rousted by an in-house security guard: 'Ya can't sleep here ya bum ... make a bet, buy a drink or get out!'

George stopped a moment to pull at the heels of his chaffing loafers and tug down his cotton briefs, which had sucked up uncomfortably into his ass crack. It was mercilessly hot. Human soup bubbled and seethed everywhere he looked, all meandering pointlessly back and forth, back and forth. On and on through mile after mile of designer shopping malls. Gucci and Armani and Yves Saint-Laurent. Expensive clothes for people with bad taste.

He tried to stay within the air-conditioned walkways linking the hotels, but had to leave these occasionally for pedestrian footbridges at major intersections, joining once again with the shuffling throng under the unforgiving desert sun. Waiting for the lights to change he was relentlessly proffered small cards with pictures of busty women, a phone number on the flip side. Greasy types touted photo-ops with sedated pythons and iguanas, multi-coloured to look like Mohicaned punk rockers.

A young black man gave witness, a microphone and speaker slung over his shoulder: 'I don't want your money. I don't want nothing from y'all but to help y'all. It pains me, it saddens me that y'all are going to hell. But you can change all that today, right here, right now.' George thought he sounded sincere. No one was listening.

It was getting dark, night-time desert dark. He trudged on and on, looking for black faces in the endless crowd, looking for Jaffé Losoko. On past the Flamingo where Bugsy Siegel had started it all, past Caesar's Palace, with its mock ancient decadence, and the Venetian, where motorised gondolas were steered by out-of-work actors in striped shirts, singing 'O Sole Mio'. He reached the fringes, the eastern periphery of Circus Circus, the Algiers and the Sahara, hanging on by their fingertips at the edges of the whirling, flashing, gushing, surging, money-mad mega-strip. He walked all the way to the Stratosphere Tower, rising up like a neon-jewelled hard-on over a thousand feet into the air, splitting the ink-dark sky.

He had come further than he'd intended. He was almost at Fremont Street. Downtown – Glitter Gulch, Old Vegas. The covered pedestrian mall looked like an Aladdin's cave of X-rated sparkle and twinkle. 'Vegas Vic', the huge neon cowboy, winked at him, pulled on his cigarette and gave him a thumbs-up.

Above him more than twelve million LED lamps illuminated an overhead video-art installation canopy. Even though it was night, they created a replica of a beautiful, benign Mediterranean blue sky, tinged with dusk at the boundaries. The clarity and authenticity of the image was astounding. Suddenly it changed to a video of a fat-bodied passenger jet roaring across the canopy above him. He tilted his head back until his neck hurt. It was quickly followed by a fighter plane, rockets blazing. It seemed familiar and unnerving. The image changed again to a bursting fireworks display, then a sky filled with benign cherry blossom and the sound of birdsong.

George felt done in. All day, as he walked, he had been staring into the faces of everyone in his eyeline, hoping to register the striking countenance of Jaffé Losoko. All day he'd thought of little else but the fact that she hadn't left the country as he'd hoped, but had taken his money – Beatrice's money, the abortion money – and found her way here to the Vegas sex industry.

Beatrice. She would have loved all this. He wanted to believe that she was in mourning for him, grieving for the man who had gone ahead without her, who she thought was now atomised, at one with the fuselage of United Airlines Flight 93 and the clay of Somerset County, Pennsylvania.

A wave of fatigue swept over him. His feet hurt; his chest hurt. He felt desperately lonely. He longed to walk back into her life with all the associated joy and forgiveness that any resurrected prodigal son might hope for.

He sat down on a concrete bollard but stood up again almost immediately. The sharp point of the Digital8 in his pocket had dug uncomfortably into his groin. He pulled it out and held it in the palm of his hand. 'Webcore.'

His attention was caught by a loud electronic braying, triggered by a shop door opening and closing. The owner must be stone deaf, or spend all his time at the rear of the store.

'Phil the Greek's Electrics', said the storefront. The window was full of audio and visual devices. It seemed incongruous among the fast-food outlets, casinos and strip joints. He walked toward the orange glow and saw instantly what he was looking for: a Hitachi 500X Digital8 Camcorder. At last he would be able to see what that prick Lou was keeping under lock and key and maybe get a handle on this whole Webcore business. Now that the little bastard was here in town somewhere it seemed more pressing than ever.

The door said 'Push' but he found that it pulled open toward him. 'Eeeeee … Awww' brayed the door. He stood alone in a small, brightly lit space surrounded by glass cases and cabinets containing cameras, mobile phones, MP3 players and fake Rolex.

'One minute. Give me one minute,' said an accented voice from the back room.

George reached into his pocket for Beatrice's American Express card. For the first time it occurred to him that if he continued to use it, the card statement would let Beatrice know that he was still alive. That wouldn't do. He wasn't ready to come back from the dead just yet. He was about to turn around and leave the store when a shuffling of feet made him stop.

Looking up, George winced. Before him was a stoutish man in his mid-fifties, wearing a T-shirt with the logo, 'What would Jesus bomb?' He had a purplish-blue eight-ball haemorrhage in his left eye that seemed to pulse. His lips were cut and cracked. George had some trouble forcing himself not to stare.

'Whad-ken-i-gedcha?'

'Ummm, can I see the Hitachi camcorder … the one in the window?'

The man reached down below the counter and slid back a glass partition. Reaching in, he produced the model George had asked for and placed it in front of him on the counter.

'One-hundred-thirty-nine-ninety-nine. I give you for one-hundred-twenty-five dollars. No tax.'

George picked it up and flipped the lens cap. He peered into the viewfinder and inadvertently hit the zoom button. The window filled with the blotchy red and purple haematoma of the shopkeeper's eye, the semi-solid mass of blood clot and tissue gently undulating. George almost dropped the camera.

The man smiled knowingly. 'Careful whad you point dat at.'

'That's some kind of a shiner you got yourself there.'

'Fuckin' redneck bastards!' He mimicked a spitting action on the floor.

'You get beat on?'

'They beat me cuz they think I'm a dirty fuckin' Muslim. Me, whose family fought against those Turk motherfuckers as far back as 1922. ME! A GREEK!'

His bad eye seemed to enlarge and contract as if it were breathing.

'Because of New York you mean, because of the towers?'

'Those fuckin' raghead bastards!' He placed both his hands on the counter for support. The knuckles were bloodied and bruised. He took a deep breath and got control of himself again.

'One-hundred-twenty-five-dollars.'

George thought for a moment and fished out the cassette tape from his pocket. 'Will it play this?'

The man held out his hand. George gave him the tape and the Greek held it up close to his face.

'No problem. Can play, but tape is electronically locked.'

'What do you mean?'

'No copies, can't make copies.'

'That's okay.'

'One-hundred-twenty-five-dollars. Will throw in earphones for listening.'

George reached into his pocket for the card, still unsure if he should use it. When he withdrew it, it was wrapped in two crisp hundred-dollar bills. His amazement must have been visible.

'Whad, ya don't know how much ya worth?'

George smiled, mystified. 'Cash okay?'

'Always.'

'I'll take it in the case, as it comes. No need to box it.'

'Comes with lead for play on TV screen.'

'Thanks.'

'Staying local?'

'The Luxor.'

The man shook his head. 'Now dat's just asking for trouble.'

'How d'ya figure that?'

'That pyramid, it's Egyptian. That would be sacrilege to dem, no? I mean, the light beams straight up into the air. Flying in at night, those crazy Muslim fucks – it's perfect for dem.'

'I hadn't figured it that way.'

'Go figure it my friend!'

The cab ride back to the hotel was sticky and uncomfortable. He pressed the button to open the window but the sullen driver insisted on closing it again. He almost left the video camera on the back seat, remembering just in time before the car edged out from the kerb. He'd already put the stolen Webcore tape into it.

With the camera firmly lodged under his arm, George made his way back to his room. He passed through the pool area again, so different to this morning. Deserted now, velvet ropes stretched between short brass poles with a notice announcing 'Pool Times 8 a.m.–8 p.m.' Sun loungers and tables had been rearranged with military precision into straight lines, and bins and ashtrays were emptied and tiles hosed down, ready for the next morning's early-bird activity. There was a faint whiff of chlorine and coconut suntan oil. Illuminated from underneath, the surface of the water shimmied with a pale blue light. It appeared irresistibly cool and inviting.

He looked around furtively for any sign of staff or guests. Some music from a hotel bar floated on the late-night air over the low hedges and through the collapsed parasols. No one stirred.

George pulled the elasticised top of his underwear up above the waistband of his pants and looked down. Black button-front boxers … perfect. He set the camera down under a recliner, took off his shirt, shoes and pants and placed them on top. He crept stealthily to the pool's edge and squatted, his toes gripping the edge.

Suddenly he froze.

The hissing of what sounded like a hundred serpents surrounded him on all sides. The water sprinklers had kicked in, spraying the flower beds and grassy knolls with rotating jets. He breathed out.

With one last quick look around the pool area, he took a deep breath, clamped his nose closed between thumb and finger and tumbled head over heels into the silver-blue pool. He touched the bottom with his feet and pushed off. The shock of the cold felt delicious and affirming. He broke the surface, failing to suppress a boyish giggle.

Shaking his head free of excess water, he bobbed up and down, the waterline just below his nostrils. He trod water and turned full circle, noticing that he had manoeuvred his way to the centre of the pool. For a moment the ladders fixed to the four corners seemed disturbingly far away. The water was colder in the centre and George felt unexpectedly vulnerable.

He started out for the poolside but felt that something was amiss. He reached up to his throat in what had become a reflex action. His St George medallion, the one that Margie Kaufman had asked him to wear, was missing. He trod water, trying to look down through the brightly lit surface. There it was, catching the light, winking its presence from its resting place on the patterned tiles at the bottom of the pool.

He dove down, kicking his feet behind, hoping to propel himself downward. To his amazement he sank like a stone to the bottom of the pool. He squinted into the water and clutched at the chain. But he kept missing it, over and over again. Just when his lungs were about to burst he hooked it between his fingers at last. He was on his way to the surface when a dark shape entered the periphery of his vision. He twisted around to see it more clearly.

At first his rational mind rejected what appeared to be a row of three airplane seats resting on the bottom of the pool. In each

244

THROUGH HOLLOW LANDS

was someone he recognised. They were fellow passengers from Flight 93.

The man wearing the 49ers cap sat at one end, talking on a mobile phone. In the centre sat the elderly woman, now bizarrely squeezing a tube and applying hand cream underwater. No air bubbles escaped from her nose and mouth as she smiled at George. On her other side sat the air hostess who had refused him a drink.

He blinked hard and looked again. The man on the phone now seemed to have what looked like octopus tendrils reaching out toward him. To his horror George realised these were his intestines, unfurling and snaking across the distance between them.

He violently propelled himself backward through the water. The last thing he registered was the air hostess turning her face away from him. Half her head was missing, the gaping wound scorched black, small fragments of flesh and bone, like sticky shark chum, clouding the water around her.

George exploded to the surface, gasping for air and retching, and clasping the medallion. He flapped and splashed his way to the side of the pool and grabbed desperately at the metal ladders. Linking his arm through them, anchoring himself for a moment, he looked in terror over his shoulder to where he had just fled. Nothing. There was nothing to see but the pristine waters of the pool, rising and falling from his own exertions. All around him was still, save for the lapping of the water and the tinkle of the silver medallion on the pool rail.

When he turned around again to climb the ladder, George caught the scent of what he recognised as Polo cologne, while right in front of him was a pair of black-and-tan Bally Wingtips, topped by absurd lime green socks. He slowly looked up. Wearing leather pants and waistcoat, a crushed velvet shirt, bootlace tie and reverse Kangol cap, a tall, thin black man was looking down on him disdainfully.

Lamont Riddle stroked his pencil-thin goatee thoughtfully, then smiled slowly, revealing a mouthful of gold crowns.

'Believe you be the dawg askin' all over town 'bout Jaffé Rossetti.'

NEVADA

Lucian de los Santos couldn't sleep. He'd adjusted and readjusted himself under the clammy sheets a dozen times. He'd reversed the pillows to the cool side, then back. He'd cast off the coverlet and pulled it back up to his chin again. But his mind just wouldn't switch off. He had that same old feeling again, the one where he felt guilty for no obvious reason – or, at least, for no reason that he hadn't already reconciled himself to. He couldn't shake it. As Captain of Detectives, it was a decided disadvantage for a man in his position.

He thought of Sheriff Fox McKinley and immediately felt even more culpable. He tried to salve his conscience with mental images of the Webcore yacht moored in some Florida key or Caribbean bay, gorgeous, bikini-clad Eastern European hookers, primo coca, the works … but it was no good. McKinley was what a public servant was supposed to be – a law enforcer, protecting and serving. An influence for good.

Lucian thought of the hardships he'd endured in the barrio, of the black blood pooling under his dead father's head and how white society owed him and his kind. It owed him for the jungle of discrimination and prejudice and disdain and humiliation that he'd had to navigate before even being allowed to compete in their fucking meritocratic society.

He tried to visualise political power and how that might feel. But it was still no good. No matter how he tried, it was his mother's face that returned to sit behind his closed eyelids, his poor, long-suffering, sainted mother who, heartbroken after the violent death of her husband, hadn't lived long enough to see Lucian join, then scale the heights of law enforcement. Never before had she visited his nocturnal thoughts in this way, and God knows he'd done plenty that would have made her blanch with shame and mortification. What was so different this time, to cause a visitation from the dead matriarch?

He'd felt uneasy since Minos Baboov and his entourage had hit town. Despite the celebrity brouhaha and after-fight festivities, something didn't feel right. It was different from the other times. Lucian had a feeling that something else was expected, something beyond the general debauchery and privileges that those Russians associated with Webcore had become accustomed to, some special favour in the service of those way on up the food chain.

The weird pale kid, the pimp and the fat toad-man – what had they to do with any of this? The unrest at the Martin Luther King Elementary School had spooked him good. That crowd had got right up into his personal space. He had been just one more finger-jabbing, saliva-spitting black face away from calling in the riot squad that day when someone, probably Fox McKinley, had kicked in the sprinkler system and brought the whole event to a damp if timely conclusion. Those people were scared, and with good cause.

Lucian turned on his side and reached across a cluttered bedside table for the light switch. He squinted into the soft glow and groped around in the tossed bedclothes for the copy of the *Las Vegas Sun* that had probably contributed to his restlessness in the first place.

'Police Clueless in "The Black Herod" Killings', screamed the headline. The editor, Archie Monroe, had picked up on the biblical angle with the discovery of the third victim, little Morton Fender. It was undoubtedly the *Las Vegas Sun*, along with the Reverend Jonas McCord, who took most responsibility for whipping up the black community of West Vegas into a fervour of Old Testament proportions. When the fuck did the *Las Vegas Sun* grow itself a racial conscience, he wondered. He felt like going round there and confronting that ginger-headed, freckled-faced fuck Monroe, demanding to know how many African Americans they actually employed in his goddamn rag of a paper.

Under the headline was a photograph of the scene earlier that day – McCord, eyes closed, hands clasped in prayer as the sprinkler's deluge fell on him. There was Lucian, standing off to the side, linen suit sodden, stained dark, his hands raised to placate the crowd rushing for shelter. Beside the photo was a black-bordered shot of the recently murdered Curtis Owens kid proudly holding aloft his spelling bee trophy. All in all it was an unmitigated fucking disaster.

No wonder Lucian de los Santos couldn't sleep. The Atlanta crew who had worked the murders there were flying in next week. The FBI were hovering on the edge of things, reigning in their enthusiasm only because of the conventions of protocol and territoriality.

Why, then, had the skinny young Russian, who had joined them at the fight, sought an audience with de los Santos on arrival? And why did all of them, including Baboov, seem to show him such respect? Crucially, why did the weird Russian kid give Lucian an unused, still-packaged cell phone, instructing him to keep information flowing in regard to anything the Atlanta cops might turn up in the 'Black Herod' case? Why also had he insisted that on no account was the Met to hand the case over to the Feds?

Lucian could feel a migraine coming on. He pushed hard at his eye sockets with the heels of his hands. Stars and circles exploded like fireworks behind his eyelids.

He knew Fox McKinley and the Sheriff's Office would be all over this by now, official clearance or not. McKinley's hard-on for the Russian crime syndicates was common knowledge after the high-speed pursuit, crash and injuries he had suffered some time back.

Could Webcore really be tied up in some way with murdering innocent black kids?

He thought about it, lying there in the dark for hours on end, and still couldn't find a fit. Whores, porn and drugs were their MO. It didn't seem to make sense, save for one very chilling, indisputable fact. He harboured no doubts whatsoever that these were dangerous and depraved men who were capable of absolutely anything.

His mind was racing. Knowing it was going to be impossible to sleep, Lucian wearily got dressed. The large green neon digits on his alarm clock read 02:07. He wanted strong coffee and a smoke. He was up now and staying up. *Jesus*, he thought, *who else goes to work at this time? Drug pushers and whores, cops and … newspaper men. Time to pay Archie Monroe a visit.*

He knew he'd still be working on the next morning's edition of the *Sun*, and that some of his hacks blew off steam in Kenny's Bar, around the corner from the newspaper office.

He heard Monroe's New Jersey bluster the minute he walked into the place, saw his thinning ginger head nod in eager affirmation at some story a features writer was sharing with the pack.

One of the company saw Lucian approach and leaned in toward his boss to whisper a warning. Lucian pulled up a stool.

'A man with as many enemies as you, Monroe, should never sit with his back to the door.'

Archie Monroe turned sideways on.

'Captain de los Santos.' He smiled round at his posse. 'You dried off yet?'

The men bent forward conspiratorially, covering their mouths, coughing, their shoulders shaking with suppressed laughter.

'We're happy to pick up your dry cleaning bill, Captain. I mean, it's the least we can do.'

'I need five minutes, Archie, and bring coffee.' Lucian walked off to a booth at the far end of the bar.

Monroe stayed talking to his colleagues just long enough to appear nonchalant. Then he walked to the percolator, poured two mugs of coffee and followed de los Santos, banging them down on the table so they splashed a little.

'You want I should get Danish and some napkins to clean that up?' he said sarcastically.

'Sit.'

'How can I be of service, Captain?'

'It's this "Black Herod" shtick you're peddling. How'd you come up with something like that?'

'*Las Vegas Sun* … one dollar seventy-five cents, Captain. The store across the street's got so many copies they're sellin' 'em!'

'Look, Monroe, save the wise-ass routine. This is some serous shit we're talkin' about here.'

'Due respect, Captain, most folks feel it's you and your fat buddies who ain't takin' this nearly serious enough. I think you saw that this afternoon. I mean … any leads?' He arched his eyebrows and turned his palms upward, knowing the answer already.

'It's a slow business, requires painstaking and sometimes unpleasant work, like comin' down here in the early hours to hang with you sleazes.'

Monroe laughed. 'All right, all right. I've got a paper that won't put itself to bed and you … I guess you've got to get back to the other members of the Justice League of America. Cut to the chase.'

De los Santos leaned in closer. 'The Herod thing – is that hinting at what I think it is?'

Monroe smiled. 'Whadaya think it is?'

'That this isn't some race war against the black community. That whoever is doing this is knocking off spade kids in the hope of getting to one in particular.'

Archie Monroe's face darkened. 'I never said that. Show me where I said that.'

'*I'm* saying it, saying it now. Killing the first born – biblical shit to make sure he gets the one he's after.'

'That's scary stuff, Captain, and that's what I told your buddy.'

'Whadaya mean?'

'What, you thought I came up with this angle – the Herod thing?'

'Then who?'

'An unnamed source.'

'Don't jerk me around, Archie!'

'Jesus, don't you guys ever talk to each other? What are we paying taxes for?'

'Whose idea was it?'

'Why Sheriff McKinley's. He came into the office a couple a weeks ago.'

All the colour drained from Lucian's face. That irritant; that crusty discharge in the corner of the eye, that blister on the sole of the foot, that splinter under the skin. There was no doubt: McKinley was conducting his own enquiries and cutting him out of the loop.

Now he knew why he couldn't sleep.

Chapter 34

Deputy Sheriff Harry Shankill Bailey ran a finger along the wall of video cassette tapes. The shelves contained nothing but movies and TV series of classic Westerns. He noticed that some of the labels, written in a variety of inks and pens, now fading, were curling in on themselves at the edges.

Official box sets of John Wayne and John Ford movies and some Gary Cooper bookended the rows in their mock-leather vinyl and gold-embossed self-importance. In between were recordings, mostly from TV: *Rawhide, Bonanza, The Virginian, The High Chaparral, The Rifleman, Branded.* On the lower shelf was lighter fare – *F Troop, Alias Smith and Jones, The Little House on the Prairie.*

He rubbed a film of grease between thumb and forefinger while he considered what to settle down with and adjusted his wire-rim glasses on the bridge of his nose more comfortably.

From above, factory-framed and autographed photographs of 'The Duke' in full Western regalia looked down protectively on the room. Neville Brand and Chuck Connors, the Cartwright, Montoya-Cannon and Ingalls families all dutifully smiled out from their glossy Hollywood studio promotional shots. Purchased through mail order, they were mass issue prints that anyone could easily obtain. Yet they felt like real family to Harry, the family he never had. They were as real as any portrait of grandparents, parents or siblings.

He coughed to clear his throat of the saliva and mucus that invariably gathered there. His hand automatically went to the thin pink keloid scar that ran right across the front of his neck. He rubbed the protrusion at the angle of the thyroid cartilage surrounding the larynx. The line seemed more pronounced every year around this time. Harry fought a rising tide of resentment against a foggy past that offered no explanation for the person that he had become.

The one-bed apartment had been sourced and provided by Fox and Rita McKinley. It was located over a liquor store and next to a pizza joint, laundromat and video rental shack. It was perfect for any young man who might use it as a base for hanging out with friends or seducing young women. Both activities were actively encouraged by his surrogate parents, the McKinleys. But Harry remained a dedicated loner. Unable or unwilling to maintain relationships with either peers or female companions, Harry dodged the teasing and criticism of his community by being good-natured and open.

The other deputies in the Sheriff's Office had known him since he was a boy and felt naturally protective toward him. But of late, Harry had become acutely aware that no one really knew him, least of all himself.

He squinted hard at the faded writing on the spine of a box and slid it out. *The Horse Soldiers* was a 1959 John Ford civil war classic. Most of the pertinent details he had meticulously transcribed onto a sheet of lined paper placed inside the sleeve. He had watched the movie so often that he knew the script itself verbatim.

He put popcorn in the microwave and removed a beer from the refrigerator, then slipped the video into the slot of the machine. It clicked and began to play. He removed his glasses and felt his way to the bathroom. After turning the shower on, he undressed in the adjoining bedroom and stepped into the water jet. He vigorously worked the soap in his armpits, in his ass crack and between his legs, a rite that routinely took less than two minutes.

The full-length mirror opposite the shower normally steamed up instantly, but not today. For no good reason and to his complete amazement, Harry could see himself clearly. Despite his poor eyesight and the rising steam, he could make out his tall, pale, hairless body perfectly. He moved in slow motion, and could see the suds as he washed in and around his groin and the sweaty ravines that should have flanked his ballsack. He stopped and let the soap drop. It clunked to the bottom of the enamel tub.

He stared at his secret shame. His testicles had still not dropped. His penis, a tiny worm, scrunched up into nothing more than a concertinaed foreskin, barely broke the smooth lines of his groin.

He rubbed hard at his eyes, hoping to return to the myopia that rendered such routine exercises a little more bearable. But it didn't work. Inexplicably, the surrounding bathroom, the door leading to the bedroom beyond and the hallway – everywhere except the mirror and its reflection of his sorry state – remained familiarly and reassuringly blurred, out of focus. Only the body of the pale, pathetic man-child stayed in sharp definition, staring back at him accusingly, taunting him with its inadequacy, trapping him in a place that he couldn't recall, couldn't return to, couldn't escape.

Harry stood under the shower for what seemed an eternity as the hot water turned cold, the popcorn popped, the ice in the glass melted and the movie played on. He stood there staring at his reflection for an age.

From the front room he could hear a sequence he knew off by heart. The young boys of Jefferson Junior Military Academy were falling in to march on the Yankee soldiers and buy time for the Confederate army. As the band played a call to arms, he acknowledged a familiar refrain: 'The Bonnie Blue Flag'. Harry's body began to shake and heave in anguished gulps of tears.

The shower water suddenly became very hot.

As his eyesight began to deteriorate once again, and condensation fogged the mirror, he thought he could make out a shape in the foreground, a reflection of what looked like a bone-weary man hunched over a cot or small bed. He was playing a harmonica. Harry recognised his father who was serenading him to sleep with 'The Bonnie Blue Flag'. He felt this more than remembered it. But he was sure.

When he shook his head and squinted again, Harry was staring at the pale, sodden body of a young boy, the child in the reflection self-consciously covering his nakedness in the way he himself was doing now. The mirror image of the child mimicked his every move and gesture.

For no reason he could understand, and with words that made no sense to him, he balled his fists and wailed aloud in primal torment, 'Daddy, Georgie, why did you leave me? Where did you go?'

Chapter 35

'You know Jaffé Losoko?'

Lamont Riddle sucked his teeth in disapproval and held out a bony hand toward George, his wrist wreathed in gold chains.

'I don't know no Jaffé jungle-bunny Losoko shit. I'm talkin' 'bout some prime dark meat here, my man. Mmm, mmm.' He licked his lips, lizard-like. 'Jafféeeee Rossettiii … mmm, mmm. Rising queen of the Vegas skin-flick scene, you know what I mean.'

George ignored the man's proffered assistance and pulled himself up by the metal steps. He stood dripping and vulnerable by the poolside while Lamont looked him up and down disparagingly.

'Too much woman for you, that's for goddamn sure,' he said with a sneer.

'We go way back.'

'Uh huh?' Lamont arched his eyebrows and didn't seem so convinced.

'Can you give me her address?'

'I can do better than that. I can take you to her.'

George was cautious. 'Why would you do that exactly?'

Lamont's face darkened. He looked like he'd been struck. 'Don't y'all be disrespecting me now, ya hear? I come up here to do you a fuckin' solid and you givin' me attitude, standing there like some drowned fuckin' rat, runnin' ya goddamn mouth!'

George folded his arms across his chest pathetically. His paunch hung over the top of his boxers.

'Ya wanna meet with her or not?'

'Sure, yeah. Just let me get dried off and I'll be right with you.'

Lamont looked indignant. 'Well, all right then.'

'Twenty minutes, okay?'

Lamont took a thin cigarillo out of a leather case in his waistcoat, bit the end off and spat it out. 'See that fine piece of Deutsche technology in the parking lot?'

George looked across to where Lamont had gestured with his head. A pimped-up white BMW stood out from the rows of rentals.

'That be the Riddlemobile. You get your skinny white ass over there in fifteen or forget all about it.'

George gathered his clothes hurriedly; the video camera dropped to the ground with a clatter. Lamont Riddle looked around instantly, his entire frame seeming to expand and tense like some long-limbed mantis.

'Anything I can help you with there, Georgie?' His teeth sparkled.

George swept the camera up under his bundle. 'No, no, I got it.'

'Well, all right then.' The man retracted again.

'Seeing as you know my name, mind telling me yours?'

'Oh, lots of folks know you, George.' He chuckled unnervingly and his voice dropped. 'Lots of folks keen on this here ... uhhh ... family reunion too.' His face darkened.

'What was that? I didn't—'

'Lamont Riddle ... the Riddler. You gonna remember me, and that's for goddamn sure.'

Laughing, he loped effortlessly through the stacked sunbeds and folded parasols and was gone.

George headed back to his room to get dry underwear. On his way, he stopped at the concierge's desk. The man was writing and peered up over his glasses.

'Can I help you sir?'

'Sure. Can I bother you for one of those large envelopes?'

'No bother at all, Mr Bailey.'

George took the video cassette out of the camcorder and put it into the envelope, licked the flap and sealed it. He put the envelope in a security box at the main desk, and took the elevator to his room, his mind racing at the prospect of meeting Jaffé Losoko once again.

What did he want to say to her? Wallow in mea culpas and accept responsibility for the predicament he put her in? Apologise for his inability to keep his dick in his pants? Offer help in some way that he himself couldn't yet guess at?

Guilt, guilt and more guilt. Between Jaffé Losoko's legs – that was where all his recent troubles had begun.

Fuck it! He'd just know what to do when he saw her. That was all there was for it. It didn't make any sense. It just felt irrefutably right.

Having deposited the camcorder in his room and wearing fresh dry clothes he headed for his date with destiny. The casino was buzzing with activity when he stepped out of the elevator. George suddenly stopped in his tracks as he passed the roped-off high-rollers' poker area. Sitting in a wheelchair, propped up on elaborately embroidered baroque cushions, was Father Francis 'Gusher' Geryon.

He was sucking at a mojito from a straw, his face frozen in the unmistakable maniacal leer of a stroke victim. He had aged, of course, and was more corpulent than ever, but there could be no doubting the pervert tormentor of George's school days.

Geryon was being tended by a young acolyte who periodically bent forward to wipe his mouth and chin. Both wore clerical collars, Geryon in the burgundy silks of high ecclesiastical office, a golden crucifix around his neck.

The old bastard looked directly at George, his tight lips tugging at the corners into a partial, mocking smile.

'Can I help you?' said the young priest, noticing George's disbelieving stare. He had an Italian accent.

'We know each other,' said George, warily advancing.

'Oh! Were you one of Father Geryon's boys?' The young priest sniggered. 'If so, you must know each other very well.'

Some subliminal deference to the collar kept George's rising temper in check. 'Due respect, Father, but I should take that mojito and shove it down that fat fuck's throat!'

The old man chuckled – a sort of chesty, mucus gargle – his folds of fat rising and falling, jiggling with mirth.

'Dearie me,' simpered the fresh-faced curate. 'To err is human, to forgive divine.'

George felt his gut tighten with rage. Memories of St Augustine's came back, banging loudly on the walls of whatever locked and buried compartment he'd banished them to.

Geryon dropped his drink to the ground, ice and liquid spilling across the carpet and pooling at George's feet. His right hand jerked and oscillated in an almighty effort to indicate something to his helper. The young priest bent in close, pressing his ear to Geryon's mouth.

'He wants to say something to you.'

'Tell him go fuck himself!'

The old priest chortled and green sputum ran down his chin.

'He's not deaf.'

The young man bent in close again and, slowly straightening

up, smiled malevolently. 'He says, "How sharper than a serpent's tooth it is to have a thankless child".'

It was too much. George balled his hands into fists and stepped forward menacingly. The young priest raised his hands in alarmed supplication.

'He says he has a message for you.'

'He doesn't have anything to say to me that I could possibly want to—'

'He says it's from Beatrice.'

George felt the room begin to swim and fold in on itself. How could this be? The two were polarities of light and dark in his life. That Geryon knew of her existence – or she of his – made his stomach knot and his bile rise.

'He wishes to tell you himself. Come closer ... closer still.'

Fighting an urge to vomit, George inched his face nearer to the fat mouth, caked with spittle and rank with a lifetime's residue of putridity and corrupted innocence.

In an instant, giving the lie to his infirmity, the gargoyle raised both withered hands and clamped George's head between them, then slipped his plump, viscous tongue into his ear, working it there, exploring the orifice like a slug, deeper and deeper. The sudden act and the fat priest's strength took George unawares and he struggled to break free. Geryon inhaled deeply, as if trying to suck in his captive's very essence, then released his grip with a sigh, whispering softly the unmistakable words 'Baby-killer'.

George recoiled as if shot, falling backward onto the ground and into the icy puddle of spilled mojito. He pushed himself away, hands and feet propelling him backward across the floor while both priests leered after him. Pulling himself to his feet on a passing cocktail waitress, sending her tray of drinks tumbling, George ran for the parking lot.

Once outside he gasped, sucking the dry night air deep into his lungs, his body rising and falling with the effort. He looked over his shoulder only once.

The brilliant spotlight beaming into the sky from the apex of the Luxor was partly eclipsed. It was engulfed by a breathing, pulsating black cloud, moving this way and that in what seemed like one giant choreographed flourish after another. A magnet for desert flies, the shadowy pyramid appeared to be sucking this plague of insects down the shaft of light into some awful vortex of darkness.

George was badly shaken. But the sheepskin seat covers of Lamont Riddle's car smelled of marijuana smoke and cheap aftershave and he welcomed this as a return to the tangible, knowable world of mundane familiarity. He collapsed back into the passenger seat as Lamont moved off.

'Shit, dude, you look like you seen a ghost.' Lamont was driving with one hand on the wheel while patting his pockets for something.

'I think maybe I did.'

'Wouldn't be unusual for this shithole, maaan.'

'How's that?'

As soon as the question was out he wished he hadn't asked.

Lamont was incredulous. 'You serious, Georgie? Don't you know about the Luxor's rep?'

'No, but you're gonna tell me, right?'

'Dude, the Luxor is a jumper's paradise! They be queuing up to launch offa that muthafuckin' atrium that runs around the inside. Twenty-sixth floor – that's their favourite. Landing in the buffet bar and the express checkout area and shit. It was raining junkie hookers for the first three years after it opened, maaan!'

'I didn't know that.' George sank deeper into the sheepskin and placed a hand over his eyes. His head hurt. His ear was still wet where that fat fuck had despoiled him. He rubbed at it absent-mindedly with his sleeve.

'You best believe it,' Lamont said, smiling.

Lamont Riddle, it turned out, loved to talk. He produced another cigarillo, bit off the end and spat it out the window.

'Marvel of modern engineering, my ass. Six guys killed on the construction alone. Wall fell on three of 'em. Place is jinxed, dude. Fact! Something 'bout that pyramid shape. Magically sharpens razor blades or some such shiiiit.'

'You believe that stuff?'

'Look, man, I heard' – he leaned sideways toward George conspiratorially – 'that until the image of an eye is installed at the pinnacle of the tower the place will stay cursed. Ancient raghead magic or whatever.'

George continued to rub his ear with the sleeve of his shirt for the forty-five minutes it took Lamont Riddle to arrive at his first port of call – the Southern Nevada Las Vegas Aids Clinic. He squirmed uneasily when he read the plaque.

'This is where Jaffé is?'

'Someday, but not today,' Lamont said. 'No, today it's me. I got an errand to run. Come on in with me.'

Lamont noted George's reticence. He laughed. 'Walk on the wild side a little, Georgie boy.'

The clinical corridors of the facility seemed sterile and unyielding, a less than welcoming environment for the line of black men and women who sat along the walls, clutching papers and forms, waiting to be called. One woman looked distracted and picked at a scab on her arm. Several men, stick-thin with tattoos and body piercings, studiously examined the floor beneath them or the posters on the opposite wall. Eye contact was diligently avoided.

Lamont went to a window in the wall with a sign above it saying 'Inquiries'. A heavy-set Latina nurse was scratching off the columns of a lottery card with a quarter.

'Riddle. I had an appointment,' stated Lamont officiously.

'Through the double doors, turn left. Dr Silva will see you in a moment,' she said without looking up.

Lamont turned and strode off in that direction, his long legs outpacing George.

'Will I just wait here?' George asked half-heartedly.

'Shit, no son. Come with me. Ya might learn something.'

George reluctantly followed Lamont into a small cubicle. There was a bed of sorts on a gurney, a table, and various medical appliances placed around the cramped space. Charts and posters warning about the effects of STDs covered the walls, and featured graphic depictions of genitalia in advanced stages of decrepitude. George tried not to look at them.

A harassed Hispanic doctor breezed in, drawing a curtain behind him with a trailing hand. Lamont had already sat down, taken off his jacket and rolled up a sleeve in anticipation. Saying nothing, the doctor pulled on some latex gloves, tied a piece of rubber hose around Lamont's upper bicep, slapped his arm, broke a hypodermic out of a paper sachet, held it up to the light and jabbed it into a raised vein.

'This might sting a little,' he added as an afterthought.

Drawing a small amount of blood, he removed the needle and deposited the contents into a test tube. The blood made a squirting, gurgling noise as it filled. Casually he dropped needle and syringe in the waste bin, a bright yellow plastic bucket bedecked with an array of red warning stickers: 'BEWARE!' 'TOXIC MEDICAL SUPPLIES! NEEDLES! DO NOT HANDLE!' A red triangle containing a drawing of a hand with a big X through it left no one in any doubt.

'Is this your boyfriend?' asked the doctor. He was writing on a label and sticking this on the tube with the blood, but looking at Lamont while nodding toward George.

'Sheeeeeit,' spat Lamont with derision.

'Just asking. I'll do him now as well if you want. One-stop shop.'

Lamont smiled. 'What you say, George? You been a bad boy? You got a little stink on ya Johnson there?'

'Eat me!' said George indignantly.

In an instant the medic was out through the curtain and gone, saying over his shoulder, 'Check back in a week for the result.'

Lamont rolled down his sleeve and touched George fraternally on the knee.

'You intend spending any quality time with Miss Rossetti? If so, I suggest you make an appointment here yourself.'

George was suddenly impatient. 'You promised to take me to her. Instead' – he held up his arms and swung round in a circle – 'this!'

Lamont Riddle's eyes narrowed to slits. He reached into the jacket of his pocket and brought out a small silver door key with a skull-head key ring and a paper tag attached.

'Know what this is?'

'The key to your heart?'

'This is a key to her apartment with the address attached. Want it?'

George put out an upturned hand. Lamont drew the big yellow waste needle bucket to him with his foot and, holding the key up by its paper tag, dropped it through the gap in the lid. It clinked as it slid down through the used needles.

George groaned and peered in. A forest of hypodermic spikes criss-crossed each other, a jungle of glistening shards forming a barrier of blood-to-blood infection. He could see the silver metal of the key glint at him near the bottom.

'What the fuck.'

Lamont was leering. 'Sometimes ya gotta speculate to accumulate.'

The longer George stared at the key the more he felt compelled to thrust his hand in deep, just jam it right down in there, then swirl it around. Taking his chances. Letting God decide.

He pulled his fingers and thumb in tight together to make his hand as small as possible and held it over the lid.

'Oh what, now you gonna make bunny shadows on the wall?' Lamont laughed.

George's hand hovered above the winking needle pit.

Lamont Riddle shifted in his chair, ready to watch the show.

In one quick movement, George grabbed the base of the bin and tipped the whole thing out over Lamont. Needles and swabs rained down about his head and shoulders and tinkled onto the tile floor. The container bounced to the ground as George lunged for the key. He hugged it to his chest, anticipating an assault from Lamont. But it never came.

Instead the skinny pimp shook with amusement. He bent double and hooted with laughter, his lips pulled back over small, sharp gold teeth. In between gasps for air he shouted, 'Security ... Security!'

George didn't get it. 'What's so fuckin' funny?'

'You, George. You are.'

'Me? Why me? You're the one with shit all over you?'

'Cuz ... cuz I know that catchin' AIDS ... well, it's the least of your fuckin' worries ... haw, haw, haw.'

'Yeah, well now I got this.' George tossed the key in the air and caught it triumphantly. 'I don't have to look at your ugly mug no more.'

'Sure. Fine. But she ain't there.'

'What?'

'You heard me. She's out earning, man. She's a working girl, ya know?'

'Look, I'm gonna find her anyway, so—'

'Save it, George. She works at the Thunderbird Lounge, ten minutes from here ... SECURITY!'

A lardass hospital guard in khaki uniform pulled the curtain aside with his nightstick and peered in.

'This muthafuckin' cracka gone crazy, destroying hospital property and shit. I want you to take that stick and beat on his ass!'

The black guard looked embarrassed and unsure how to react. 'I'm not really on duty until six a.m. I'm just helpin' out.'

Lamont slapped his thighs in exasperation. 'See? Nobody willin' to do their muthafuckin' job no more. Place is going to hell in a handcart.'

'And you can go to hell with it. I'm goin' to the Thunderbird Lounge,' George announced.

He went to manoeuvre around the fat guard, who warily placed a hand on his baton.

'Maaaan, you won't even get through the door, you sorry piece-a-whitetrash,' Lamont said. 'They see a white man in there, they gonna goddamn cook and eat him!'

George stopped in his tracks, tiring of the Riddler's relentless know-it-all cockiness.

'So what do you suggest?'

Lamont stood up, pulled on his jacket and brushed himself down. 'Well, I just happen to be going over there myself. Why don't you come along.' He threw back his head and roared with laughter.

The Thunderbird's small, lone neon sign glimmered feebly among the darkened warehouses and shady corners of West Vegas's seedy underbelly. They paused at a brightly lit steel cage surrounding the main entrance. Lamont instructed George to look up into the CCTV camera on the wall above. A dull metallic buzz indicated that the electronic door was open. Lamont pushed on through and they were in.

The Thunderbird Lounge was just another black, blue-collar West Vegas dive bar, but what set it apart was the strange feeling that you'd stumbled into the setting of a Chandler novel. The vintage wood bar and chrome bar stools proved unremarkable enough, but nothing prepared the casual lush for the enormous mural painted in lurid reds and purples depicting Hieronymus Bosch's *The Seven Deadly Sins and the Four Last Things*.

A number of muscular black men in gold chains, wife-beater vests and basketball shirts played poker, drinking booze and ogling the big-tittied women who waited to do their fifteen minutes on the pole of the tiny burlesque stage. It was decked out in fairy lights, glitter balls and strobe flashes. Freddie King and Jimi Hendrix pumped from the small PA system. It was enough to make any ordinary Joe's pulp fiction fantasies take flight and soar. The club was about half full.

'Welcome to my world,' said Lamont, all the time nodding in this direction and that, pausing to high-five and knuckle bump, occasionally squeezing the ass of some girl or other. The heavy-set guys at the poker table barely looked up.

A single chair, ornate wrought iron with a heart-shaped back and covered in stained burgundy velveteen, sat on stage in front of the pole. Lamont leaned over the bar and shouted above the booming blues beat into the ear of a bored barman.

'Where Jaffé be at?'

The barman looked at George suspiciously, then back to Lamont. 'If you came for her gig you just missed it. She's backstage changin'.'

'Okay, if I we ...' Lamont gestured to George.

'Go right ahead, man. Be my guest.'

George felt his adrenaline pump. Why was he here? What did he have to say to her? Would she even remember him? What would Beatrice think about all of this? The whole thing suddenly felt like irredeemable folly.

Lamont led him through some double doors and into a kind of chill-out room.

'Passing through. Passing through. Don't get up,' he said to its inhabitants.

There was an unmade bed in the corner and smoke hung in the air from a large hookah on a centre table. Arranged around this, in various states of repose, were half a dozen young men. They looked Middle Eastern or Mediterranean.

George squinted through the dim light and low-hanging smoke, thinking they looked vaguely familiar. He grabbed Lamont by the arm.

'Hey, I know those guys. They were on my flight!'

They were already moving through another set of doors and out of the room.

'What, those guys? Stupid camel-jockey fuck-heads. They come around here every night, saying somethin' 'bout how they've been promised seventy-two virgins for services rendered. Seventy-two fuckin' virgins no less! Maaan, ain't been a virgin back here since ... well, probably never! Every night it's the same thing with these guys. They end up bangin' the skankiest whores in the place, then bawl their eyes out. Nessus – he's the owner – he only allows 'em to hang here cuz they spend money like it's goin' outa fashion.'

They passed down a narrow corridor which smelled of pee and disinfectant due to its proximity to the toilets and came to a door with a sad single silver star pinned to it. It suddenly swung open.

A swell of girly laughter rose and fell, and a young woman not much older than seventeen with braces on her teeth came pushing through.

'Gangway. Gotta show to do,' she said.

She passed in a trail of feather boas and a big frizzy afro. Silver tassels were fixed to her nipples and she wore a silver G-string. Her body shone with baby oil and glittery stars.

George remembered Jaffé Losoko, the quiet, religious Muslim girl he had met seven years ago and how she had lacked the confidence to show her cleavage or dress with hemlines above the ankle. Had his dalliance with her started her down a path that led her here?

Lamont stood in the doorway, making it difficult for George to see around him.

'Jaffé, honey?' He spoke as if he was talking to a toddler. 'It's the Riddler. I brought somebody to see you.'

A voice, soft and seductive with only a hint of accent, floated back. 'Lamont, baby, you know that's not the way I do business. Customers gotta make an appointment.'

'It's not business, babe. This guy says he knows you … from way back.'

There was a long silence.

'Ain't nobody knows me from way back, Lamont. I don't go way back.'

George stood on tiptoes to get a glimpse over Lamont's shoulder.

The room, long and narrow, had mirrors down both sides with naked light bulbs arranged around them. The tables in front of the mirrors were a riot of powder puffs, lipsticks, moisturiser tubes, mascara pencils, hairsprays and pill bottles. A framed, signed photo of Eddie Murphy sat beside a box of tissues. In semi-shadow at the far end George could just make out the figure of a woman seated with her back to them. A curtain was pulled across a rail off to the side – some kind of makeshift changing room.

'Sweetness, do this one thing for me, huh?' Lamont pleaded.

For the first time since they'd met, George began to wonder why Lamont Riddle was being so accommodating, why, in fact, he was so keen to bring George and Jaffé together.

The woman's voice seemed tired all of a sudden. 'Okay, but no private dances on the premises. You know Nessus. Your guy will have to cop for a hotel room like anyone else.'

She stretched slowly like a cat, her fingers linking her long arms above her head. She rolled her head one way, then the other. Even though she was sitting down and George was viewing her from behind, he could see that same firm body and those long, lean legs.

Yet he was convinced there had been a mistake. There was little about her tone, her body language or her vocabulary that suggested this was the same shy young woman who had sought political asylum from her war-torn homeland, the same young woman who had so naively fallen in love with him and denied him nothing, the same woman who had carried, all too briefly, their terminated child.

In one seamless movement she swivelled round on her chair, agilely throwing a long fishnet-stockinged leg over the back in a high dancer's arc, and faced both men in the small room.

Jaffé Rossetti was in full-on 'Sally Bowles' chic. She looked stunning – a tight lace corset pushing up her cleavage, a velvet choker around her throat, endless legs, suspenders, stilettos, the works. Her make-up was dramatic, lightening her skin tone. Her eyebrows arched, her lips were impossibly red, impossibly shiny. She had arranged her long hair extension into a ponytail and tied it over her shoulder.

'Okay,' said Lamont, 'I'm gonna leave you two lovebirds together. I guess you gotta lot of catching up to do.'

'Ohhh honey, don't go,' said Jaffé in a cooing tone while looking in a hand mirror and re-applying lip gloss.

She tilted a bowler hat on her head for full effect. She was flirting shamelessly.

George was fascinated by the sheer 'Americanisation' of her. It was undoubtedly Jaffé Losoko, but in her dress, her mannerisms, her worldliness was an inversion of the innocent girl he'd taken advantage of back in Florida.

Lamont crossed to her and bent low, kissing her affectionately on the cheek.

'Gotta go, baby girl. Webcore bullshit to attend to.'

George bristled at the name, remembering the porn movie featuring Jaffé, the Baboov's tattoo, the video he'd stolen from Lou Plutus but hadn't yet watched. He might have guessed that Lamont Riddle would be involved in some way.

George was still half in, half out of the room. Lamont walked toward him and placed a hand on his shoulder, pulling him closer.

'D'ya wanna fuck her, Bailey?' he whispered. 'Do ya wanna? Well, just go right ahead. You only get one life. There's no God, no rules, no judgements except those you create or accept for yourself. And once it's over it's over. Dreamless sleep, forever and ever and ever. So why not be happy when you're here, Georgie. Really, why not?'

'The temptation of George Bailey,' said a sardonic voice in his head. He recognised it as Margie Kaufman's.

'Beatrice won't care,' Lamont said as he walked out the door. 'She's forgotten you already.'

It shook George to the core.

*

'George-muthafuckin-Bailey!'

Jaffé stood up, placed her hands on her hips and shook her head slowly from side to side in disbelief or, perhaps, disapproval. George stood sheepishly before her, shifting his weight uneasily from foot to foot, trying to pull off his best obsequious little boy look, batting long lashes and coquettishly flashing puppy-dog eyes.

'Hi Jaffé! Howya been?'

She looked gorgeous. Somehow the quality of innocence that had always drawn him to her was still present. It was there in the lingerie flourishes, and permeated through her immaculate cosmetic sheen in a way that rendered her desirability even more undeniable.

She was still slowly shaking her head.

'Well, seems like you've grown a pair at last!'

George was slapped out of his veneration. 'Excuse me?'

'You've got some balls, running all over town shooting your goddamn mouth off about me. I don't need no attention on me, you understand?'

He was offended and perplexed. Already this wasn't going the way he'd planned. 'Well, if you'd let me explain.'

'Especially after the fix you left me in!'

There it was, and without a chance for him to get to work on her, to soften her up first. He raised his palms placatingly.

'Okay, look, that's why I'm here, all right? To maybe try to make things right between us.'

Jaffé looked incredulous. Her eyes widened at his audacity. Her jaw dropped. But then she recovered.

'Ha! What a piece of work you are, George Bailey!'

George allowed a smile to tug at the corners of his mouth. For a moment she sounded like she used to. During their short time together, it was how she had always reacted when she'd caught him out on a falsehood or some mischief: 'Ha!' A loud sigh escaped him and he regretted it instantly, regretted the inference that maybe, just maybe, he was off the hook.

'I can't believe you're here – in the US I mean. I thought after you … got yourself right … you'd be going back home.'

'Oh, did you now? Just clean up your mess for you and disappear? How convenient,' she said, sneering.

'Jaffé, it was six years ago. I … we … did what we thought was right at the time.'

'I was a child, George. I could barely speak the language. You fucked me seven ways from Sunday … and got me to thank you for it!'

He lowered his head again. 'I know.'

'What kind of a man does that? Takes advantage like that?'

'You're right.'

'You filled my head full of shit, George, and went back to your woman. Your white woman.'

'Please.'

'Left me with nothing, no one. So if you're gettin' ready to ask me how it all came to this' – Jaffé gestured around the room – 'how I came to be doin' what I'm doin'—'

'Stop!'

'I swear to God, George Bailey, if you're gettin' ready to judge me, if you pull some shit about taking me away from all of this …'

'It's been six years. A lot of water—'

'Lotta water! Now that is for goddamn sure!'

She dragged her handbag to her and, reaching in, pulled out a lighter, a pack of cigarillos and a NAA .22 Magnum Pug 5-shot mini-revolver. She lit a cigarillo and blew smoke in his face, then looked down at the gun and back at him so there could be no mistaking her fortitude.

Seeing his expression change from one of alarm to hurt, she softened a little.

'I mean … I don't even … I never ac-tu-ally knew you. Who the fuck are you, George Bailey?'

'Good question.'

The dull thud of drums and bass, which had been the soundtrack to their conversation, had stopped. Now a flute played a haunting, floating refrain that drifted on the hot air, snaking down the corridors and through the rooms from the main bar. A conga drum flicked like a forked tongue, in and out, punctuating the rising and falling tone. It changed the mood completely – slow, graceful, seductive. It was her default setting.

He watched her cross the small room and lift an electric-blue silk kimono from a coat stand, wrap herself in it and fasten the belt. She moved effortlessly and with a sensuous poise. George had to force the image of Jaffé performing the dance of the seven veils from his mind. He caught himself wondering how much she might actually charge for that service and reddened a little. She caught a glimpse of his lechery and let him have another broadside.

'What-the-fuck-you-lookin-at? You do know, if I wanted to I could have you put in the trunk of a car and buried right out there in the desert?'

'Jaffé, I—'

'Oh shut up, George, you pussy-mutha-fucka! You never should have come here!'

Among the cosmetics strewn around her dressing table, he noticed a jar of skin-lightening cream. Back in Florida, in his self-appointed role as her guru, he'd remonstrated with her that her African blackness was a beautiful thing, that she didn't need to be like Halle Berry, Mariah Carey, Whitney Houston – her American heroines.

He reached over and lifted the jar, holding it up for her to see. 'You don't need this junk, you know.'

Jaffé Losoko stared at him. Was she trying to decide whether to shoot him in both kneecaps, George wondered. Instead, she shook her head and half-laughed.

'Are you for fucking real?'

'Remember how we used to talk about not being an Oreo, dark on the outside and white on the inside?'

She stared at him like he was from another planet. 'Are. You. For. Fucking. Real?'

'Look, I just wanna help … wanna do something to make up for, you know, what happened.'

'You think it's enough if we have clean water and a pair of Nikes? Well, why can't I have what American women have, what white women have?'

She walked slowly toward him and stood really close. 'You want to help, huh? So you got any money?'

The smell of her scent, her breath, was intoxicating.

He swallowed hard. 'I could maybe get some.'

'Oh yeah?' She sounded less than convinced.

'I'm sitting on something … could be worth a lot of money to some people.'

'The only thing you're sitting on is your raggedy ass, and it's cheap and nasty.'

'What do you need?'

Jaffé got up even closer. 'I'm in the market for some corrective surgery … tightening here.' She grabbed his hand and thrust it between her legs. 'Well, let's face it, johns don't wanna fuck water down there now, do they?'

She cackled, and spittle flew onto his face. George pulled away. It was as if she were deliberately trying to shock him, to hurt him.

'You legit? I mean … you got papers now, a green card maybe?' he asked.

'What's it to you?'

'Maybe I could help with that.'

She mocked him, rolling her head on her shoulders. 'Whadaya gonna do, George – marry me?'

He heard himself say it, almost involuntarily. 'Maybe, if that's what it takes.'

Jaffé's expression changed now. She stared hard at him.

Just then, a noise came from behind the curtain of the improvised changing room. It sounded like a high-pitched cough. They met each other's eyes while the noise of something tumbling to the floor filled the cramped dressing room. Small multi-coloured plastic blocks spilled out from under the curtain and into the room.

'I thought we were alone,' George blurted out.

Jaffé said nothing. She went over to where the curtain was and pulled it aside, then gestured for George to join her. He went across and looked down.

A small boy of about six years old looked up at them with big brown eyes from underneath impossibly long lashes. His hair, tousled and curly, framed his chubby face, and his perfect, coffee-coloured skin was lightly flushed.

George's mind raced. He dared not believe it. The words, barely audible, formed on his lips and came out in a breathless whisper.

'Who … who is this?'

Jaffé, squatting down to the boy's eye level, ran a hand through

his hair. 'This here is Habibi Losoko, but you can call him lil'
George if you like.'

They were the words of salvation, of impossible redemption;
manna from the city of second chances.

Chapter 36

The 29th Safety, Security, Technology and Equipment Exhibition and Trade Show was in full swing down at Conference Centre 1 of the Bellagio Hotel. It was one of the most popular events on the circuit and one of the biggest days of the year for professional security and law enforcement personnel, and for the companies chasing that increasingly lucrative surveillance dollar.

The event was well attended and the predominantly white, middle-aged, male onlookers clustered around the expo stalls and stands, hungry for the latest demos and free gifts. High-profile speakers addressed the key topics of the industry: covert surveillance, anti-counterfeiting technology and non-lethal containment measures. Some guys from Wichita had crowbarred in a seminar on counter-terrorism measures as an afterthought. The place buzzed with talk of what had just transpired back East.

Lucian de los Santos knew he would find her here. Since she had been 'retired' from the LVMPD, Evelyn Mulvihill had not let the grass grow under her feet. The humiliating intervention of friends, work colleagues and family had 'taken', and she had attended her subsequent AA meetings for alcohol and prescription drug abuse religiously. While no one could contest that in the intervening years she had become a poster girl for the rehabilitation process, it was not enough to secure her reinstatement to the force. The term 'functioning addict' would not go away.

'Shit,' Lucian had observed at the time, 'if every cop with a drinking problem were shown the door, you could probably fit the entire remaining department into two black-and-white cruisers!'

Evelyn's major offence had been to pass out in the back of her own squad car while thoroughly soaked on oxycodone and tequila. The fact that she had a known felon in custody at the time, and that said scumbag had absconded with her firearm and a laptop containing personal details of every cop in the division, sealed her fate. Some kids found her comatose and phoned it in. Up to that point, she had been the beneficiary of innumerable blind eyes turned by Lucian and his predecessors. But even the attending officer thought it a bridge too far and filed the report.

As Lucian looked at her now from the coffee dock across from her stall he thought again of the one-night stand they'd drunkenly fumbled their way through following the funeral of a brother officer, killed in the line of duty. She wasn't a bad looker back then. Tall, thin, pale skin, freckles, long legs, long copper-coloured hair. She had avoided the lard ass that most female cops seemed to develop, and carried herself with a certain poise and grace that made her look younger and men look twice.

Now, he figured, she must be pushing forty-five. Her features seemed pinched, her lips tight and colourless, her gait a little stooping. She had her hair pulled back from her face, and she wore a dark business suit that made her look drained and androgynous. It wasn't as if she had let herself go, but rather, thought Lucian, that the struggles on a daily basis with her demons had taken their toll.

She had just finished explaining to a fascinated Korean guy how a new NSA microphone could pick up vibrations from window glass unfeasibly long distances away, when he decided to make his move. He had held back this long because of the gravity of the favour he was about to ask of this woman who he hadn't seen or spoken to in three years, and because he was far from certain that what he was doing was for the best.

'Could that thing prove that my wife's having an affair with my neighbour's Afghan hound?' Lucian asked.

She had returned to sit at her desk behind the stall and was stacking some information leaflets. She squinted at him.

'Christ, Lucian! Is that you?'

'The very same.'

'That's soooo weird. I was just talking about you to my buddy … she's gone for coffee. I saw a photo of you in the *Sun* the other day.'

'Yeah, not my finest hour I'm afraid.'

'This business with the black kids, it's just … urrgghh'. She winced and seemed to shiver.

'It's a helluva bad situation.' He looked down at his shoes. 'In fact, it's a not unrelated matter I want to talk to you about.'

'You came here to see me?' She checked the buttons on her blouse nervously and smoothed it down.

'Sure. Why not?'

'Oh, I thought you were maybe just at the convention.'

'How the hell are you, Evie? You look good.'

'Oh, you know, makin' a buck like everyone else. But what about you, mister! Captain of Detectives! Didn't see that comin' when we were partnered up in that piece-a-shit black-and-white back in the day.'

'Good days, Evie, good days. Listen, is there somewhere we can maybe grab a coffee, have a talk?'

'No can do, Lucian. I can't leave the display until my partner comes back. My boss is a ball-breaker and he's around here somewhere.' She glanced around. 'But what about this?'

She stood up and crossed to the front of the small exhibition area with its glossy display photos of long-range camera lenses and minuscule listening devices and pulled across a beaded divider on which hung a sign: 'Back in 10 Minutes!'

A young man in his early twenties who had been loitering in front of the stand, undecided on his next move, seemed glad that his mind had been made up for him and walked away.

Evelyn pulled out a chair for Lucian and invited him to sit.

'I thought I saw you at the Baboov fight the other night,' she said.

'You were there?' Lucian bristled a little, uneasy that his profile was currently so high.

'Of course not, dummy. On the TV news. In the ring, after the fight.'

'Yeah, perks of the job,' he mumbled self-consciously. 'Anyhow, so what happened to Tony?'

She laughed wryly. 'Yeah, Tony Baloney … that's what you used to call him.'

'Always the man with the million dollar plan.'

'That sorry piece of trash. Let me tell ya, that got tired real quick.'

'Tanning spray booths at the beach, retractable earphones to stop the wires tangling …'

'Yeah, and always looking for some mug like me to bankroll him. Last I heard, he wanted to patent a battery-powered pooper scooper that hermetically sealed the shit in the bag.'

The ice was well broken now. They were both laughing freely.

'Yeah, that seems about right. That's Tony!' said Lucian.

There followed a moment's silence that was in danger of becoming an awkward pause, so Lucian leapt right in.

'Evie, I gotta call in a favour. I don't like to have to do it, and

it could be dangerous, but I need someone outside the loop …
someone I can trust.'

Evelyn started to shake a little. She had always suspected that
Lucian could be wayward with rules and regulations but she didn't
like to dwell on the extent of his peccadilloes. He had stood in
her corner when she'd appealed her dismissal and she knew he
had been influential in winning her a small pension entitlement.
Christ, he'd even provided a character reference for her current job
as sales rep with this security firm.

'Sure, Lucian. What do you need?'

'You remember Fox McKinley?'

'The sheriff? I thought he'd retired.'

'No. He's one tough son-of-a-gun. They'll have to carry him out
when the time comes.'

'You been pissing off our law enforcement brethren in the
Sheriff's Department, Lucian?'

'Shit, wouldn't be the first time! No, I need some information
to find its way to McKinley but it can't come from me, you
understand?'

'What gives?'

Lucian drew closer to her. 'Before I say any more, Evie, you
should know that what I'm going to tell you could put us both in
harm's way. It implicates some very heavy people. You get me?'

'I'm a big girl. If I can do you a solid, I'll do it.'

He reached over and squeezed her hand, more in gratitude than
anything else. Was it his imagination or was there a little frisson of
half-forgotten intimacy?

For the next ten minutes, he rapidly outlined a scenario that
was barely credible. Even to his own ears it sounded outlandish,
far-fetched. He found himself admitting to weaknesses that had
compromised his ability to effectively exercise his obligations. It

was a euphemism that he had been mulling over for some time. He couldn't hold her gaze as he talked about Webcore, the role of the Russians in the national sex trade, and the part he played in receiving favours to look the other way. Christ, he even found himself talking about how he couldn't sleep at night and how his late mother came to him in his dreams. When he'd finished, his shirt was sticking to him and he had to ask her for tissues to mop his brow and face.

'You know, I thought this might make me feel better – getting this stuff out in the open – but to hear myself say it out loud, it makes me sick to my stomach.'

Evelyn rested her hand on his arm. 'You know I'm the last one to judge – it's not my style. And I'll listen to you all day if you want me to, Lucian, but I still don't get where I come in?'

'It gets worse.' He sighed heavily and thought briefly about getting up and walking away. 'It goes deeper, higher. It's not just about skanks and stroke movies. It's about oil – oil and power.'

Evelyn looked puzzled but was hanging in there. 'Okaaaay.'

'You've heard of Enron, right? Enron is Webcore. They own it, but not in any way that can ever be proved, you understand?' He met her eyes this time. 'Evie, I'm talking high-ranking members of the administration in Washington, Texan royalty, Wall Street adrenaline junkies. These people – some of the stuff they're caught up in ...' His voice trailed off.

She swallowed hard. 'I still don't see where McKinley and me come in?'

Lucian took a deep breath and blurted it out.

'I think they have something to do with the kids – the Black Herod murders. I don't know why, but ... I have a name ... George Bailey. He's some guy holed up in the Luxor. He has something they want. I haven't made the connection yet but ... those kids,

Evie … the things they did to those kids.'

Evelyn had started to tremble. 'What can I do?'

'You must think I'm a louse, a coward.'

'What can I do?' she repeated firmly.

'I can't go to my own people with this, or to Fox McKinley. It would take me down with them and I can't do time, Evie. A cop inside? Forget about it! You know that!'

She looked away.

'You've got to let McKinley know what's going on,' Lucian went on. 'They're on their way to Vegas … may already be here. McKinley can't be bought. He'll hear you out. And Bailey, someone needs to warn Bailey. Evie, something very bad is coming.'

She stood up and turned her back on him for a moment. Then she faced him again.

'If you can help, your mark would be a low-life called Lamont Riddle. He's easiest to keep tabs on. He won't be far away from anything going down,' Lucian added.

A shadow crossed her face, then she smiled. 'Of course I'll do it. I'll start tonight.'

He stood up, grateful, worried, remorseful. 'And Evie, don't be surprised to see me there too.'

'Yeah, well maybe you'll arrest yourself! Failing that, you'd best come down with a virus or some such and miss the party. One thing's for goddamn sure, don't expect Fox McKinley to cut you any slack.'

He smiled wryly. 'Do you still carry protection?'

She paused for a moment, her eyes narrowing. Then she gave him a lopsided smile. 'What, right here on the desk, Lucian? Jeeze, time was you'd have bought a girl a drink first.'

They both laughed. It was empty, hollow, anxious.

'You know what I meant, Evie. Don't be jerking me around now.'

Evelyn sprang open the catches of a standard black briefcase on the tabletop and turned it toward him. A nickel-plated, snub-nosed .38 revolver lay on top of the day-to-day detritus.

'Once a cop always a cop.'

An exaggerated woman's cough came from the far side of the curtain. 'Coming in, ready or not!'

Lucian and Evelyn turned to see a woman carrying two cups of coffee in styrofoam containers duck between a gap in the curtain.

Evelyn smiled. 'It's my partner. I don't mind saying – and I won't spare her blushes – she's been a rock to me over the past year and a true friend. Lucian, meet Margie Kaufman.'

Chapter 37

NEVADA

'Vegas Classics Radio ... all of the classic hits, all of the time ...'
Van Morrison sang on about sweet Tupelo Honey.

For the fourth time in ten minutes, an angry driver blared his
horn and flashed his lights in irritation at George Bailey. Once
again he'd had to swerve to miss a car turning right, or another
merging out into traffic. He just couldn't pull his eyes away from
the rear-view mirror and keep them on the road ahead.

The reason for this distraction was sitting in the back seat of
George's recently acquired hire car. The boy was concentrating on
staying within the lines of the elephant he was colouring in with
green and pink crayons.

Habibi Losoko had not said one word from the moment George
laid eyes on him. Jaffé had assured George that he had not spoken
a syllable from the moment he'd been born in the emergency room
of the hospital in Ybor, Florida. Doctors had assured her that there
was nothing amiss with his vocal cords or cognitive ability. The
child had simply chosen not to speak.

'I prefer it that way,' said Jaffé. 'He don't give no backchat. He's
a good boy.'

George's gaze fell again on the little man strapped into the back
of his Chevrolet. Every once in a while, his big soulful eyes would
look up and meet his. George found himself looking away quickly,

almost frightened to hold the boy's gaze.

When he'd asked her straight out, Jaffé had refused to say one way or the other if Habibi was his son. He figured that crack about 'Lil George' was designed to hook him and reel him in. She'd laughed at him when he'd begged her to know, citing the boy's lighter features and his age as possible proof. All she would offer was a cryptic, 'White man, white woman: white baby. Black man, black woman: black baby. Black man, white woman: black baby. White man, black woman: black baby.'

Jaffé then dismissively suggested that if he'd like to get to know Habibi better then why didn't he babysit the child the next day as she had several 'appointments' she needed to keep.

Initially petrified at the prospect, George eventually agreed that he would take the boy to *Star Trek: The* Experience at the Vegas Hilton. Habibi had seemed happy when he heard the news and flashed George a killer smile. George's heart felt like it would explode.

Could this really be the child who had been on his conscience and racked him with guilt this last few years, now miraculously reborn? Did second chances really happen this way? Could this actually be his flesh and blood? His own son?

He thought of Beatrice Hatcher. Poor Bee, who had wanted nothing more than to bring a child into this world. His fecklessness and shameless manipulation of her brightest hopes and worst fears had left her broken and unfulfilled. But as always with George, his sense of culpability didn't last.

He looked again at Habibi. Might it be that he was being given the chance to realign some awful cosmic wrong by doing right by the boy and by his mother? It seemed a chance too fortuitous to pass up.

He had begged Jaffé to allow him to make amends. She had clearly been interested when he brought up the question of a green card, and George, the dreamer, began to entertain notions of them all living happily ever after together.

Her first 'condition' was that George showed her a good time, and they had agreed that on returning from the *Star Trek* event he would deliver Habibi and pick her up for a night on the town. To have Jaffé Losoko on his arm as they frequented the nightspots of Vegas was an attractive proposition to him. Jaffé, however, also presented him with a bill: a $750 escort fee. She assured him it was a friends-and-family rate.

When they arrived at *Star Trek:* The Experience, George was concerned that the large crowds, many dressed in the fearsome costumes of characters from the show, would be too much for the young child. However, Habibi displayed a placidness beyond his years and wandered around at George's side, clutching a large cotton candy and a Sprite, his eyes wide with curiosity at the spectacle. When he patted George's leg for attention, then reached his hand up so he might take it, George felt a warmth wash over him that he had simply never known before. He swung Habibi up and around onto his shoulders, and the boy clung to him about his neck, giggling.

Afternoon was turning to early evening. Following the show, where they enjoyed a shuttlecraft simulator ride and a session on the transporter pad, Habibi, now clutching a *Star Trek* backpack containing a scale model of the USS Enterprise, was rubbing his eyes. George kept asking him questions in the hope that the child might break the habit of a lifetime and reply. But he just continued to look back in silence. It was clear, however, that he was flagging.

'Do you need to go, buddy?'

George gestured to the sign for the toilets. Habibi nodded enthusiastically and George felt guilty that he hadn't thought to ask him earlier. His next challenge was to determine the required protocol about taking a young boy to the lavatory.

When they entered, the room was empty save for two Trekkies taking a leak at the urinals. One was dressed as a Ferengi, the other a Klingon. They seemed in deep conversation about matters of the day.

'I've got a boy in the forces. I don't see how rushing off to war in Iraq is gonna fix anything. Besides, how do we know it was them?'

'Believe me, Bush Junior just wants to impress his daddy, so anything is possible.'

Habibi gestured at one of the cubicles and George obliged by holding the door open. The boy immediately closed it behind him and locked it. He himself needed relief but the only urinal free was between the two aliens. He squeezed in, apologising self-consciously and feeling just a little absurd.

'QaqIHneS >sup, qaqIHmo' jIQuch,' said the Klingon as both shook off, turned and left.

The lights in the bathroom were activated by sensors and as only Habibi and George remained they dimmed a little. George heard a noise above his head that began as a soft pitter-patter but rose to a more strident drumming sound. The lights now strobed in time with the tattoo. Before he could look up, a voice addressed him.

'Good evening.'

He swung around and found himself face to face with a tall man, waxy in appearance and dressed in a Star Fleet uniform. He was made up as the synthetic lifeform Lieutenant Data. His eyes were rendered otherworldly by the application of coloured lenses. He smiled at George disconcertingly.

'Jesus, you surprised me there!' said George, moving toward the sink. The noise above his head got louder. 'Okay buddy,' he shouted in to Habibi. 'Best we get going.'

In the mirror he noticed that Data didn't move. He stood stock still, staring at George intently.

'Jesus? Jesus is just the wetback who cuts my lawn.'

The man spat it out with such contempt that George immediately tensed.

'I'm told that you've recently acquired an enthusiasm for procreation,' Data went on. 'Most unlike you, Mr Bailey.'

George froze, the water still running over his hands.

'What … what did you just say?'

The noise overhead grew louder. George looked up. Above him, what looked like a large gecko or lizard seemed to be trapped behind the opaque light cover. It reminded George of the dragon on his medallion and he put his hand up to his throat to touch it. It thrashed and writhed in panic or agony, beating out a percussive racket that seemed impossibly loud. As George returned his gaze to the man, an air freshener dispenser puffed out a cloud of cloying perfume. It stung George's eyes, and he gagged and spluttered.

In a moment Data was upon him, clawing at his neck with sharp nails, whining and grunting in equal measure. George felt the skin at his throat tear and sting. He covered up as best he could but the man bore down heavily on him. George slid further down the wall, hitting his head against the basin and ended up spreadeagled on the floor.

Data did not press home his advantage. George, squinting through smarting eyes, made out the shape of his assailant slowly turning toward the cubicle where the boy was.

George pushed himself to his feet, flailing blindly, hitting nothing but empty space. 'Noooooooo!' he screamed.

Suddenly the room grew brighter and the terrible beating in the ceiling ceased. George ducked his head into the nearest sink in desperation and splashed water into his eyes, drying them off on his sleeves. When his vision cleared, the toilets were empty, the only noise the pneumatic howl of a hand dryer.

The cubical where Habibi had been was empty.

George ran to the door and back into the main vestibule area, looking feverishly in every direction. Had he really lost this child again? And who had taken him?

He didn't see the boy at first, just his shape and that of a tall, thin woman standing beside him. But when Habibi dropped his backpack and ran across the space separating them, flinging himself into George's arms, his heart nearly burst with relief and joy.

'I found him wandering around here on his own. You really have to be more careful with young children, George. It is George, right?'

He looked at her bewildered.

'Evelyn Mulvihill is my name.' She extended a hand. 'I have a message for you from someone who has your – and his own – best interests at heart.'

George was still disorientated. His eyes stung like hell. 'Did you see someone come out of there – a man in a *Star Trek* uniform?'

'No, I've just arrived. Besides' – she gestured round the foyer – 'virtually everyone's in uniform here!'

'Sorry, what did you say your name was?'

'Evelyn. I'm a private investigator. I've been trailing you two most of the day.' She ruffled Habibi's hair, then looked at the scratches on George's throat and his torn collar. 'Oh, before I forget – is this yours?' She held up the silver St George medallion and chain.

George touched the wounds on his throat. 'You wanna tell me what in Christ is going on here?'

'Sure, but I gotta meet my partner. She drives me crazy – there one minute, gone the next.'

'I have an appointment at nine p.m. to drop off Geordi La Forge here. You wanna walk and talk?' George scooped the boy up into his arms and hugged him tightly to his breast. 'Okay buddy? Grab his bag for me will ya?'

All three moved off toward the parking lot.

In a closed and locked cubicle in the toilet block, Lieutenant Data, slack-jawed, head tilted at an impossible angle, stared blankly into oblivion.

Elsewhere in the building, in the Alhambra lounge to be exact, a woman sat surrounded by characters in Federation Star Fleet uniform all laughing and carousing uproariously. She rubbed her elbow and flexed her arm a little to relieve the efforts of an earlier violent exertion.

'Hey Scotty, beam a lady up a gin and tonic, rocks, why doncha!'

'Aye, aye, Margie.'

Fox McKinley didn't know whether to laugh or cry. A lifetime in the Clark County Sheriff's Department had tempered shows of emotion of any kind. Sure he felt vindicated. And justified. And goddamn self-righteous, for that matter. He'd been telling anyone who would listen, for the longest time, that the Russian mafia had infiltrated law enforcement in Nevada, and that they had their red fingers in porn, sex-worker trafficking and God knows what else. The fact that, years ago, he had been left a near cripple by the side of the road in a car wreck following a pursuit of those commie sonsabitches had focused his mind on the matter.

Now this lady PI waltzes into his office unannounced and corroborates everything he'd suspected. And it got better. It seemed that the 'Herod Killings' could be laid at those Russki bastards' door as well. Throw into the cocktail some shady, unnamed property developer with New York links and a whole mess of camel jockeys … well, Christmas had come early!

Fox waited patiently until Evelyn Mulvihill had unpacked her story.

He checked her bona fides and reluctantly accepted that she would not give up her source. Then he took some contact information, thanked her kindly and, as he watched her walk back to her vehicle, considered putting Harry to tailing her, something he decided against for the moment.

When he got back to his office, he buzzed his intercom for Deputy Sheriffs Harry Bailey and Luis Fernandez to join him. While he waited, he did a little two-step dance around the floor, linking his thumbs in his belt and whistling the trumpet refrain from 'Ring of Fire'.

When the men arrived, he motioned them to sit.

'Ain't often I enjoy the prerogative of telling one and all "I told you so",' he began. He stood in front of them and leaned down toward their faces. 'But I one hundred per cent, twenty-four carat gold, and lord God almighty TOLD YOU SO!'

The young men looked at each other, bemused.

When Fox finished relaying a synopsis of what Evelyn Mulvihill had told him, his excitement and enthusiasm at the news communicated itself easily to the young officers.

'You want we should put the armoury on notice? You want we should move on them?' asked Fernandez.

'Sounds like these sleazes have it comin'!' said Harry, keen not to be thought slow to pursue the quarry.

Fox McKinley raised both hands to placate them. He was inwardly berating himself for his rash and unprofessional display of eagerness. He drew up a chair so that he sat in front of the boys.

'Hold on a minute here, this ain't no all-guns-blazing, last-man-standing situation. This is a very delicate set of circumstances we have to contend with. Besides, what do you babes in arms know about killing a man?'

Luis Fernandez pushed his hat back on his head and stared at his boots; Harry Bailey cupped his hands on his belt buckle and appeared pensive.

'Maybe you've had to put down a mangy dog or a lame horse or whatever. Well, let me tell ya, paper targets on the shooting range don't shoot back, boys!'

Neither spoke for a while until Harry, clearing his throat and looking meditative, said, 'It's a hell of a thing, killing a man. You take away all he's got and all he's ever gonna have.'

Fernandez stared at him in disbelief, like they had just met for the first time. Where was this coming from?

Fox McKinley shot him a look, a mixture of pride and surprise. 'Them's some heavy, heavy words for a young man, son.'

Harry immediately brightened, like a puppy that had pleased its owner. 'Not mine. Clint Eastwood's … in *The Unforgiven*.'

Fox covered his eyes with his hand in exasperation. 'Boy, would you get yer head out of yer ass with this cowboy shit!'

Harry reddened and sank down in his seat.

'Have you been listening to anything I've been sayin?'

'Yes sir,' they chorused.

Fox looked worried for the first time. 'We can't go to the Met with this – gotta fly solo on this one. And I don't mind tellin' ya, these guys scare the shit out of me, so that means they sure as hell should scare the shit outa you two pussies. So start acting like goddamn deputies!'

'Yes sir,' they chimed in unison.

'We're talkin' stone-cold killers, heavy-duty career criminals, connected, lawyered up. And if what Ms Mulvihill says is true, there's no knowin' where this could lead.'

'Yes sir.'

'All right then.' Fox seemed somewhat placated. 'Harry, she mentioned someone called Bailey, George Bailey, as the patsy caught up in the middle of this shitstorm. Ring any bells?'

Harry flushed immediately. He suddenly felt bewildered, confused, defensive. 'What … you think cuz we have the same name?'

Fox McKinley sighed heavily and brought his hand to his

forehead. 'No, no son. I'm not asking if you're related. Don't you think I know your family history, or lack of it?'

It was out of his mouth before he knew and he instantly regretted it. In his mind's eye he could see Rita glare at him for being a first-class A-hole.

Harry's face darkened. The welt on his neck ballooned and turned a livid red.

'What I meant to say, boy,' Fox went on in a more conciliatory tone, 'is that maybe you recognise this guy from the big fight the other night. Might he have been in their company?'

Fox crossed to the desk and returned with a photograph taken surreptitiously by Evelyn Mulvihill earlier that day when she'd been following George Bailey at the Vegas Hilton. It showed George awkwardly holding the hand of a young black boy who was eating cotton candy.

When Harry looked at it the room began to spin. Beads of sweat broke out on his face and he quickly passed the photo to Luis Fernandez.

'You okay, son?' enquired Fox.

'Sure. Just need a little fresh air.'

'Well, you know this guy or not?'

'No, never seen him before,' Harry shot back. Rising unsteadily to his feet and staggering toward the door, he called back over his shoulder, 'Bad enchilada. Blame this dude!'

Fernandez looked baffled. 'We had McDonald's!'

Around by the trash cans and gas tanks, beside the pens where they kept the canines, Harry Bailey doubled over and threw up. His airway burned and it felt like it was closing over. He tore at his shirt collar and grabbed at his throat, desperately sucking down as much air as he could. The normally placid police dogs set to barking and howling. One repeatedly threw itself at the wire door of its cage.

Harry was reeling. When Fox mentioned the name of George Bailey a flood of unease had swept through him. On seeing the photograph, he had felt overwhelmed, like he had been before with the flashbacks, if that's what they were. The buried past was flirting with him, taunting him again. But the most daunting aspect of the experience was the sure and certain belief, born more from raw emotion than memory, that he did indeed know this man, that this George Bailey had betrayed him, and that, one way or another, he would betray him again.

✳

At precisely the same time across town, in a back room of the Thunderbird Lounge, Lou Plutus, Lamont Riddle, Minos Baboov and Virgil sat down together to discuss the absence, and thus questionable dependability, of Captain Lucian de los Santos.

Lamont seemed particularly agitated. He threw a fistful of pills into his mouth. 'Apologies. Purely for recreational purposes, you understand.'

Virgil spoke softly. 'Calm down. I will try him again.' He flipped open his phone and punched a number.

'Maybe the guy's just late,' said Lou.

'No, no.' Lamont got up and paced the room. 'Just because he is who he is he thinks he can jerk us around, thinks he can't be got at.'

Virgil pocketed his phone with no result. 'Everyone can be got at, as far as *he* is concerned. Captain de los Santos knows this very well.'

Minos Baboov sat at the table eating pistachios, apparently disinterested.

Lou seemed bored. 'I say we lift 'em both – Bailey and the boy,' he said. 'Have them all ready for when the boss man arrives.'

'The boy's easy. My bitch, she trust me with him. I can pick him up any time. Bailey as well, if you want me to.' Lamont still paced while speaking.

Virgil had grown tired of the company he'd been keeping. He sighed.

'Mr Bailey and his protector have already proved quite resilient on more than one occasion. No, our instructions are clear. Wait for his arrival. Recover the tape by any means necessary. Secure Bailey and the boy for subsequent … retribution.'

'What about the merchandise?' asked Lou. 'No way will he have it on him.'

Baboov stood up slowly and lumbered across the room to where Virgil stood. He bent low and whispered something in his ear.

Virgil nodded. 'Minos is confident that he can convince Mr Bailey to part with this information. You, Mr Plutus, will be required to dispatch both parties – on camera – as per previous instructions, unless, of course, you can convince Bailey to deal with the boy in the manner of the others. *He* would particularly like that.'

Lamont's agitation was getting the better of him. 'This is the one, right? After this one no more killing of the little brothers, correct? I mean, black lives matter y'all. It's a community thang, know what I'm sayin'?'

Lou snorted. 'Who fucking died and made you Martin Luther King? Oh yeah – Martin Luther King!' He guffawed at his own joke.

Virgil was searching for an appropriate Americanism. Eventually he said, 'It is what it is. We have our instructions.'

'But if the opportunity presents itself to nab 'em sooner rather than later …' Lou said.

Virgil could see that Lou now dwelt in a place he could never return from. His descent was complete.

'Then we would be foolish to look a gift horse in the mouth,' he said.

'Then let's stop sitting on our asses and go out there and create some opportunities.' Lou glared at Lamont, provoking him. 'I can taste me those Yardbird Dixie Wings!'

George and Habibi were greeted by the overpowering smell of flowers as soon as they got out of the elevator.

Initially, George had taken the boy back to the address that Jaffé provided, as instructed. But a stoned fifteen-year-old youth with an enormous bong and a sullen attitude had given him a message that she would instead join him at the agreed time in the reception area of the Luxor. So he was bringing Habibi back to his room until then.

The child was struggling to keep his eyes open now. It had been a long day. Following the incident at *Star Trek:* The Experience, and after what George had heard from Evelyn Mulvihill, he had retrieved the video cassette from front desk security with all the trepidation of a man arriving to identify a corpse. It sat in his pocket, burning like a hot coal through the lining. He would happily give it back to Lou Plutus, or anyone else, just to end this whole thing. But he didn't have the first idea how to go about that, and besides, from what he could gather, this crew wanted their pound of flesh. Evelyn Mulvihill had been quite clear – the boy, too, was in danger.

The key card mechanism flashed green and he pushed his hotel door open, guiding Habibi through. They were both immediately assailed by the sickly sweet scent of hundreds of lilies. They had been arranged around the room in bowls and vases; bunches were strewn across the bed and the floor.

Instantly George tensed. He moved cautiously toward the bathroom. Water beat hard against the sliding door of the shower cubicle and soap suds flecked the walls. George motioned to Habibi to sit on the bed while he edged further into the bathroom. It was filled with steam. He steeled himself and slid the shower door open. It was empty. He reached in and turned off the taps, soaking his arm in the process.

Returning, he cleared a space on the bed, carrying some of the lilies into the bathroom and leaving others outside in the hallway. The room still resembled the opulent boudoir of Louis XIV. He opened the window for some fresh air. The twilight desert heat rolled in with it. George turned the bed down and plumped up the pillows. He removed Habibi's jacket and shoes, and took away his *Star Trek* backpack, which the boy was loath to part with.

'You look beat out, sport,' he said. 'Your mom will be here soon.'

Habibi remained silent. He gestured to the bag for his colouring book and crayons, which George provided. But soon his head fell backward and the steady rise and fall of his breathing indicated that he had fallen into a deep sleep.

George quietly lifted the receiver to the front desk. The revelation that the hotel knew nothing of the flowers in his room came as no surprise. Since the events of 9/11, as it had been dubbed, a new world order seemed to hold sway and George Bailey was in thrall to its idiosyncrasies and impossibilities. The illusory had become commonplace, the inexplicable, the norm. It made much more sense now to simply take things at face value, no matter how fantastical they appeared.

So when, on returning to the bathroom, George saw in the mirror that a heart with an arrow through it had been drawn in the condensation, and that the words 'BH loves GB' had been written inside, well, there seemed nothing else to do but to sit down on the lavatory seat and cry. In the midst of all the insanity, uncertainty and danger, one simple, immutable fact remained: *Yes, Beatrice Hatcher does love me. Yes, she always has. Yes, she always will.* It was the only thing he was sure of any more, the only constant, the only fact that mattered.

Why did it have to come to this? Why hadn't he realised what was at stake all along when he'd undermined her time and time again? It was all there right in front of him and he'd trampled on it, spat on her and expected her to clean it up.

His whole body was racked with sobs now, his face, hot and wet with blubbing. He had to cram his fist in his mouth, just to avoid waking the boy. He was sure he'd never see Beatrice again, not even to tell her how sorry he was for the way he'd shit on her dreams and wasted her life.

In due course, he reached for a towel and, wiping away the snot and tears, realised that, more than anything else, he just longed for her company – as simple as that. Just to be near her again. She had been his best friend – his only friend – and her friendship and love had been a gift to him beyond all reckoning. The feeling swept through him so powerfully that his gut flipped and his head swam with regret.

Eventually he gathered himself and looked in on the boy.

Habibi was fast asleep. 'Away with the fairies' was what Beatrice used to say when watching over her young nieces or nephews. George wondered what she would make of this little fella, especially if he was indeed George's progeny, even if by another woman. Another wave of emotion overwhelmed him and he smiled forlornly to himself, for he knew without doubt that Beatrice Hatcher's heart was big enough for all of that and much,

much more. It might take a while, but she had too much love in her to do anything but adore this child.

But those things were gone from him now, and gone for good. Lost forever. He felt wise after the event. A day late and a dollar short.

Slowly his expression darkened. The answer to his predicament might be closer than he imagined. That fucking tape!

He reached into his pocket and removed it, held it in the palm of his hand, turned it over. He considered flushing it the fuck down the toilet or hurling it out of the window, as far away as he could. But he knew he would do neither of these things. He just had to see what was on it. Besides, it was no longer about money. The PI had made it clear it was about survival, and this was the only bargaining chip he possessed.

Time to see what all the goddamn fuss was about.

He checked again on Habibi and dimmed the lights further so as not to disturb the boy's sleep.

He connected the leads from the camera he'd purchased to the television set, the same set where he'd watched Habibi's mother perform acts no child should see. He plugged in the earphone jack, slid the tape into the camera, found the right channel on the TV, and settled himself on the floor with his back against the bed and pressed 'PLAY' on the device.

The screen flickered into life and two words appeared: 'Hotel Girl', then an image, at first dark and blurred but continually auto-correcting and tracking to come into sharp focus.

A young girl of about sixteen was undressing awkwardly beside an open bathroom door in a hotel room much like the one George was currently in. She hopped around on one leg, then the other as she tugged off her purple socks. The words, 'Webcore International' trailed in a banner along the bottom of the screen. George felt the first stirrings of dread far down in his innards.

The girl removed her sweater, T-shirt, sweatpants, bra and panties, fastidiously folding each item and placing them on the back of a chair. She looked around once at the camera and giggled self-consciously before saying something to whoever was in the room with her. George thought the words sounded French, the accent French Canadian. The girl was skinny, with long hair and small breasts and wore heavy eye make-up.

Wearing only long dangling earrings, she gestured to the bathroom: '*Je prends une douche?*'

There was no reply.

The scene cut to a bathroom. The girl climbed into the bath and turned on the overhead shower attachment, running the water until it was warm. Holding the shower head between her knees, she tied her long hair up in a top knot, then washed herself down. There was nothing especially sensual or erotic about this action. It was merely a young girl at her ablutions. Unlike the porn movies George had seen before (and working for Lou, he'd seen quite a few), the girl had no 'tramp-stamps', as Lou called them – no tattoos or markings of any kind. Just the earrings and a gold ring on the middle finger of her right hand.

She accidentally knocked a switch and rerouted the water from the shower attachment to the bath. She looked at the camera, and laughed nervously. The brass fittings in the bathroom and the room lamps looked quite ornate, leading George to surmise that this was no road motel. She smiled at the camera, as though it were her boyfriend or someone she knew behind it.

This shot faded out and a new image slowly faded in. This time she was sitting naked on the edge of the bed, her long hair still wet. She faced a mirror. In fact, virtually every wall in the room was mirrored.

The torso of a big man entered the frame. He was wearing a conservative, pinstriped business shirt, red tie and dark suit pants. It was clear from his physique and deportment that he was middle-aged. He lined himself up in front of the seated girl's face and began to undo his belt, then stopped and indicated that the girl should to do it for him.

She obliged, looking at the camera, then back up to him. He stepped out of his pants and pulled his shirt over his head. All the while the shot stayed below his shoulders. She then removed his boxers.

When he was naked, his considerable paunch overhung a semi-flaccid penis. He said something to the girl who got to work on it, eventually taking it into her mouth. This was the modus operandi of a million skin flicks.

George remembered that Habibi was in the room. He pulled out the earphones and quietly raised himself on one hand to check. The boy was far off in dreamland, his little chest rising and falling with gentle regularity.

Back at the movie, the oral was still monotonously in progress. The john repeatedly pulled the girl's long hair away from her face for the cameraman to film without encumbrance. Then he lay on his back on the bed, shot only from the waist down. The young girl propped herself up on his well-fed belly with one arm while supporting her chin with her other hand. Occasionally the man stroked her back or breasts. All the while the cameraman moved around the room, changing the angle, capturing images as reflections in the different mirrors.

The girl's head bobbed up and down mechanically. She made absolutely no attempt to appear alluring or erotic. This is no pro, thought George. In fact, it was incredibly tedious and uninteresting. Christ, she must have a crick in her neck by now! On instruction, she tried something sensual with her tongue but it seemed amateurish and contrived.

As mundane as all this was, George couldn't escape the feeling in the pit of his stomach that something was not altogether right here. A sense of dread had been rising in him because of, not despite, the banality of the scene. Why did Lou want this recording back so badly? There must be a reason.

The action cut to the bed again. There followed the obligatory three or four position changes as the girl was slammed from behind, above and below. As the pace intensified, she let go a few little gasps and 'oohs' and 'aahhs'. The big man ploughed away, all the while pulling her long hair back from her face.

Then unexpectedly, the camera cut to a completely different scene.

The girl was framed in a soft-lit moment of introspection. Still naked, she lay on the bed, absent-mindedly pulling at the strands of her hair. She gazed pensively off into the distance until the man came back into shot. He roughly pushed her legs up into the air and turned her head toward the camera.

Something had changed in the girl's demeanour. Before, she had smiled and asked questions, now she seemed morose and listless. As her body juddered with his rhythmic thrusting, she closed her eyes, wrinkled her nose in displeasure and looked like she might cry. She had been reduced to meat, and had never seemed younger and more vulnerable than at that moment.

George noted for the first time that the man had an advanced case of eczema, a cluster of red scabs showing at his elbows.

Suddenly the girl was protesting about something and raising her hands to her face in an animated, protective fashion. Clearly unhappy, she was saying something like, '*Non, non, pas ça!*'

George reflexively raised his own hand to his face in silent solidarity.

The man forced her hands back to her sides, clamping them there, and arranged himself into position for the 'money shot'.

The girl continued to protest, looking pleadingly at the camera. 'Je ne veux pas regarder ce,' she said. She closed her eyes tightly.

Suddenly, in the big man's hand there was a long, curved blade similar to a Gurkha kukri. He held it up to the camera, showing it off. It caught the light and flashed for a second. Then he held it in front of the girl's eyes and clamped his hand across her mouth.

Her expression registered her instant blind terror.

George knew what was coming now but he couldn't look away.

She struggled. The weight of the big man pinned her to the bed.

His first pass left little more than a pencil-thin red line across her pale white throat. But in seconds, the line thickened and blood spread out like a liquid flower, crimsoning over the white sheets and duvet.

The girl's efforts to suck in air became more desperate, and she was making gurgling noises like a farmyard animal in an abattoir.

George pulled himself into a foetal position but still didn't look away.

The big man then began sawing, backward and forward, backward and forward, until in no time at all the girl's thin neck had been cut clean through, her head separating easily from her body. Blood gushed out and saturated the bed.

The man lifted the decapitated head by its long hair, now matted with gore, and lurched toward the camera, knocking the cameraman backward. The camera swept wildly around the room for a moment, then back onto him.

Behind the big man, the figure holding the camera was reflected in the mirrors. He still held the camera up to his face, obscuring his features, but he was clearly wearing the white ankle-length thobe usually worn by Saudi men. His headdress was a large square cloth in red and white checks, kept in place by a double black cord. But that wasn't what held George's attention.

He suddenly learned why this video was so important, for now all attempts to protect the killer's identity were abandoned. The big man, clearly crazed with blood lust, made no effort to hide his face. Instead he dipped his hand into the purple pool of blood, tasted it on his fingers and smeared his face and chest in a bestial gesture. In his other hand, he still held the young girl's head, her eyes upturned, her tongue protruding. He thrust himself toward the camera, a groaning, grunting abomination.

The film ended there in close-up freeze frame.

George stared mutely at the infernal visage that now filled the screen. It was the billionaire property tycoon, his mad eyes stretched into slits, his lips pouting outrageously.

At last George Bailey realised what all the fuss was about. At last he appreciated why he was a dead man walking.

He scrabbled around, desperate to find the control that would shut off the image. Adrenaline coursed around his body and vomit rushed into his mouth. He began to gag. He stood up and the earphones ripped painfully from his ears.

Then he noticed the flowers. Every blossom in the room had withered and died. They lay all around him, lifeless and rotting.

George turned to look at the child. Habibi was sitting bolt upright against the bedframe, eyes wide open in shock, his mouth an open oval of horror, staring at the now blank screen in abject dismay. Beside him lay his colouring book. Across the picture of a kangaroo were scrawled the words, 'Long is the way and hard that out of hell leads up to light.'

THROUGH HOLLOW LANDS

WELCOME

Part 3

NEVADA

George held Habibi's hand tightly as they moved through the crowded lobby of the Luxor Hotel. The boy squirmed and was able to extricate himself repeatedly from his sweaty hand, but George reasserted his grip each time.

After what he had just witnessed on the tape, he felt an undeniable obligation to safeguard the innocent out and about in a world such as this. If the boy was in fact his own child, he wasn't about to lose him again after he'd tried to get rid of him via a backstreet abortion. Redemptive opportunities such as this were surely to be grasped and held close. But there was another reason, just as pressing, to keep Habibi near.

While the boy had used the bathroom, George, still overwhelmed by what he had just witnessed, ransacked the room in a near frenzy. He no longer felt it prudent or desirable to be walking around Vegas with such an incendiary item on his person. The room safe, the minibar, the toilet cistern, behind the pants press – all seemed too obvious or woefully inadequate hiding places.

Then he'd spotted Habibi's backpack. Unzipping it, he removed the model of the Starship Enterprise. The dome on top came off to reveal the main deck, complete with a tiny, scaled-down captain's chair, James T. Kirk at the helm. George forced the tape into the space, pulverising the little Spock and Uhura figures in the process. Then he replaced the dome until it clicked into place and put it back in Habibi's bag. Not perfect, he reasoned, but it would do for now.

In the crowded lobby, the boy broke free again and this time ran off, clutching his *Star Trek* backpack over one shoulder. George could see immediately who he was making for. There, imperious in the centre of the polished marbled floor, between the tall bevelled pillars, fake palms and plaster pharaohs, stood his mother.

Jaffé Losoko looked stunning. She was wearing a habesha kemis, the traditional formal attire of Ethiopian women. It was a white ankle-length dress made of chiffon and around her shoulders was a multi-coloured silken netela. Her black hair hung in oiled ringlets, and about her neck was an array of brightly coloured wooden beads and engraved brass and pewter discs. So striking did she appear – like some Nubian princess – that guests passing by dallied to look, nudging each other as if she were a hotel attraction.

The boy ran to her immediately and flung himself at her, hugging her around the waist. Jaffé smiled and simply rested one hand on his curls. With the other, she summoned George imperiously.

He was angry with her for so readily leaving the boy in his care and for her apparent indifference toward her son's well-being. But 'That's quite a look' was all he could manage.

'I hope you're pleased, George Bailey. You promised me a night to remember.'

'Of course, of course. I owe you big time … for everything.' He looked down at Habibi and back at her, hoping she'd give him some indication of who the boy's father was, but she turned her back on him.

George had noticed that, in the short time they'd spent together, her manner and speech had increasingly harked back to the young girl he'd first met in Florida, not the nightclub seductress of the previous evening. He was happy to believe that their reunion might have touched something deep within her, rekindling an earlier innocence. But he had no sooner had that thought than she slapped him down, reverting back to her street persona.

'Damn right you do!' she snapped.

'It's been a crazy day, Jaffé. I've seen some things that I wish I hadn't.'

'Well, welcome to my world, sugar,' she said dismissively. 'Now let's get this party started.'

'You know this place better than I do. Where to first?'

'Cocktails at the Mandalay.'

She walked off through the crowd, on through the double doors and headed in the direction of the parking lot, the boy trotting behind her. George caught up and walked alongside toward his hire car.

'But the Mandalay is over there, just down that walkway. Why do we need the car?'

She reached into her bag, took out a cigarillo and lit it, blowing smoke back in his face. 'What? You think we're bringing him with us?' She nodded down at the boy.

George was appalled. 'You can't be serious. Leave him in the car?'

'Sure, he'll be fine. Does it all the time, don't you honey. He's used to it now. As long as he's got his colouring book and such he'll fall fast asleep in the back.'

'It doesn't seem right.'

Jaffé was becoming irritated. 'Oh, okay then, you can take him back to your room, but don't expect to be getting jiggy with me later if he's in there. I have standards!'

George despaired. What kind of life had this kid been living? Besides, he didn't want the boy in the room; he was convinced he could no longer stay there safely himself. Evelyn Mulvihill had been right – the threat was real and deadly.

Habibi looked at the car, then around the parking lot, as if oblivious to the conversation. He unhitched his bag and stood looking up at the adults, waiting for them to unlock the car door like he had a hundred times before.

George felt tears sting the corners of his eyes, but he pushed the keyring fob. The lights flashed and the doors clunked open. The boy climbed into the back seat and set to unpacking his crayons. George thought about retrieving the tape from the child's bag but figured it was as safe with Habibi as it would be with him – maybe safer.

Jaffé ducked down, pecked the boy on the cheek and then turned back to George.

'You're in luck, Georgie. It's happy hour!'

The Mandalay Bay Resort and Casino was tired and in need of a facelift. It was Cuban Night, and the salsa dancers in their outfits, cut high at the crotch, revealing stubble and fake tan, worked hard for the half-full lounge crowd. But their Botox rictus grins and hair plugs made the whole affair seem rather sleazy.

Jaffé demanded champagne and, having quaffed this with an indecent amount of haste, she set to gorging on mojitos. George noticed that it didn't seem to affect her. It was hard to imagine this was the same girl who had once eschewed alcohol for religious reasons.

They decided to take a walk along the Strip for some twilight desert air. The longer the evening went on, the more morose Jaffé became. By ten thirty, she seemed browbeaten and self-reflective. Having ranted all evening, cussing at clients, pimps, and her sister pole dancers, George was surprised to find her tempering.

She talked about her family in Africa and her girlish dreams when she'd arrived in Florida. He felt her transmute to the optimistic, trusting young woman he had first encountered, so much so that he felt emboldened to ask her about their last meeting all those years ago. When she broke down in floods of tears and threw her arms around him, he was disarmed.

'Oh George, I couldn't do it … kill something that had hurt no one. The money you gave me … I bought an airline ticket, but I couldn't go home. I had a premonition of my own death there. It was horrific, awful. They came for my brothers. They weren't at home so they took me. They beat and beat me. Then one … he was just a boy … he took a machete … and … and hacked and hacked. I saw my own blood run into the sand. They left me there alone. No one should have to die alone, George. I couldn't go back.'

They had stopped under a street light in a quiet corner set back from the glitz and razzmatazz. A car cruised by slowly, the passengers looking hard at this distraught, beautiful African woman and the dubious older man who was seeking to comfort her.

George steered her into the doorway of a storefront shrouded in after-hours darkness.

'But everyone dies alone,' he said lamely. 'Don't you know that? We all die alone.'

'I believe that when I die it is the world that will end, not me,' she replied defiantly, pulling herself together and shaking off her vulnerability to become Jaffé Rossetti again.

But George didn't notice and moved toward her with outstretched arms.

'Back off!' she snapped and pushed him hard.

Surprised, he stumbled backward and thudded against the window of the store. There was a loud electronic click, then the buzz of fluorescent tubes stirring into life. The interior of the store slowly illuminated, clunking section by section, from front to back, into light.

When they looked around they discovered they were in front of the window display of a large bridalwear store. Naked, tanned, headless mannequins in regimented rows stretched back as far as the eye could see. In the middle at the front stood one lone black figure. It was fully dressed in an elaborate white lace wedding gown.

Jaffé smiled mischievously. 'Guess it's about time to put your money where your mouth is, Georgie boy. I be 'bout ready for my green card.'

She stepped back a little from the glare of the lights, the better to fix her hair in the reflection from the window.

George swallowed hard. 'You serious?'

'You sure got a short memory, white boy!'

He winced. 'I know, I know. I promised … whatever it takes.'

She hitched up her bosom defiantly. 'Well, all right then.' She smirked. 'Relax, it'll be painless. I won't make ya get a tattoo nor nuthin.'

'But Jaffé, it must be after midnight and—'

She cackled. 'Fool! This is Vegas. You just leave all that up to little ol' me.'

Around the corner and out of sight, Harry Bailey sat in shadow on the dark side of the street. His engine idled and a country station buzzed low on the radio as he gripped the wheel with both hands and tried to determine his best course of action.

He had been trailing them from the Luxor parking lot, adopting the plaid shirt, casual jacket and glasses 'disguise' that had served him so well at the fight. He'd seen them lock the small boy into the car and for a moment considered calling social services. But he knew that was exactly the kind of boneheaded call that always seemed to land him in trouble. It would only lead to a shitstorm of questions and paperwork, not to mention blow his cover. And then there would be the wrath of Fox McKinley to contend with.

In not consulting the sheriff and heading out solo to further explore the vexing conundrum of George Bailey, he was going against everything the older man had taught him. It was nothing short of disrespectful and criminally insane. Not even Rita would intercede this time. Shit, he wouldn't be surprised if Fox chose to kick him out of the department post-haste, such was the sheriff's anger at the recent turn of events. Christ, hadn't he been working on a strategy, waiting on an opportunity, dreaming about this for years?

But as Harry had tracked the pair through the Luxor and the Mandalay, and now to this part of town, he became absolutely certain that he had to stick with them at all costs. Something was compelling him toward this man, this neurotic, stressed-out individual who was running around the parking lots and city streets of Vegas with an African woman and black child in tow. He seemed so familiar.

The Herod Killings, the Webcore angle, Mulvihill's unidentified source – where did George Bailey fit into all of this? And what was it about the man that Harry felt so drawn to? Whatever it was, there was no going back now.

Chapter 41

The term 'low rent' might have been invented for the Casino Wedding Chapel on 3rd Street. Outside was a wooden porch with steeple, two backlit faux stained-glass windows, and a flashing neon sign saying '24 Hour Betrothals'. Plastic hedging and a rusty wrought-iron love seat were intended to offer the happy couple some post-vow photo-ops. Downtown LV real estate was at a premium, so the porch shared space with a huge flashing arrow pointing next door where a sign proclaimed 'Topless Girls'.

The chapel itself was a monument to tacky. In a narrow room, numerous prints of casino legends hung on peeling gold and yellow wallpaper. Four leatherette divans sat at right angles. The ceiling was mirrored, and the loud red and black carpet depicted a hodgepodge of poker cards, dice and 777 images. A functioning fifties slot machine blinked away in the corner, occasionally blasting out a few bars from Chuck Berry's 'You Never Can Tell'.

At the far end of the room were two tall plinths, one labelled 'Love' and the other, 'Las Vegas'. A crescent-shaped table, with playing cards and casino chips lacquered into the surface, sat between them. On the wall behind, where the pastor presumably stood, was an oversized representation of a slot-machine window and handle. In it were three hearts, two red and one black.

As they walked toward this 'altar', George could feel the carpet suck at his feet, the accumulated soak of spilled beer from numerous inebriated couplings. The whole room smelled of stale alcohol and cigarettes.

'Let's get on with it!' snapped Jaffé.

She was becoming increasingly hostile and aggravated as the night-time moved into the wee small hours – no more confessionals, no more regrets; just thinly disguised contempt and bile.

'You got somewhere to be?' he shot back at her.

'Yeah, well maybe I do … and maybe he's more of a man than you'll ever …'

She was interrupted by a twitching of the gold and silver lamé streamers to one side of the altar. Two hands pressed together as if in prayer slipped through to part them and a small man with white hair and beard appeared in front of them. He wore an oversized white linen suit, black bootlace tie, a trilby and Ray-Ban Wayfarers. He seemed a little baked on pot – or something stronger.

'Ahhh, the happy couple,' he said, smiling.

'Well hi, Colonel Saunders,' said Jaffé sarcastically.

'Ready to get 'er done?'

'Sure are.'

'That'll be one hundred dollars American … ummm, up front if you don't mind.'

Jaffé looked at George, who passed over the money.

'Sorry to be a stickler about that.' The man took off his glasses, pocketed them and looked contrite. 'Too many young couples, drunk and loved up, scamper outa here without paying. You know how it is.'

George nodded wearily. He felt profoundly depressed. This was all so wrong. Here he was, doing more than he had ever been prepared to do for Beatrice Hatcher who had loved and supported him across the years. She had wanted little in return – security, a family, a life together with him. Now he stood in front of some funky Las Vegas preacher and was offering it all up to a hooker. A virtual stranger. It seemed profane; sacrilegious to the memory of Beatrice.

The small man pocketed the money and flipped on a switch, which brought solemn, celestial organ muzak flooding into the room through hidden speakers. He removed a small harmonica from his pocket, blew into it to register a key, then began to sing 'Shall we gather at the river'.

George felt increasingly ill at ease. 'Ahh, excuse me, what do I call you? Pastor …?'

'You can call me whatever you want now you've paid. My name is Anastasius. Alphonse Anastasius.'

'Well, Pastor Anastasius – Al – can you give us just a minute?'

He took Jaffé's arm and led her off to the side. She looked offended and like she might strike him.

'I need a few guarantees before I go through with this. The boy … Habibi. Is he mine?'

She smiled at him, slowly, malignantly, and sucked her teeth to express her disgust. 'How can he be yours when you tried to have him killed?'

It was intended to hurt him, to put him back in his place. But he was beyond that now. He'd seen the boy, and how she treated him. He was done fucking around.

'If we do this do you promise to give him my name, and to take better care of him?'

Anastasius cut in. 'If I may just intrude: many couples get cold feet at the last minute, in my experience. Life, death … they both happen so fast sometimes we have to be careful not to miss them. Ever consider that?'

George wasn't listening. He was starring apprehensively at the rage gathering behind Jaffé's eyes. Pastor Anastasius was determined to deliver his homespun homily regardless.

'When you think about it, everything in life is about death, and vice versa. It's all tension and release, you see. Things in motion, things at rest.'

George and Jaffé looked at the man as if he were a simpleton, then resumed hostilities.

'Fuck your green card, George Bailey, and fuck you!' Jaffé said, almost growling at him. 'I need to be among my own. I'm going back to the Luxor. I need a fucking drink! Or are you bailing on that promise as well?'

She turned around and walked out.

Chapter 42

They passed through the casino in full swing. The place was packed. It was 'Celebrity Impersonator Dealers Night', always a favourite with the punters.

At various crap tables, roulette wheels and dice pits sat Cher, Ozzy Osbourne, a Red Indian Chief, Superman, Stevie Wonder, Marilyn Monroe and Jack Nicholson. All eyes were on a Michael Jackson lookalike who was doing his *Thriller* thing on a makeshift stage beside the Texas Hold'em tables. People whooped and clapped along.

George paused to watch; the performance was uncannily accurate. When he turned back again, Jaffé was disappearing up a flight of stairs at the far end of the casino. He quickened his pace and followed her.

The house DJ of Pharaoh's nightclub upstairs was pumping it out big style: 'Beastie Boys in full effect y'all!' Professor Plugg and his Boogie Angst Roadshow had held down a residency at the Luxor for a year or so. The huge Honduran bounced his sweaty six-foot-five frame around the stage, unfeasibly agile among the turntables and mixing desks.

George, who was still trying to keep up with Jaffé, could hear the bass booming long before they reached the rope line and security.

 THROUGH HOLLOW LANDS

The walls narrowed into a corridor and were covered in garish-coloured graffiti. Most of the sprayed comments seemed to be in Italian, but George recognised the phrase in English, 'Eternal, and eternal I endure. All hope abandon ye who enter here.'

Jaffé bypassed the queue effortlessly and reached the shaven-headed bouncers first. She stood on her toes to whisper something in the ear of one of them, then they all looked around at George and laughed. Jaffé was handed a fluorescent wristband, and she slipped quickly between the thick drapes. George was stopped in his tracks by a solid palm to the chest.

'Can I help you?'

'I'm with her.'

The man smiled, showing a mouth of uneven teeth, a diamond inset in the front. 'You sure about that?'

'Sure I'm sure.'

'Well, all right then.'

The man handed him a wristband with a skull-and-crossbones motif, stepped aside, and bowed, making a theatrical sweep of his arm in the direction of the curtain. George passed through and immediately had to readjust his focus to take in the Bacchic scene that met his gaze.

He stood in an area raised above the main room that was packed with people, a sweating swell of humanity rising and falling with the pounding beat of the music. He looked for Jaffé, but manic strobe lighting made it difficult to discern individuals among the pulsing, heaving, gyrating crowd.

George's immediate inclination was to turn around and leave again, but, to his horror, in place of the drapes where he had entered, there now stood a solid wall with a mounted TV screen. He turned back to the nightclub, tamping his panic down into the pit of his stomach.

All around him were scenes of debauchery and excess. He caught sight of a group of young men dressed as angels, in togas, wire halos and elaborate feather wings strapped to their backs. A cluster of young women were dressed as comic devils, with red make-up, horns and pitchforks. There were nuns and bishops, Batmen and Jokers, French maids and cops. All whirled and shook on the dance floor as if possessed.

Huge TV screens were dotted around the room, flashing up various pornographic images, war victim footage and looped videos of the collapsing towers. Dancers stood on tabletops and in cages, thrashing about as if an electric current were passing through them. Bubbles, soap suds and balloons fell from the ceiling above. The volume was merciless and the music incessant. 'Get Your Freak On', 'Sabotage', 'Pappa's Got a Brand New Pigbag'. Klaxons and whistles screamed relentlessly. The smell, too, was overpowering. Sweat and sick and – dying flowers, the cloying smell of his room when he had left it.

The tempo slowed a little and the strobe lights were replaced by a dim red satin wash that cloaked the room. The dancers slackened to a more sensual merging of limbs and bodies. 'Dream on', urged the singer of a more seductive beat, who then told them to 'Reach out and touch faith.'

George could make out a number of well-dressed, society types dotted around the fringes of the dance floor. They held ornate cocktail glasses and threw their heads back with exaggerated laughter. He understood why he could smell vomit. Each one in turn leaned forward and, forcing fingers down their own throats, forcibly made themselves puke. Others provided the service for partners who got splattered. The edge of the dance floor was a vomitorium of steaming sick, the patrons better able to sluice down more champagne and canapés from the tables around them.

George was still struggling to find Jaffé or register a familiar face. Then his eye was drawn to the hotel's resident act, 'The Redskins', two of whom were bitch-slapping each other in some kind of mock vaudevillian routine. The third stood staring directly at George, like before, grinning manically, his eyes so wide that the whites appeared huge against his red face. Again he raised a single finger, pointed it at George and then drew it slowly across his throat.

The wet suds and bubbles had soaked the crowd in a sticky lather. Heat seemed to rise off them and they pulsed together as one, a human stew of squelching, slick amoeba, altering and shifting shape in time with the beat.

He looked behind him for the way he'd come in but there were only TV screens, flashing now at a rate the eye was barely able to register. For a moment, they all seemed to freeze on one image of plain text which he was sure read: 'Let the little children come to me, and do not hinder them, for to such belongs the kingdom of heaven.'

When he turned back to the crowd he saw Jaffé.

She was rocking backward and forward in time to the music, thrusting her hips and pelvis in a sensuous bump and grind. Her eyes were closed in ecstasy, her pink tongue protruding from between her teeth. He could see her mouth the words, 'It's sweet, it's sweet.' Behind her stood a tall figure, moving with her every thrust in perfect time. They looked locked together, coupled like street dogs.

Light fell on the features of the man. It was Lamont Riddle. His gaze seemed to meet George's, his smile more of a leer. Then George discerned that he wasn't looking at him at all, but behind him. He swung around to see the towering figure of Minos Baboov move slowly, menacingly toward him, and beside him was Lou Plutus, smiling, his arms outstretched in a malign welcome.

'Spoken to Beatrice lately, George?' Lou asked, taunting him. 'What's the matta? Can't you raise her?' He sniggered.

George was dumbstruck. He looked desperately around the hall for a means of escape. There was a green neon 'Exit' sign flashing in the far corner of the room. How had he missed it before?

There was no time for hesitation. He pushed into the crowd of wet, oozing humanity. Faces loomed – desperate eyes, slack jaws, gnashing teeth – bony fingers pulled and clawed at him as he pressed on and out the other side, covered in spit and sweat.

Under the flashing sign was a pair of double doors with a push-bar release. George allowed himself one look back over his shoulder. The crowd was parting like the Red Sea, allowing Baboov and Lou easy passage; they had been joined by Lamont and Jaffé.

He felt his heart sink. Had she deliberately led him here? To them? And they to Habibi?

George threw himself at the doors and they exploded open. He stumbled and fell, rolling forward and hurting his shoulder in the process. When he got his bearings again he found himself looking at a pair of giant moccasined feet. Gazing upward, he saw the Red Indian Chief, in full warpaint and headdress, who had been working the blackjack table back at the Luxor. The man glared down at him.

Convinced he was between a rock and a hard place, George reverted to his customary gallows humour.

'Who the fuck are you supposed to be – Geronimo?'

He closed his eyes and awaited the blow.

'No,' said the man, in a higher pitched voice than might have been expected from a man of his size. He grabbed George by the collar and hoisted him up. 'My name is Manto and I'm the Hopi brave who's gonna save your sorry ass!'

Chapter 43

Manto half-trailed, half-lifted George through a trade entrance that led out to where George's hire car was parked. The cool late-night desert air felt good.

'Wait!' George screamed. 'That way. I'm parked over there!'

'No time,' shouted the big man. 'That's my pick-up.' He led him toward a beat-up Nissan.

'No, no! The boy … the bag!'

George broke free and ran to his car. Manto let out an audible groan and followed.

The trade door they had just come through shot open. George sprinted toward his rental. His shoulder hurt like hell. He fumbled for the keys, dropped them, picked them up again, then stopped short. The car was empty. Both boy and backpack were gone.

George felt like rolling into a ball right there and then and letting these people do their worst. But before he had time to turn and face the music, he was swept off his feet again by the Indian chief.

'Keys!' he demanded.

George pushed the key fob and the car lit up.

'Get in. I drive,' said Manto.

Not far behind them came their pursuers, but they were walking now, in no apparent hurry, sure of their quarry. Their lack of haste was even more chilling.

Manto reversed out of the bay at speed and spun the steering wheel. The car righted itself, brakes screeching, before coming to a momentary stop, sending smoke and the smell of rubber into the night air. He straightened it up just as the shadows of their predators began to emerge from between the parked cars in the lot.

Manto reached inside his tunic and produced something that resembled the butt handle of a whip. It was woven from reeds and decorated with strips of calico and beads; wrapped around a loop at the end was what appeared to be horse hair. He leaned across George and, opening the window, kissed the charm and threw it onto the asphalt at their pursuers' feet.

They stood still, silent, oozing quiet malevolence, Lou Plutus grinning, Minos Baboov clenching and unclenching his fists, Lamont Riddle grinding his teeth. Behind them stood Jaffé with Habibi in her arms. He still carried the backpack.

George reached across and placed his hand on the steering wheel, indicating that he wanted Manto to wait a moment. Manto revved the car, aching for flight, but held it teetering on the clutch.

A man George didn't recognise stepped into the light. He slowly pulled down his hood. His white hair was luminescent against the dark sky.

Manto immediately shielded his face with the side of his hand and muttered under his breath, 'Fallen angel.'

The white-haired man did not look at George directly, and when he spoke it was with tired resignation. 'Mr Bailey, it's simple. The boy for the tape.'

George felt a surge of incredulity, relief and fear, but he battled to hide it. So they believed he was still in possession of the tape. Perhaps the child had a chance after all.

'Jaffé – the boy,' he called out. 'It's not too late. Come with us. Come now.'

Her face was expressionless. 'I love him, but I have chosen darkness,' she said. 'He belongs to them now.'

She turned with Habibi and walked back into the shadows.

'Drive!' barked George Bailey.

*

The ridges of Deputy Harry Bailey's glasses bit deep into the bridge of his nose. He was dying to scratch it. But he remained where he lay, completely immobile, flat out on the collapsed seat of his unmarked sheriff's car.

He had circled the parking lot until the space, one down from George Bailey's car, had become free, then pulled in and waited. He noted that the boy was no longer in the car where Bailey and the African woman had left him.

Beside him lay a pizza box with a half-finished pepperoni deluxe and at his feet, a Gatorade bottle containing his warm pee. He was determined to wait all night if he had to.

When he heard the running feet, the banging and screeching of tyres, he was half tempted to blow his cover and reach into the glove compartment for his revolver. But he stayed low and waited. He heard the conversation about the boy, about the tape. He heard the woman turn Bailey down and walk away.

It wasn't much to go on but he thought that the voice making the deal betrayed the traces of a Russian accent. He also believed that any bartering involving a young black child, in the current climate of the Herod Killings, warranted investigation. All in all, it had been a good night's work. And he was convinced that Sheriff McKinley would agree, after he got through chewing him out about heading off on his own accord without backup or any word of his movements.

Harry was just about to shift from his uncomfortable position when four waists appeared, one at each side window of the car: a fat belly in elasticated slacks, someone in loud, baggy pants held up by red suspenders, a broad, solid torso in sharp suit pants, and a skinny kid in combats with a snake-head belt.

For what seemed the longest time, no one spoke. Eventually, Harry Bailey gritted his teeth and forced his best nerdy smile. He decided he would shoot for the "innocent bystander who had fallen asleep in his car" story.

He pushed himself up and began to crank the back of the seat to its upright position.

'Can I help you gentlemen?'

When he saw their faces, he knew he was a dead man.

George could have sworn that the sun had been coming up about seventy miles back and over an hour ago. But as they drove at speed down dusty back roads, through rocks and a desert resembling a moonscape, the twilight semi-darkness clung on around them.

Avoiding Route 93, they were heading north-west on roads little better than rutted tracks. George kept looking over his shoulder to see if they were being followed, but unilluminated darkness was all he could see for miles. Their own headlights threw up stark images of twisted cacti and shape-shifting rock formations.

Manto remained in flinty silence since they left the parking lot at the Luxor. If George's jumpiness irritated him, he didn't show it. He had lost his elaborate headdress in the melee and his long black hair, streaked through with silver, was tied into a ponytail that reached far down his broad back. His knuckles were white on the steering wheel.

George stared straight ahead as the car bumped up and down on the dirt track, his mind still reeling from the nightclub encounter. He had more questions than answers. But that had been the case since he set foot on the asphalt at McCarran International Airport two days and a lifetime ago.

He had to believe that the Digital8 tape was still undiscovered, wedged in under the dome of the USS Enterprise in Habibi's backpack. Otherwise, why would the Russian still be seeking to trade for the boy? As long as the kid didn't prise open the lid, Lou Plutus and the others would believe that he still had something to parley with.

He chanced a sideways glance at his companion. As grateful as he was for the man's intervention, he still had little idea who he was or why he had interceded on his behalf. More worryingly, he had no idea where this man-mountain was taking him.

'Correct me if I'm wrong,' George ventured, his voice sounding loud after the long silence between them. 'But wasn't that the boxer back there?'

Manto said nothing. George's words hung in the air.

'You know, the big guy … "The Beast from the East" … Baboov?'

Still Manto said nothing.

'I dunno,' George muttered, resigned to talking to himself, 'maybe you don't get pay-per-view. Does the tribe have cable?'

There was another long silence. Then, while George considered his next bon mot, Manto spoke.

'I don't do sports.'

George was a little taken aback. 'Okay, but you like the ladies, right? Job like yours … I'll bet you're beating those cocktail waitresses off with a tomahawk.'

Manto kept looking straight ahead into the darkness, his eyes squinting occasionally as a jackrabbit or lizard crossed the beam. 'I'm gay.'

'Ya don't say! Is that allowed among your people … your tribe, I mean?'

Manto turned his head slowly to look at him through narrowed eyes. 'It's 2001, George, for fuck's sake. Get a life!'

For a moment their gaze held. The car bucked violently, throwing them both up in their seats, then returned to its course.

George exploded with laughter. He couldn't help himself. It was like all the dread and panic that had preceded their escape from Vegas just poured out of him.

It was infectious. The Indian cracked a smile.

'In fact, your question isn't so crazy,' said Manto. 'My forefathers often had a role in our tribe that we called a "contraire". This meant that they adopted behaviour that was deliberately the opposite of other tribal members. So to my grandfather, for example, "no" meant "yes", and "hello" meant "goodbye". To tell my grandfather to go away would have been an invitation for him to come.'

'And are you a "contraire"?'

'Not really. I find the whole thing much too confusing, but it means they understand me not taking a squaw. And they allow me to spend time on my other … passions.'

'Boys?'

'No, fool. Melittology!'

George nodded sagely. 'I'm just gonna pretend I know what you're talking about there. What did you say your name was again?'

'Manto.'

'Well, you're all right, Manto. You'll do for me, chief.'

The night-time desert air was cold and George worked the blow-heater settings for a while, as much for distraction as necessity. They journeyed on for another few miles in silence, the orange glow from the dashboard offering them the comforting semblance of firelight, until George pitched in again.

'I just want to thank you … for back there, I mean. Getting me out of that mess.'

Manto didn't answer.

'I'm guessing you know a lot more about what's going on than I do – about the tape.'

'Guess again,' said Manto.

'Well, I mean why else help me out?'

'I don't know much, and I don't want to know,' said the Indian. 'But I do know them. I know what they are, what they've become.' His face twisted in disgust. 'I know that the innocent is in grave danger while he remains with them.'

'So why pitch in? What's in it for you?'

Manto smiled. 'Let's just say that somebody up there likes you.'

They travelled on, the darkness becoming more impenetrable the further north they went. It made no sense. It was as if daybreak had come, peeped over the threshold of dawn and changed its mind, seen off by the gloom pursuing them from the very bowels of Sin City.

George kept looking over his shoulder for tails.

'No one will follow us,' Manto said with a marked degree of certainty.

'Yeah? How's that?'

'Because they already know where we're going.'

'I'm glad someone does!'

'You must be curious yourself.'

'Buddy, I've learned to wait and see. Nothing surprises me any more.'

'We're going to the home of my people. It's under Meeker Peak, in the Worthington Mountains Wilderness. Have you heard of it?'

George looked at the man to see if there was any sarcasm present, then threw in some of his own. 'Ummm, not exactly. I'm not from around these parts.'

'They know they can't enter there, so it's the safest place for you until …'

The car jolted to a stop. George could make out the outline of a tall mountain range, jagging up into the sky and framing the landscape all around them. Snow speckled its highest peaks. They had arrived at a campsite at the foot of a tall mountain, the clearing forming a natural amphitheatre of sorts. It was lit by dozens of storm lanterns placed on the ground and hanging from spindly trees dotted around the clearing.

The sun was definitely on the rise now, and as it crept up further, shafts of dawn light shot out from behind the peaks and bluffs. George could make out white buckskin tepees standing erect, perfect rows of pristine triangles raised to attention. Colourful drapes and blankets hung on wooden frames outside the tents, and orange earthenware pots were set out around a truck and large aluminium trailer next to large puddles and patches of damp earth.

The dawn chorus was warming up, small birds chirping, crickets sawing and large crows cawing. Two mongrel dogs came close to sniff George and Manto, then wandered off again, uninterested.

The flap from the nearest tepee was pulled back and two old men slowly emerged. They were dressed in gingham shirts and denims; one wore a baseball cap with 'Salt Lake Bees' with the logo of a cartoon bee wielding a baseball bat on it. Their dark skin wrinkled into full smiles when they saw Manto. All three hugged, then they exchanged a few words, looking back at George while they talked. Manto said something; they all laughed. He said something else, and George watched their expressions become morose. They nodded and looked at him again, more in pity, he thought.

George was too tired now to care much. His eyes were struggling to stay open and he swayed a little where he stood. The adrenaline and angst of earlier had subsided, leaving him exhausted and drained. He yearned to fall spreadeagled into the vortex of sleep. Then he spotted the lights in the desert sky off in the distance.

Hundreds and hundreds of sky lanterns, like miniature hot air balloons, floated slowly upwards from the ground, unhurriedly winding their way into the breathless early morning sky. Up and up, higher and higher they drifted, until they finally disappeared off over the horizon. It was strangely uplifting. They were like spirits set free, returning home. George was entranced.

He snapped alert when the first man hugged him. They had come up close and, one after the other, embraced him warmly. And as Manto stood to the side, George could see others – men, women and children – slowly emerge from their tepees and form an orderly queue in single file. To his amazement, each walked forward to look into his eyes, then embrace him. Some of them smiled; others looked at him in wonderment. A few old ladies cried quietly. Small children hugged his legs. It seemed as if the whole tribe had turned out. Although he had only just arrived, George had an overwhelming feeling that these people were saying goodbye.

It was too much for him. A surge of emotion like nothing he had ever experienced before shot through him. His eyes filled with tears, then the sky spun and his legs gave way and the darkness subsumed him.

When he awoke some hours later, dressed in a pair of sweats and T-shirt, he was shocked to see a man in a head-to-toe white suit and netted helmet standing over him. In his hand he held what looked like a watering can. It was leaking smoke. George thought he looked like an Olympic fencing champion.

He pushed himself up in the small cot he'd slept in. The inside of the tepee smelled of woodsmoke and incense. The man removed his helmet. George was relieved to see that it was Manto.

'You went deep,' he said.

George stretched and yawned. 'Christ knows, I needed it.'

'The sleep of the dead.'

'Yeah, out for the count.'

'Let's get you some breakfast. You'll need sustenance and resolve. You've journeyed through hollow lands, but your journey is not over.'

Manto pulled aside the flap of the tepee and held it open. Sunshine flooded in.

'I'm going somewhere?'

'Yes, to where you've been headed all along.'

George, recalling the previous evening, was becoming a little irritated with all the cryptic bullshit. 'Sure, and where's that?'

'Why, to the Mountain Lying Down, of course.'

'Of course,' said George sarcastically.

They emerged from the tent under a cloudless blue sky. It seemed like early morning but the desert heat was already beginning to rise. Several of the tribe were wearing the same uniform as Manto; the temperature inside the suits must be unbearable, George thought.

'What's with the getup?' he asked.

'Seeing is the best answer,' said Manto and led George back to the rental car.

They drove for twenty minutes or so through the same kind of terrain they'd covered on their previous journey until they reached the most wonderfully verdant meadow on a plateau.

George was amazed that such luxuriant foliage could prosper, right here in the middle of the wilderness. Birdsong filled the air and, nearby, a stream of white water cascaded down the mountainside, crashing into a translucent emerald pool below. Clusters of purple and red crystals jutted out in layered, interlocking columns around the rock walls of the pool, catching the light and glittering in the sunshine.

As George took it all in, Manto, opening the trunk of the car, threw him a towel with a bar of soap wrapped inside.

'Trust me on this!' he said, gesturing toward the cascading water and waving his hand in front of his nose. 'Woof!'

After washing, George felt reinvigorated. His folded clothes sat on the hood of the car and seemed to have been washed and pressed.

A large rug was laid out on the ground, on which Manto had arranged bowls of fruit, nuts, berries, smoked meats, corncobs, goat's cheese, honey and unleavened bread. A metal bowl sat over a small fire of hot coals, boiling water and coffee grounds.

Manto sat cross-legged on the ground and indicated that George should join him.

George sat down with an exaggerated groan and sigh. 'Ahh, gettin' old, gettin' old. You might have to help me up again!' he joked.

Manto nodded his head sagely. 'Sedentary lifestyle,' was all he said.

They ate in silence for a while. George felt awkward.

'Healthy breakfast. Great food ... delicious. Beatrice is always ...' He tailed off and a shadow of regret passed over his face.

There was silence again. Then Manto spoke.

'This is a big day for you, a very big day.'

'There you go again,' said George, laughing and slapping his thigh in mild irritation. 'Everyone knows more about me than me!'

Manto smiled, shrugged and popped a berry into his mouth. He offered no further explanation.

'And what about this ... this getup?' George pointed to Manto's suit. 'You said seeing was believing or something.'

Manto threw the remainder of his coffee into the grass and stood up. He signalled for George to follow him. They walked across the meadow until they reached the edge of the plateau.

'Down there,' Manto said and spread his arms proudly.

Far below them stretched a valley that ran off into the distance. It was filled with column after column of identical little white houses with sloping roofs. Trees grew here and there in between the little houses, offering cover and shade.

'Bees!' exclaimed George, as if answering a question on a quiz show. 'That's what melittology is … bees!'

'Honey bees,' corrected Manto.

'Amazing!' whispered George, genuinely impressed.

'My people, like many tribes before them, believe the honey bee is a sacred animal that bridges the natural world and the underworld.'

George wasn't listening. He was shaking his head in disbelief and laughing at the sheer audacity of what lay in the valley below.

'Goddamn beehives … hundreds of 'em!'

'Honey bees, signify immortality and resurrection. The ancient story goes that a bee carried a mantis across a river. Exhausted she left the mantis on a floating flower but planted a seed in the mantis's body before she died. The seed grew to become the first human.'

Manto nudged George to get his attention. George almost lost his footing and went lurching toward the precipice. Manto caught his sleeve and pulled him back.

'Pay attention! This is important!'

'All right! Okay! Jeez!'

Manto's face darkened. 'The bees are dying.'

'That's sad,' said George, not sure how he was supposed to react to that news.

Manto pushed him again, this time catching his sleeve before he staggered.

'Hey, quit that!' George said.

'Sad? Sad? It's a catastrophe!' boomed Manto. 'Foolish men, poisoning everything around them. How did you enjoy your breakfast?'

George was thrown by this new line of questioning. 'What?'

'Your breakfast?'

'It was delicious. What's that got to do with this?'

'Grains are pollinated on the wind, but fruits, nuts and vegetables are pollinated by bees. Seventy out of the top one hundred human food crops, which supply about ninety per cent of the world's nutritional needs, are pollinated by bees.'

George went quiet. He could see the pain in Manto's eyes and felt bad for not listening.

'If the bees vanish from the earth, then the wars for control of our failing resources ... well, they would be unprecedented in history.'

'Okay, professor, I get it,' he whispered gravely.

Manto had turned and was already packing the utensils into the car. 'A single bee colony can pollinate three hundred million flowers each day,' he said over his shoulder. 'That's what you're looking at down there.'

George scurried after him. 'Say, can we go down ... for a closer look, I mean?'

'No, George, you have to get going. It's a seven-hour drive, if you take the 93 to Coyote Springs and change for I 15. There's a map in the glovebox.'

'Wait. Enough,' said George, catching him up. 'Where the hell am I supposed to be going, and why?'

'I told you already ... to the Mountain Lying Down.'

'What the hell is that?'

'You'll know it as the Grand Canyon.'

'What? Why am I going to the Grand Canyon?'

'To get the boy back, of course.'

This stopped George in his tracks. He was speechless.

Manto turned to face him. 'You have the look of a beekeeper yourself, George Bailey. But one who has neglected the queen.'

On the short journey back to the camp Manto told him what little he knew.

'The elders have chosen the Mountain Lying Down as the place for you to make the trade. They have good reasons.'

'No disrespect,' George butted in, 'you people have been aces and all, and I really appreciate it, but what the hell has this got to do with you? And besides, how will those bastards get the message to bring Habibi there?'

Manto shot him a stern sideways glance. 'You're welcome!' he drawled dryly. 'They already know. They're probably there now, waiting for you and your tape.'

'About the tape …' George began.

Manto cut him off abruptly. 'I don't want to know.'

'Yes, but I don't have …'

'Do you understand? No one here wants to know about that.'

George was taken aback by his insistence. They travelled in tense silence, then Manto spoke again.

'There are ancient energies in the Mountain Lying Down, electromagnetic energies from the vortexes, from the earth's core itself. You might call it a "spiritual hot-spot". The elders think the energy exists in another dimension but that it crosses over into our world.'

George resisted his default flippancy and listened intently. He was in no doubt that this man was trying to help him – and the boy. His gut tightened at the prospect of what lay ahead of him and the adversaries ranged against him. He needed all the help he could get.

'It's our ground, not theirs. Remember that – ours. It's important for what you have to do today.'

Back at the camp, the two elders who had met him on his arrival were waiting. One held a shawl and the other a small canvas sack. Manto approached them and stooped so that each man could touch his forehead gently with their fingertips.

He took the shawl and handed it to George.

'Unfold it. Our people have worked through the night to have it ready.'

George shook it fully open.

It was delicately embroidered with a pattern of many small red crosses on a white background. George looked puzzled.

Manto reached up to his throat and, nodding for George to do the same, said, 'It's the crest, the symbol of your protector ... the banner that you fight under.'

George fingered the St George medallion that Margie had given him. He smiled but his knees got a little weak. They were preparing him to do battle.

'Thank you so much. Please tell your people thank you ... for everything.' He was emotional and started to feel a little teary. 'Okay, so I guess we better get going.'

Manto walked toward him and, to his surprise, lifted him up in an enormous bear hug.

When he returned to the ground, a slightly embarrassed George gave the brave a hug that seemed feeble by comparison. 'Hey, right back at ya big guy!'

The old men smiled.

'This is your journey, George. I cannot come along. You must make it yourself.'

'I figured you might say something like that.' George's voice shook a little.

'One more thing. I believe there's an important phone call you've been putting off … to someone back East?'

One of the elders stepped forward carrying a small canvas sack.

'We don't really have much use for telecommunications out here.' He smiled and said something to the old men in his own language. They laughed heartily. 'So the tribe has collected all the quarters in the village.'

George took the sack from the elder and weighed it speculatively. 'There's about fifty dollars-worth here I'd say. Who knew?'

The men threw their heads back and laughed.

'About one hundred and some miles down the trail you'll come across an old truck stop that has a payphone,' said Manto. 'It's run by a Christian lady and her boy. Doesn't have much, but you should fill up with gas … and, George Bailey, make that call.'

✳

George drove back over the same terrain they'd covered the previous night. The sun was climbing higher and the desert heat was rising. He was surrounded by scrub, cactus and sand for miles in every direction. The road was little more than a dirt track that improved steadily the further he progressed.

He had the map open on the seat beside him. The winding blue line of the Colorado River snaked through the brown and green of the massive crater. Manto had sketched his route in red magic marker all the way to the North Rim of the Grand Canyon itself, then further to Angels Window on the Cape Royal Trail. Here he had drawn a large X. It could not have looked more ominous.

As George drove he thought about what he might say to Beatrice and wondered if she would be shocked or surprised at hearing from him. Should he mention Jaffé and Habibi? What if she slammed the phone down, called him a womanising, cheating motherfucker and hung up? But how could he tell his fantastical story, the things that had happened to him, without mentioning them? And what of his need for forgiveness, for another chance. Could a conversation over a long-distance line do justice to his mea culpa? Could he convince her of his absolute certainty that she, Beatrice Hatcher, was the only woman he had ever loved and ever would? And could he persuade her that he was absolutely committed to making amends for disrespecting her love for him?

He spotted the weather-beaten sign from some way off. 'Homer's Truck Stop & Diner'.

There was a garage forecourt with two gas pumps, a low-level one-storey building set at the back, and a rusting, aluminium hangar that presumably passed for a workshop of sorts. In the corner was a telephone kiosk. Overgrown sage and brushwood covered much of the concourse; the whole place looked to be in an advanced state of disrepair and neglect.

George pulled the car up to the gas pumps, passing over the rubber line that rang a bell somewhere. A boy of about thirteen sitting at the foot of the pumps reading a comic book looked up and gave George a wide, toothy smile.

'How ya doing today?'

'Middlin' son, just middlin'.'

'What can I getcha?'

'Fill 'er up.'

'Sure thing.' The boy jumped to his feet, the comic book falling to the ground.

'Any good?' asked George nodding at the book.

'Just started it. Zombies and vampires ... or maybe zombie-vampires. Too soon to say.'

While the boy pumped the gas, George let his gaze wander around the yard. He could hear the noise of metal hammering on metal coming from the hangar.

'Things pretty slow?'

'Always pretty slow around here.'

'You running this show yourself?'

The boy smiled bashfully. 'No, my grandma's the boss, but she don't talk much. She mostly works on transmissions and such.' He nodded toward the hangar. 'I'm kinda front-of-house.'

George laughed. He liked the kid's openness. 'I'm George,' he said, offering his hand.

'Tyrone,' said the kid, shaking it.

George pointed to the phone booth across the yard. 'That thing working?'

'Sure is. I check it every morning for tone. Grandma uses it now and again.'

George wandered back to his car to collect the sack of quarters. As he passed the hangar, he couldn't resist quickly looking in.

From behind he could see a small woman, in stained dungarees and work boots, bent so far over the open hood of an old gold-coloured Chevy Impala that her feet dangled off the ground. Along with the occasional grunt, George could hear the sound of a wrench seeking torque on a stubborn, unlubricated bolt head.

He walked on toward the phone, his apprehension welling up again. What should be his first words? 'It's me … don't hang up!' seemed the most pragmatic opening.

He loaded the phone with quarters and listened breathlessly for the ringtone. When it began to purr he felt his throat constrict and he forced himself to swallow spit.

The tone clicked to answer, but before he could speak, Beatrice cut in: 'Hi y'all. Me and my man George are off to San Francisco.

If we don't leave our hearts there, we'll get back to you soon. Bye, y'all!' Just before the line disconnected he could have sworn he heard his own voice in the background say, 'Beatrice, honey, the cab is here already.'

He forced himself to concentrate on the sound of her voice and not what she had said – how happy she had seemed, how excited to be going. To consider anything else was to court the very real possibility that he had finally lost his mind. Given what was ahead of him that day, he could not afford to crumble now.

In a daze he returned to Tyrone, who was cleaning bugs from the windscreen.

'How much, son?'

'She was nearly dry, so I'd say sixty bucks even.'

George gave him two fifties and told him to keep the change.

'Are you sure?' asked the boy.

George was already in the car and pulling away. 'Sure kid. And regards to your grandma.'

He moved off fast, kicking up dust into the air.

The metallic banging from the hangar ceased and the woman, her grey hair tied up in a red bandana, emerged, rolling down her sleeves. She picked up a petrol-soaked rag and rubbed her oily hands with it. Then she walked to the middle of the forecourt and, hands on hips, looked off down the road at George Bailey's disappearing tail lights.

A storm was gathering toward the east and dark clouds sat ominously over the far-off mountain range. A peal of thunder rumbled remotely in the distance.

Margie Kaufman chewed anxiously on the skin around her thumbnail and pulled Tyrone close to her.

Their journey had been uneventful, Virgil driving one car, with Lou and Habibi as passengers, Lamont Riddle driving the other, accompanied by Minos Baboov. Jaffé had been left behind.

The road narrowed and became more winding as they climbed a wooded valley and passed over undulating land that linked the Kaibab and Walhalla plateaus. After a sticky last few miles through the thick pine woodland, the road ended in a loop around to a large gravel parking area without any visitor facilities. All save the boy got out to stretch and ease the kinks and stresses of the journey.

Lou Plutus stood in the baking late afternoon heat of the Arizona sun. He had discarded his sunglasses to better appreciate his surroundings. But he was in poor health; his guts hurt and unsightly boils had erupted overnight on his arms, neck and face.

The vista that lay around him was simply breathtaking. Despite the evidence of his own eyes, the sheer scale of the red rock formations, stretching out to the horizon and sweeping down to the river, took on the surreal majesty of some massive artificial, painted backdrop. Candyfloss clouds of all shapes hung in a perfect blue sky, occasionally drifting by and casting vast moving shadows over the landscape. To one side was the Angels Window, a natural hole in the Kaibab limestone that, from this vantage point, framed a section of the Colorado River some six miles distant and five thousand feet below.

A path, protected by a railing, led across the narrow neck of land on top of the Angels Window and stopped at a viewpoint right at the edge of the cliffs. The best views westwards were to be had by climbing over the railings and walking a few steps downhill, and as the metal wire fence was bent in places, it was clear that tourists had been doing just that. Vertical cliffs lay below; the drop was sheer.

When Lou looked over his shoulder again he saw that he was standing alone. Lamont and Baboov had returned to the cars to cool off in the AC. The boy sat in the rear seat, staring silently ahead, as he had done since they left Vegas. There was no sign of Virgil.

Then Lou noticed three huge black SUVs, Chevrolet Suburbans, with darkened windows, sitting abreast in the parking area. Their exhausts tremored as the vehicles idled, AC on max. He was sure they hadn't been there when his group arrived. It was probably the Triptych, thought Lou.

Sure enough, when a door slid open on the middle SUV and Virgil slipped out the narrow gap, Lou caught a glimpse of the black porcelain doll, Mikhailavich, and Baba Yaga's tiny red and gold satin slippers.

Virgil came and stood beside Lou, shielding his eyes as if looking for something way off in the distance. Lou followed his gaze, squinting into the bright light. He could just make out a small black dot – like a hovering insect, shiny and menacing in the heat haze – slowly making its way up the middle of the canyon. It seemed to drop altitude, then pick up speed as it swept over the hills, trees and rock stacks far beneath.

A faint *whop-whop-whop-whop-whop-whop* throbbed in the still air. Then, as the MH-6 helicopter got closer, the sound of the thrumming rotor blades drowned out any other sound. The chopper came in low over Angels Window, taking a wide sweep on its approach, inspecting the flotilla of vehicles beneath it. The blades sent up dust and sand, and Lou and Virgil covered their eyes.

All the cars activated their hazard lights in unison, forming a kind of landing strip as the chopper hovered there like some giant flying cockroach. It bore the Webcore logo.

'It's him! It's really him,' Lou squealed like an excited child.

'And the Lord said, "The fear of you and the dread of you shall be upon every beast of the earth",' Virgil pronounced. He turned away.

*

Watching all of this from a distance was George Bailey.

He'd had the prescience to park back at the pine woodland and make his way on foot. In his sweating hand he held a C90 cassette tape of *The Eagles' Greatest Hits*, which he'd found in the glove compartment of his rental car. It was rectangular and it was black; at a distance he hoped this would be enough to carry off the biggest bluff of his entire life.

As sundown had progressed and the dust particles in the air caught the evening sunlight, the canyon was burnished in a copper glow. The red rocks seemed to be luminous, like smouldering embers, and every cliff face as far as he could see, glowed in shades of burnt sienna and ochre.

The helicopter settled on the large gravel parking area, its blades throbbing to a slow whine, then stopped. A door slid open and the Ogre disembarked adroitly. He wore a khaki-coloured sweater and slacks, and looked for all the world like he was heading to the golf links. He was followed by a man dressed as a high-ranking Saudi.

George recognised the Arab from the snuff movie. And, of course, there could be no mistaking the big man, his bizarre straw-coloured hair held down by a red baseball cap, his face pancaked orange like the rocks around him. Yes, he had been the one who decapitated the young girl in that accursed video, although George knew him from the TV shows and interviews, the hundreds of newspaper columns and magazine articles over recent years.

Virgil, Lou, Lamont and Baboov stood in a line as the billionaire property tycoon screwed up his face, pouted his lips and pumped handshakes, offering a word to each. Then he said something to the Saudi, who went over to the car that Habibi sat in, opened the door and led the boy to where the others stood. The child remained wide-eyed and mute as always, but George could see immediately that he didn't have the *Star Trek* rucksack with him.

The big man said something and they all laughed, all except Virgil who was looking to where George Bailey now stood on the fringes of the parking area, terrified and shaking.

'The circle is complete,' said Virgil. 'And my work here is done.'

The men all turned to look at George. He feared that he might wilt under their gaze.

'I'm here for the boy,' he cried, the words catching in his throat. 'I'm here for Habibi. I have what you want.'

He held the fake tape in the air, his hot fingers closed around it. *Do they know I'm bluffing?* Sweat ran down his forehead and stung his eyes. When he wiped it away and looked again, Virgil had gone.

When the boy saw George, he beamed a huge smile and flung his arms open in desperate entreaty but did not move. George thought he felt his heart break.

The Ogre said something, then the Saudi led the child to the first SUV. Heat shimmered from the glossy black hood of the car. The Saudi took the boy's hand, hesitated for a moment to allow George to register what was happening, then pressed it down hard on the baking metal and held it there.

The child didn't make a sound or show any sign of pain. Instead he stared directly at his tormentor, fixing him with an unbroken, puzzled gaze. No one else spoke.

It was George who reacted. 'God, no! Stop it, you bastard!'

Lou Plutus sniggered.

George was horrified. 'Lou, for Christ sake, look at yourself. This isn't you.'

'Hey,' said Lou dismissively, looking to his associates for approval. 'Pity the sinner, hate the sin.'

George's disgust turned to anger. 'Can any of this be worth it, whatever it is you're trying to—'

'It's business, George, just business,' the Ogre said matter-of-factly. 'My people tell me that there will be a nigger president in the White House in the next ten years, a woman in fifteen, and that's just not good for business now, is it?' He looked down at Habibi.

'He's a child. He's hurt no one,' pleaded George.

'Oh, there, there, George. Don't you know what happens in purgatory stays in purgatory?' The big man shook with laughter.

The others joined in, like a band of cackling hyenas.

George held the dummy tape above his head again. 'Give me the boy or—'

'Or what?'

'I've seen this …'

'Oh, have you now. And what did you think of little Veronique's performance,' asked the Ogre. 'Amazing? Outstanding? A star was born, truly.' He formed an 'O' with his thumb and first finger.

'Since the towers, everything changes. Our time … my time is coming. Time to make America great again!'

'Inshallah!' exclaimed the Saudi.

'By the way, did you know that my building is now the tallest in lower Manhattan?'

George was wilting in the face of the man's callous certainty, the power that he exuded.

He waved the tape again.

'Yes, George, you have my tape. Well, not mine exactly … my Russian friends'. It's something they call a "Kompromat", and we would very much like it back.'

'I've made a copy,' George lied. 'I've sent it to the press!'

'Nobody cares, George, really. Believe me … nobody.'

'Then I'll throw it down there.' He gestured toward the canyon, now aglow with the setting sun.

'Please, be my guest. That will do us all a favour.'

George was cornered. How had he ever thought he could pull this off?

'I've contacted the Sheriff's Department. They're on their way.' It was a last throw of the dice.

The big man raised his left hand in the air and the door of the middle SUV slid open. A beaten and shaken Deputy Harry Bailey fell out onto the ground, his hands secured behind his back. His cracked glasses fell from his face and into the dust.

Baboov crossed to him and jerked him to his feet. The door of the SUV slammed closed again.

'My glasses,' pleaded Harry.

The Ogre nodded and Baboov put them back on for him. 'Let him see what he's got coming to him.'

'Do you mean *this* Sheriff's Department?' Lamont Riddle said as he fashioned a noose from a long length of rope taken from the trunk of his car. He placed it around Harry's neck, then led him over to the safety railings at the very edge of the canyon and fastened the other end of the rope to the metal barrier.

Beating him violently about the head with his revolver, he forced Harry to climb on top of the railings and balance there precariously. The Riddler held him by the arm, Harry teetering on the rail, the soles of his cowboy boots failing to find good purchase. A simple shove would send the young officer over the edge, down the sheer face until his drop was arrested by the snap-jerk of the line.

'Woooooweeee, that's a helluva long way down,' said Lamont, peering over the side. 'Lucky for you you've got something to break your fall with!'

He yanked on the rope, causing Harry to sway wildly. Lamont steadied him again.

'Ring any bells, Mr Bailey?' asked the Ogre.

George stood open-mouthed in disbelief. Instead of the young officer, what George saw was a small boy in a cowboy outfit, his straight, blond pudding-bowl haircut framing a pale, freckled moon-face with large cobalt-blue eyes and a rope around his neck.

'Harry?'

'Georgie?'

The big man looked from one to the other. 'Another catastrophe on your watch. Another young life lost. Would you like to trade? White for black?'

'No, it's impossible. It can't be.'

The big man turned to his retinue, then back again. He sighed in an exaggerated fashion. 'All right then, George Bailey. You're a loser, but your entreaties have moved us.'

Lamont and Lou giggled maliciously.

'We'll let you have the little monkey as a gesture of good faith.'

The Saudi man pushed Habibi in the small of the back. He stumbled but regained his balance, then began running toward George. But halfway across the space between them, he abruptly stopped, turned around and walked back to his captors. George was incredulous, dismayed.

'Habibi, it's okay. Come on … come to me!' he called out to him

But the boy was marching purposefully toward the car and audaciously pointing at something. Baboov lifted the boy's backpack in his huge fist and handed it to him. Habibi took it and ran toward George.

George scooped him up and, hugging the boy, grabbed the backpack from him. Before unzipping it, he looked at the men, then hurled the phoney tape high into the ravine. He pulled the bag open, expecting to find the USS Enterprise model with the concealed, despised cassette. Instead, he found himself looking at dozens of tapes, all identical. He tipped it upside down and shook them out onto the dusty ground around him where they fell with hollow, clattering smacks.

The posse of men roared with laughter, bending over to wheeze and howl in delight. Then, ominously, they fell silent. And in the silence George knew it was all over for him and the boy. And for Harry.

George fell to his knees, exasperated. He clasped his hands together. 'Please, I'm begging you, let Harry go. Take me.'

The big man's face darkened. 'Take you? *You*. Wow, how appropriate. How totally amaaazzzing, George Bailey, cuz it was never about the tape now, was it? It was always about you … and the boy, of course. All those other sweet little cherubs on the chopping block, even bringing that fat slug Plutus here … it was always all about you.'

'Always you,' they all said together like a chant. 'Always you.'

The Ogre reached into the nearest SUV and pulled out a knife that looked like the one he had used on Veronique.

'Now take the blade and open the child at the throat.' The man's voice had changed. It echoed and boomed. 'Do this ... or else Plutus will!'

Suddenly Lamont Riddle casually and indifferently pushed Deputy Sheriff Harry Bailey over the edge. He disappeared from view, and the rope went taut with a ferocious lurch. But in that instant it snapped with a loud whiplash crack, giving way where it had been attached to the railing.

George swept up Habibi and ran to the edge, looking down for any sign of his brother. The child clung on tightly around his neck. He spotted the young Harry some way down, lying on a ledge.

Just then, Lou Plutus bent forward and puked. More boils appeared on his skin, some rupturing and bursting. Lamont Riddle crossed to him and wrinkled his nose at the stench rising up from the man.

'You don't look so good,' he said as he peered more closely at Lou's afflictions.

Something seemed to be emerging from the crust of one of his sores. It squirmed and writhed in a shiny, viscous ooze. It was difficult to see at first. Then another appeared. And another. Lamont tentatively plucked one from a wound between finger and thumb and held it up for closer inspection. It was a bee.

Baboov also seemed in some discomfort. He pawed at his ears and scratched his nose in irritation. Then bees began to appear from Baboov's nostrils and wriggle out of his ear canals. He looked for all the world like he was back in the boxing ring as he ducked and weaved, swiping blindly and in panic at the air around him.

Lou retched again and evacuated a puddle of foul-smelling vomit that contained hundreds of the insects. Soon, the bees got their bearings, then rose from the sick and began to attack him. Like Baboov, he flailed at the space around him in panic, yowling in pain from the stings.

Minos Baboov fell to his knees and, throwing his head back to the sky, let out a guttural roar. A torrent of the insects exploded from his mouth in a column of buzzing fury and enveloped the man, almost obscuring him completely.

The Ogre and the Arab made for the chopper, and almost immediately the engines of the big SUVs gunned up and revved loudly. The blades on the helicopter started to whine and whirr.

Lamont Riddle had run to his car and locked himself inside. But he was not quick enough to shut out all the creatures entirely. Already they buzzed around the interior, and were joined by others that flooded in through the ventilation system.

The space where the men had stood was now black with swirling, flying insects, the buzzing, droning din blocking out their screams.

George saw his chance. He had noticed a faint trail, pale as chalk, winding down the cliff beneath him, a silver thread, meandering over the rock face. Where did it lead? Who had used it before him? It didn't much matter. He felt compelled to follow it to its conclusion.

He looked again for Harry and saw movement on the ridge far below. But where there had previously been a boy in a cowboy outfit, now stood a young man in sheriff's uniform. He had freed his hands and was urgently beckoning George and the child to join him.

The maelstrom of buzzing, stinging chaos had intensified. Clouds of insects were rising from the depths of the canyon itself, blocking out the remaining sunlight and moving across the sky in sheets. Squadrons passed over George's head, twisting into vast cones in the air and diving onto the vehicles and men in the parking area. Blankets of the insects settled on every surface, undulating like molten ore.

But George and Habibi remained untouched as they descended into the deep drum of crimson rock, Habibi sitting securely on George's shoulders. Intermittently, they caught a glimpse the clay-red Colorado River. It looked swollen and was moving fast.

As they descended further, chasms of deep shadow appeared around them. George looked above. The bluffs and overhangs of ochre stone seemed to close in over their heads. He couldn't believe they had come so far, so fast. Below, sweeping red plateaus of limestone swelled like marbled padding from the canyon sides, and bands of rocks – deep purple, orange, red and pink – revealed their ancient origins. 'The banners of God,' Manto had called them.

Suddenly, George lost his footing and slipped. He struggled to regain his balance, the child lurching wildly but clinging on, his hands over George's eyes.

'Habibi, I can't see!' George shouted in alarm.

To his amazement, the boy put his mouth to George's ear and whispered in a quiet, authoritative voice, 'I will guide you, dragon slayer.'

Astonished, he tried to turn his head to look at the boy, but Habibi's grip became as strong as a man's and held his head firmly, his hands still covering George's eyes.

'Keep to the middle,' came the calm instruction. Then, 'Go left', or 'Go right.'

George complied meekly, fearful at first, but became more and more assured until he was but a child himself, walking between the hands and feet of the small boy.

It was like treading water, but each blind step was a secure one and George began to smile. They journeyed like this for a long time.

Gradually the steep descent down the incline lessened, then levelled off. The ground beneath his feet became softer and more pliable. And so they continued.

After a while, George became convinced that they had begun an almost imperceptible ascent again, their path now leading gradually upward. It felt as if he was now walking on loose, deepening sand and it took a much greater effort to keep walking forward. The ground pulled at his feet and sucked the energy from him.

He felt bushes and trees flick and brush his face and body and he held his arms out in front of him to protect himself.

The incline grew ever steeper. The muscles at the backs of his calves and thighs tightened and burned in pain. He thought of stopping and turning back, of ripping Habibi's hands from his eyes. But the weight of the small boy on his shoulders bore down on him, pushing him on. After a while it became almost impossible to lift his legs even to take a single step, as if the force on his shoulders was grinding him deeper into the sand. The child grew heavier and heavier with every step. Soon it took a superhuman effort just to stand upright.

Then George thought he caught the smell of fried bacon and eggs.

And the sound of a harmonica playing.

And shower water beating on a plastic curtain.

Far off in the distance he heard Beatrice goofin' on Elvis in her inimitable Southern drawl: 'Treat me like a fool, treat me mean and cruel, but love me ... doo, waa, waa, ooo.'

Then abruptly:

SWISSSSSZZZZZZUUUUUPPPPP!!!

It was as if all the air around him had suddenly imploded, been sucked back in.

When the boy at last removed his hands and George Bailey turned to look up at his face, he had to squint against the piercing, dazzling radiance of the brightest, brilliant light.

Epilogue
NEVADA

When the first responders arrived at the field near the Diamond T. Mine in Stonycreek Township, Somerset County, Pennsylvania, clumps of still-smoking metal fuselage lay strewn in every direction.

Flight 93 had fragmented violently upon impact.

Most of the aircraft wreckage was lying around the crater itself. All human remains were found within a seventy-acre radius of this, but many of the bodies had been consumed by the impact.

Two F-16 fighter jets from the 121st Fighter Squadron of the DC Air National Guard were scrambled and had been ordered to intercept Flight 93. The official finding was that they never reached the flight in time and didn't learn of its crash until hours afterwards.

By the time the second wave of investigators had arrived at the scene in their bright yellow forensics suits and gloves, the terrible task of identifying the victims had begun. Black plastic body bags now grimly dotted the rural landscape.

It would be December 21st before all those on board the flight were identified.

The heartbreaking task of gathering up and returning personal effects to the victims' families was also underway – cell phones, bunches of keys, wallets, spectacles, laptops – the modern flotsam and jetsam of everyday life. They were tagged, identified where possible, and placed into individual plastic containers.

The young Federal Agent consulted his clipboard containing the passenger manifest. It was his third month out of training academy, top of his class, but nothing could have prepared him for this. As gruesome as the task was, he consoled himself with the thought that at least he wouldn't be the guy knocking on some poor wretch's door with the worst news that anyone could receive.

He spent most of the day indexing, filing and tagging fragments of the lives lost, and was just logging the effects of his final passenger. For some reason he could locate very few items belonging to No. 19, one George Bailey: a scorched jacket, its pockets containing a set of keys, a boarding pass stub, a wallet with a credit card in the name of 'Beatrice Hatcher', a watch inscribed with the message 'Love always, B', its face smashed, the hands frozen at 10.03, and a book of matches, Big Apple Strikes.

Not much to recover here, he thought forlornly. Not much to salve any loved one's cherished memories. Not much to show for a life lived.

He turned the book of matches over in his hand. They had a drawing of the Statue of Liberty on the cover sleeve, and there was a quotation on the back. It read:

'That's the great thing about the American dream ... when it ends, you get to dream it up all over again!' M. Kaufman.

In Memoria

NEVADA

Minos Baboov (1976–2001): death by gunshot wounds.

George Bailey (1965–2001): killed, terrorist attacks, Flight UA 93, Sept 11th.

Beatrice Hatcher (1967–2001): killed, terrorist attacks, World Trade Center, Sept 11th.

Gabriella Henderson (1960–2001): killed, terrorist attacks, World Trade Center, Sept 11th.

Damir Igric (1972–2001): death by suicide (bus/auto wreck; responsible for the deaths of seven others).

Margie Kaufman (1939–2001): died, lung cancer.

Lou Plutus (1952–2001): killed, terrorist attacks, World Trade Center, Sept 11th.

Lamont Riddle (1957–2001): died, AIDS-related illness.

Daniel Stockton (1995–2001): killed, terrorist attacks, World Trade Center, Sept 11th.

Flight Lieutenant Bradley Streep (1976–2001): death by suicide.

Evelyn Mulvihill (1947–2000): died, liver failure.

Corporal Virgil Shevchenkov (1973–1998): killed on active service with Russian Special Forces, Chechnya.

Jaffé Losoko (1973–1996): murdered, Asmera, Ethiopia.

Habibi Losoko-Bailey (1995): pregnancy terminated, Ybor, Florida.

Deputy Sheriff Fox McKinley (1929–1979): killed in the line of duty (auto wreck).

Harold 'Shankill' Bailey (1968–1976): death by misadventure (hanging).

Lucian de los Santos (1959–1971) and Hernandez de los Santos (1931–1971): murdered, Miami, Florida.

Manto (1969–): unknown.

Dr Thomas Paul Burgess was born in Belfast, Northern Ireland.

He is a published academic, novelist and songwriter / musician with his bands Rufrex and Sacred Heart of Bontempi - with whom he achieved commercial and critical success – through the release of eight singles and three albums. Most notable amongst these was the scathing commentary on American funding for Irish Republican violence, 'The Wild Colonial Boy' which entered the UK top thirty. The British music press, comparing his work to that of Yukio Mishima, described his writing as, "...a line of poetry written in a splash of blood." And described Ruefrex as "...the most important band in Britain" at the time.

His first novel, 'White Church, Black Mountain' (Matador ISBN 9781784621612) is a political thriller, dealing with the emerging 'post-conflict' society of Northern Ireland and exploring the legacy of 'the Troubles' and how its residue impacts on those who seek to build a personal and communal future in their aftermath.

His second novel, 'Through Hollow Lands' is a dark thriller with political undertones and follows survivors of the 9/11 attacks, through the seeming purgatory of the Las Vegas underworld.

He holds degrees from the Universities of Ulster, Oxford & Cork and has published a number of academic books dealing with aspects of Education ('A Crisis of Conscience: - moral ambivalence and education in Northern Ireland' ISBN 1 85628420 4) Social Policy ('The Reconciliation Industry: - community relations, community identity & social policy in Northern Ireland.' ISBN 0 7734 70441) and Cultural Identity ('The Contested Identities of Ulster Protestants' ISBN 9 78113745393 8) as well as a number of treatises on Youth participation in European civil society.

His book, *'The Contested Identities of Ulster Catholics'* will be published by Palgrave MacMillan in the summer of 2018.

He lives in Cork, Ireland, where he is a Senior Academic and Director of Youth & Community Studies at The School of Applied Social Studies, University College Cork.

Urbane Publications is dedicated to
developing new author voices, and publishing
fiction and non-fiction that challenges, thrills and
fascinates.

From page-turning novels to innovative
reference books, our goal is to publish what
YOU want to read.

Find out more at
urbanepublications.com